continued . . .

For Coach Derek – Yoda!
Thank you for being
in our corner.

PLAGUE
WAR

Enjoy.
JEFF CARLSON

Jeff ☺

John

Ben

Diana

ACE BOOKS, NEW YORK

THE BERKLEY PUBLISHING GROUP
Published by the Penguin Group
Penguin Group (USA) Inc.
375 Hudson Street, New York, New York 10014, USA
Penguin Group (Canada), 90 Eglinton Avenue East, Suite 700, Toronto, Ontario M4P 2Y3, Canada
(a division of Pearson Penguin Canada Inc.)
Penguin Books Ltd., 80 Strand, London WC2R 0RL, England
Penguin Group Ireland, 25 St. Stephen's Green, Dublin 2, Ireland (a division of Penguin Books Ltd.)
Penguin Group (Australia), 250 Camberwell Road, Camberwell, Victoria 3124, Australia
(a division of Pearson Australia Group Pty. Ltd.)
Penguin Books India Pvt. Ltd., 11 Community Centre, Panchsheel Park, New Delhi—110 017, India
Penguin Group (NZ), 67 Apollo Drive, Rosedale, North Shore 0632, New Zealand
(a division of Pearson New Zealand Ltd.)
Penguin Books (South Africa) (Pty.) Ltd., 24 Sturdee Avenue, Rosebank, Johannesburg 2196,
South Africa

Penguin Books Ltd., Registered Offices: 80 Strand, London WC2R 0RL, England

This is a work of fiction. Names, characters, places, and incidents either are the product of the author's imagination or are used fictitiously, and any resemblance to actual persons, living or dead, business establishments, events, or locales is entirely coincidental. The publisher does not have any control over and does not assume any responsibility for author or third-party websites or their content.

PLAGUE WAR

An Ace Book / published by arrangement with the author

PRINTING HISTORY
Ace mass-market edition / August 2008

Copyright © 2008 by Jeff Carlson.
Maps by Meghan Mahler.
Cover art by Eric Williams.
Cover design by Judith Lagerman.
Interior text design by Laura K. Corless.

ISBN: 978-0-441-01617-4

ACE
Ace Books are published by The Berkley Publishing Group,
a division of Penguin Group (USA) Inc.,
375 Hudson Street, New York, New York 10014.
ACE and the "A" design are trademarks belonging to Penguin Group (USA) Inc.

PRINTED IN THE UNITED STATES OF AMERICA

10 9 8 7 6 5 4 3 2 1

This one is for her, too.

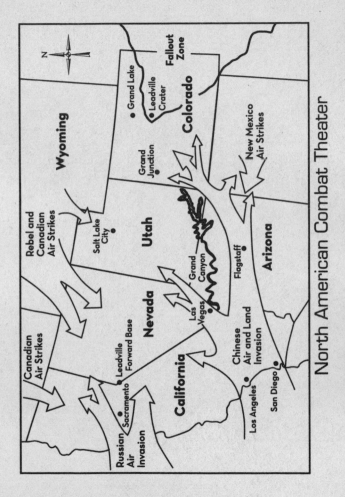

North American Combat Theater

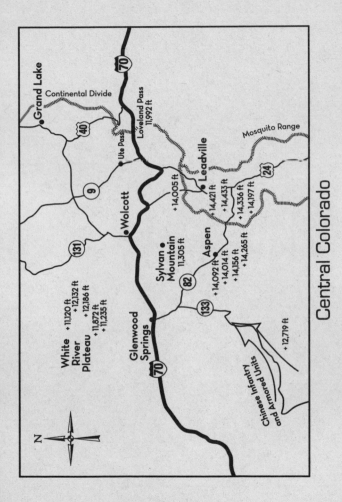

Central Colorado

1

Ruth kicked her way through another tangle of bones, stumbling when her boot caught in a fractured chunk of ribs and vertebrae. Interstate 80 was a graveyard. Thousands of cars packed every mile of the wide road, each one full of slumping ghosts— each one pointing east.

Always east, toward the mountains.

Ruth hiked in the same direction, huffing for air against her face mask. Her movements were less like walking than dancing. She lunged and sidestepped through the wreckage, because many people had also continued on foot as far as they were able. Everywhere their skeletons huddled among endless garbage. Some still held boxes or bags or rags or jewelry. Most had gathered in clumps wherever the standstill traffic pinched too closely together, blocking the way.

Each step was made more difficult by her broken left arm. The cast affected her balance. Worse, she never wanted to look down. The skulls were a silent crowd. Ruth tried to avoid their gaping eyes, so she blinked constantly and glanced sideways and up as she walked, letting her gaze move like a pinball. In three days, that dizzy feeling had become normal. Ruth barely remembered anything else. It helped that she always had Cam in front of her and Newcombe behind, walking single file through the ruins. The steady clumping sound of the men's bootsteps were markers for her to follow.

Then they came to a clot of vehicles that had burned and exploded, throwing doors and bodies into the confusion. The spaces in between the cars were thick with splintered bones, steel, and glass.

Cam stopped. "We need to try something else," he said, turning his head from the raised Interstate toward the neat, sprawling grid of the city below. All three of them were wrapped in goggles and face masks, so Ruth couldn't tell exactly where he was looking, but the streets were even worse in the downtown areas. The neat lines of the city were deceptive, full of traps and dead ends. The carnage was unimaginable. The human debris filled hundreds of square miles just here in the greater San Francisco Bay Area, mixed with dogs and birds and every other warm-blooded species.

"This way," Newcombe said, pointing past the blackened cars to the downward slope of the shoulder.

Ruth shook her head. "We'd be better off pushing through." Several drivers had tried to escape by ramming the guardrail, only to overturn on the hill below. She didn't want to start an avalanche of cars.

"She's right," Cam said. "We'll just take it slow."

"Then let me and him go first," Newcombe said to Ruth, stepping past her.

Mark Newcombe was twenty-two, the youngest of them, younger than Ruth by more than a decade, and he had trained as an Army Special Forces soldier for two years before the machine plague. The end of the world had only continued to harden him. His assault rifle, pack, and gun belt weighed fifty pounds—and barely slowed him at all.

Cam's stride was more uneven. He was hurt, like Ruth, which she thought made him a better leader. Cam wasn't so sure. He worried about things, and Ruth liked him for it. He was more willing to admit he was wrong, which was why they were still on the Interstate. The road was bad, but at least it went through. Their small trio had tried to hike cross-country more than once, wherever the residential areas or commercial buildings eased back from the highway, but they'd encountered too many fences and creeks and brittle gray thickets crowded with beetles and deadfalls. Even the burned traffic was better.

Newcombe cut his elbow and both knees before they were through. "Let's keep moving," he said, but as soon as they cleared the burn, Cam made him stop and immediately flushed the wounds with a canteen, trying to outrace the plague. Then he bandaged the cuts, wrapping Newcombe's pantlegs with gauze.

Cam stood up before he was done. "Wait," he said, tilting his head to listen to the sky.

It was a clear blue May afternoon, sunny and calm. Goose bumps prickled up the back of Ruth's neck. *I don't hear anything,* she thought, but the cool, vulnerable shiver in her spine made her turn to stare behind them. She glanced through the dead cars, seeking any threat. Nothing.

Cam shoved at her. "Move! Move!"

They ran beneath the twisted metal bulk of a truck rig. Cam and Newcombe had their guns drawn but Ruth needed her good arm to crawl under the wreckage, suddenly half-blind out of the sun. Her glove crunched in a litter of glass and plastic.

"What—" she said, but then she felt it, too, a low, menacing drumbeat. Helicopters. Again. In the vast ruins of what had been Sacramento, California, there were no longer any sounds except the wind and the rivers and sometimes the bugs. It was a small advantage. So far they'd always heard the choppers while they were still tens of miles away.

Closer this time, and coming fast.

"There was a culvert about a quarter-mile behind us," Ruth said, her mind jumping. Twice before they'd gone underground because the enemy had infrared.

Newcombe grunted, *huh.* "I saw it. Too far."

"Oh." Cam lifted one glove to the inhuman shape of his goggles and hood. "Ants," he said.

Ruth turned to see but cracked her head in the tight space. The crumpled bulk of the trailer read SAFEWAY in letters as long as her body and she said, quietly, "It's a grocery truck."

"Christ." Newcombe scuffled back toward the sunlight, moving on his elbows to keep his rifle out of the grit and dust. But his backpack caught on the metal above him and he had to squeeze even lower, pushing his weapon in front of him.

Ruth clenched her teeth. The cutting roar of the helicopters, Newcombe's struggle just to gain a few inches—it set the fear in her spinning and she realized there was another noise all around them, creeping and soft. The dead had begun to live again. The bones and the garbage vibrated in the rising thunder, rattling, sighing. Somewhere a car door wailed as it sagged open.

"Go," Cam said, just as Newcombe hissed, "Stay back."

Ruth shifted urgently. She had to move even if there was nowhere to go. She had seen ant swarms in the heart of the city like impossible black floods, surging over ceilings and walls, stripping entire buildings of carpet glue, rubber, and upholstery. If they were on top of a colony now, it would be a hideous death.

"We need to get out of here," she said.

"Go," Cam agreed.

Ruth tried to ease past him, shoving herself between the broken asphalt and the white-and-red bulk of the trailer. Then she saw two tendrils of ants.

The choppers slammed across their position, overwhelming her pulse and her mind. Everything in her shook. Everything was noise. The trailer overhead echoed with it and Ruth thought to scream—and then the thunder tipped away, sliding by like a falling building or a train—and Newcombe grabbed her arm.

"Goddammit, stay back!" he yelled as the crushing sound continued past. "They might not be sure! They might only be following the highway!"

Ruth made herself nod. She couldn't breathe. She tried to look out, but when the truck rolled it had hit at least one other vehicle. There was a badly dented beige sedan in front of her, and yet the noise was still a solid thing and easy to follow. It hadn't gone far. It was landing.

Suddenly she could see through a gap between the car's torn fender and wheel well. At first there was only sky and trees. Then she saw two helicopters. Maybe there were more. The aircraft dropped smoothly, meeting the ground with almost perfect symmetry. The side doors on both helicopters were open, spilling men in green containment suits—men without faces or shoulders, deformed by long hoods and air tanks.

"They're down," she said.

There were open fields on this side of the highway, an irregular stretch of flat brown earth where the commercial buildings stopped short of the road. Ruth saw a chain-link fence that might slow the soldiers, but it was leaning over in one spot where they could probably shove it down. The sound of the choppers echoed and rapped from the tall face of a warehouse.

Cam pushed in beside her, craning his neck to see. Ants covered his shoulder. "We can't make our stand here," he told Newcombe.

"The bugs," Ruth said. "Get the bugs between us and them."

"Okay, yeah. Move." Newcombe rolled over and began to pull off his pack.

Ruth turned and scrambled away, looking for Cam as soon as she hit daylight. He came out slapping at one sleeve and they ducked into the motionless cars together.

The glinting she had seen, sunlight on air tanks and weaponry, were there ten soldiers? Twenty?

"Here! Stop!" Cam pulled at her and they circled behind a white Mercedes. "If they come up the embankment we can try to force them back toward the truck."

Ruth nodded, dry-mouthed. Where was Newcombe?

Waiting, she became intensely aware of her exhaustion, old bruises, new hurts. Waiting, she drew her pistol. In another life this much pain would have stopped her already, but she was not who she had been. None of them were. And that was both good and bad. In many ways Ruth Goldman was less complicated now, thinking less, feeling more, and there was real strength in her anger and frustration and shame.

She owed it to her friends to fight. She owed it to herself, for every mistake she'd made.

Panting through the bitter taste of her face mask, Ruth kicked aside the small, partially melted ribcage of a child to reach the car's rear bumper, where she brought her pistol up and braced for the assault.

A lot of survivors called it Plague Year, or Year One, but it wasn't only human history that had crashed in the long fourteen months since the machine plague. The invisible nanotech devoured all warm-blooded life below ten thousand feet elevation. What remained of the ecosystem was badly out of whack, with only fish, frogs, and reptiles left to whittle down the exploding insect populations—and the land suffered for it. Entire forests had been chewed apart by locusts and termites. Riverways were forever changed by erosion.

States and nations had been obliterated, too. The plague had left few habitable zones anywhere in the world, the Rockies, the Andes, the Alps, the Himalayas, and a few scattered high points here and there. New Zealand. Japan. California.

Leadville, Colorado, was now the U.S. capital and the greatest military force on the planet. Their capabilities had been reduced by several orders of magnitude, but on every other continent the refugee populations were entrenched in savage land wars, devastated by each other and two winters.

The civil war across North America was tame in comparison. The rebels declared independence and claimed possession of the nearest cities below the barrier, and for the most part everyone had been able to recover enough food, fuel, medicine, and tools to get by.

Mammals and birds could dip into the invisible sea for a time, sometimes hours. Without host bodies, the nanotech was inert. Then it got into the lungs or the eyes or any microscopic break in the skin. It multiplied and spread and multiplied again, disintegrating soft tissue, muscle, and bone to build more of itself.

Scientists everywhere had made huge strides during the past year, especially in the consolidated labs in Leadville, using the plague itself to learn and experiment. The *archos* tech was a versatile prototype, meant to target and destroy cancerous cells. It could have been a godsend. Instead it had killed all of its design team except one when it broke loose in the San Francisco Bay Area—a small tragedy inside the global extinction. No one knew where to find their lab. When they died, their computers and their secrets vanished with them. The one man who escaped had been caught on a high island of rock in the California Sierra until just twenty-nine days ago, when he dared to run for another peak with a ski patrolman named Cam Najarro.

He was dead now, but first he'd devised a cure.

Using his ideas, Ruth and other top researchers became sure they could put together a nano capable of protecting the body from within, like a vaccine—and the slow American war turned hot. The Leadville government thought the situation was too far gone to simply share this new technology and trust in any peace. Overseas, starving armies ate each other's dead and kept prisoners like cattle, and there had been atrocities here as well.

Leadville saw an opportunity to control the only way down

from the mountains. It was a chance to own the entire planet, ensuring loyalty, establishing new states, leaving every enemy and undesirable to gradually succumb to famine and war unless perhaps they agreed to come down as slaves. The prize was too great, after too much hardship.

But not everyone felt this greed. The strike team that flew out of Colorado to ransack the *archos* lab was full of moles. A few men and women in key positions disagreed with Leadville's plan, sacrificing their own safety and well-being to get the right people on the plane. All three nanotech experts, all three pilots and seven of the twelve soldiers who landed in Sacramento had gone there hoping to grab the new technology and take it north to Canada, spread it freely and end the fighting. Things went badly. The good guys came out on top only to find themselves trapped in the city, more than half their number killed or captured.

In the end they chose to strip off their containment suits and gamble on the vaccine nano, a hurriedly built, first-generation construct. It proved not to be absolute protection against the plague. At times the vaccine was overwhelmed, which left them vulnerable to some pain—but they could stay. They could hide.

Three days ago, Ruth and Cam and Staff Sergeant Newcombe had set out on foot through the never-ending destruction to carry the nanotech to survivors everywhere. They thought they'd won. But they were still ninety miles from elevation.

The pounding scream of the helicopters increased again, tilting closer, and Ruth gaped up at the clear May sky for an instant before she turned and shut her eyes, dizzy with new fear and adrenaline. The choppers would come overhead, she realized. They would cover the squads on the ground. The idea took all the strength out of her and she leaned against the Mercedes—the heavy Mercedes, which Cam must have picked because its solid design might stop rifle fire.

Please, God, she thought.

Newcombe came dodging through the wreckage and bones. He was covered in ants. Unfortunately he couldn't slap at them, clutching his pack against his chest with both arms. He twisted and bucked, banging off of a big gray SUV.

Cam tackled him. The two men hit the ground and then they seemed to be fighting. They flailed at each other, frantic to crush as many ants as possible. Bugs weren't only dangerous because of bites or stings. After all this time, the ants would be enshrouded in nanotech. Every tiny puncture wound might also inject the plague directly into Newcombe's blood, but there wasn't time to hunt out every ant hidden in his gear. Newcombe was already scrambling for his rifle, which he'd dropped, and Cam got one hand on Newcombe's pack and dragged it behind the Mercedes.

"Here, over here!" Cam yelled.

The choppers had definitely lifted off now, cutting the air with their thick, pulsing thunder. Any moment they would rise beyond the truck. Ruth looked at the Mercedes, wondering if she and Cam would fit beneath. Not with their packs.

Then her gaze shot back to Newcombe's gear and froze there in sudden understanding. The top flap was unbuckled and Ruth saw their radio inside, a med kit, socks. No food.

The decoys had been Cam's idea, exploiting this strange environment. Struggling to feed themselves, they'd found stores and homes scoured clean, everything in boxes or paper bags demolished, so Cam and Newcombe had included as many cans of lard and syrup in their packs as they could carry. It was a clever plan. There were no other living heat sources down here, which could have made them comparatively easy to spot. Six times now, Newcombe had run north or gone back west to leave food traps, drawing in huge frenzies of roaches, ants, beetles, and flies. Frenzies of heat and noise. Two days ago he'd rejoined them as a hazy black storm swelled on the horizon, a violent fog of competing species and colonies, and that had been at least a mile away. How many cans had Newcombe just hacked open?

Cam regularly dosed them with a foul mix of bug spray and perfume, yes, perfume, to hide the mammal smell of their sweat and pheromones, but they weren't more than twenty yards from the truck. If there was a swarm, they would be in the middle of it.

Ruth clenched her left fist, a new habit to fight for control— to punish herself. Several days ago, both bones had been snapped at the wrist, and the grind in the break was always a distraction. She wanted to be more like her friends. She wanted to be as relentless. Her own pack was the lightest and she clawed at it now, too clumsy with her arm in its cast. Somehow her filthy mask had pulled down and she gulped clean-tasting air without regret. Dust and hot sun.

Ruth carried the data index from the *archos* lab, a few computer discs and a sample case of nano-structures. She also had a grenade. She believed it was better to destroy the index than to let it be captured. A brutal choice. The design work might be used to truly defeat the machine plague, but it could also lead to advanced new weaponized nanotech and Leadville had already used a crude nano "snowflake" to liquefy sixteen hundred men and women on the White River Plateau, rebels who dared to try to race them to the *archos* lab. If the soldiers overran her, if the bugs tore her apart—

She closed her fingers on the hard, wire pin of the grenade as the choppers ripped into the sky, sunlight flashing from metal and Plexiglas.

There was no way to keep the vaccine itself from them. Even if she and Cam and Newcombe set a hundred cars on fire, consuming themselves, the microscopic nanotech could still be harvested from their remains, and the human race had been pushed too close to the brink to destroy the vaccine outright. It was better to let Leadville have it than no one, but that was a dangerous idea. It felt like failure.

Ruth stared at the roaring aircraft and let her hatred and bitterness fill her. In that instant, she knew she could do it. She tensed her hand on the arming pin.

"Down!" Cam hit her bad shoulder and Ruth fell, gasping. She was vaguely aware of Newcombe behind him. The other man had hidden against a red commuter car and then Cam blinded her, throwing his body over her head and chest.

She fought him, trying to get to her pack again. He didn't understand and kept shouting, *"Down, stay dow—"*

Above them, the deafening thunder veered away. The change was abrupt and distinct. At the same time, a blast wave of twitchy black muck spattered across her bare face and goggles. Ants. Shredded ants.

Ruth bent back from it and screamed, trapped between the road and Cam's weight. Then he swiped at the black rain with his entire upper body and she was free.

A huge spout of insects jetted into the sky. They were carpenter ants, well out of their normal reproductive cycle. Maybe they were always breeding now. The nests and passageways of their colony extended fifty yards in every direction beyond the berm of the highway and the ground there had exploded with thousands of winged males and immature queens, although Ruth saw only the aftereffect of the swarm's collision with the helicopters. The billowing hole immediately filled in again, a cloud of small bodies ready for war.

They were protecting the food that Newcombe had left out. The truck formed a crumpled wall near the center of the storm, fortunately. It deflected most of the flying ants as well as the warriors and worker drones that boiled across the earth. Backwash from the helicopters had dragged the upper layers away, too—and on the far side, the bugs also found competition.

Fourteen months ago, in the space of a few weeks, the ants' food supply had skyrocketed and then dropped off again and the tiny scavengers had evolved to meet the change, ravaging every opportunity, surviving by aggression alone. The Leadville troops would have only a residue of human scent on their containment suits, but they were new. They were moving. And they were nearly on top of the colony.

Dark threads swirled together in the air and lashed down out of Ruth's sight, twisting up and back in the cyclone winds. Both helicopters had swung away but one went low as the other climbed, its engines straining, clogged with ants. In some brief gap in the noise Ruth heard the rattle of submachine guns on full auto, the soldiers fighting back any way they could.

Then she recoiled, her cheek and neck burning with half a dozen bites. *"Aaaaa—"*

The wet blast of ants that painted her were not all dead. Not by far. Many had been chewed apart by the rotors and many more were stunned, some of them stuck in the moisture of their own pulverized companions, but some were still free, and confused and enraged.

Ruth fell to the ground, clubbing at her face and neck. One thought stayed with her. *My pack.* She looked for it as she tottered back onto her knees and Cam was there, stumbling through the junk of his own upturned pack. He had a handful of little glass bottles. He fumbled off the caps and made a pitching motion at her. Perfume. Sweet. It scalded her nostrils and Ruth clutched at her face mask, roughly dragging the fabric up to dislodge any ants still on her cheeks.

"Where—" she said, but he caught her arm, shaking the rest of the bottles out over their heads.

Newcombe joined them, bumping hard. He had a squeeze

bottle of insect repellant and punched it against her, crushing ants, spraying juice. It was like breathing turpentine.

"I don't think they've seen us!" Newcombe yelled.

But the drumbeat of the choppers changed again, coming back.

"Run for the culvert!" Cam shouted at her.

"Where's my pack?"

"No, stay down!" Newcombe yelled. "If they see—"

"I have more trap food! There!" Cam yanked at Ruth even as he knelt, propelling her toward the Mercedes and her backpack. "If we stay here we'll die!" he shouted.

He was right. The sun was fading as the bugs thickened. In the shifting new pitch of sound, Ruth understood that one of the chopper pilots must be using his aircraft like a powerful fan, blowing the swarm off of the ground troops.

Off of them and onto us.

"Go! Run!" Cam hollered, jamming a knife into a can of milk. But she hesitated.

He threw the dripping can as hard as he could and bent to stab at another, ignoring the haze of ants on his gloves and knees. He was like that, quick to make the best decision. Cam Najarro was neither a soldier nor a scientist, but he had lived through the entire plague year on a barren, isolated peak where eighty people were ultimately reduced to six by starvation and cold and bugs and madness, and that was an education of a kind that few could match.

He was a good man, though profoundly wounded—and maybe not entirely sane, Ruth sometimes worried. He was so single-minded. He had committed himself to her even before she suggested that advances in nanotech might someday rebuild his damaged body, taking on every role available to him. Scout. Bodyguard. Friend. It was wrong that he should stay while she escaped. Wrong to waste his effort.

Go, she told herself, hefting her pack. The two men were puncturing every last jar and can and they'd finish in seconds. They'd be right behind her.

Ruth jogged into the maze of cars and skeletons, trying to keep her head down. The choppers hadn't moved and she angled away from the noise as much as possible, staggering once when her boot caught in a drift of bones. Then she ricocheted off a brown minivan and hunkered down, coughing, sick with exhaustion. Her face and mouth throbbed but she was mostly free of ants. She rose just enough to peer through the dusty windows of a sedan, trying to spot the enemy.

Some of the soldiers had fallen in the low, living fog. They staggered up, but somehow one man's suit had ripped. Maybe he'd caught it on the fence. Ruth thought his rubberized sleeve was flapping at the elbow, although it was impossible to tell in the leaping black mass of ants.

His ragged arm swung up like a flag, trailing a dark mist of blood and insects. The bugs were inside him. His shape barely looked human anymore, knotting and jerking as he was eaten alive. Two of the other soldiers tried to lift him away but a third soldier rammed himself into the bleeding man and knocked him down, pointing his submachine gun at the man's chest.

No, Ruth thought. The realization left her stunned. *No, he's aiming at his friend's arm.*

The weapon blazed, amputating the furious buldge of ants but leaving the man's body wide open to more. Ruth couldn't watch. She jerked her eyes away, looking for Cam and Newcombe. But there was another horror behind her. New eruptions had come up out of the earth and covered the road like smoke. There was also a reddish streak pushing in from the northeast, beetles or something else. At the same time, another phenomenon stirred through the haze of ants. The machine plague. Even the bugs were not immune, as Ruth had long suspected. In their frenzy, the ants were generating too much heat despite the cool May afternoon—and within the cloud, holes burst open like fireworks as the ants disintegrated.

Ruth stared in mute awe. Then her heart leapt as a human form sprinted between two cars nearby. Cam. He ran with an odd limping motion, swatting at his collar and hood. Newcombe appeared close behind. Ruth waved frantically even as she cut her eyes back to the enemy, trying to see the wounded soldier again.

One glimpse convinced her. Newcombe was right. Leadville had almost certainly detected some trace of her group, but as the helicopters flew in, the larger heat signature of the ant colony had deceived them. Now they were done. It was a spectacular mess. Dense spirals of ants whipped through downdrafts and currents as the last men on the ground fled, hauling the bloodied soldier aboard a crowded flight deck. He was limp now, dead or unconscious, but the writhing shadow of ants remained attached to him even after his friends kicked and slapped at his body.

The other chopper was already lifting away and Ruth allowed herself a small, savage smile.

It looked like her luck was holding.

2

The water gleamed in the sunrise, white and treacherous. "Stop," Cam said, even as he took several more steps himself— but now he moved sideways instead of forward, feeling wary and restless.

There was no wind this morning and the valley below them held a flat inland sea, dazzling in the light. The highway disappeared into it, although he saw the road hump up again briefly about two miles off. The water wasn't deep. It was rotting and stagnant, cluttered with buildings and power lines and cars. Spiderwebs. Small patches of silk clung to the ruins by the thousands.

"Where are we?" Ruth asked behind him, and Cam said, "Stop. Stay there." Then he realized his voice was too harsh and he shook his head. "Sorry."

"You've been here before," she said, her eyes searching for his through their dirty goggles.

"Yeah."

He knew she'd lived in Ohio and Florida, and Newcombe said he grew up in Delaware, but there was little question that Cam's parents and brothers lay dead somewhere on these same roads. Maybe they'd even made it this far. Northern California had once rivaled Los Angeles for bad traffic, however, because the greater Bay Area sat in a massive delta crammed with rivers and gullies, which meant bridges, levees, and bottlenecks.

He was not as sad as she probably thought. The land down here was too strange and dangerous to be home. More than anything, Cam felt frustrated, trying to grasp the scale of what they were facing.

Their goal looked close enough. They wanted to spread the vaccine to other survivors, and the Sierras made an imposing band across the horizon—brown foothills, dark mountains—like a wall of pyramids with the highest peaks still capped in snow. In another life he'd driven there in three hours. But those memories were deceptive. As the land rose, it buckled, and walking all the way there would have been an up-and-down nightmare even without the traffic and other wreckage.

The city in front of them was Citrus Heights, one of the nicer suburbs that made up the dense urban sprawl all around Sacramento. It had burned before it drowned. Despite the name, most of the Heights sat on the same low plain as its neighbors. This quiet marsh must have seen a torrent of water when it first went under, judging from the debris wedged against the slumping homes and telephone poles as high as three feet up. There were mud banks among the overturned cars and snarls of brush and charred lumber, all of it softened by the glimmering white silk of webs and egg sacs. The water kept the spiders safe from the ants.

"Let's check your map again," Cam said, but Newcombe had the same idea. Newcombe was unbuttoning a pouch on his jacket as he strode closer.

Cam looked back at the glinting sea. They had been lucky not to run into other new basins and swamps before now. Hundreds of miles of earthworks spread across northern California, channeling the flow down from the mountains. Two winters with no one at the gates had been too much. Everywhere they'd seen plant life sick or destroyed entirely—and without grass and reeds, the levees were vulnerable.

"What do you think," Cam said. "North, right?"

"We have to go north anyway." Newcombe crouched easily and set his map on the asphalt, moving his glove to the hooked line of pen marks he'd drawn.

Cam bent more slowly, careful of his right knee. Ruth settled down with a thump. She was clearly desperate to rest, but so awkward with her cast. He saw her raise her good hand to her face mask to scratch her bites.

"I don't like it," he said. "Look." East of the city, the American River had been dammed on two sides to form a giant, square-cornered lake. Some part of that huge berm must have given way. Cam covered a section of the map with his glove and said, "If this whole valley is flooded, we'll actually need to go *west* to work around it. That could take forever."

"North was our direction," Newcombe said.

"Cam knows the area," Ruth said, and he was glad.

It was childish, but he was glad. He said, "We don't want to be down here any longer than we have to."

"We stay north," Newcombe said, drawing his finger south across one short inch of map. "The other guys must be around here, maybe a little farther. It's just not smart to bunch up and make it any easier to find us."

Cam only nodded, sifting through his doubt.

There had been two more people with them in downtown Sacramento, Captain Young and Todd Brayton, another scientist like Ruth. The division was obvious. It meant a better chance that someone would reach elevation with the vaccine, so they had angled away from each other as quickly as possible. But they faced another problem. By the second day, Newcombe became certain that Leadville had established a forward base in the Sierras, probably straight east of Sacramento. There was no other way they could mount so many helicopter searches. The range from Colorado was too far.

Avoiding that base meant a detour either farther north or back south again, and Cam didn't think Ruth had the extra miles in her. Maybe not him, either. Newcombe didn't see that. Newcombe was too strong, whereas Cam knew very well how an injury could change and limit everything about a person. Mood. Imagination.

He admired her. She was tougher than anyone would have guessed, but the truth was that the two of them were a ragtag disaster, Cam with body-wide damage from old nano infections and his left hand thickly bandaged after a knife wound sustained during the fight in Sacramento, Ruth with her busted arm—and until just sixteen days ago, she had been the centerpiece of a crash nanotech program aboard the International Space Station for over a year, losing bone and muscle mass despite a special diet, vitamins, and exercise.

She tired easily, which had been holding them back. They were still barely twelve miles from where they'd started, although they must have covered twenty or more. Their path had been a back-and-forth zigzag through the jammed streets and bugs and other hazards. Cam estimated their total hike to be a matter of weeks, not days.

It should get better. In theory, Leadville's search grids would grow too big and they could spend less time hiding. Ruth pushed herself mercilessly. She knew she was the weak link. And yet if she dropped from exhaustion or developed a fever or something, Cam honestly didn't think they could carry her. He shared her impatience, but it was important for her to get the rest she needed, no matter if that increased other dangers. Newcombe only encouraged her, though, with all the best reasons in mind, and Ruth was too driven to say no. It had to be Cam who protected her.

"What if we find a boat," he said. "A motorboat. Every other guy around here was a fisherman or something. We could cut straight across or even go upriver."

"Mm." Newcombe turned and Cam followed his gaze to the submerged homes and wreckage.

"We have to try," Cam said, rising to his feet. His back hurt and he had ant bites down his neck and shoulders, a pinched nerve in his hand, but he bent to help Ruth anyway.

They fell into a familiar rhythm, Cam in front, single file with Ruth between him and Newcombe. They went south, drifting back the way they'd come but off the highway.

The new shore was fickle. In places the water stretched inland, filling the streets—and everywhere the houses and fences were a problem. They wanted to look into yards and garages, but each neighborhood was its own trap, either dead-ending in the water or choked with debris from the larger flood or both. Several times Cam dodged around fields of spiderwebs. Once he saw ants. Everything took time. They needed food and cautiously entered a house that looked normal except for the dry band of muck wrapped around its foundation. They wanted to siphon gas into a few extra canteens and Ruth immediately sat down as Newcombe stopped beside a small Honda, shrugging out of his pack.

"You okay?" he asked.

Ruth bobbed her head, but Cam wondered what she looked like behind her goggles and mask. Her twisted posture wasn't right.

"I haven't seen any reptiles," she said. Typical Ruth. Sometimes it was hard to know what she was thinking, only that she'd definitely latched on to something.

"Me either," Cam said.

"But you did in the mountains," Ruth said.

"Yes. Not at the top, but we saw way too many snakes and whole fields full of lizards at eight thousand feet. Seven. Six." That was as far down as he'd gone. "They were definitely below the barrier."

"Maybe the ants are attacking their eggs," she said. "Or their hatchlings. The bugs might be getting to their young before they're big enough to fight."

"I can't figure out why there's anything alive down here at all," Newcombe said.

"They don't get as hot as people," Cam said.

"But they do," Ruth said. "Sometimes hotter. Cold-blooded things aren't actually cold. They just don't generate their own body heat, except from running or flying. Basking in the sun. They can be very precise. I think most reptiles keep themselves between seventy and eighty degrees, but insects are usually about the same temperature as the environment."

Cam nodded slowly. The machine plague operated on a heat engine. When it hit ninety degrees, it activated. And yet in his experience, the plague took as long as two or three hours to power up after it was absorbed into a host. At midday, in summer, the nanotech might begin to decimate the bugs—but as the day cooled, so would these creatures. Obviously enough of them had survived, and they would breed uncontested in autumn, winter, and spring.

Fish and amphibians were safe in rivers and lakes. He'd seen it himself. They remained below the critical threshold, and at altitude it was the same. Lower temperatures protected the reptiles and insects in the foothills and mountains. They must have continually repopulated the world below in haphazard migrations.

"My guess is they're always on the edge of disaster down here," Ruth said, "but it makes me wonder if the whales might have survived. Dolphins and seals." She shook her head. "We looked sometimes. Up in the space station, I mean. They're insulated in a lot of fat, but if they stayed cold enough . . . maybe way up in the Artic or down at the South Pole . . ."

It was a nice thought. "I hope so," Cam said, trying to encourage her.

Then he leaned back to stare past the houses. Cam had grown accustomed to the feeling of being watched, surrounded by empty dark windows and ghosts, but this was different. A noise. The dead had mostly settled long ago, but rot and imbalance were always itching away at things. Buildings shifted. Garbage moved. And yet his subconscious had pulled this one sound out of the soft whispering all around them, a low, distant sound like the breeze, even though the late morning sky was clear and still.

"Hey," he said.

Newcombe looked up from the Honda. "What?"

The noise reminded Cam of the storm winds in the mountains, but there was no wind here and the rising *shhhhhhhhhh* seemed localized. He turned to follow it, afraid now. It was very big, he realized, somewhere north of them. The environment had changed so drastically, the land stripped and baking, was it possible that some temperature differential between this muddy sea and the dead earth was causing tornados?

"Oh God," Ruth said, just as Cam finally recognized the echoing drone way out across the water.

Fighter jets.

They holed up inside a sewer drain, musty but dry, crowding in one after another. Newcombe thought the concrete box and the dirt-pack above it would conceal them from airborne sensors—and as the jets swept back again, crisscrossing the sky, he said they might as well settle in. Their allies in Colorado had transmitted bad commands to all of the U.S. spy satellites under Leadville's control, causing those eyes to tumble and burn down through the atmosphere, but Leadville still had a thermal imaging sat which would pass overhead twice during the next two hours... unless they'd moved it.

Hiding from the sky was complicated. Leadville might have used some of the satellite's fuel reserves to alter its orbit and its timing, and spy planes could pass so far overhead as to be invisible. The space station was still up there, too. Even uninhabited, the ISS made a fine satellite with its cameras operated remotely from Colorado. Newcombe didn't have good intelligence on what its last orbital path had been.

They could only work with what they knew. That was one reason they got moving so early every day, to gain a few miles before finding cover again. In his systematic way, Newcombe had even taken five watches from a store, still ticking perfectly. He kept three for extras in his pack and wore the other two— two for safety—having set both alarms to give them at least thirty minutes to look for a place to hide before the thermal satellite passed overhead. The bugs also seemed worse in the afternoon, mindlessly responding to the same heat that made them vulnerable to the plague, so it wasn't a bad time to go to ground. They always needed to eat, reorganize, and nap.

First they emptied a pint of gasoline over the street above them, trying to cover their smell. Then they shared five cans of greasy uncooked soup and it was good beyond words, rich in fat and sodium. Cam's stomach cramped. He ate too much too fast, dragging his mask down to gulp straight from the can, but slowly that knot relaxed as his body sang with new energy. Unfortunately all they'd found to drink were stale, odd-tasting boxes of juice, and they were leery of the water, certain it was teeming with bacteria and common household toxins like weed spray, detergents, and motor oil. Boiling it would at least kill any parasites, but they couldn't risk a fire.

"Insects don't have hemoglobin, either," Ruth said, resuming their conversation from before. She was tenacious if nothing else, and Cam smiled to himself.

"What does that mean?" he asked.

"They don't have iron in their blood like we do, and the plague uses both carbon and iron to build more of itself. That could give them a little more protection. It might confuse the nanotech." Her good hand shrunk into a fist. "Places that get hotter than this must have been absolutely wiped out, though, Arizona and New Mexico and Texas. Large parts of the South."

"Yeah." Cam thought of Asia and Africa, too, and everywhere along the equator. In jungles, the air would be hot and thick, which might increase the odds that bugs and reptiles would be susceptible to the plague.

There was nothing they could do about it. Ruth was still taking on more than she could handle, he thought. Or maybe she was only using the problem to distract herself.

The two jets crossed back again, trailing great wakes of sound. Newcombe identified the aircraft as F-22 Raptors and wrote briefly in his journal, one of several little notepads he'd picked up. He expected to have to account for himself, providing a report of everything they'd seen and done, and Cam appreciated the man's confidence more than he could say.

Ruth was already drowsing. "I'll keep watch," Cam said, and Newcombe lay down to sleep.

Cam felt surprisingly good. He was hurt, worn down, tense, and filthy, but also full of purpose and self-worth. Companionship. Yes, they squabbled constantly, but it was for the best, everyone contributing. The redemption he needed was here with these two. He believed in what they were doing.

Still, it was damned odd. They were so dependent on each other. Day-to-day their survival was an intimate experience, demanding cooperation and trust, and yet the three of them were hardly more than strangers. There had never been time for more than a few words here and there, always on the run. Cam hadn't even seen their faces for days. He only knew them by their actions.

Newcombe. The man was smart and powerful, with stamina to spare, but his pack was the heaviest and he'd already hiked twice as far as Ruth and Cam, ranging outward to set their bug traps. He had also suffered the most yesterday. He was peppered with bites, and Cam wanted him to nap because Cam needed him to stay sharp. It troubled him that their dynamic was uneasy. Newcombe was an elite and a combat vet. A sergeant. He naturally expected to take charge of two civilians, and yet Cam and Ruth each had their own authority.

Ruth. Cam turned to look and found her curled up against her pack like a little girl. His gaze lingered.

She was completely out of her element. Her power was in her intellect but she was changing, he knew, becoming more physical and more aggressive. Becoming ever more attractive. What he remembered most were her dark eyes and curly hair. Ruth was not what anyone would consider gorgeous, but she was trim and healthy and genuine.

He didn't understand her guilt. Nothing that had happened was her fault, and the work she'd done was miraculous, and yet she clearly felt she was lacking. That was something else they shared—something else that set them apart from Newcombe. Newcombe had never failed. Yes, their takeover at the lab had ended in a bloodbath with five of his squadmates killed, but Newcombe had reacted as well as possible to every obstacle. None of the mistakes were his. He simply wasn't hurt as deeply as the two of them. It was an awkward bond, but it was there.

Cam looked away from her and a brown spider fled from his movement, scurrying across the concrete. He crushed it. He watched the ruins and the gossamer webs, fighting inside himself for quiet.

He had learned to contain feelings like hunger and fear, but Ruth was something else. Ruth was warm and bright, and Cam was too starved for anything positive. He was too aware of what they could achieve together. The potential for improving the nanotech, the potential for new uses, was both stunning and dark. There was far more at stake than their own lives.

The world they knew was dying. Today was May 19th, and yet they'd seen very little new spring growth and not a single flower, not even resilient weeds like poppies or dandelions. The grasshoppers, ants, and beetles were devastating, but a lot of plants appeared to be wilting or extinct simply because they'd gone unpollinated. There didn't seem to be any bees left, or butterflies or moths, and it was the same in the mountains.

If they were successful, if humankind ever reclaimed the world below ten thousand feet, it would be a long struggle to survive as the environment continued to fall apart. Generations from now, their grandchildren would still be waging war against the bugs and sterile deserts and floods, unless they developed new nano tools—machines to fight and machines to build. Ruth had said that wasn't at all impossible, and Cam realized he was watching her again when he should be looking outward.

"Shit," he said.

The man-woman thing had already played some part in their relationship. If nothing else, she peed away from them, whereas Cam and Newcombe were as casual about it as boys could be. But there were other nuances—her hand in his, climbing over the bent wire of a fence, or her nod of appreciation when he opened a can of pears and gave it to her first. Had he ever done the same for Newcombe? He supposed so. More than once he'd grabbed the other man's arm to help him past a car wreck. Last night he'd even offered Newcombe first chance at a jar of chocolate syrup because Ruth was still eating from a tin of ham, but with Newcombe these gestures were straightforward and thoughtless.

With Ruth, he read more into everything. He felt hope, and it was good and it upset him at the same time. Cam had no expectations that she regarded him the same way, not with his rough, blistered face. Not with his ragged hands.

He could have been angry, but he had seen what that kind of bitterness did to so many others. Sawyer. Erin. Manny. Jim. All of them dead. Cam had come far enough from those memories to see those people in a different light, and to see himself differently. Either you discovered how to live with yourself or you self-destructed, in hundreds of little ways or all at once, and Cam was thankful to be a part of something so much larger than himself. To be someone new.

But you can't tell her, he thought. *Things are too complicated as it is, and there's no way she could—*

Explosions pounded the earth. The vibrations hit in three or four rolling impacts and Cam jolted onto his knees and peered up out of the drain, looking for fire or smoke.

Newcombe wrestled past him. "Let me see."

"It was that way."

A steadier noise washed over them, a collection of howling engines that cut out of the southwest. The fighters. Cam realized that what he'd thought were missile strikes had been sonic booms as the jets accelerated close above the city, ahead of their own sound, but then he saw two specks briefly, darting east at an angle that did not correspond with the direction of the turbulence overhead.

There were other planes in the sky, maneuvering for position. They were already miles away and Cam held still as he tried to picture the chase in his head, seeking any advantage. Should they use this chance to run? Where?

"Fuck, I'm an idiot," Newcombe said as he turned to grab his pack. His radio.

"What's happening?" Ruth asked, blocked in behind them.

"The first planes are from the rebels, maybe Canada," Newcombe said. "That's good. They'll help us. I just never thought they'd risk it."

Cam frowned as he glanced at the other man, sharing his disgust. They had all made the wrong assumption, always afraid of the sky, but it had only made sense to act as if they were alone. Except for Leadville's new forward base, there were no organized forces here along the coast, either rebel or loyalist. The mountains in California and Oregon offered little more than a few scattered islands above the barrier, with few survivors. Their nearest allies were in Arizona and northern Colorado and Idaho, where the refugee populations had declared their independence from Leadville. But with the lion's share of the United States Air Force, Leadville had claimed military superiority even before developing weaponized nanotech. Cam and Newcombe had never expected anyone to interfere.

Their radio was a small, broken thing—a headset and a control box. It was designed to be worn with a containment suit, the earpiece and microphone inside, the controls on the suit's waist. They had cut it free of Newcombe's gear on the first day, splicing the wires back together again. They'd also packed up Ruth and Cam's radios as extras.

Newcombe held up the headset and then there was a woman whispering inside their little concrete box. The same woman as always. Every day, every night, Newcombe worked to find a signal other than the loop broadcast cajoling them to surrender, but the suit radio was more of a walkie-talkie than a real field unit. It had limited range and only operated on ten military bands, and Leadville was jamming all frequencies except this one.

Her words were calm and practiced. ". . . come for you anywhere, save you, just answer me . . ."

In the city and on the highway, they had also found police, firefighter, and army radios for the taking. Rifles, too, although Cam couldn't use a larger weapon with the knife wound on his hand.

During the first days of the plague, local and federal forces had tried everything to meet the threat, often with opposing intents. There were roadblocks. There were eastbound convoys and escorts. Once they'd come across an old battlefield where an armored Guard company had turned back CHP and sheriff units, uselessly. It was all just part of the mess.

Good batteries were a problem, though. Many of the civilian and military radios had been left on as their operators fled or died, maybe hoping, impossibly, that help could still come. Even when Newcombe got something working, the civilian frequencies were deserted, and the Sierras made it easier for Leadville's forward base to override the military bands. Sitting on top of the immense wall of the mountains, Leadville could block out every other voice.

The woman taunted them. "If you're hurt, if you're tired, we have medical personnel standing by and we . . ."

Newcombe switched through his channels rapidly. Static. Static. "Those jets have been trying to reach us this whole fucking time," he said. "That's why they're down so low, to get under the jamming. To stay off Leadville's radar net."

"But what can they do?" Ruth asked. "Would they land?"

"No. Not fighters. Not here. But they can give us information and they can keep Leadville off our backs. We had contingencies. We—"

A lot of things happened fast. Two of the planes roared back again almost directly overhead, an invisible pair of shock lines that hammered through the ruins. It was as if a giant hand dragged two fingers across the houses and the water, lifting waves and debris—and inside this hurricane, a flurry of white-hot sparks tumbled down toward the sea, so bright that a conflict of shadows rippled over the drowned city, stark and black even in full daylight. It was chaff, a defensive tool intended to blind and distract heat-seeking missiles. But if there were missiles, Cam didn't notice. A smaller line of destruction chased after the jets, stitching its way through mud banks, buildings, and cars. Gunfire. Cam saw the large-caliber explosive rounds kick apart an entire home, tearing through wood and brick like it was paper, before he winced and ducked away and three more jets screamed past.

At the same time Newcombe grunted, *ha*, triumphant. Beneath the noise, the radio was chanting in a man's voice loud with popping static:

". . . air is against the wall, the chair is against . . ."

It faded out. The jets were gone. Cam didn't understand the

weird phrase, but Newcombe was nodding. Newcombe clicked twice at his SEND button, a quick and untraceable signal of squelch, acknowledging the message even as he looked back and forth at Cam and Ruth. "Good news," he said.

3

Ruth woke up hurting. Her fingers. Her wrist. The feeling was a hard, grinding itch and Ruth thrashed out of her sleeping bag, frantic to move away from the pain. It was a reflex as basic as lifting your hand off of a fire, but these embers were inside her. The machine plague. She knew that but she moved anyway, screaming in the dark.

"Get up! Get up!"

The stars were intense, close and sharp, like a billion fragments of light. Even through the bronze lens of her goggles, Ruth could see the neat, open canyon of the residential street around her—but as she tried to stand, she cracked her knee on something. Then the ground rocked and clanged beneath her. She nearly fell. She grabbed with both arms and struck Newcombe as he sat up.

The two of them were in the truck bed of a big Dodge pickup, she remembered. They'd found a boat at last, well before sunset, but spent forty minutes looking for a vehicle capable of towing it. Negotiating the truck through the ruins cost them another hour. By then they were losing daylight and Cam suggested using the truck itself for camp, two of them sleeping as the third stood guard. The tires were as good as stilts and they'd soaked the road beneath with gasoline in case ants or spiders came hunting.

"What—" Newcombe said, but he stopped and stared at his gloved hands. "Christ."

He felt it, too.

"We're in a hot spot!" Ruth cried, wrenching her bad arm as she staggered up again. "Cam? Cam, where are you!? We have to get out of here!"

A white beam slashed across the darkness from inside the long, thin fishing boat, parked on its trailer. Then the flashlight jogged higher, reflecting on the beige paint as Cam stepped onto the bow. "Wait," he said. "Take it easy."

"We can't—"

"We'll go. Just wait. Get your stuff. Newcombe? We'd better splash ourselves with more gasoline. Who knows what the hell else is awake right now."

His methodical voice should have helped Ruth control herself. He was right. There were too many other dangers to run blindly into the night, but the pain was bad and growing worse and every breath carried more nanotech into their lungs.

Their ski gear was only designed to repel snow and cold. Jackets, goggles, and fabric masks could never be proof against the plague. In fact, the masks were nearly useless. They wore their makeshift armor only to reduce their exposure, but it was an impossible battle. Thousands of the microscopic particles covered each short yard of ground, thicker here, thinner there, like unseen membranes and drifts. With every step they stirred up great puffs of it, yet even holding still would be no help. They were deep within an invisible ocean. Airborne nanos blanketed the entire planet, forming vast wells and currents as the weather dictated, and this fog would be its worst down here at sea level. The wind might sweep it up and away, but rain and runoff and gravity were a constant drag on the subatomic machines. Newcombe hadn't wanted to drink the water because he was afraid of bacteria, but even if he'd had purifier tablets, Ruth would have stopped him because this shoreline must be dense with the machine plague.

Their only true protection was the vaccine nano. But it could be overwhelmed. In an ideal scenario, it would kill the plague as soon as the invader touched their skin or lungs. In reality, its capacity to target the plague was limited, and it functioned best against live, active infections. That was a problem. Inhaled or otherwise absorbed into a host body, the plague took minutes or even hours to reactivate, and in that time it could travel farther than was easily understood. A human being was comprised of miles upon miles of veins, tissue, organs, and muscle—and once the plague began to replicate, the body's own pulse became a weakness, distributing the nanotech everywhere.

The vaccine was not so aggressive. It couldn't be. It was able to build more of itself only by tearing apart its rival. Otherwise it would have been another machine plague. Ruth had taught it to recognize the unique structure of the plague's heat engine, which it shared, and she had given it the ability to sense the fraction of a calorie of waste heat that plague nanos generated repeatedly as they constructed more of themselves, but the vaccine was always behind its brother. It was always reacting. It was smaller and faster, able to eradicate its prey, but only after the chase.

Fortunately, in one sense, the plague had a tendency to bunch up in the extremities and in scar tissue, attacking the body's weakest points first. The vaccine gathered in the same way, but more than once they had all suffered some discomfort as the endless war continued inside them.

With Ruth, it was her broken arm. The swollen, clotted tissue there seemed to act as a screen, trapping the nanos in her wrist and keeping them down in that hand, eating her away a bit at a time. She was terrified of being crippled. She worried about it almost compulsively because anything more was unthinkable. Hemorrhaging. Stroke. Heart attack. Death.

For an instant she stared at Cam, shaking all over. But behind the white light in his hand, he was only a shadow, faceless and distant. Ruth bent and grabbed her pack, pushing off of Newcombe as he switched on his own flashlight. There was no chance she'd bother to pack up her sleeping bag. She immediately began to climb down from the truck, swinging her foot over the side.

"Ruth—"

"You're sixty pounds heavier than me!" she screamed, wild with fear and envy. "Goddammit! I'll always have it worst! I'll always be closer to maxing out!"

"Just let me get in front," Cam said, jumping down from the boat. He landed hard. The beam of the flashlight splashed over his chest, but he quickly gathered himself and took one step away from the truck.

Ruth gritted out words. "We need to get inside. Somewhere clean."

"Okay." Cam played his light over the street and changed direction, glancing back once at Newcombe. "Move," he called. "We can douse ourselves on the move."

Newcombe hustled after them, a second wand of light. He caught up as they reached the sidewalk and gestured with his free hand. "Stay here," he said. "I'll check this house. You two stay here."

Ruth made a sound like laughter, like sobbing. It felt insane to wait out at the edge of the patchy dry lawn beside the mailbox. In the dark, this small space looked so normal and perfect, even as she burned, but Newcombe's decision was inarguable. His sacrifice.

If there were skeletons inside, the home would be packed with nanotech. The plague was bad along the highway, where so many people had been disintegrated, but it had also been swept by wind and rain. There were safer pockets here and there, and they tended to settle down on the upwind side, using their own nerves to gauge how thick the plague might be. They'd had mixed luck trying to camp inside. A sealed room was priceless, but a single body could be exploded into millions of the damned things and they needed to avoid concentrated spikes in exposure. Worse, it might not be obvious that anyone was dead inside a building. In the final extreme, most people had hidden themselves away, crawling into corners and closets.

Opening every door was a good way to overload the vaccine, but that kind of inspection was necessary. Houses with bodies were also houses with bugs. Either the ants had come through, often leaving a colony behind, or the rot eventually made the place more attractive to termites and beetles.

Hunched over her arm, Ruth watched Newcombe approach the two-story home. He skimmed his light along the front of the building, making sure there were no broken windows.

Cam said, "What else can we do? Ruth? What else?"

"Nothing. Wait." *Oh God,* she thought. Maybe she said it out loud, too.

"Here's another mask. Put it on over your other one. You need help? Here." He dropped his backpack and carefully snugged the band of fabric down over her hood and goggles. "I'm going to check next door in case we—"

"Bones!" Newcombe shouted, and Cam pulled at her.

"Go," he said. "Go."

They were all speaking as if surrounded by a loud noise, re peating words for clarity. They were each alone, Ruth understood. She hurried alongside Cam as Newcombe's bootsteps ran up behind them and it was eerie and horrific to feel *caged* when there was nothing around her except the open street— caged on the inside.

Then she was in darkness. Both men had aimed their flashlights at the next house. Its front door hung open and Newcombe said, "Skip it, keep moving."

Ruth dropped one foot off the edge of the sidewalk. She fell, ramming her shin, but she scrambled up again with the dogged focus that had served her so well in her career. Her thoughts narrowed down to one rigid point. *Keep moving.*

Cam seized her jacket. "Slow down," he said. "We need to be careful."

She ran after Newcombe's light. She knew too much. Few teenagers and no children survived any significant infection. Their smaller bodies were a liability, and Ruth would always be closer to major trauma than the two men.

The hate she felt was senseless and crazy and yet it was there, crashing against her pain. She tried to hide it. "Come on!" she yelled. She had nothing to gain by accusing him, but why hadn't Cam warned them? He had been awake. *He was supposed to be awake,* whispered the new hate. Then she fell again. Her boot stubbed on something and she rolled over a brittle hedge and collapsed. It was like being slapped.

Ruth didn't move, trembling, quiet, listening to the agony in her arm. Even the seesaw of emotions had left her.

"I said slow down!" Cam's light strobed up and down her body. The beam was full of swirling dust and Ruth saw a little black yard lantern tangled around her shin, its power cord uprooted. "You could break your fucking leg," Cam said roughly, kneeling. He yanked at the cord and for the first time she realized he was twitching. He snapped his head again and again, trying to rub his ear on his shoulder.

Ruth looked up at a nearby *whump*. Newcombe was at the front door, putting his shoulder into it. Suddenly the frame splintered and he stumbled in.

"We're going to be all right," Cam said, but the words were just useless sounds. Helpful sounds.

Ruth nodded. None of this was his fault. The truck might simply have more nanotech adhered to it than the boat, and Cam had his size advantage. Long ago, he'd also suffered considerable damage to his feet and hands and one gruesome ear. He was unlikely to notice an infection before her. It was just that she'd come to expect everything of him, fair or unfair.

"Can you get up?" he asked, reaching for her.

"Clear! I think it's clear!" Newcombe yelled inside the house, and Ruth and Cam hurried to the neat front walk with its WELCOME mat still in place.

The entry hall had a dark wood floor. Ruth glimpsed the open space of a dining room. Newcombe was at the stairs to the second floor and waved for them, his fingers spasming. "Here," he said, leading the way. His flashlight sparked on a collection of small glass pictures. Family. Faces. Ruth forced her legs to carry her. She banged against the wall and knocked down two pictures and Cam kicked into one, shattering the glass.

Newcombe went left at the top into a boy's bedroom. It was blue with two silver-and-black posters—football players. Their flashlights cut back and forth. Cam shut the door. Newcombe leaned over the twin bed and pulled up the blankets, then knelt at the door and wedged the loose mass into the crack at the bottom.

"The window," Ruth said.

Cam tore open the dresser drawers, throwing them onto the floor. He took great handfuls of clothes and jammed the shirts and underwear into the windowsill as best he could. They were all breathing hard. "Good?" he asked.

Ruth shook her head and nodded in a confusion of pain. "Best we can do," she said. "It'll get worse."

In this safe room, their vaccine only had to deal with the plague already in their blood and the particles they'd carried with them on their clothes and in the gust of motion. Still, running and sweating had accelerated their absorption rate.

Ruth wept. There was a new thread of plague scratching through her left foot and the blades within her arm had turned to molten fire, consuming the bone, cramping every muscle. Her fingers made a palsied claw. In the half-light, the destroyed room matched her thinking exactly, a tight, haphazard mess packed with restless bodies. Her claustrophobia became a living thing like cancer, numbing her intelligence and leaving only childish terror and remorse.

Cam endured in silence, but Newcombe beat his hand on the wall.

"Don't," Ruth whispered. "Don't."

At last the burning faded into more normal pain. It was done. They tugged off their masks and goggles and luxuriated in the stale air, but Ruth avoided their eyes, feeling too vulnerable, even ashamed. She felt grateful, and yet at the same time she was repelled.

Cam was a monster. Old wounds. His dark Latino skin had erupted dozens of times, often in the same places, leaving dull ridges on his cheek and patchy spots in his beard. His hands were worse. His hands were covered in scars and blister rash, and on his right he only had two strong fingers and his thumb. The pinky there was only a weak, snarled hook of dead tissue, nearly eaten to the bone.

Ruth Goldman was not particularly religious. For most of her adult life, she'd let her work take up too much time to bother with Hanukkah or Passover unless she was visiting her mom, but the emotions in her now bordered on the mystic, too fervent and complex to understand at once. She would rather die than suffer as he had, but she wanted to be like him—his calm, his strength.

Cam dug out the last of his water and some peppered jerky and crackers. Ruth's belly was an acid ball, yet he urged her to eat and it helped a little. He also had a bottle of Motrin and shook out four apiece, a minor overdose. Then they all tried to settle down again, beyond exhaustion. The men let her use the narrow bed, clearing a little space on the floor for themselves, but Ruth did not sleep any more that night.

The room looked bigger in the yellow-gray dawn and still had some semblance of neatness above the floor. The posters. The toy robots and books on the shelves. Ruth tried not to let it affect her, but she was very tired. She hurt. She mourned this anonymous boy and everything he represented—and wrapped up in her misery was a cold, stubborn anger.

She was ready to keep moving.

She knew it was worth it.

Even as hard as life had become in the mountains, there was no excuse for the decisions made by the Leadville government. If they won, if they left most of the world's survivors to die above the barrier, in many ways it would be a crime worse than the plague itself. What this place and every graveyard like it deserved was new life. A cleansing. The ruins should be bulldozed where they couldn't be repaired, repopulated where the damage hadn't been so bad, and there were desolate cities across the globe, far more than could be reclaimed for generations. They'd forgotten. The leadership was too insulated, trapped on their island fortress.

Ruth made herself eat with grim focus, even though her stomach still felt like a knot and breakfast was a few cans of cold, gluey potatoes and beef. Cam ate like it hurt him, and Ruth wanted to say something, she wasn't sure what. Her taste buds stung at the fresh reek of gasoline. The stench made her head ache, but at least she could barely smell the corner of the closet they'd had to use as a toilet.

"Show me your map again," she said.

Newcombe set down his can and unbuttoned his jacket pocket. He invariably folded his map and tucked it away, in case they had to run—but his neatness was also about control, Ruth thought, watching his long, hawk-nosed face. Sandy blond eyebrows and beard stubble. Newcombe looked so young, even beneath the ant bites and dirt and the flaking raw pink spots that were being worn into his skin by his goggles and mask.

She didn't like his silence. Newcombe was impatient, jerking at the map when a corner of it hung up in his pocket. Yes, they were all sore and irritable, and they'd already talked through their options after the planes had gone, but they couldn't afford to make the wrong choice.

Their plan was to sprint back to the truck and drive out of the hot spot as fast as possible. The boat trailer was already attached and Newcombe had ripped open the truck's ignition, so that starting it was a matter of pressing two wires together. Even after fourteen months of disuse, the battery had kept enough power to crank the engine once. Then they'd run it for more than an hour to generate a charge. *We built good,* Newcombe had said with surprising softness, leaning his hand on the truck's tall, broad hood. He might have only been talking to himself, but

Ruth believed he'd felt the same melancholy pride that haunted her now, sitting in the wreckage of this child's room. She was glad. Even the relentless Special Forces soldier wasn't untouchable.

Newcombe was confident the truck would start again, and the boat's enormous motor had also fired right up. The question was where were they going.

The chair is against the wall. That strange sentence had changed everything, shifting the balance between them. It was almost as if there were suddenly other people among the three of them, just when she'd finally begun to adapt to being so utterly on their own. Ruth had become accustomed to outnumbering Newcombe. Cam always backed her, but now Newcombe had new power, and Ruth thought Cam was wavering.

The radio code was a rendezvous point. Despite the chaos of the plague year, it was still the twenty-first century. The Canadians had their own eyes in the sky. The rebels controlled three American satellites themselves. The surge of radio traffic in Leadville could not be hidden, especially in this now-empty world. Nor could the sudden flux of aircraft. Even if the Canadians hadn't been involved in the conspiracy, promising aid and shelter, they would have known something big was going on.

Newcombe's squad had gone into Sacramento with no less than eight contingency plans, five of which led to open stretches of road where a plane could touch down, and Ruth did not doubt that those men could have reached one of their rendezvous points long before now if they'd been moving on their own, even wearing containment suits, even hauling extra air tanks.

The Canadians planned to intercept them, lancing down out of British Columbia. The two North American nations had co-existed as friends and allies for nearly three hundred years, but now Canada would raid across the border in force, committing four full strike wings as a curtain against any Leadville fighters. Newcombe wanted to head for Highway 65 just north of Rose-ville, and Ruth was tempted. She yearned for it. Safety. Warm food. Oh God, and a shower. But it would mean pushing farther north once they were across the sea, staying in the lowlands rather than hiking east into the mountains—and there was a deeper fear in her.

"Look." Newcombe laid out the map with his naked hands,

his knuckles bruised and scabbing. Then he edged his finger slightly from Citrus Heights to Roseville. "Look how close. We could get there in a day or two."

"I just don't know," Ruth said, touching the rough patches on her face where her own goggles had pressed in. She was thinking of the paratrooper ambush that had destroyed Newcombe's squad. "They'd come in one of those big cargo planes, right?" she asked.

"Not necessarily. I'd send something small and fast."

The thought of cramming herself into a plane made Ruth claustrophobic again and she glanced uneasily at the walls of the room. Not all of the ISS crew had survived the crash of the space shuttle *Endeavour.* "All it takes is one missile to bring us down," she said, "and Leadville will do anything to keep anybody else from getting the vaccine. They've already shown that."

"There are ways to defend against air-to-air missiles, especially if our escort doesn't let anyone close," Newcombe said. "And if we don't do this, we'll have to keep playing hide-and-seek with the helicopters. We've been lucky so far."

"But we're so close to the mountains here!" Ruth met his blue eyes, pleading with him. "The whole idea is to spread the vaccine to as many people as possible, so no one can ever control or keep it." She worried that the Canadian government would prove just as selfish. Overall, their losses had been even worse than those in the United States, and they might view the nanotech as the same opportunity for conquest and rebirth.

"We're not that close," Newcombe said. "Look. Look where we are. It's still a hundred miles to the Sierras and it's going to keep getting more and more uphill. You have to realize we're still weeks away from elevation. You don't even know if anyone's alive up there. We could wander around for another month just trying to find a mountain where someone's survived this long."

And they might be dangerous if they did, Ruth thought, unable to stop herself from glancing at Cam. It was a real concern. Lord knew some of those survivors would be too desperate to care why or how they'd come, but she didn't say it. She wasn't going to give Newcombe anything else to use against her. Ruth genuinely believed that most people would help them, and once they'd reached four or five groups they would be unstoppable, dispersing in every direction, filling the dead zones of the plague like a new human tide.

"This is our best chance to get somewhere," Newcombe said.

I'm stronger than you are, Ruth realized, but she needed to be careful. She couldn't afford to make an enemy of him. "I just don't like it," she said.

Cam finally interjected, and Ruth was grateful. "I know what I'd do," he said. "This isn't usable ground for them, not if we get away. If I was Leadville, if I thought the Canadians were going to take off with us, I'd just nuke the whole area. Here. Oregon. Wherever they could drop a bomb in front of us. There's no way a plane can defend against that, right?"

"That's crazy," Newcombe said. "This is their own ground—it's American soil."

"No. Not anymore."

"They'll stick to conventional weapons," Newcombe insisted. "Look, it's a gamble either way, so we take our best bet. We get the rebels and the Canadians behind us."

Ruth clenched her arm in its cast, wondering how deeply his training had affected his thinking. The need for structure. Newcombe was an incredible asset, a great soldier and obviously comfortable improvising in any situation, but he was still a soldier, with the expectation of fitting into a larger command.

He was going to be a problem.

"Do you want to get left down here?" he asked, gesturing at her broken arm. Had he seen the fist she'd made?

The infections last night scared him, she thought. *Me, too.* But at least she knew how rare it should be to hit a concentration that bad, especially once they got out of the delta.

"They're willing to put a lot of lives on the line," Newcombe said. "Fuel. Planes. Taking you north was always the plan, get you into a lab, make the vaccine better and then spread it everywhere."

"We can still do that," Ruth said, slowly. "We can do that after we've given the vaccine to a few people out here."

Cam surprised her. "We could split up," he said.

She was right that he had been uncertain but wrong about the biggest question on his mind. She'd thought he was halfway to agreeing with Newcombe to jump on a plane. Instead, he had

found another way out of the box. He was willing to leave her—
and it upset her more than she would have guessed. It made her
angry.

"Why don't we split up," Cam said. "I can try for the mountains while you guys go to the rendezvous."

It felt like betrayal.

4

They were on the water before the sun lifted clear of the mountains. They were well-practiced by now and stripped the house in five minutes, finding a case of bottled water in the kitchen and a good haul of disinfectant, gauze, tape, and perfume in the bathrooms. Then they ran to the truck. Newcombe started it easily as Cam and Ruth climbed into the boat behind him. Everything looked good. But they were more silent than usual, Cam noticed, and he knew he'd frightened Ruth. Fine. She had to understand. He wasn't her dog and he wouldn't always say *yes*. Still, he caught himself looking for her eyes as Newcombe drove away from the house.

She ignored him. Armored in her goggles and mask, Ruth held tight to her seat, turned almost sideways because she could only use one arm.

The boat was a twenty-two-foot Champion, lean like an arrow and nearly as thin. With a hull less than three feet deep from top to bottom, it was more of a bass fishing platform than a riding craft. It had only two seats set in its smooth deck. The Champion was designed to speed fishermen from one good hole to the next, and that was perfect. Cam guessed that even the motor shaft wouldn't stick more than a couple feet below the surface, which would be crucial out there in the ruins.

Newcombe drove to the shore slower than Cam expected. They must have reentered the hot spot as soon as they left the house, but the street barely had any downward slope and the waterline had crawled up and back many times, leaving thirty yards of muck and garbage in lines and dunes.

"Hang on!" Newcombe shouted. They crunched through styrofoam and plastic, a lamp shade, empty soda cans, and stinking damp clothing and paper. Endless skins of paper. Ahead of them, the shallow edge of the sea was thick with bobbing junk, clogged in between the homes on either side. Newcombe intended to drive straight in. The truck was a big monster. Newcombe thought it would keep churning until the water was deep enough to float the Champion off its trailer. He didn't want to risk getting caught on something if they backed in like you were supposed to do.

Then the truck hit the water, clattering through the debris. They shuddered over something big. The trailer rocked up on one side and the boat slid the other way, almost bumping loose. They'd already removed the rope ties that secured the Champion to the trailer, not wanting to miss any surge that would carry it free. Now that seemed tremendously stupid.

But it worked. Newcombe dragged on the steering wheel and the truck hooked even further to the side, its engine spluttering. The Champion slid away and drifted a few yards. All around the boat, the surface clunked with charred, waterlogged bits of lumber.

Newcombe killed the engine. He got out of the truck and slogged over cautiously, dirty and wet while they were dry. Cam helped him into the rocking boat and said, "Nice work, man. You do nice work."

"Got a little sketchy there for a minute," Newcombe said. That was all. Still, Cam sensed a chance to rebuild everything between them, rather than allowing Ruth's mistrust to continue to push them apart. He could make a new beginning. But he wasn't here for Newcombe. He turned from the other man and glanced at Ruth and then past her at the cluttered sea, wanting more than anything to talk to her alone.

He didn't want to fight. Every minute in this place was enough of a struggle without losing her.

* * *

The motor echoed strangely. The sound yammered back at them from every housefront but raced away into every gap, bouncing in and out of broken windows and open doors as they eased through residential streets.

Newcombe drove with the 260-horsepower Mercury throttled down. The Champion wouldn't go any slower than five miles per hour and coasted effortlessly. Too often they bumped and bounced into tight spots, the propeller grinding once on a submerged car and then blasting through a door window in a slosh of bubbles and glass. Several times they scratched against drifts of dead brush and lumber and garbage. The ruins formed an incredible maze. Cam used it as best he could, always looking east for a way out. Sometimes that was easy. The flood had come from that direction and knocked down fences and cleared yards, often leaving bars of debris and mud on the lee side of the buildings—the west side. Streets that ran east tended to have been swept clear.

They had to know if they could boat up the river, even if it meant another argument. Newcombe must have realized what Cam was doing, but none of them had any interest in going west and the two men worked well together. Once they struggled to lift aside a snaking mess of utility lines. Once they took turns leaning out of the boat to kick away a long sheet of aluminum. There were still odd little things floating in the most stagnant corridors, a toy farmhouse, shoes, a perfectly sealed Tupperware container blotched on the inside with mold.

The sun flickered everywhere, clean acres of light on the dirty sea. It shimmered in patches of chemicals. It sparked on glass and metal and lit up every scratch in the lens of Cam's goggles, turning his head, making shapes that weren't there.

Again and again they were caught in delicate threads. Hundreds of strands flagged out from thousands of spiders. Newcombe accelerated suddenly after they idled through the collapsed shell of a home and found themselves within arm's reach of a wall full of silk and white nests, all of it packed with tiny brown bodies. The water not only protected the spiders from the ants. It also kept this region cool enough that they were probably never affected by the plague, even in summer, and Cam wondered again at the niche evolution they kept seeing. It seemed to him that the remnants of the ecosystem were pulling further apart rather than working toward any new cohesion, but he was too tired to think how it might end.

Moving east was a waste of time. After forty minutes Cam and Newcombe were finally able to study that shore through binoculars. What they could see of it was an impassable mud slope, raked through with dozens of narrow trickles of water. It made the decision for them. North.

An hour later Newcombe chose a spot to run the Champion aground. They sped into the cramped swamp beneath a massive highway interchange where the boat would be hidden. Newcombe unlatched the motor's cover and Cam helped him dump more than thirty canteens of water onto the engine, dousing its heat. There was no sense leaving a bright heat signature at the shoreline, pointing the way they'd gone. Cam figured they'd covered a little less than twice the distance they would have hiked on foot, but that was partly the point—to give Ruth every opportunity to rest. She had even lain down for a while against the coil of rope at the nose of the deck, totally withdrawn.

They needed to talk about what she wanted him to do.

They could have had the chance. As soon as the three of them cleared a fence and made their way onto the Interstate again, Newcombe called a halt and knelt, checking his watch. He quickly reorganized his pack. On the outside were mesh pockets where he kept one of their little radios, his binoculars, and a squeeze bottle of gasoline. Now he tucked away the radio and binoculars and put jars of maple syrup into those pockets instead, preparing to range off by himself and set more food traps.

Cam stopped him. "Wait."

"I'll catch up."

"That's not what I'm worried about," Cam said, aware of Ruth's gaze switching back and forth between them. Her posture had changed as soon as it became obvious what Newcombe was doing. She'd stood a little straighter, but now that bent, worried tension returned to her shoulders again.

Cam felt badly. He wanted to reassure her, but this was more important. "We can't set any decoys on this side of the water," he said. "Not right away. Think about it. When you put them all over downtown, the swarms couldn't have formed much of a pattern. But if Leadville notices the worst swarms are moving north, they'll realize we're causing it."

Newcombe stared at him. "Okay."

"C'mon," Cam said to Ruth, gently touching her good arm. She looked at his hand and then raised her face to his, her busy eyes trying to read him. He nodded once. It was the best signal that he could give her, hidden in his goggles and mask.

They walked. They walked and every minute it got harder. Stress and fatigue poisons left them sluggish and the sameness of the hike was wearing in its own way, the endless cars, the endless dead. Newcombe was the first to see the few spots of clouds in the west. Cam hoped it would thicken up. A good overcast would be some protection against satellites and planes. Any drop in temperature would slow the bugs, too. More important, their jackets and hoods were individual sweat shells. They were always dehydrated.

It was close to noon before they went to ground, much later than they wanted it to be. At last they found a wide, dry canal that ran beneath the highway. Five minutes later there was an explosion in the distance like a sonic boom.

"Oh, please, God, no," Ruth said, lifting her head from where she'd curled up to nap.

"You think they tagged us?" Cam asked Newcombe. The soldier only shrugged. They gazed out from their hole in silence. Cam made Ruth drink as much water as she could hold. They all had salty chips and tuna fish and Newcombe quickly updated his journal, looking at his watch twice again. The man took real comfort in the time and date, Cam had noticed. He supposed it made sense. Those numbers were reliable in a way that nothing else could be.

Finally, Ruth and Newcombe settled down to rest again. A pack of helicopters swept through the valley, unseen—a distant rolling thunder. But there was nothing more. The hunters never came closer.

"Don't leave me," Ruth whispered, her small hand on Cam's shoulder. He turned and opened his eyes to darkness, unsure if he'd been asleep or only in and out of waking. He wasn't surprised to find her leaning over him.

He felt the hair rise on his arms and neck. It was as if he'd expected her and he realized he'd been having his nightmare again, the same nightmare of Erin bleeding out as ten thousand grasshoppers covered the sun. The sky beyond the canal was black, like in his dream, and the two of them were positioned exactly as he and Erin had been, one on the ground, the other kneeling, except their positions were reversed. In his dream he'd been in Ruth's place, staring down at his lover as she drowned in her own eroded lungs.

Cam sat up, frightened. It was early in the night and the sky really was a solid dark mass, except where the quarter moon radiated light way down on the horizon. The clouds must have come in. Good. He glanced over at the other man, listening. Newcombe was only four feet away, but in the darkness it seemed farther. His breathing was soft and regular.

Ruth had volunteered to take the first watch, explaining that she'd napped in the boat and again when they first reached the canal. That was the only reason Cam and Newcombe had agreed, when normally the two of them let her sleep the whole night.

She'd wanted this. She'd wanted him.

"Please," she said, laying her fingers on his shoulder again. It was about as meaningless as contact could be, her glove on his jacket. She was barely more than a shadow herself, misshapen by her goggles and mask, but Cam remembered the shape of her mouth and her quick, intelligent gaze.

She doesn't know, he thought. *She can't. No one would ever guess I could still feel that way about anyone, because no one could ever feel that way about me.*

And if she did . . . If she was aware of his attraction, he would hate her for using it against him.

"Newcombe wants out of here," Ruth whispered. "I can't blame him for that, but he hasn't been through what you and I have. He doesn't realize."

Cam nodded, brooding. He wanted more reasons to be closer to her, even bad ones, and not for the first time he wondered how she must have felt watching the planet go dark from the space station. Watching it stay dark, the cities on every continent abandoned and lost. She had suffered in different ways, more like a prisoner than a refugee.

"Don't leave me," she repeated.

"I won't." It was a promise. But at the same time, he knew it was very possible that Newcombe would force the issue. What else could the soldier do? Let them walk away? Newcombe had almost as much on the line as the two of them. He would never jump on a plane without Ruth or her data index.

Cam turned to regard the other man again as an old, animal feeling stole over him—an empty sort of clarity that he hadn't known since he murdered Chad Loomas, the man who was the first to steal and hide food on the small mountain peak where Cam had survived the plague year.

If it came to a fight, Cam thought Newcombe had every edge. Newcombe was stronger. He had the assault rifle. Rather than confronting him face-to-face, Cam knew he would be smarter to shoot the other man in the back.

Before dawn they continued north. It was necessary no matter what they decided. They had to assume there was a forward base, either on the mountaintop where Ruth and Newcombe had first met Cam or somewhere in Tahoe or Yosemite—or all three. They needed to be that paranoid. The helicopters yesterday might have only been on a random search grid, but Newcombe didn't think so. Fuel was too precious.

The morning sun was still burning off the clouds when they discovered the reason for the helicopter patrol. There was only one body, a whole body, crushed and burned but whole, so immediately different than the thousands of bare skeletons strewn across the road.

"Stop," Cam said. They were at least sixty yards away and he climbed onto the bumper of a station wagon, digging his binoculars out of his jacket.

"What is that?" Ruth asked, craning her neck.

It was a young man in uniform, wrapped in gear and still tied to a paraglider. A ripped glider. His clothes and skin were scorched and there appeared to be wounds caused by shrapnel. It was difficult to tell because there were already bugs in him, an undulating haze like a ghost. Worse, he'd fallen to his death. Fallen a long way. Some of him had splashed and the rest was only held together by his uniform, belts, and pack.

"Christ," Newcombe muttered.

Cam was already looking out across the horizon for the rest of the crew and the plane itself. *That was the explosion we heard before the helicopters came to clean up,* he thought. But he saw nothing. He supposed the aircraft could have gone down miles from here, depending on its altitude and direction when the missile struck.

"Is that a pilot?" Ruth asked.

She must think he ejected, Cam realized as he stepped off of the car. He gave Newcombe the binoculars, occupying the other man's hands. "It's a paratrooper," he said. "What do you think, Newcombe? Is he Canadian?"

"But he's not wearing a containment suit," Ruth said.

"He's American." Newcombe appeared to recognize some articles of the man's clothing, although there were no unit patches or insignia that Cam had seen. "A rebel, probably."

"But he couldn't last more than a couple hours down here," Ruth said. "He would know that."

"He probably expected to meet us," Cam said.

"What?" She turned from the body to stare at them, although Cam was only aware of her peripherally. He kept his eyes on Newcombe, who made a vague, restless motion with the binoculars, but Cam didn't reach for them and Newcombe set the binoculars down on the hood of the car.

"Bringing in more people is a great idea, actually," Cam said. "They fly in a whole plane full of their best guys. We inoculate them. Then everyone spreads out with the vaccine."

"You've been talking to them?" Ruth asked Newcombe.

Newcombe carried all three of their radio units. The components didn't weigh much, but it had seemed like another team-oriented gesture, sharing his strength. Now Cam realized that the soldier's decision was entirely selfish.

"He's probably just acknowledging messages," Cam said, "tapping on the send button again, like Morse code. Right? If you broadcast too much, Leadville could zero in on it," he said, just as another idea hit him. "That's why you wanted to get away from us yesterday. You knew we couldn't set any more food traps. You just wanted to use the radio without us around."

"Listen," Newcombe said, holding his arms away from his sides. It was an open, nonthreatening posture.

"What else aren't you telling us?" Ruth asked, trying to put herself between them. Cam was proud of her, fleetingly, even as he kept his attention locked on Newcombe's hands.

"The fighting's escalated," Newcombe said. "It's total war. If we get the chance, we have to get out of here."

"This man," Ruth said. "His plane was shot down?"

"The rebels and the Canadians are putting as much pressure on Leadville as they can, one offensive after another," Newcombe said. "And it's working. Most of Leadville's attention is back in Colorado right now."

"But this man," Ruth said.

Cam's heart beat hard in anticipation and his head swam as he imagined jets and helicopters spearing across the Continental Divide, down from British Columbia, up from Colorado. There would be others dodging west into the gray sky above him, engaging each other over the deserts of Utah and Nevada.

"Even if someone managed to reach us," he said, "we'd be crazy to get on a plane right now."

"That's our best bet," Newcombe said.

"No."

"You said it yourself," Ruth said. "Leadville is distracted. This is our best chance to run into the mountains."

"But then you're still nowhere," Newcombe said. "It still leaves you an easy target."

You're. You. Newcombe was already separating himself from them in his mind, Cam realized. Should he say it? *You go.* He and Ruth could keep hiking while Newcombe made the rendezvous. Maybe that would be best. Splitting up was a way to double the odds that someone got away and Newcombe would have his success, completing at least some of his mission goals.

"Our first priority has to be to spread the vaccine," Ruth said, never swerving. "That has to come first."

"Christ, lady, that's exactly what I'm trying to accomplish," Newcombe said as his gaze slid away from Cam to her backpack. To the data index.

"You go if you want to," Cam said quickly.

"My job is to see you safe," Newcombe said.

What did they tell him? Cam wondered. *What kind of promises would I hear if I had one of the radios at night?*

"We have to get you back to the labs," Newcombe said.

Cam raised his left hand like a schoolkid with a question,

his bandaged hand. A few inches of gauze had come loose and dangled from his glove, stained with dirt and one rust streak from the fender of a car like blood. He raised his hand in a big distracting gesture and then drew his pistol with the other.

Newcombe flinched. It looked like he almost went for his rifle, but he froze with both palms out.

"Give me the radios," Cam said.

5

Major Hernandez moved carefully, trying to keep the weight on his shoulders from riding him sideways down the hill. It would be easy to turn an ankle, especially with his legs and body encumbered in gear.

Up on the Continental Divide, above thirteen thousand feet, even a sunny May afternoon was icy and brisk—and the nights were lethal. Weapons jammed in the cold. Dental work and glasses and rings could burn. Like all of the troops in his command, Hernandez dressed thickly, wearing more layers than fit well inside his olive drab jacket. They would rather be uncomfortable than dead. But it made them clumsy.

"Gaaaah—" A man screamed behind him, and Hernandez heard a clang of metal. His pulse jumped, yet he caught himself, hefting his canvas sling away from his back before he let go of his rock. The forty-pound boulder crashed down as Hernandez stepped away from it, looking for his trooper.

Private Kotowych was on his knees against the wall of the gorge, squeezing his arm. Hernandez saw a dark splatter on the ground and a crowbar that had instantly congealed with blood and skin. "Hey!" he yelled at Powers and Tunis, who'd also hurried over. There were only eight of them in the gorge and Hernandez glanced at Powers.

"You're my runner," Hernandez said. "Go tell the doc. *But go slow.* We don't need to pick you up, too, understand?"

"Yes, sir," Powers said.

"The fucking bar went through my hand," Kotowych groaned.

Susan Tunis lifted her own pry bar like a club. "You can't make us keep working like this," Tunis said. Her breath came in short, heavy gasps and the steel bar rocked in time with her body.

Kneeling beside Kotowych, Hernandez gazed up at her without moving. "Why don't you help me," he said.

"We should be using explosives instead of digging like this!" Tunis said.

Hernandez looked past her for support, but he barely knew any of these soldiers and none of his noncoms were present. His T/O was a mess. His table of organization was devoid of company-level officers—he had only himself, three sergeants, and a corporal—and he wanted to make at least six field promotions if he could identify the right people.

He couldn't ignore the insubordination. He stood away from Kotowych and held Tunis's eyes. "Get your head straight, Marine," he said.

Her face was white with tension.

"Help me." Hernandez was careful not to make it an order. If she said no, he would have to enforce it. So he tried to divert her. He shrugged out of his jacket and swiftly removed one of his shirts. Kotowych had nearly stopped bleeding as glassy red ice formed outside his fist, but it was still important to apply pressure. If they didn't, he might continue to hemorrhage inside his arm.

Hernandez put his jacket back on before he felt for breaks in Kotowych's fingers and wrist. There were none, but the hand was a disaster. Hernandez used his knife to cut his shirt into three strips. He folded one into a square and forced the bandage into Kotowych's palm, then wrapped the other two as tightly as he could.

"That'll have to do," he said. "Can you walk? Let's get you down the mountain."

"Yes, sir," Kotowych said, gritting his teeth.

Tunis echoed the word suddenly. "Sir," she said. "I'm sorry, sir. It was. We."

"You were upset," Hernandez said, giving her an out. Tunis nodded. He let her fidget under his gaze for another instant, then looked away from her and called, "The rest of you get back to work. But for God's sake, pay attention to what you're doing."

The men hesitated. Hernandez almost snapped at them, but he hid his frustration—and he realized he didn't want to leave Tunis with them. She was trouble.

"Take his other side," he said.

Supporting Kotowych, Hernandez and Tunis worked their way from the gorge into a bleak, moss-softened rock field. Nothing grew taller than the coarse grass and a few tiny flowers. Mostly there was only the spotty brown carpet of moss among pale rock darkened by lichen. A lot of rock. Rock and snow. In many places, in fact, the snow never melted completely.

Up here, the air was frigid and thin. Every survivor had acclimated to elevation or they hadn't survived, but headaches and nausea were very common among the population in Leadville, and that was down near ten thousand feet. More than half a mile higher, any physical effort made it necessary to gasp to get enough oxygen, breathing too fast to let the air absorb any warmth in the sinuses. It didn't take much to scar your lungs or even freeze from the inside out, dropping your body core temperature almost before you knew it. Anxiety was also a common side effect of hypoxia. Not getting enough oxygen, the brain naturally created a sense of panic, which did nothing to help people who were already under a lot of strain. In fourteen months, Hernandez had seen a lot of soldiers ruined as outposts and patrols sent their casualties back to Leadville.

These mountaintops were dead and ancient places, never meant for human beings. The orange-gray rock had been worn smooth and broken and worn smooth again. The elements could do the same to them in far less time. Hernandez had issued orders to dig and build only in the few hours of midday, and only on staggered shifts. No one worked every day, no matter how urgent their situation. His command had reached this slope just forty-eight hours ago. Already he had three troops on sick call, plus Kotowych, and there was little sense in having superior fighting holes with no one capable of fighting from them.

That goes for you, too, he thought. His back hurt, as did his hands and shins. Frank Hernandez was barely on the wrong side of forty, but the cold made everyone arthritic.

He was committed to doing more than his share of the grunt work, rather than sitting back and passing out bad jobs. He was too worried about morale and too many of his Marines were strangers to each other, thrown together from the remnants of five platoons. There were too many rumors and fears.

"We're almost there," he told Kotowych.

Their bootsteps faded into the clear, brittle sky. Hernandez kept his eyes on his footing, but the mountainside fell away so dramatically that it was impossible not to see the immense up-and-down horizon, a collision of dark peaks and snow and far open spaces. It was a distraction. Panting, Hernandez glanced west. There was nothing to see except more mountains, of course, but he imagined reaching across the basins of Utah and Nevada to the heavily urbanized coast, where everything had gone wrong for him in one minute.

By necessity, the American civil war was mostly an air war. The urgent struggle to claim and scavenge from the old cities below the barrier was dependent on the ability to maintain their helicopters and planes. Infantry and armor could only cross the plague zones if they were flown over, and yet this patch of ground he'd been ordered to hold was still a frontline assignment, when just a week ago he'd been the security chief for Leadville's nanotech labs and a liaison between the scientists and the highest circles of the U.S. government. Hernandez had been tapped to lead the expedition into Sacramento because they relied on him, because that confidence was more valuable than food or ammunition. Now he was on the outside. The hell of it was that he understood.

Their mission hadn't been a total loss. They'd returned to Leadville with a stack of computers, paper files, and a good deal of machining hardware. The hidden cost was the conspiracy itself. All except five of the fifteen traitors had been accounted for—six dead, four captured—but their betrayal screamed of larger problems.

Who could be trusted? The rebellion had finally reached the innermost circles of Leadville itself, although no one had said anything so blunt to Hernandez. He'd seen the doubt in their eyes. The fact that he hadn't been called in to meet with General Schraeder or any of the civilian leaders was also telling. The top men had distanced themselves from him. They couldn't help but suspect the possibility of his involvement. His friendship with James Hollister was too well-known. As the head of the labs, James had been instrumental in substituting the wrong scientists aboard the plane. Worse, Hernandez's Marines failed to put down the takeover by the Special Forces unit.

No one in the leadership had anticipated their betrayal either. That was beside the point. Hernandez had been the man on the ground, and if he'd kept the vaccine, the rebels almost certainly would not have launched their new offensives against Leadville.

Hernandez had been the linchpin. Resources were too scarce to waste an officer, however, especially with the sudden surge in the war. The irony of it annoyed him. The fighting had saved him. There were no courts-martial. There was not even an outright demotion. Instead they'd given him nearly twice as many troops as before, a mixed infantry-and-artillery detachment of eighty-one Marines supported by a Navy communications specialist and a priceless medic, a conscript who had been a firefighter in another life.

The rebels in New Mexico were said to be mounting an invasion by helicopter and ostensibly that was why he was here, ready to rain fire down on choppers or ground troops coming through the pass. It could be seen as an opportunity to prove himself again. They were positioned on a southern face nearly twenty miles from Leadville—twenty miles as the crow flies, which in this upheaval of land was more than twice that distance on foot. The trucks that brought them to the base of this mountain were long gone. Hernandez had a lot of independence out here. He wanted to believe that the leadership wanted to trust him. Realistically, though, his people were only a speed bump. A small deterrent. They might launch a few shoulder-mounted missiles at incoming enemy aircraft but then they would be irrelevant or dead, either passed by or devastated by bombs or rocket fire. And his troops knew it. They had been condemned to hard labor and a potential death sentence for no other reason except that they were infantry and therefore disposable.

"Hey! Hey!" A man yelled below them and Hernandez saw four troops hustling across the slope, including Powers and the medic. They carried extra jackets and a canteen.

"Nice work, both of you," Hernandez said to Tunis and Kotowych. Then the others closed around them.

"What happened?" the medic asked.

"Let's get him back to the shelters first," Hernandez said. "I've stopped the bleeding."

"That gorge is fuckin' killing us," another man said.

Hernandez stiffened, but this wasn't the time to assert himself. *They're frightened,* he thought. *You have to let them complain.* And yet he couldn't allow open dissent.

They were excavating rock from far up the hill because he didn't want to mark their position with a field of open scars. It required more effort but their shelters blended in fairly well, piles of granite among piles of granite. The waiting was the hardest part. They had a few decks of cards and one backgammon set and he knew his troops had taken to drawing names and pictures on themselves with ballpoint pens. It was better to work. Lugging rocks wasn't much of a challenge, but it made them plan and it made them cooperate. It gave him a chance to evaluate them. He could have ordered the use of more explosives, and he supposed it might still come to that. The ground here was like concrete, hardened by eons of short thaws and long winters. The only way they'd gotten their bunkers started was to detonate too many of their AP mines facedown against the earth, but he wanted to save as much ordnance as possible.

It was a threadbare camp that Hernandez saw as they helped Kotowych over a low ridge—a few scattered troops, a few green tarps nearly lost on the mountainside. Their shelters would never be enough. Even if New Mexico attacked somewhere else, their tents and sleeping bags could not protect them from the cold indefinitely. Still, Hernandez felt pride. He felt as good as he thought was possible. They'd built this together and that counted for something, although he couldn't help surveying their positions and reanalyzing the distribution of heavy machine guns and Stinger missiles.

The troops were right to worry. Fortunately, helicopters always had difficulty at this altitude. The weather was their ally. They could expect New Mexico to wait for a high pressure front to get as much lift as possible. The terrain was their friend as well. It would channel any approach into the pass below, where the slope tumbled away into a valley lined with the flat, winding ribbons of Highways 82 and 24.

They took Kotowych to Bunker 5. Two more soldiers emerged from inside and one of them said, "I've got him, sir."

Hernandez shook his head, wanting to stay with Kotowych.

The soldier insisted. "Please, sir."

Sergeant Gilbride surprised him. Gilbride appeared from the

downhill side of the bunker, flushed from exertion. His bearded face was red in his cheeks, nose, and ears. He looked like he'd jogged all the way across camp and Hernandez felt a bright tick of alarm.

"Major, I need for you a minute," Gilbride said.

"Fine." Hernandez separated himself from Kotowych. "I hope you're all right," he said.

"Yes, sir."

Gilbride had already started down the hill again and Hernandez went after him. Then he heard two high, clean notes of a woman's voice. He glanced back. Powers and another man were watching him and quickly averted their eyes.

They didn't want me inside, Hernandez realized. *Damn.*

Nearly all of his troops had been garrisoned inside Leadville before being redeployed. They'd lost lovers and friends along with any sense of safety. His noncoms reported that there were at least three women smuggled in among his eighty-three troops—three women who were not Marines—but Hernandez had kept quiet. Only eleven of his troops were female themselves, so the disparity was bad. There hadn't been more than a couple fistfights, though, and Hernandez didn't want to start a battle of his own, being heavy-handed about fraternization. The extra mouths were a demand he couldn't meet, but he also didn't think he could afford to take away the few good things in their lives, even if he was afraid of where it would lead. They couldn't deal with pregnancies.

He kept hiking, his face bent with a frown. He'd left someone behind himself, a younger woman named Liz who was fortunate enough to have a job in town. Liz was a botanist, in charge of an entire floor of greenhouses protected within one of the old hotels. That was a big deal, but when he thought of her, what he remembered was her tawny hair and the way she tucked it behind one ear, showing off her neck and the long, perfect line of her collarbone.

He wondered again if he should have brought her out of Leadville. Would she have come if he asked?

"Stop," he said, reaching for Gilbride's shoulder. They were halfway to the command shelter, alone in the slanting field. Hernandez saw no one else except a lone sentry at the edge of Bunker 7. "I get it," he said. "There was somebody in 5 they didn't want me to see."

Gilbride shook his head and gestured for him to follow.

"No," Hernandez said. "I have to make at least one more run for more rock."

"Please, sir." Gilbride's voice was rough and wet. His sinus tissues had reacted to the desiccated air by generating mucus, which was choking him.

That wasn't what made Hernandez search his friend's eyes. *Sir.* The formality was unlike Gilbride. He knew it wasn't necessary when they were alone. Nathan Gilbride was one of the four Marines who'd flown into Sacramento with Hernandez, and even before then Gilbride had earned every privilege. They'd been together through the entire plague year. The guilt that Hernandez felt went deep, shot through with anger and more. Gilbride didn't deserve to be out here, but Hernandez was glad to have him, which made him feel guilty in a different way. He trusted Gilbride even if the leadership in Leadville did not. He knew Gilbride was a good barometer of how the troops were doing, and Gilbride was nervous.

"You're no good to us if you're exhausted," Gilbride said reasonably. "Come on. Take a break."

Hernandez knew better than to ignore him, but he dug into a jacket pocket to check his watch. 1:21. It was early to quit for the day, and if he did, he'd have to get a runner out to tell everybody to stop. And then tomorrow's shift had better be short, too, or people would bitch, which meant he'd lose two afternoons' worth of work. *Damn.* "All right," he said. "But then we need to pull everyone in."

"Not a problem," Gilbride said.

The command bunker was no different than the rest. It was simply a trench with two tents stitched together, surrounded by rock. They hadn't been given lumber or steel. There had been an impossible amount of stuff to drag up the mountain anyway, so the bunkers had no roofs. That made them more vulnerable to rockets and guns—and snow. At this altitude, it wasn't uncommon to see storms at any time of the year.

There was one benefit to the cold. As they laid down their rock walls, they shoveled dirt into the gaps and then poured urine on it. The freezing liquid cemented earth and stone together. Drinking water was too precious, even though they'd found eight good trickles and seeps in the area.

"I pulled some coffee for you," Gilbride said, unzipping the flap of the long tent.

Their home was dim and crowded with weapons, sleeping bags, a bucket for a toilet that gave off almost no smell at all in the thin, biting air. Still, Hernandez was surprised to see only Navy Communications Specialist McKay inside, sitting with a tattered paperback close to her face. It was torn in half to allow another trooper to read the other part. She barely glanced at them, but then looked up again. Hernandez realized there was something like fear in her brown eyes.

"Sir. Afternoon, sir," she said.

"Was there a call on the radio?"

"No, sir."

But she's jumpy, too, he thought.

Their furniture consisted of steel ammo boxes and a wooden crate that served as his desk and their kitchen. Gilbride had their stove out, a civilian two-burner Coleman. It was unsafe to cook inside, not only due to the fire hazard but because of carbon monoxide poisoning, but no one stayed outdoors if they weren't on duty. Hernandez hadn't tried to enforce this rule, either, although he encouraged his noncoms to constantly harass the troops about opening a few vents before lighting a stove.

"McKay, I need a runner," Gilbride said, rasping. "Tell everyone to knock off for the day. Short shift."

McKay nodded. "Aye aye, Sarge."

She's too ready to go, Hernandez thought. *And where is Anderson?* He knew that only Bleeker and Wang were up the hill, mining rock. Gilbride was too efficient. The setup was too perfect and now Hernandez was nervous himself.

It's bad news, he thought.

6

Hernandez felt as if he'd walked into a minefield. He could only wait. Lucy McKay stayed just long enough to get an insulated mug of coffee, then ducked through the flap of the tent, the zipper rattling.

Gilbride tipped his head toward an assortment of MRE pouches. Most were slit open, their contents eaten or traded away. "Sugar?" Gilbride asked.

"Right. Thanks." The whole sit-down was uncharacteristic, not the brotherly gesture itself but the extravagance of it, the using today what they wouldn't have tomorrow. If there was a tomorrow. Sipping their mugs together in the chill green light of the tent, Hernandez deliberately gave voice to the thought. "Might as well live it up, right? If this is what you call living."

"Yeah." Gilbride fidgeted, moving two pots and a canteen for no reason except to move them. "This is already about the last of it, by the way, until we're resupplied. The troops have been going through it fast."

"Freeze your balls off," Hernandez agreed.

"We will be resupplied, right?"

That must be the new rumor, that we're on our own, Hernandez thought, and he was glad again for Gilbride's friendship. His noncoms were the best way to get information to and from the rest of his command. "It could be a while before coffee makes their list," he said, "but yes. Of course. They know we can't live on moss."

Leadville wouldn't have dumped this much firepower on him if they were afraid his troops might come back with it, hungry and mad, and yet too many of their supplies had been pilfered before they opened the cases. Nearly every Meal, Ready to Eat packet had been cherry-picked of its best components: candy, coffee, toothpaste. Even some of the ammo cases had been light.

"They need us," Hernandez said.

"Sure."

"You know you can say anything to me," he told Gilbride after another moment, curt now, even impatient. "It goes no further. Just you and me, Nate."

Gilbride set his dirty mug on the board where Hernandez had tacked his area map, putting it down on the Utah border where there wasn't any fighting. No. Where it rested near the high region of the White River Plateau, where rumor said their own forces had used a nano weapon against the rebels, disintegrating two thousand men, women, and children for the crime of repairing a commercial airliner. White River had hoped to beat Leadville to the labs in Sacramento. Instead, they'd been annihilated as an object lesson to the other rebel forces.

North America resembled a different continent on his maps. Nothing lived in the East or Midwest or the long northern stretches of Canada. Even the surviving populations were limited to two spotty lines up and down the West. The band formed by the Rockies was much thicker than the Sierras. Otherwise there was nothing.

Red spearheads had been drawn to show air assaults out of Wyoming, Idaho, and British Columbia. Red squares showed advance armored units from Loveland Pass, plus circles and numbers for projected unit strength down in Arizona and New Mexico. A few of the numbers were black, from old Mexico. Leadville stood nearly alone against so much effort, except for three islands of loyalists.

"There are just a lot of people pissed off at things," Gilbride said. He indicated the map, pretending that was what he meant.

Hernandez could see how much it cost his friend merely to edge around the idea. He respected Gilbride for it. Using their brains was the best of what the Marine Corps had schooled in them, after all, and the war scattered across the Continental Divide was no longer about food and resources. Not anymore. Everyone wanted the vaccine. He knew he should absolutely condemn Gilbride for even hinting at rebellion . . . but all he said was, "Yeah. Yeah, it's a mess." And that itself was a small kind of encouragement.

Hernandez had only limited information, which he knew was intentional, another kind of leash. He was a career man and he smiled thinly at the traditional foot soldier's complaint: *I am but a mushroom. They keep me in the dark and feed me bullshit*.

Leadville wanted him to have no other options. Leadville had seen far too many deserters, so they not only intended to keep every field commander short on food and dependent on them. They also wanted their people to know as little as possible: the reasons for the war, and whether it was being won or lost. Hernandez had been ordered to maintain radio silence and quarantine, supposedly to prevent the rebels from discovering his location, but also to deafen him to the other side's propaganda. They were all American. They all had the same equipment. The leadership had put Hernandez and other southern front commanders on frequencies once used by the Navy, yet it would be simple enough to listen to the enemy. To talk.

Lucy McKay was here to decrypt any messages received from Leadville and to encode their own reports. Back in town, there were a thousand techs like her combing radio traffic across the continent for patterns and clues. A thousand more studied intercepts from all over the world. Most of the civilian and military communications satellites were still up there above the sky and Leadville was top-heavy with personnel from agencies like the NSA, CIA, DIA, FBI, and smaller intelligence groups like those of various state police.

The rebels had those experts, too. Hackers on both sides had fought to lock out, retake, or destroy the satellites. The information war was just as real as the bullets and bombs.

Sitting beside Gilbride, Hernandez was careful not to turn and look at the radio. Was it possible that McKay had heard something she wasn't supposed to? Could she have made transmissions? He left the tent for hours at a time and there was so little for anyone to do in this goddamned place. The temptation must be huge. All of her training, the whole reason she'd been assigned to his command, was to be a radioman—and there was no question in his mind that she and Gilbride had a secret.

Hernandez breathed in from his mug, reluctant to finish it. The coffee had cooled but its taste was a luxury, as was the rich, bitter smell. In a way its goodness hurt. It touched the lonely feeling in his chest that he constantly fought to ignore.

He waded into the silence again. "We'll do okay," he said. "We always have, right?"

Gilbride only nodded, protecting his ragged throat.

"You know this hill is about the most forgotten corner of the map. It's a vacation." Hernandez laughed suddenly. The notion was absurd. "Hell, this is a garden spot," he said. "We'll probably sit out the whole war."

He was babbling. He was scared, and Gilbride looked away from him as if ashamed.

There was real dissent among their Marines. The question wasn't if there was a problem, but how bad was it? That it had reached the command tent told Hernandez a lot.

Over at Bunker 5, Gilbride had probably saved him from a confrontation he'd only begun to worry about. His troops were close to outright defiance. The injury to Kotowych could have been a catalyst. The more they saw themselves becoming hurt and sick, the quicker it would go. Tunis had said what many of his troops must be thinking. They wanted to stop working. They wanted to get out of here. Hernandez was lucky that word had spread in time for Gilbride to run to 5 and pull him away.

He drained his mug and stood up, losing the heat of his friend's shoulder. Then he stepped to the door flap, wrestling with his disappointment. He did not take a weapon. "Thank you," he said cautiously, looking at the green fabric instead of Gilbride's face. He tried to put as much meaning as possible into those two simple words.

"Sir," Gilbride began, rasping.

Hernandez interrupted. "I need some air," he said. "Just for a minute." *I'm sorry,* he almost said, but there were too many ways to interpret an apology. Gilbride's little sit-down had been an overture. Hernandez was sure of that now.

He drew open the tent's zipper and ducked through, wincing at the change in temperature. A breeze had come up and the invisible cold swirled in and out of the rough shape of the trench. Then he closed the flap, half-expecting Gilbride to follow. But no. Thank God. And there was no one waiting outside to stop him. So it was just an overture.

Frank Hernandez hiked away from the bunker, feeling very much like a man making an escape. At best it was only a delay, and quite likely a mistake. He didn't want Gilbride to misunderstand. *It's a mess.* But he didn't go back. Not yet.

There were more troops out than usual, the work crews just returning. Laden with shovels and rock, they moved in twos and threes, heading for their shelters. Hernandez had no trouble avoiding them. He was trudging up while they were going down, but it felt like the wrong decision. Normally he went out of his way to exchange a few words or a smile, anything to bridge the space between officer and enlisted.

He could see how the insurrection might have started. Each of his sergeants had three bunkers to supervise. That was as many as eighteen troops each, many of whom were on their own every night and for most of the day. If all of those men and women felt a certain way, one voice in opposition would not be enough, especially if that one person spoke up too late. It was a smaller model of what was happening to him now. The influence from below was too strong. A smart leader only chose directions in which his followers were willing to go. Pull too hard, and they might break away.

But what choice do we have except to stay? he wondered. *Where else do they think we can go? Back to town?* They were under orders. They had a job to do, no matter how unlikely it was that they would actually be of use in the air war.

Hernandez stopped beside a hunk of granite. There was a thin, warmer spot against its face and he worked to slow his breathing, taking in the empty sky again. Then he turned and hiked to the nearest summit. The wind tore into him, humming over the low, storm-blasted nubs of rock. His pantlegs and sleeves slapped like flags.

Talk to Gilbride, he thought. *Settle him down. If I can convince him first, then the two of us can work on everyone else in the command tent. If there's still time.*

If a single trooper was impatient, if any one of them was too angry or tired or careless, it could force his hand. If someone refused an order, what would he do? He couldn't spare anyone to put people in custody, much less assign guards. Even if the crisis didn't break his command, it would kill his effectiveness.

Morale was bad now. Imagine if he had ten people locked down in one of the shelters and a rotation of at least two more holding them at gunpoint day after day.

I need more time.

He couldn't see Leadville beyond the serrated peaks, although at night there was the faintest glow of electricity like a pink fog seated down in the earth. Still, he stayed. The compulsion was too strong. The need for certainty.

Things had been moving fast since the decision to abandon the space station. There had been rumors of a shake-up in the general staff and Hernandez still wondered what had happened to James Hollister. Did he get away or was he in custody? Or shot for treason? Hernandez suspected the president's council was afraid of a coup.

He also wondered if the vaccine nano really worked. It must. Otherwise the rebels wouldn't be pressing so hard, burning through their few resources . . . and without that immunity, Captain Young and the other traitors wouldn't have run off into the graveyard of Sacramento and refused to surrender. Would they? Maybe they were dead. Maybe they'd been captured and were being held out in California or in Leadville itself. He didn't know. That information had been tightly suppressed, because if it got out . . . If it was true . . .

The loyalty of the diverse troops surrounding Leadville was tied to the city's riches as well as the habit of command, but mostly to its riches. There was nowhere better to go.

What if people could walk below the barrier again?

No. It was too easy to blame Leadville for everything. Even if the leadership changed, should they really be doing anything differently? Leadville had the best labs on the planet. They should control and develop the vaccine. Hernandez believed this. If the other new nano weapon was real, they should have it as well. The wars on the other side of the planet could spread here too easily. Habitable ground was too scarce, and there had to be a center to hold.

Not so long ago the president's council had been true representatives of the people, duly and fairly elected. They had made the best they could out of a very bad hand of cards, and yet . . . And yet he respected too many of the men and women who'd worked against him, James Hollister and Captain Young, Ruth Goldman and the survivor, Cam.

Hernandez shifted miserably in the cold and saw one dark bird flitting through the wind. He wondered again. How would all of the squares and arrows on his maps begin to rearrange themselves if the vaccine spread? There had been too many atrocities for America to easily reunite as one nation. All of them had seen too many good reasons to hate, and there would still be populations on other continents who were desperate for the vaccine. The only real question was the scope of the conflict to come, who against who, on what ground, and when. He could almost grasp the shape of it. In many ways the new tide would be as vicious and all-consuming as the machine plague itself, and he was aware that small units like his own could be a deciding factor in the civil war, adding their weight to the final balance.

Frank Hernandez still had to decide where he would stand.

7

Ruth lifted her binoculars and grimaced, sweating inside her goggles and mask. The three of them had found a patch of shade beside a FedEx truck, but it barely helped. The truck had been soaking up heat all morning and now it radiated warmth as well as the odd, pasty smell of the packages baking inside. Cardboard and glue. The crowded highway was like a stove top. For a day and a half the sky had been utterly still, the clouds forgotten. Spring seemed to be giving way to early summer and the land was hot and windless, the sun like a white torch. They tried to avoid the darkest vehicles. Ruth could feel a black car through her glove or her jacket just leaning against it. Repeated contact had left her good hand feeling raw and pink. The outsides of her thighs were almost as bad, her knees, her hips, anywhere that rubbed constantly in the maze of cars.

Aching, she peered at the rows of homes below the highway. There was only a small chance she'd learn anything, but so far small things had made the difference—and she could not pretend that the ugly fascination in her didn't exist.

More than a mile away, a steel meteor had furrowed through two residential blocks, hurling shrapnel as it went. At least a dozen houses had exploded or slumped open, leaving only hunks of walls and ceilings and great drifts of white plaster and furniture. Here and there were also torn segments of metal. This was the booming they'd heard the day before, the missiles that had brought the plane down. The aircraft must have been closing on their rendezvous point on Highway 65, although they were not. They were past Rocklin now, farther east and north.

The debris field was lost in a tornado of bugs. Attracted to the blood and bodies strewn among the wreckage, ants and flies flooded the ground and pillared up into the air, lifting and swirling. The three of them had tried to avoid the storm without realizing what was causing it until Newcombe spotted the fuselage within the haze. The largest piece was most of the nose-end of a big C-17 Globemaster III cargo plane. It must be the aircarft that had carried the dead man they'd found yesterday, and it was nearly ten miles from that first corpse.

Lord God, my God, she thought, trying not to imagine it. The plane coming apart. The men thrown away into the sky. There would be more craters wherever the other parts of the C-17 had slammed down. Even roasting inside her jacket, Ruth felt a chill. It didn't matter that she hadn't asked them to come. These men had died for her, and their heroism was something she could never repay.

She closed her eyes. She wanted to pray but she didn't believe in it. *God* was only an emphatic word to Ruth. Still, going through the motions made her think of her step-father and his calm faith and then she was angry and jealous and she looked up again, her breath thick in her chest.

She reeked of gasoline and repellent. They all did. Cam had grown uneasy at the number of flies persisting at them despite the perfume, bumping at their goggles, squirming to get inside their collars and hoods. He'd done the only thing he could think of to further conceal them. He'd soaked their jackets with fuel and entire bottles of bug repellent and it made the pain in Ruth's head like a dull nail.

"What do you think?" Cam asked. "Forty guys? Fifty?"

"Let's get out of here," Newcombe said, hefting his pack. Then, too loudly, he turned back and said, "Yeah. Which means there were probably a hundred altogether."

Scattered like the first man we came across, Ruth thought, but she didn't say anything. She didn't want to provoke them. Cam and Newcombe were still learning to read each other as well as she understood the two men herself, and they clashed even when the argument was already said and done.

Ruth tried to end it before it started again. She hurried after Newcombe, and Cam fell in behind her. They hiked hard and fast, pushing themselves. Ruth saw the skeleton of a dog and a wad of money and then a red blouse that hadn't faded at all. Otherwise the carnage was numbing—cars, bones, garbage, bones—and her mind caught in a loop as she struggled on.

A hundred men, she thought. *A hundred more, dead for me.* She knew that wasn't fair. Her role had always been defensive, reacting to the holocaust. She could never be blamed for the machine plague, but it felt like the truth. It felt like she should have done more. She should have done better.

"We need to rethink what we're doing," Newcombe said.

Cam shook his head. "Let's not waste the time."

"That plane was a show of commitment."

"I don't want to talk about it, Newcombe."

Every hour the temptation to agree with Newcombe was stronger. Ruth was unspeakably tired. She obsessed about her arm. Was it healing straight? Cam needed medical care even more, and yet he remained single-minded.

"I don't know what more you want," Newcombe said. "That mess back there, that was a hundred guys who knew they had pretty bad odds even if they actually found us—and they never even got that far, did they? But they came anyway."

Ruth turned her head. More and more, the gesture was becoming a habit, denying what was in front of her. Nothing had changed despite the snatch of rebel broadcasts they'd picked up last night. They were still down here beneath a sky full of aircraft, no matter if the rebels declared themselves the legal American government. Both sides had made those claims before. So what? It was only words, and yet it had given Newcombe something else to argue with.

Newcombe hadn't given up on persuading them. He probably wouldn't. They had made the radio even more important to him, because he had no other friend, and Cam admitted it was smart to listen as much as possible. Whenever they stopped to eat or nap, the two men monitored the airwaves together. Cam had to be sure Newcombe never transmitted. He kept their radios in his pack and slept against it, and his hard pillow also included Newcombe's pistol.

"Every day we hike east is another day we'll have to hike back out again," Newcombe said. "They'll never try to get us right up against the Leadville base. It was high-risk for them already."

"High-risk is the problem," Cam said. "Listen to yourself. We're not getting on a plane just to get shot down."

He walked left suddenly into an open pocket like a strange asphalt meadow. Then they crunched through a puddle of glass alongside a Buick that had veered into a tiny Geo, smashing it against two other vehicles.

"Shit." Newcombe waved his arms helplessly. "Pretty soon they'll scrub the whole operation if you stay off the radio. They'll think we're dead."

"We can make contact when it's time."

"This is crazy."

"It's already decided, man. Stop working against us."

Ruth huffed for air against her mask. Her boots clattered through a broken femur and a torn suitcase and then the three of them dodged left again to avoid a small oil slick where an SUV seemed to have accelerated and reversed and accelerated again, bashing through the other cars all of thirty feet until its tires went flat and the engine seized because its radiator had burst. The ramming was something they'd seen again and again—dying people trying anything to escape—and every time it made her feel anxious and lost.

She kept moving, holding on to her thoughts like a beacon. They ducked under a torn bike rack and Ruth stumbled. She was immediately up again, woozy and dry-mouthed. She turned to stare back at the cloud of bugs. Was it leaning toward them? Her vision leapt with black threads and she twisted away—

She never seemed to hit the asphalt. She came awake in the damp, hot cocoon of her jacket and face mask with a new pain spiking through her arm.

Cam leaned over her. "Easy," he said.

I passed out, she thought, but the realization felt dim and meaningless until he tried to help her up. He was obviously close to dropping himself, bent beneath his pack and the assault rifle. His left arm trembled as he grabbed the front of her jacket.

Newcombe stepped in to help. Cam bristled. Even with his face and body concealed, it was unmistakable, like the way her step-father's dog had tensed if anyone except her step-father approached the numbskull little terrier after it stole a pillow or a shoe.

Cam tipped a canteen into his glove and dripped the water over her hood and shoulders. Ruth frowned, confused. She was thinking too much of the past and she tried to avoid Cam's eyes and the concern she saw there. She had seen the same look in her step-brother's gaze when he asked if they were going to tell anyone about the two of them, that they'd slept together while she was home for Hanukkah and then again for a week in Miami. The excitement between them had become a lot more than just fun and convenient, but neither of them knew how to tell their parents. Ari. She hadn't thought of him in what felt like a very long time and yet she understood why the memory came. The tangle between herself and Cam and Newcombe reminded her exactly of that wild, trapped feeling.

They'd made a bad situation worse. Their trust was gone and they could never relax, not even in camp at night when they needed it most. None of them had been resting well, not even with pills, and sleep deprivation was another ever-growing hazard. It made them stupid. It made them paranoid, but they were forced to work together. There was no other way out.

They were bound more tightly than she and Ari had ever been and her mind whirled as she fought for some kind of answer. Then she saw both men glance beyond her, leery of the bugs. Ruth nodded once and shoved herself to her feet, the nail in her head throbbing with new frustration.

They'd made their situation almost unworkable. Ruth accepted that she was as much to blame as the other two. She could have simply obeyed Newcombe, instead of encouraging Cam to stand against him. She could have let Cam go east alone and taken her chances on a plane.

They were long past the rendezvous. Rocklin was miles behind them, along with all but the farthest outskirts of the greater Sacramento metropolis. In fact, they'd talked about leaving the highway soon, striking out across the dry brown oak-and-grassland hills. Cam thought they'd make better time off the road, and yet it would also become more challenging to find supplies. Newcombe and Cam were sure they could carry enough food for several meals, but each of them needed at least two quarts of water a day. Some of their canteens also had to carry gasoline. They had no idea how bad the insects might be in the open hills. Better? Worse?

There were other unknowns. Ruth still had yet to decipher her feelings for Cam. It was impossible not to be grateful and impressed. The difficult choices he'd made were the only reason she was alive and free, and a huge part of the success she'd had so far. She didn't want to hurt him. She felt real affection and loyalty, but she was also wary. In his protectiveness was also a possessiveness, and Ruth worried at that. She was also disturbed by how easily he'd turned on Newcombe. She'd thought he would argue, but instead he seemed very comfortable with the idea of betrayal. It made her wonder again what it must have been like for him on his mountaintop, surviving at any cost.

Maybe he'd only agreed for her sake. He was obviously smitten with her—not because she was so great, she thought, but simply because she was there, because he wanted so badly to be accepted and to feel normal and whole.

It was very human to join with whoever was available. Fear and pain only made that instinct stronger. Their predicament reminded her of Nikola Ulinov. As the space station commander, Ulinov had tried to separate himself from Ruth even as they traded glances and found reasons to touch each other, bickering in her lab or helping each other through the corridors and habitation modules of the ISS in zero gravity.

Her moments with Ulinov had been easy compared to here and now. Ruth couldn't imagine pursuing anything physical. After so many days on the road, she was encrusted in dirt . . . and she and Cam were both wounded . . . and his face was so badly scarred, his body must be blistered and burnt as well. Plus he was just a kid, really, maybe twenty-five, whereas she was all of thirty-six with another birthday coming soon.

Cam hadn't said anything. She didn't think he would push. Maybe he even believed she was unaware of his feelings. He must be painfully self-conscious, wrapped in his scars, and he was often quiet with her. Shy. They didn't need the distraction, this little spark growing between them.

Just by itself, the long walk was too much. The two of them weren't enough people to watch Newcombe and still look out for bugs and other hazards, watch their maps and compass, find water, find food, make camp. They'd had to talk it out with Newcombe and ultimately they'd had to trust him. He didn't have any great options, either. What could he do? Wrestle with Cam to get his rifle back, then shoot Cam and keep Ruth as a prisoner, tying her legs to keep her from running?

In this at least she and Cam had the upper hand. In camp they always lay down close together. Two would be harder to overpower than one, but the implications of bedding down side by side were only deepening that particular trouble. In the cool spring nights, Cam was warm. Even wrapped up in his gloves and jacket, he was much softer than the ground. Last night Ruth had burrowed against him, knowing she was wrong to encourage him but unable to forsake the basic comfort of it.

Of everyone who'd been a part of her life, Ruth missed her step-brother most of all. Not her parents, not her few close friends. Ari had always been her favorite distraction. They still had yet to resolve their relationship and never would, not with him killed or, less likely, lost among the scattered refugees. He was the perfect memory, good and strong. He was safe. She recognized that. Even the cruel things he'd done were part of the easier world before the plague. He'd hurt her badly, in fact, because he was never quite in reach. Legally they were family and they'd been scared of what people would think. So he'd left her. Twice. A third time, she had been the one to call things off. It was messy. It was intense.

Ruth Ann Goldman had been an only child. Probably that was for the best. Her father was an independent software programmer/analyst, brilliant at his work and in high demand. He had few hours for his daughter and less for his wife. That he could have hired on with one company and settled into a steady nine-to-five, yet chose not to, wasn't something Ruth understood until much later. She was a loud girl, antic and capering, hungry for approval at home and therefore everywhere else—in school, with her peers.

After the divorce her mother found a better man, not so driven. Her step-father was a lot like her dad, enthusiastic and smart. He was more disciplined in giving of himself, however, more appreciative, having lost his first wife to cancer.

It wasn't the Brady Bunch, no matter how many times her mother made that idiotic joke. Ruth shared a bathroom with Susan and Ari, which was both excruciating and thrilling for a thirteen-year-old who had always had a toilet and a shower to herself. The Cohen kids were casual about busting in on each other wearing only underwear or a towel. There were glimpses of skin and slammed doors and apologies, and it was all very dramatic. Both of them were older than Ruth, Susan by four years, Ari by two, and they were always running around getting ready for dates or, in Ari's case, cleaning up after baseball and basketball. Ruth managed to get in the way often enough.

If love is indeed just chemistry, it shouldn't have shocked anyone that step-brother and sister ended up together. His dad and her mom made a good fit. There was an echo of that attraction in the next generation and they circled each other for years, Ruth pushing him back with sarcasm and drawing him close in a thousand ways, teasing him and herself by asking about his girl-friends, by flaunting around the house in her pajamas, by sitting with him and his math homework—a low-charge erotic tension much like she would develop with Nikola Ulinov nearly two decades later. Alone in the house, they wrestled for possession of the TV remote, and they played dunk wars in the community pool in front of everyone, smooth skin on wet skin.

Ari was popular and athletic. Ruth was more on the outside of the social scene, a brain. She had a decent body and great hair but a face that looked like she'd borrowed an adult's nose and ears.

They first kissed when she was seventeen and still a virgin, after she came home unhappy after a bad time at a school dance. The boy she liked hadn't been interested in her. Maybe Ari took advantage of that. Maybe she let him. He touched her through her clothes and she grabbed him once. But it was awk-ward the next day. Confusion drove them apart and silence filled their friendship. Fortunately, Ari went off to college. They only saw each other over holiday breaks and the next summer, after which Ruth left home herself for Cincinnati U. Then he had a serious girlfriend. Then she had her first internship.

Ruth was more experienced when they both came home for Hanukkah the year she was twenty-one. She made eyes at him over dinner and across the living room while the family watched TV. After the house had settled down for the night, she left her light on, pretending to read a book. He rapped quietly on her bedroom door and it was exciting and nice and romantic as hell.

Things went on like that for years, stealing an afternoon or a few nights together. They certainly could have tried harder to make a relationship of it, but Ruth was too busy and Ari never had any trouble talking other women into bed, which flustered her.

It was that unsettled karma that kept him in her heart.

Most of what Ruth knew and believed about religion, she'd learned from her step-father. She had hardly grown up Orthodox, eating tasty animal by-products on pizza with her friends, her dad banging away on his computer on the Sabbath, but this part of her life underwent a change after her mother remarried. Ari often had games on Saturdays and her step-father happily drove the family to attend, and yet the Cohens disdained pig meat as proscribed. They also made some effort to avoid work and to leave the TV off on the Sabbath. Her step-father's faith was less a matter of worship than a practiced respect for all things. If pressed, he could boil it down to one cliché not typically perceived as Jewish. *Do unto others as you would have them do unto you.* It wasn't scientific or even particularly logical, given human nature, but it had balance and it appealed to her.

Ruth had been a child at first with Ari, and later she had been selfish. She couldn't afford to make that mistake again.

The fact of the matter was that Ruth had gone out of her way to grab a box of condoms from a Walgreens while the men were three aisles over in the canned-foods section, wondering what the hell she was going to say if they caught her. *Because I have to.* Even if she said no, Cam might say yes, and her choices were limited. She'd encouraged him.

She resented him. Sometimes it was no fun being a woman, being smaller, being alone.

As she followed Cam past a dented van, Ruth willed herself not to ask him for a rest. More and more, she was afraid of appearing weak. She reached for the vehicle's side mirror to balance herself, glancing up to regard Cam's back. Then she reeled away from the broken skull pressed against the glass, its teeth smashed into an everlasting scream.

Ruth felt her doubt swelling, and new shame. *Try not to think about it.* Unfortunately her body hurt in too many places to ignore, and where she didn't hurt she itched. She didn't understand how Cam could get up and keep moving every day.

Don't think. That's the trick. Don't think.

There were too many decisions to make among the cars. Cam stepped over a skeleton, but she had to walk around. Then he backtracked from several vehicles crammed together into a dead end, whereas Ruth was far enough behind that she could shortcut to his new path.

She stopped suddenly, gazing past him with sick disbelief. They had neared the top of a low rise and in front of them the Interstate swept upward for more than a mile, cutting in between steep hills of grass and gnarled oak trees. The road was studded with eastbound traffic on both sides. Cars filled the shoulders and dropped into some of the lower points off-road and she could see a rockslide that had given way from one of the embankments, an iron-red vein of dirt and gravel. It looked like forever. Newcombe was right. There was no way they were going to reach elevation in less than another week or even two, laboring through every damned inch of wreckage.

Don't. Please. Please don't think, she warned herself, but the cold dread in her would not fade. Ruth couldn't help staring at the long band of road as they pushed in between the hoods of two cars—

Cam turned and caught at her as a dry, shaking sound filled her ears. Rattlesnakes. A host of muscular bodies were curled in the space in front of them, territorial and aggressive. Cam moved sideways and then backpedaled from more rattling. He'd obviously found more snakes beyond the nearest cars and Ruth glanced left and right, thinking to climb up onto something.

She struggled for words. "What do we do?"

"They like the road," Cam said. "It's nice and hot. Lots of places to hide. We might be better off going cross-country like we talked about."

"Goddammit, this is crazy," Newcombe said. "You don't have any idea what we're getting into."

"I do. We can make it."

"I can get a plane for us today!"

"They'll kill us as soon as they see it land."

"Stop," Ruth said. "Stop fighting." But her voice was a whisper and the men didn't respond, their faces locked on each other. She turned away, trembling.

The environment seemed to be changing with the rise in the land. They'd walked into an area where at least some reptiles had survived—and they were still barely five hundred feet above sea level with at least eighty miles to go in this bizarre, lethal world. She did not want to fail Cam, but what if they'd made the wrong choice?

He was already scouting a way past the snakes, hauling himself onto the hood of a Toyota to look around. The car rocked against another vehicle, screeching. Beyond him, though, the road stretched on and on, and her feet were already a mess of blisters and strained tendons and bones.

Ruth was no longer sure they could make it.

8

The intelligence agent following Ulinov carried an open flip phone down alongside his body like a knife, allowing the two of them to be tracked every step of the way through the congested streets of downtown Leadville.

Nikola Ulinov was a big man, but he constantly let himself be delayed as people shifted and ebbed around the sandbagged gun emplacements. For one thing, it made it very difficult to tail him. He'd already spotted a second agent struggling to remain unseen despite his stop-and-go pace.

Ulinov stood at a hundred and eighty-eight centimeters. The Americans would have said *six-two* in their quick slang. He normally had the edge in any crowd. The former cosmonaut was large for a graduate of the Russian Federal Space Agency, thick in the shoulders and chest. His limp only made him more imposing. Most people angled away from him without thinking, but he was in no hurry. It had been two days since he'd had an excuse to cross the city and he was taking notes.

He was a weapon. That was the basic truth of it, and that was how he felt, not hateful but full of purpose. A weapon does not hate. It only serves. His ammunition was merely what he stole from them with his eyes and ears—and yet day by day he became more dangerous.

He kept his face down like most of the civilians, hunched into his coat. Each time his gaze flickered up, he was afraid he would give himself away. Every step he took sideways or back to avoid the other men and women was more than an act. He walked among them as if he was wearing a bomb and it seemed impossible that no one could sense what was different in him, his thoughts, his poise. He was the enemy.

Perhaps that would change. He hoped for it. Nearly from the beginning, his people and the Americans had established an alliance, although that partnership had consisted of little more than words transmitted from one side of the world to the other. The Americans were too engrossed in their own survival, and by the end of the second winter, all that remained of Russia were a few million refugees with no real wealth or power. Until now.

On the face of it, that was why Ulinov had been brought down from the space station, as a proven and highly visible representative for his shattered government, bilingual, trained in diplomacy, experienced at working with and even commanding Americans. But he needed to be more. His people were desperate for any advantage.

He hadn't found it. As far as Ulinov could tell, Leadville's strength was growing. Not by much. They had their own problems, yet even a slight improvement went drastically against the global trend. He had witnessed this firsthand aboard the ISS, looking down on the planet as survivors everywhere fell silent.

You don't realize your luck, he thought, and found himself glancing up too long. He made eye contact with a sunburnt young Army corporal standing at the edge of the sidewalk in full battle rattle—helmet, parka, gloves, and submachine gun. The boy's expression tightened and Ulinov worried what had shown in his own eyes. Envy? Anger?

Ulinov didn't dare look back. It was important that the two intelligence agents didn't think he was aware of them, and yet his bitterness stayed with him like a shout.

You don't realize. You have so much.

The new U.S. capital sat at 10,150 feet on a bit of flat ground cradled among towering white peaks. There had never been many trees at this elevation—absolutely none, now, all burned for fuel during the first winter—and Leadville was a collection of old brick and modern concrete. Anchoring main street were two heritage museums and a well-preserved opera theater built in 1870.

Even in the twenty-first century, the wide boulevard still had the shape of the American frontier, designed to accommodate wagons and horses. Before the plague, this town had been home to less than four thousand people, but all of the historical buildings and breakfast cafes had been turned into command centers for civil, federal, and military staffs.

It was a foothold. Hotels, offices, and private homes had been packed with survivors, even the gas stations and the laundromat. Prefab warehouses and tents filled many of the side streets, rooftops, and parking lots. It was enough.

If he closed his eyes, the crowd almost reminded him of Kiev and Moscow and Paris, boot heels on pavement, the rustle of people wisking against each other. And yet the pace was wrong, as were the human sounds. No one ran because they were late for work or a show or lunch. No one laughed or shouted.

Ulinov came up against the back of a man who was engrossed with his cell phone, turned to face the brick wall of a bank. The man did not speak. He only texted, working his thumb on the phone's touch pad. Ulinov slipped by and immediately saw another woman tapping into her cupped hands, the bridge of her nose chapped and pink much like the young soldier's face. At this altitude, daylight seethed with ultraviolet, and there was no longer any sunscreen to be had at any price.

The important thing was the phones. The government staffers, soldiers, doctors, machinists, electricians, and other critical personnel were all linked together by a local array of cellular towers and wireless Internet built during the plague year, and yet Ulinov had never heard anyone speaking into them in more than a hush. They were afraid of infiltrators. Their war was against their own people, and how could they be sure who was on their side when the enemy looked like them and talked like them?

In many ways it was as if winter still held Leadville beneath eight feet of snow and subzero temperatures. These people were still waiting. They were frozen. Even with the fighting, too many of them didn't have enough to do, and every mouth to feed was a strain. Everyone worried that they were expendable.

For the most part, Ulinov had only seen what the government wanted him to see in the eighteen days since he'd evacu-

ated the ISS. There had been a parade. He had received superb
medical care and extra rations. But the pretense was gone.

Leadville was a fortress, walled in by layer upon layer of
garrisons, armored units, outposts, and scouts—and like a muscle,
it was flexing. The sky had reverberated for days as they launched
air sorties, the roar of jets and support craft lifting away from
the mountains. Ulinov had trouble keeping a sure count. He
couldn't always be outside or move to a window. The USAF also
seemed to be simply repositioning their planes, clearing out the
crowded little airport on the south side of town, landing many
nearby on the highways to the north instead, and some of the
short flights overhead were only small civilian craft or fat commercial planes.

Leadville was also reequipping special ground units, filling
the main thoroughfare with missile carriers and Abraham tanks,
cracking the surface of the road beneath these lumbering machines. Ulinov had counted at least six motorized units in each
of the four blocks he'd covered so far, and he glimpsed roughly
the same number on the street ahead. Motorized cannon. Squat
APCs for the soldiers who would support the artillery. Yesterday the streets had rumbled early in the day and again at night,
the vehicles moving in and out to be followed by another group
this morning. A second wave.

How many more? he wondered, and bumped into a soldier
cutting across the sidewalk to the door of a shop. A captain, he
realized. "Excuse me," Ulinov said, being careful with his enun-
ciation. He had the proper identification, but he didn't want to be
stopped for something as simple as his accent. He was already
going to be late.

The captain barely glanced at him, though, before moving
inside. Black spray paint covered the old shop name. CAV4. The
graffiti was everywhere and Ulinov tried to remember it all. FBI
F2. ODA S/S. Everything went into his reports, and to him it
looked as if Leadville was doing much more than reinforcing
what was already a powerful base. He believed they were mounting an attack. But where?

There were rumors, of course; the obvious air war; stories of
nanotech weapons and stories that Ruth turned traitor with another new device; word that James Hollister had been executed
and that many others were in jail or under house arrest.

Ulinov knew it would only be a very short time now before he was caught out himself.

In a small room in an old hotel—a small, private room with electricity and a computer and two phones—Ulinov met with Senator Kendricks and General Schraeder. His tension worked in their favor, yet there was no concealing it. Still, he tried.

Kendricks clearly enjoyed the moment, surveying Ulinov's face as they exchanged mundane greetings. "Good morning, Commander. Have a seat. Can I get you anything to drink? A Coke?" He produced a red can from his desk.

Ulinov knew the unopened soda was worth fifty dollars on the street, and Kendricks liked to do little favors. He nodded. "Yes. Please."

"And how's that leg of yours?"

"I am improving. Your doctors are excellent." Ulinov had been on the flight deck of the space shuttle *Endeavour* when it crash-landed on the highway outside of town, taking shrapnel through the windshield and killing their pilot.

"Good," Kendricks said. "Good. Glad to hear it."

Ulinov was patient, accepting the Coke and then lifting it like a salute. "Thank you."

Kendricks nodded his head and his broad cowboy hat in a slow, serious movement. The white Stetson was his signature mark and he also dressed himself in string ties on plain blue work shirts. He was clean-shaven. Ulinov suspected the man had worn a suit in Washington, but Colorado was his home territory and most of the survivors in town were local or at least from the surrounding West. A good part of the military had also been based in this state.

Ulinov didn't think there had been any elections, nor did he suspect there would be, but it must be easier, playing the caricature. People wanted the traditional to steady themselves against so much loss and suffering. In his mid-fifties, fit and strong, Lawrence N. Kendricks made a good father figure.

General Schraeder might have tried to model himself in the same image, learning from the senator. He kept his dark hair longer than the cliché military man, softening the stern image of his Air Force uniform, ribbons, and insignia. The extra length also partially hid the strip of gauze on his ear, where Ulinov guessed that a precancerous melanoma had been removed.

Schraeder lacked the ego that gave Kendricks his unshakeable confidence, however. Maybe it was only that Schraeder had witnessed more destruction and failure up close. He was usually as tense as Ulinov, and today it showed. The general was stiff and quiet. He was a henchman.

But don't ignore him, Ulinov thought, drinking from his sugary, fizzing Coke. *The two of you have more in common, and Schraeder may actually want to help if the senator lets him.*

Since the first days of the plague, Kendricks had never been farther than eight slots from the pinnacle of the American government. A helicopter accident had killed the president in the evacuations out of the East Coast, the vice president assuming that role himself, and in the chaos the Speaker of the House ended up in Montana, which soon went over to the rebels.

The end of the world had been good to Kendricks. And if there was a coup attempt that was put down in recent days, the senator appeared to have come out of it even more perfectly positioned. Kendricks and Schraeder already held two of the seven prized seats on the president's council, and Ulinov suspected the top leadership had recently been pared down to four or five. In his prior meetings he'd sat down with the whole group, but two days ago that had changed.

Kendricks was adept and opportunistic, extremely sharp beneath the show of being a lazy cowboy. *The man is a bear,* Ulinov thought, *afraid of nothing and always hungry.*

How can I use that against him?

"Well, it looks like it's as bad as we were thinking," Kendricks said at last, rapping his knuckles on his desk and then gesturing with the same hand at Schraeder. "We can't afford to give you any planes right now."

"It is difficult," Ulinov agreed blamelessly.

"Still, there's no question that it's in our own best interest to help your folks way over there," Kendricks continued, folding his hands. "It's just a matter of how many planes we can dedicate to the job. How many and when."

Ulinov only nodded this time, struggling with his resentment. *Does he want me to beg?*

He'd known this was coming. Two days ago Kendricks had

given every signal that their deal would change, calling Ulinov in to lecture him on the problems presented by the rebel uprising . . . and yet the American civil war was a trifle compared to what Ulinov's people were facing.

Their motherland had been abandoned almost completely. The tallest peaks in the Urals fell short of even two thousand meters. Otherwise Russia possessed only a handful of icy mountains very close to the Chinese and Mongolian borders, plus a few small safe zones in deepest Siberia and along the Bering Sea. From the first reports out of California to the time that the machine plague swept into Europe, the Russians had barely a month to relocate their entire nation even as dozens of other countries claimed and then fought for elevation.

By accident, humankind had begun global warming in time to do themselves a lot of good. There was evidence that the trend was at least partly natural, easily blamed on volcanic activity and a pendulum-like cycle from warmer eras to ice ages and back again—but eighty years into the greatest population boom the world had ever seen, endless gigatons of smoke and exhaust had tipped the balance in the atmosphere.

It was the upper reaches of the planet that began to show the effects first. There were still cold spikes, but by the late 1990s the evidence was too conspicuous to disbelieve. Snowfall became rain. Frozen ground relaxed and thawed. There were also more landslides and floods, but the acceleration of greenhouse gases had made every difference between life and death in the plague year. The warming created more useable ground for survivors even if it was just a few meters at a time.

All of Europe clashed in the Alps. China and India rose over the central Himalayas like human tides. There were also safe zones within Iran, and Russia had economic and political ties there, but the Iranians detonated fourteen dirty bombs along their borders to beat back their Arab neighbors. The wind was wrong. Fallout left too much of the Iranian high ground contaminated, not at lethal levels but deadly in the long run.

The Russians fled to the mountain ranges of Afghanistan and to the Caucasus, a sheer jag of rock thrust up between the Caspian and Black Seas. They were outnumbered in both places by refugee hordes from across the Middle East, but at the same time, they were correct in believing they would outgun their enemies. It didn't last. Air superiority meant nothing without reliable maintenance, fuel, and ordnance. Their tanks and their artillery also wore down. On some fronts the pitiless land war was already being fought with rocks and knives, and the Muslims' numbers quickly gave them the advantage.

Negotiations with the Americans had begun months ago, still in the heart of winter. Everyone was aware of what the spring thaw would bring—new fighting, new horror—and the Russians were both distributed badly and surrounded everywhere. Let the Afghanis, Chechens, Turks, Kurds, Jordanians, Syrians, Lebanese, Palestinians, and Iraqis battle among themselves. The Russians had bargained their way out, offering their veteran armies to India in exchange for a sliver of real estate in the Himalayas as a buffer against the Chinese.

That would be a brutal fight itself, of course, but with only one front instead of twenty. Their hope was to establish a stalemate, a cold war with entrenched borders. But to get there, they needed many more planes and fuel.

The United States had been spared as always by its geographical isolation and, ironically, by the fact that the plague broke loose in California and spread across North America first. They only had themselves and the Canadians to save as the rest of the world stayed back. Other countries waited and hoped, and then it was too late. Even close allies like the British, with no high ground of their own, had been forced to airlift themselves into the crowded war in the Alps after the nanotech was suddenly everywhere.

There were a few other somewhat calm zones. In fact, most of the South Pole was safe. Antarctica had endless ranges and plateaus above ten thousand feet. The freezing weather also came with low pressure fronts, leaving vast, high stretches of ice that were often free of the plague. But it was just ice. There was nothing to sustain anyone there.

Greenland took in some of the Norweigans and the Finns and their militaries, establishing a separate peace. The survivors out of Australia joined with New Zealand, and Japan still held a few peaks at the heart of their island.

Elsewhere the fighting was mixed and savage. In Micronesia, millions of people fought for a handful of island peaks. The entire population of Africa tried to shove up onto Mt. Kilimanjaro and the very few other high points on the continent even as the Israelis airlifted south into Ethiopia and burned clear several peaks for their own.

Ulinov often wondered if the Russians should have planned to run farther themselves, but it was hard. They'd wanted to stay close to their cities, their industrial base, their military stockpiles—and they were not without experience in fighting on Muslim land. He knew they were using their few remaining jets and helicopters to scavenge beneath the barrier, desperate for weapons and food.

The weight of it was like hundreds of years pressing down on him, millions of lives, the history of an entire nation. His people had been pushed to the last extreme. Their existence itself was at risk. There were still more than fifteen million of them alive, but unless the fighting saw a dramatic turnaround, they would be lost, utterly gone except perhaps for a small collection of slaves and a few scattered souls like himself, bred out in a generation. And here he sat in his plush chair with a Coke.

"What we need is everybody on the same page," Kendricks said, making an open gesture with one small hand. "We need to work together if we're ever going to get things straight again. Right now it's up to India to make the right choice. We've told 'em that."

"And what did they say?"

"Well, they're playing hardball. They think they're doing enough by giving you people some land, and that's a good deal for you. Sure it is. Them, too. But what about us?" Kendricks tipped his head forward, bringing the peak of his hat down in an aggressive posture. "What do we get for all those pilots and planes and the guns we'll bring over? Maybe even some food. Why are we sending our boys all around the world when we've got a whole stack of problems of our own?"

"The nanotech," Ulinov said, like a good pupil.

"Exactly. That's it exactly." Kendricks smiled. "India's got some good folks and they've got a lab full of gear or two. But they're exposed. The Chinese could ruin what they're doing at any time, and they're way behind what we're doing here anyway."

"So you consolidate their labs with yours."

"Yes. It's too hard to do everything on the radio and there's no way we're going to keep flying planes back and forth. It's just smart. It's win-win."

"Then you are making progress with R—" He didn't want to say *Ruth's work.* "With the nanotech."

"Yes. I think I can tell you we're getting close to something that'll protect us all—us and our allies. I mean below the barrier. We can change the whole planet."

"A weapon?" Ulinov looked at Schraeder, but the general's expression betrayed nothing.

Kendricks frowned before making his face smile again. "People have been talking, I guess," he said. "I know you're in the radio room a lot."

Did he expect names? Someone to punish? Ulinov would give him that, if he wanted. "A new plague is what they say." Ulinov shrugged. "Talk on the street. Everywhere. They say it's a new plague that works above ten thousand feet, but controlled, like a gas."

Kendricks just shook his head.

"They say it goes away and the land is good," Ulinov said, shifting cautiously in his chair. He did not want to play his next card . . . to take this gamble . . . but it felt good to show strength. "We know it exists," he said. "We know you used it on the White River."

"What are you talking about?"

"We still control a few satellites," Ulinov said. When he imagined them, it was always with pride and hurt—his countrymen in dirt holes and ice caves, using laptops and a ragtag collection of transmitters to control impossibly complex machines beyond the sky, machines that were now beyond their ability to replace. "We have high-gain video of the assault," he said. "We have analysis of how the nanotech . . . how it consumes." The Americans called their weapon the snowflake, perhaps because of the way it reacted to living tissue, swirling and clotting. "We know its dispersal rate. The heat it gives off. We have even been able to determine its *shape*."

"The assault was necessary," Schraeder said.

"Yes." Ulinov would not argue that. "But we wonder if the Chinese also had a satellite in position. There has been some speculation if they could use that information to advance their own nanotech."

The rest didn't need to be said out loud, the array of threats within those words, not if Kendricks understood that the Russians could choose not to protect India after all. Kendricks had to realize that the Russians still had the option of making a very different deal to save themselves, trading their muscle for real estate as shock troops *against* India instead of for it. They could sell their satellite videos to the Chinese as a good part of that bargain.

Ulinov knew this proposal had already been made. Envoys had gone not only to the Indian Himalayas but also to the southern range to bow before the Chinese premier.

Kendricks responded easily. "I've got my doubts that anyone could learn much from a few pictures," he said with a shrug. "Either way, that's just all the more reason for India to help us out. Our side's got to keep the upper hand if everyone doesn't want their babies to grow up talking Chinese."

"Before we fight them we want the snowflake," Ulinov said, and he smiled at the small shock in their eyes. Orbital analysis was one thing. That he also knew the name of the nano weapon revealed a much deeper level of espionage, and that he would be so bold about it should indicate something even more worrisome to them: a willingness to fight.

Kendricks remained cagey. He scowled at Ulinov, but his voice was steady. So were his eyes. Nothing would shake the man. "Well, the problem there is we're having a hard time manufacturing enough of the nanotech," Kendricks said. "That's another reason we need India's gear."

Ulinov nodded slowly, bitterly, measuring his own position and knowing that it was weak. But his orders were clear. "We want the snowflake," he said.

9

It was a feint, of course. His government must know the Americans would never hand over a weapon of such magnitude, although before the end of their meeting Schraeder made a few noises about possibly sending over a few Special Forces advisors in control of the snowflake.

What were his people truly after?

Ulinov grimaced in the wind and darkness, squinting up at the rash of stars. Tonight his old friends felt very far away and he tried to summon the memory of their real beauty. Even at ten thousand feet there were a great many miles of atmosphere between him and space, altering and dimming the starlight.

From the viewports of the ISS, those distant suns had never wavered, and Ulinov missed their bright, steady perfection because he didn't dare allow himself to miss it in himself.

He was a tool. He accepted that. There was a great deal more at stake than his personal well-being, but this new gambit was worrisome. By pushing Kendricks for the nanotech, Ulinov had revealed that he had a secret channel of communication, because his conversations with the Russian leadership were always closely monitored. Without question, the tapes were replayed again and again by NSA analysts. There had never been any charade of diplomatic privilege. Each time a talk was scheduled,

Ulinov sat among a gaggle of American personnel. For him to disclose new information was a surprise.

By now, the Americans would have triple-checked their radio room for bugs and viruses, searching everywhere until they cut him off. He didn't like it. He was already so isolated. Worse, it felt very final, and Ulinov rubbed his thumb against the hard shape of the 9mm Glock inside his jacket pocket.

The night was frigid, especially on this third-floor balcony. Ulinov was exposed to the breeze, but the main doors of the hotel were locked and he hadn't even considered trying to get into the courtyard. Hardly anyone was allowed outside after curfew. Leadville had hunkered down until sunrise, with only a few windows glowing here and there.

"No signal," whispered the shadow beside him, holding a cell phone in the dim light. "Still no signal."

Ulinov nodded curtly, wondering at the white slash of teeth on Gustavo's face. Some of that grin was fear, he thought, and yet there were also equal amounts of defiance and self-confidence. Gus had tricked the Americans before. He swore he could do it again.

Gustavo Proano was a thin man and no more than average height, but Ulinov was still learning to remember their size difference. In zero gravity, it hadn't been so obvious, and Gustavo had been his communications officer during their long exile in space, left aboard the ISS to appease the Europeans.

Gus had a big mouth and busy hands. Ulinov had warned him twice to stay quiet and yet Gus still commented on the obvious as he tapped at his phone. His free hand rustled and scratched at the back of his wool cap. Beneath it, he had a bald spot that he liked to rub as he worked.

Ulinov was calmer, even melancholy, motionless except for his thumb on his pistol. The sidearm had not been hard to come by in this war zone. Four days ago in the mess hall, the pistol had found its way from the gun belt of a weary Marine into the folds of Ulinov's sweater.

"This damn thing," Gustavo muttered, holding himself awkwardly to reflect what light there was onto his keypad.

Acquiring a phone and a PDA was easier. The Americans seemed to have saved many, many millions more of their fun little gadgets than they had of their own people. Nearly everyone was connected to their grid by cell phone, iPhone, Bluetooth, or Blackberry. Again, Ulinov had stolen a phone, while Gustavo traded outright for several more.

"Shall we stop?" Ulinov asked, almost smiling himself.

"I can get in," Gus said.

"If they shut down the entire network—"

"Let me try another phone."

Ulinov shrugged and nodded and made certain his smile did not show. It seemed to him that the Americans had missed a good bet with Gus. If they'd trusted the man, he could have been a significant asset. If nothing else, Gus was a familiar voice to survivors everywhere, but the Americans had more radiomen than radios and Gus was a foreign national.

After confirming access and control codes to the space station, they'd left Gus unemployed. It was a problem he'd anticipated. The Americans had wanted all of Ruth's files and the entire backlog of Ulinov's surveillance work. They wanted the use of the cameras and other instruments. Even empty, the ISS made a valuable satellite—and Gus, like Ulinov, had reprogrammed his computers long before they disembarked, knowing it might be useful to leave open a few back doors.

Gus had deliberately created a bug that only he could correct, blaming the problem on the avalanche of data relayed through the ISS in the past year, not all of which was clean. "Fixing" the bug gave him two days to send code back and forth from the station after the Americans got frustrated. Two days to study. Two days to rig his patches.

Ulinov had always planned to act alone in his mission, using the ISS databases to store, send, and receive messages. The Americans agreed that he could still access the station to provide photos and weather reports for the Russian defenses, which gave him every excuse to transmit complex files—but the Americans watched too closely. They recorded every keystroke. They made sure they had experts on hand to "help" him, combat engineers and meteorologists who were unquestionably CIA computer techs, no matter how competently they discussed demolition efforts or high pressure fronts.

Ulinov's only transmissions to the secure database had been a weather report and then a duplicate of the same report, a clear signal to his countrymen that nothing else was safe.

His next message, however, was a short burst of text via wireless modem, reestablishing contact. Gustavo had three ways to pirate into the local system, delay-and-relay programs that attached packets of data to larger transmissions. Whenever the Americans uploaded commands to the ISS, which was constantly, Ulinov's notes leapt into the sky as well.

Gustavo had shared this trick with Ulinov for reasons that Ulinov never fully trusted. For friendship, yes. And to keep busy. And yet he knew that Gus had been cooperating with American intelligence almost from the start of their twelve months in orbit . . . surely on orders from his own people . . .

What game were the Italians playing?

The situation in the Alps was not much better than in the Middle East. There were multiple battlefronts, a patchwork mess of alliances and counter-invasions, with Italy holding on to a few small shards of land against the French, Germans, Brits, Irish, Dutch, Poles, Greeks, Czechs, Belgians, Swedes, and Slavs. Ulinov had to trust Gustavo's resentment. The whole world wanted to bring the Americans down a few notches to better their own chances of begging or buying help, but Ulinov was also aware that Gus could win favor by exposing him. The Italian spy agency, SISMI, had surely tried to copy all of Ulinov's messages. If they'd succeeded, by now they must have broken the simple encoding.

The relay through Gus was never more than a short-lived chance to update and confirm contingency plans. Gustavo would betray him. Perhaps it had already happened. The Russian leadership must know this, and yet twice in the past twenty-four hours they'd alluded to their envoys to the Chinese. They'd also instructed Ulinov to demand the nano weapon, making certain the Americans learned of his deceit.

He was a tool that had been sacrificed, but to what purpose? Why did they want him in trouble and how did they want him to act? To try to minimize the problem? Make it worse?

"I'm in," Gus said, beckoning for him to move closer.

Ulinov reluctantly took his hand from the pistol inside his heavy jacket. His bare fingers tensed in the breeze as he accepted Gustavo's phone. He had never felt so vulnerable.

"Thank you," he said.

Gus nodded and grinned. He stepped away to give Ulinov a margin of privacy and Ulinov forced himself not to stare after his comrade. His enemy. It wasn't that he expected men to crash into the room behind them, shouting, like a drama on American TV. Not yet. How did they say it in their Old West? They would hand him enough rope to hang himself.

Ulinov stabbed his finger expertly over the tiny face of the cell phone, holding it and his PDA in his left hand, using his right to enter his own codes now that Gus had keyed him into the Trojan database across town. He needed the PDA to remember his passwords and to encode and decode his messages, even though the cipher was very basic, substituting numbers for the Cyrillic alphabet. Again, it was only meant to keep the Americans guessing for a few days.

He used shorthand and abbreviations, perhaps three words in a row without most of the vowels, then one fully written out. He ran the numbers together so that 25 might as easily be a 2 and a 5. Also, the number substitution began arbitrarily, 1 for *R*—but only for messages transmitted on Sunday. The number representation shifted forward and back depending on the day of the week.

Ulinov was good with data, but he couldn't instantly make sense of a hundred numerals squeezed together. Composing his reports wasn't any easier, encoding a hundred letters after deleting vowels at random. He needed to organize his messages ahead of time, then key them into the phone as he read off of his PDA. Likewise, when he received text he transcribed it into the PDA as rapidly as possible and only later worked through it.

Even before he'd returned from talking with Kendricks, the Americans had disturbed his few belongings in the thin private area that was his living space, the back part of a suite that had been walled off with plywood. It wasn't much, blankets and a mattress on the floor, two spare shirts, underwear. And they hadn't searched too hard. They'd moved things just enough to show they'd been there—to see what he would do, if he would panic—but Ulinov had stashed his contraband elsewhere in the old hotel. He'd found a small slot behind the exposed studs of the wall in the second-floor stairwell where the paneling had been removed for firewood.

The gun was not to kill Gustavo, nor himself nor anyone else. It was not for fighting at all. There was no chance for Ulinov to escape Leadville, nor any reason. He intended to use the weapon to destroy his PDA and the pitiful few files he'd created and received, no matter that the Americans might already hold copies of most. Let them think there were more. Let them worry there were real secrets.

I can make everything worse, he thought, glancing out at the night again and the muted white points of the stars. Much closer, he saw the red beacons of a comm/radar plane returning from patrol.

Ulinov believed the Russian leadership was using the link through the Italians to create confusion and fear. He believed it was a backhanded test of strength. They were pushing in order to be pushed back. They wanted to be slapped down. They wanted the Americans to feel confident, and that meant . . .

It meant a double cross.

The idea was so dangerous that he tried to move it out of his head completely, but the signs were all there. He'd never expected to go home again anyway. Not *home*, that was impossible, but he'd always understood he had little chance of rejoining his people no matter where they ended up. His duty was here. That was acceptable as long as he succeeded in doing his part.

Were they selling their loyalty to the Chinese after all? Something different?

Nikola Ulinov turned his eyes to the pockets of light in this cold, small, overcrowded city, his pulse beating with guilt and conviction at the same time. First he tried to access new messages, but either there were none or the Americans had intercepted them. Then he began his text with his authentic sign-on, *Charlie*, perhaps someone's idea of a joke. It had been given to him months ago by the Russian foreign intelligence agency, SVR. Broken down into English, his message would be ominous, and his leadership would realize he was playing along. *No bargain yet on ntech but U.S. pressed hard by rebels. Suggest you download all ISS files. Make offer to—*

He interrupted himself, breaking the connection as if the cellular system dropped him or his phone had failed. Let the Americans make a mountain out of that. Ulinov could sell them enough bullshit in the meantime to keep them occupied.

Something awful was going to happen.

10

Helicopters thudded in the darkness and Ruth crawled into
the flat tire of an Army truck before she was awake, scraping
her cheek and forehead against the lug nuts.

"Here," Cam said. "Over here."

She moved to his voice, shuffling in the dirt. They'd left the
highway to make camp, settling down against an old troop carrier that had gone no more than four hundred yards before bog-
ging down. The vehicle's nose canted into the earth, which had
been mud at the time. Now the conflicting angles of the hillside
and the truck added to Ruth's disorientation. She bumped into
Cam. He held Newcombe's rifle in both hands but leaned toward her for an instant, like the beginnings of a hug. She pushed
against him, needing more physical contact.

The helicopters were far away and seemed to going farther.
Ruth glanced wildly into the night, not believing it. Then a man's
silhouette blocked out the stars and she flinched. The scattered
light was mirrored in the lens of Newcombe's goggles. "They're
headed south," he said.

The noise echoed and slapped against the foothills, fading.
But there was a new sound, the hammer of guns. It was barely
audible, a *tat tat tat tat* against the larger drumbeat. *Tat tat tat.*
Assault rifles.

"Oh shit," Ruth said with sudden clarity. She and Cam jumped to their feet beside Newcombe, staring into the dark. There was nothing to see. The fighting was too distant. They probably wouldn't have heard the clash at all in a living world. The sound carried for unknown miles.

"They got Young and Brayton," Newcombe said.

Cam shook his head. "You can't be sure."

"There's no one else down here."

It changed everything. In her mind, Ruth had already quit, and she didn't know how anyone could blame her. She'd done her best. She'd decided to tell Newcombe in the morning. *Let's call your people. I can't hike any more.* Now the safety net was gone. She wasn't able to hold on to the hope that Captain Young and Todd Brayton would spread the vaccine themselves. Leadville had the nanotech, and Ruth knew exactly what the president's council intended to do with it.

One world. One people.

What would humanity look like if they succeeded? Most of the survivors in the United States were white. The immigrant and minority populations across North America had lived on the coasts and in the inner cities. Los Angeles. New York. Toronto. Detroit. It was the heartlands that had survived—and to a certain mind-set, this purity would increase the appeal of claiming the entire Earth. Leadville would share the vaccine only if they needed to expand their labor force, permitting foreign populations to come down from the mountains as farmers and slaves.

What if one of her friends had gotten away? Captain Young might have covered Todd as he ran from the choppers . . . No. Ruth was through fooling herself. The responsibility was hers. It had always been hers. She glanced at the stars again, fighting tears. Then she clenched her fist and held on to the grinding ache inside her cast.

It'll be light soon, she thought.

She walked to her sleeping bag and began to pack up.

It took them seven days to cover eighty-five miles, the last twenty-five away from any roads. Newcombe was afraid that Leadville had dropped motion detectors or even a few soldiers on every peak in the area, equipping small squads with radios and rations and then ordering them to wait. Cam pointed out how many islands there were throughout the nearest fifty square miles, and Leadville had no way of knowing they'd gone north out of Sacramento, not south. There would be countless acres of safe ground on the plateaus of Yosemite. Much closer to their real position, around Lake Tahoe, were dozens of high mountains and ridgelines. Even if Leadville only targeted the major highways that branched up toward elevation, they would need to commit hundreds of troops. Still, the chance existed, so Ruth, Cam, and Newcombe had bypassed the largest islands within reach and hiked toward a smaller line of bumps instead.

Eight more times they'd felt the burn of nano infections. There was now a dark, thready patch of subcutaneous hemorrhaging on the back of Ruth's left hand—her broken arm, the nanotech always going after any preexisting weakness. The bruise was healing but she suspected it would scar. Another mark on her. Worse, her feet were rubbed raw in her boots because she didn't want to complain. Her pack had chafed her left shoulder badly because it rode funny, the strap catching on the sling for her cast.

There were helicopters again. There were jets. They stumbled into another stretch of land that was thick with lizards and snakes, and then a dead forest littered with dead beetles, and then the hike abruptly got easier.

The Sierra range had been in its third day of blizzard conditions when the plague spread. The snow stopped a lot of vehicles. They began to see the traffic breaking apart around sixty-five hundred feet, the cars falling off the road or lined up in strange ways. Cam attributed the new patterns to bad visibility and traction. At one point Newcombe got a Ford Expedition started and they made fourteen miles in a hurry. Another time they went three miles in a van, and nearly twenty in a pickup truck. Unfortunately there were still plenty of stalls and crashes, especially wherever the road curved. In the snow, the turns had become traps. They had to leave all three of their vehicles. Thousands of four-wheel drives and military trucks and tanks had fought up through the blizzard, as had little snowmobiles and more unexpected things like farm tractors and fire engines, whatever was heavy enough to bull through the snow. But even these vehicles had gathered in clumps and fence-like formations. Wherever one stopped, others hit or steered wide and got stuck. The drivers had been hysterical and bleeding and blind.

Newcombe rummaged through most of the military trucks, not only looking for food and batteries but for clothing. They had all been in civilian gear they'd scavenged in Sacramento, but Newcombe took a stained Army jacket for himself. He had always found comfort in his training and experience. This was different. Ruth thought he wanted to have conducted himself well if they were captured or killed. He wanted to belong to his squad in the end, and she admired him for it.

She wasn't sleeping well. She dreamed too much and constantly woke despite her exhaustion, as if her mind was in overdrive trying to process it all.

That the air kept getting thinner didn't help. Any decrease in oxygen made the body anxious. The heart beat harder, and the brain reacted. Cam gave her melatonin and he gave her Tylenol PM, first a minor overdose, then as many as five pills at once. He even tried antihistamines because a side effect was drowsiness, and still Ruth muttered and twitched.

The nightmare was real.

"Don't touch anything," Newcombe said, stepping backward into the rushing wind. The sky was clear and perfect but the few, thin clouds were moving very fast. The cold ripped across the desolate earth, whistling through the gaps in the small rock structure in front of them.

Cam stared into the low hut with one hand on his gun belt, although Ruth didn't think he was aware of his defensive pose. "It looks like some kind of . . . like murder-suicide," he said.

No, she thought. *No, I don't think so.*

This mountaintop was a dead place. Walking across the barrier had been a dizzying experience. There were thousands of crosses scraped into the rock. The shape was everywhere. Hundreds of the marked stones had also been arranged into larger crosses themselves, laid across the ground. Some stretched as long as twenty feet. Others, made of pebbles, covered only a few inches. It was the work of countless days.

"Let's get out of here," Newcombe said.

"We need to bury them." Ruth couldn't bear to look at shriveled corpses anymore. She let her eyes follow the wind instead. Farther east and south, toward Tahoe, the Sierras created a high, ragged skyline as far as she could see. They'd reached ten thousand feet, but only barely. This peak stood alone above the barrier, separated by miles of open space from the nearest other peaks.

In the late afternoon, the distance looked much greater, crowded with shadows. Her grief was equally vast. Ruth's face twisted suddenly and she slumped down, catching herself on one knee and her good hand. The marked pebbles lay all around.

Cam knelt beside her. "Ruth? Ruth, whatever happened here was a long time ago," he said, but that didn't change her exhaustion or her lonely despair.

How many islands were like this one?

All this way for nothing, she thought. Then, like a different voice, *They suffered for nothing.*

These people had lived through the first winter or even longer, stacking rocks for shelter, breaking the pine trees and brush beneath this tiny safe zone for firewood. Now they were gone. There were six big graves, each too big for a single person. Two more bodies sprawled inside their pathetic little shack with no one left to put them in the ground.

A knife and a special rock lay in between the two women, a nearly round boulder etched all over with crosses. It had been used to crush the smaller woman's head and then the last survivor seemed to have sawed open her own throat.

Cam thought there had been some sort of religious holocaust. Ruth believed the crosses were something else. They had begged the sky for salvation. They'd tried to direct their souls away from this misery. Disease had taken them. The men might have missed it, because birds had been at the corpses, but the tight rotted film of their skin was distended and black behind their ears. They had endured the machine plague only to be destroyed by another contagion.

"We need to bury these people," Ruth said.

Cam nodded. "Okay. Okay. But there's no shovel."

"It'll be dark in an hour," Newcombe said.

"We can't just leave them here!"

"I know what to do." Cam walked to the shack. He set one hand on the rock wall, testing it. Then he put his shoulder against it and heaved. The corner gave. Most of the branches holding the roof fell in. He hit the wall again and the rest of it collapsed. The rubble formed a poor cairn, but it would have to be enough.

"Please," Ruth whispered. "Please be safe. Find somewhere safe." Her words weren't for these strangers, of course, and ultimately she hadn't insisted on putting them to rest for their sake, either. It was a way to try to heal a few of her own terrible wounds.

They picked their way down into the growing shadows on the east side of the mountain, moving north toward a small field of snow. They wanted to stay above the barrier, but they couldn't risk catching whatever had killed these people.

"We should scrub our boots and gloves," Newcombe said.

"Let's hit that snow." Cam gestured. "We can use some for water, too."

Ruth squeezed one of the etched pebbles in her hand. She had taken it in secret. She didn't know why, except that the impulse had been too strong to repress. "I don't understand how this happened," she said. "Everyone there . . ."

Cam stayed with her as Newcombe ranged ahead. "It won't be like that on every island," he said. "We'll find somebody."

"But that's what I mean. If there was anything good about the machine plague, it's that most diseases must have been wiped out at the same time. The flu. Strep. The population's too scattered."

"Don't people carry a lot of that stuff inside them even when they're not really sick?"

He had EMT training, she knew. She nodded. "Yes."

"So some islands would just be unlucky. The people get weak, they're always cold, a virus takes over." Cam hesitated, then said, "It's not your fault. You know that."

"You mean some diseases might have adapted." Ruth seized on that part of what he'd said because she didn't know how to answer to the rest. "Yes. We're going to have to be more careful. There might be other islands that . . . Some islands might be Typhoid Marys, where everyone's built specific immunities that we don't have."

"How do we test for that?"

"I don't know." Some islands would also be thick with rats

and fleas, pests that were extinct everywhere else for lack of hosts. "If we find anyone who's obviously sick, we might have to back off. Leave them alone." Ruth pushed her thumb against the patterns etched into the rock, her mind reeling with quiet horror.

There was another threat they were certain to find among the pockets of survivors. Insanity and delusion could prove to be an even greater problem than disease. Aboard the ISS, Gustavo had reported religious fervor in Mexico, Afghanistan, the Alps, and Micronesia. Holy men had risen everywhere in the apocalypse.

Ruth had never had much use for God. People cited the mysteries and wisdom of faith, pointing to the great understanding of their teachings, but what they'd really done was to close their minds against the true complexity of the planet, to say nothing of the incomprehensibly vast universe. The idea was laughable. What kind of half-wit God would bother to create billions of other galaxies if Earth was the focus of His energies?

It was a very human thing to believe. People were lazy. They were egocentric. Ruth understood wanting a small, controlled world. No one liked uncertainty. It tested the boundaries of human curiosity and intelligence. The monkey was still very strong in modern man. The monkey had limited patience, so people resisted time and change. They developed rationales to show that they were the center of everything, fighting to teach "intelligent design" in schools instead of biology and science. Nonsense. Tall parents tended to have tall kids. Short parents tended to have short kids. Everyone wasn't identical. It was that easy to see—evolution in a single generation. Otherwise people would have been perfect clones of each other throughout history. To think that life was immutable was a fantasy. Bacteria grew drug-resistant. Dogs could be cultivated into ridiculously specialized breeds like her step-father's terrier. Religions themselves had evolved with time, some growing more open, some more closed.

There were real answers if you sought the truth. The world was knowable. That was what she'd learned, but it was hard. She would have liked to feel that a larger hand was guiding her, but why her and not the people who died on this mountaintop? Because they were evil?

Ruth clenched down on the pebble again as a slow, stubborn fury worked its way through her. She wouldn't stop. That was what the rock meant to her. She couldn't stop even though her feet were broken and sore and her arm was throbbing in its cast.

"Hey!" Newcombe shouted. He stood on an open granite slope about fifty yards downhill, waving his arms.

At first Ruth thought he was warning them away. More bodies? Then she realized he was pointing east and she briefly glanced down at the rock inside her fist, struck by doubt and new hope.

"Look," she said, touching Cam in celebration.

Far across the valley, barely visible in the yellow dusk, a thread of smoke rose from another mountaintop.

It took them two days to hike down and up. Once they saw a large, slow C-130 cargo plane in the south, dragging long cables through the air that Newcombe said were a sensor array. Once there were more snakes.

The cookfires were repeated both days, late in the morning and again at sunset. There was definitely someone up there, but who? Would soldiers give themselves away?

Ruth jostled Cam from a dead sleep and he twisted up into the pale moonlight with his hand balled in a fist.

"Shh, it's okay," she said.

The moon was a gleaming white crescent in the valley, low enough to the horizon that it appeared nearly level with them at ninety-five hundred feet. Its light cast bars of shadows from the tree trunks—and the shadows moved, creaking. There was a chill breeze in the treetops and the forest was alive. The grasshoppers sang and sang and sang. *Ree ree ree ree.* The mindless noise lifted and fell on the wind, invading every lull in the sound of the trees.

"It's all right," she said. "Nothing's wrong."

He relaxed. His mask rustled as he opened his mouth, but he kept quiet. He only nodded and Ruth felt a small, quixotic smile. A lot of things were wrong, obviously. The whole fucking world was wrong. Maybe he'd been about to make the same joke, but there had been new tension between them.

"I'm sorry," Ruth continued. For what? She was still kneeling very close to him and she tipped her head back, trying to redirect his attention away from herself. "It's supposed to be Newcombe's shift, but I thought . . . I wanted to talk again. Without him."

"Yeah."

She had volunteered to stand guard through the first six hours of the night because tomorrow she would stay behind as the men hiked the rest of the way up without her. She would be safe down here. They knew there was no one else below the barrier, whereas the islands above might hold any number of threats.

Ruth had spent three hours in darkness before she woke Cam, three hours with the bugs and the wind. Her head was crowded with fear and loss and distance, poised on this invisible border with thousands of miles of dead zone below them and tiny safe areas above that might not be safe after all.

She didn't know how to say good-bye.

She owed Cam her life. She should have been able to give him the response he wanted, even if she hadn't felt an honest attraction. She was tempted. She had become too self-conscious of her backpack whenever she reached into it for water or food or a clean face mask, being very careful to let neither man see the glossy purple box of condoms. She needed comfort and warmth, and yet Cam still frightened her. It wasn't only the capacity for violence that she saw in him, but his own wretched hunger. She was afraid to get too near because she couldn't predict how he would react, so she was quiet, sitting beside him in the whispering night.

There was another danger that Ruth had kept to herself. She didn't want to rush Cam and Newcombe. Her science team had not incorporated the hypobaric fuse into the vaccine, so that it wouldn't self-destruct like the plague, but the vaccine was also unlike the plague in another way. It was able to replicate only by attacking and breaking down a single target—its rival. Every minute they spent above the barrier was a new danger, because without its ongoing war against the plague, the vaccine had no way to maintain its own numbers. In fact, if they stayed too long they might become trapped like anyone else after sweating it out, exhaling it, losing it by the millions each time they went to the bathroom.

After sixteen days within the invisible sea, their bodies must be thick with it. Too thick. That might explain her headaches and it might explain the discomfort in her gut. Those things might simply be the result of constant strain and bad food, but it wasn't impossible that the vaccine would hurt people, too, catching and clotting in the bloodstream, rupturing capillaries, increasing the odds of stroke and arrhythmia. They didn't know. It had never been tested.

Ruth wanted to believe they'd have days or even weeks before their immunity faded to dangerous levels, but if they had to run ... If there were soldiers waiting ... They had already been near ten thousand feet for more than eight hours and Ruth couldn't guarantee it wouldn't be a problem.

The men were just as apprehensive. Newcombe had prepared her for the chance that he and Cam wouldn't return. He broke down their packs and reassembled one for her to carry herself if necessary, mostly food and a bedroll. He carefully showed her how to use the radio and he made her demonstrate again that she knew how to fire and load her pistol, as if she'd last through a gun battle by herself.

Ruth knew she couldn't go with them but she hated the price on her skills and education, like she was some goddamned princess in a tower, too precious to be let out—so at last she forced herself to stir in the cold.

"I'm sorry," she told him.

"Me, too," Cam said. He was always surprising her.

Ruth shook her head. "Why would, no, you've been ..."

"Maybe we should have done it Newcombe's way," Cam said. "He's got training I could never ... I shouldn't have pushed so hard to hike it. Maybe you would have perfected the nanotech by now."

"Cam, no. It was my idea. Remember? I'm the one who insisted on coming here." *And then after everything else, tomorrow you're going to walk up there for me,* she thought. *You'll walk into the soldiers' guns, maybe, or find a pack of disease-ridden survivors. There's no way to know.*

Still sitting in his blankets, Cam shifted once, as if containing an argument inside himself.

I couldn't have done this without you, Ruth thought. Then she touched her fingertips to his forearm, careful not to let it be more. She was careful not to draw down her mask and kiss his cheek, no matter how deeply he deserved the gesture or her gratitude.

"Please be careful," she said.

11

Cam slipped easily across the rough terrain of granite and sparse forest. He'd dropped his pack this morning but kept his pistol and a canteen—and he knew this environment well, if not this particular mountain. The whitebark pines and junipers were a familiar world, the chokecherry brambles and wild grass.

There was a flutter of grasshoppers to his right. The insects scattered as Newcombe loped over with his rifle in hand and they hunched together behind a tangle of boulders.

They'd heard voices above them distantly. Someone up there liked to yell to his friends, a boy, alternately impatient or happy, his young voice carrying across the open sky. It seemed like a good sign, but maybe the kid was only excited because Leadville troops had recently arrived.

"What do you think?" Newcombe whispered.

Cam only shrugged. In many ways their relationship reminded him of his bond with Albert Sawyer, the man who'd taken them to the lab in Sacramento. His friendship with Sawyer had been loaded with mistrust and need and fierce loyalty all at the same time. He wanted things to be better with Newcombe. He wanted to save his energy, instead of always trying to keep one eye behind him, so he tried again to make peace. "I think you're right," he said.

"The layout here might be as good as it gets," Newcombe said, tipping his chin up at the ridges. "Let's map this drainage before we work any farther north."

"Yeah." Cam reached for his binoculars as Newcombe took a small notepad from his pocket and quickly added to his sketches. The Special Forces soldier had his own shorthand that was detailed and accurate, but Cam paused with his binoculars lifted halfway, reaching out with his ears and other senses instead, measuring the wind and the early afternoon sun. The dust-and-pine smell of the mountain. He could still feel Ruth's hand on his arm.

He itched to take off his goggles and mask, but the day was warm and clear. Without a barometer, Cam had to assume they were still in danger. The nicest weather typically came with high pressure fronts, which lifted the invisible sea of nanotech. On their maps, the nearest benchmarks read 9,985 and 10,160 feet, but Cam had learned to hold his pessimism close. They were still at least two hundred yards below the tallest peaks.

So far they hadn't been able to get a look at whoever was up there. They had a bad height disadvantage. This archipelago of high points was like a string of castles. Each of the small islands sat above a sheer, ragged band of lava. If there were soldiers, if they were forced to shoot it out, they would be very exposed.

"Stay here," Newcombe said.

"We'll go together."

"No. We can't leave her alone, and if I'm coming back in a hurry I'll need you to cover me."

Cam nodded. Mark Newcombe was a good man, despite all their disagreements. Newcombe had helped him every day with his hand, cleaning and rebandaging the wound, and Newcombe had continued to haul the largest pack even after Cam took possession of the radios.

"We'll go together," Cam said. "At least as far as the ridge. That's a better place for us to stay in sight of each other, and sooner or later . . . You know they'll spot us. The longer we sneak around, the more likely it'll happen."

"Yeah. Stay here."

"You don't understand," Cam said. "Even if there are no soldiers up there, those people will be . . . different. They could be dangerous."

Newcombe glanced briefly at the ravine again, then studied Cam for a much longer time. Newcombe's expression was hidden in his mask and goggles, but his posture was intent. For once Cam was glad to be wrapped in his own gear. He still had one secret and he meant to keep it, especially from Ruth.

"It's better if it's both of us," Cam said, finding his voice again. "Not just for the show of strength. I'll know what to say to them but you're proof that it really works, the nanotech. That could make all the difference."

Newcombe remained silent. Maybe he was thinking of the first mountain and the mad, grinding obsession that must have driven those people to carve thousands of crosses. The sight had shaken Cam to his core, because he never would have believed that anyone had things worse than on his own mountaintop. His group had only lasted eight months before they began to kill and feed on each other.

Voices echoed through the ravine and Cam ducked against a car-sized boulder, leaving sunlight for the cool shadows beneath the rock. Newcombe squeezed in beside him with a wild look, then checked his rifle's safety again. Cam had misjudged the other group's position. He'd led Newcombe too far up this gully to run back down again and there was no other route from here to the long cliff face above, where they might have scrambled into a crevice and waited and watched. The mountain had fooled him, bouncing the noise away until the other group abruptly moved past a ridgeline and their voices were redirected downhill.

They sounded very close.

"Sst," Newcombe hissed. He bumped Cam with his elbow and signaled efficiently. Four fingers. South side of the rock.

They'll cross our tracks, Cam thought, although the ground was rough and dry where it wasn't dotted with snow. He and Newcombe had avoided the fields of dirty ice and the soft new wildflowers and grass. They hadn't left much trace.

He clenched his teeth, trying to hold down his adrenaline and the stark memories of gunfire and screaming. Then the other group passed into view. They wore uniforms. Cam raised his pistol but Newcombe jammed one hand against his forearm exactly where Ruth had touched him.

"No," Newcombe whispered.

The uniforms were ragged, once green, now a sun-bleached, filthy color very much like army olive drab. The shoulder patches and other insignia were paramilitary, but they were undisciplined. One had his shirt open and another wore a frayed San Francisco Giants baseball cap. They were teenagers. They were Boy Scouts. All four carried handmade backpacks, stout bare frames of branches lashed with rope, made for stacking and hauling wood.

The boys were skinny and hard and sunburned, and in good spirits. They were laughing.

Cam barely recognized the sound, his body still tight with fear. But it was only his own nerves and the distortions of the rock that had deepened their voices. In fact, he already knew the loudest boy. After listening below them for most of a day, he identified the confident tone immediately as the kid said, "I'm gonna beat your ass today, Brandon."

"No way."

"Lose like always."

"Bite me."

They were using their chatter like a shield as they crossed into the machine plague, keeping each other brave. That was why they'd grown noisier and noisier as they approached.

Newcombe seemed as stunned as Cam at their fun, stupid banter. Both men hesitated.

It was the loud boy who saw them first, his eyes suddenly huge in his smooth face. *"Holy fuck!"* The boy's face drained white and he grabbed two of his friends, yanking them back.

Cam had hoped to meet someone else first. He'd planned to call out from a distance and give them time to react—but the loud boy was a leader. He probably took part in every scavenging mission, and his simple heroism threw his friends apart like a grenade. He shoved them away from Cam and Newcombe even though it delayed him from running himself.

Newcombe said, "Wait!"

The teens continued to stagger back. One kid had fallen over another's feet and the loud boy yelled again, dragging at his buddy on the ground. A second later there were answering shouts from above, lost and thin in the blue sky.

Cam stayed back as Newcombe slung his rifle and pushed

off his goggles and hood, exposing his freckles and sandy blond hair. "Wait," Newcombe said. "It's all right."

"Holy fuck, man—"

"—did you come from!"

Their skin was not without old blisters and bruising. Some of these scars were lost beneath sunburn, windburn, sweat, and dirt, but they'd been caught below the barrier more than once. Maybe these low islands were even submerged in the invisible sea on hot summer days. Cam could only imagine how bad that must have been, attacked by the plague with nowhere left to climb.

"They're soldiers," said the kid on the ground, taking in Newcombe's jacket and gun belt. Then he looked up abruptly, as if to check for planes.

The loud boy finished the thought for him. "You're American. You guys get shot down?"

"U.S. Army Special Forces, I'm Sergeant Newcombe and this is Najarro," Newcombe said, letting them misunderstand about Cam for the moment—and now the teenagers' movements were slower, wondering.

The loud boy began to grin at them. "Holy fuck," he said again, savoring the curse.

His name was Alex Dorrington. He was nineteen years old, with thick brown hair and a habit of squinting, an adaptation to the unrelenting sun on their islands. He also seemed short for his age. Cam remembered how Manny's growth had stunted. All of these boys would have been a year and a half younger when the plague broke loose, still in the middle stages of adolescence, and their diet had been limited and poor.

The Scouts were like Manny in another way. They were elated. They pummeled Cam and Newcombe with a hundred questions and constantly touched them, especially Newcombe, picking at his jacket as if to confirm he was real.

"Who's in all the planes?"

"—if we help you—"

"But how can you walk around below the line?"

They gave Cam a little more distance once he took off his goggles and mask, unable to hide their shock. Cam exploited it. "How many more people do you have up there?" he asked, and

Alex said, "There's four, sir. Four more. You, uh, you better talk to Brandon's dad, I guess."

"Good. Thanks."

They cautiously followed the Scouts up through the ridge, saying nothing of Ruth. Alex had sent a kid named Mike ahead of them, but there were still people yelling down from the top— a man, a girl.

The two groups met in a crack in the rough black lava and Cam let Newcombe take the lead, not because of his ruined face but because he was trembling. It scared him. The boys had been desperately friendly and yet Cam felt himself continuing to measure the situation and not liking it, pinned in the gully. His tension reminded him of Sawyer again. There had been times when his friend was as selfish and violent as a rat, all of which made him the perfect survivor, but Sawyer's strength became a crucial weakness when he was unable to stop striving, stop fighting, creating threats that hadn't existed until he imagined them. Ultimately it had killed him. Cam didn't want to be that person, and yet he wasn't fully in control of himself.

"U.S. Army Special Forces," Newcombe said, taking charge. He stepped forward to shake hands.

"I'm Ed," the man said. "Ed Sevcik." He was in his forties and dark-haired like Brandon, but with gray in his beard like salt.

Newcombe said, "Can we sit down someplace, Ed?"

"Oh my God, yes. I'm sorry. This way. I'm not . . . I can't believe you're here," the man said, glancing back and forth between them. "Thank you. Thank you so much."

Cam forced a smile, although he wasn't surprised by their enthusiasm. The arrival of new faces must be profound.

They continued back up the ravine. The girl stayed close to Ed. She had the same dark hair and snub nose, Cam noticed, and a long pair of legs she'd chosen to show off, wearing shorts when all of the boys wore pants to protect themselves from the rock.

"Are there more of you coming?" Ed asked, and Newcombe said, "No. Just us."

"They're not off a plane, Mr. S," Alex said, squinting, always squinting. Maybe it wasn't the sun but that he'd begun to need glasses.

"Then how did you get here?"

"We can show you," Newcombe said, and the kid they called D Mac added, "They were below the line, Mr. S."

"But if you didn't come off of a plane . . ."

"We'll show you, I promise," Newcombe said. "Let's get over to your camp and sit down, okay?"

They moved across the slanting face of a short, barren plateau. There was more snow here in larger patches, filthy with dust and pollen. Forty yards ahead, Brandon disappeared into a gap in the land, hurrying across to another small high point where they'd piled earth and rock to form windbreaks around a few tents. In every other direction the world dropped away, steep to the west, more gradually to the east, where other peaks thrust up across a great, broken valley. For Cam, the view was like coming home. It was endless. There was only the wind and the sun and the few tiny human beings around him, their voices loud and bright.

"Be careful on this slope," Alex said, moving to crouch at the edge of the gap. He helped Ed first and then Newcombe. He also helped the girl, which earned him a smile.

Cam watched her as they climbed down and then up again. She was thin and flat-chested. There was no fat on any of them, which must be why she drew attention to her legs. Even with a few old scabs and fresh scratches, they were her best feature.

She was the only female. *She can't be more than fifteen,* Cam thought, but if Ed was the leader here, she must be a large part of the influence that he commanded, simply by being under his control. King and princess. She would be the magnet at the center, holding all the boys, and her role only would have grown during their long isolation. Cam wondered how Ed had managed to keep the peace all this time—why there was no baby. It sounded like he'd taught the boys to call him "Mr. S," reinforcing the habit of his authority, but they'd all grown older and Cam wondered if the girl still obeyed her father completely or if she'd begun to exert her own power.

Cam was careful not to study her too closely, looking at the boys' faces instead. The girl had been quiet so far, yet the boys kept glancing at her for her reaction. For approval. That sort of charisma would be a heady feeling for such a young woman, and Cam and Newcombe were about to take it away from her.

That made her dangerous.

They had set eight boulders around their fire pit, like chairs, inside the larger ring of windbreaks. Brandon and Hiroki gave up their seats for Cam and Newcombe, and Cam finally realized that Brandon was a beta male, possibly because he was the brother of the girl. Cam would have thought Ed's son would be his right-hand man, but Alex and D Mac appeared to be the lieutenants here.

It was an odd dynamic, but it had been shaped by their circumstances. Ed very likely hadn't had the energy to spare to groom his son while protecting his daughter, which in turn had given rise to Alex and D Mac as those two worked to prove themselves and eventually dominated the rest. Brandon just didn't have the same goal or motivation. More than that, he might have put himself in danger if he'd fought to keep a place near the top of pack. A king and a princess did not need a prince to stand with them, they needed knights.

"It's not much," Ed apologized, as Brandon handed over two battered plastic canteens. Then he fetched two aluminum cups full of berries and roots. Cam had also seen a small pot and a crude canvas bag heaped with grasshopper carapaces. There was a smooth rock for mashing the bugs, along with tree bark and fresh tufts of weeds and moss, but Brandon had held back the insects and the weeds on his own initiative, offering their best instead.

"I have something, too," Newcombe said, rummaging through his jacket. From one pocket he came up with a spare notepad, which he gave to Ed. From another he produced a colorful sixteen-ounce packet of Berry Storm Gatorade powder.

Most of the boys cheered. "Oh, fuck yeah!" Alex said. Even the girl smiled.

Ed let them mix up the sweet red powder. The girl and a few of the boys choked theirs down immediately—the sports drink was loaded with salts and sugar—but Brandon drank his in sips with his eyes closed and Alex held on to his for later, demonstrating remarkable control.

"So how did you get here?" Newcombe asked.

"What? Where did *you*—" Mike began, but Alex shushed him and said, "Tell 'em, Mr. S."

Ed Sevcik nodded, recognizing like Alex that Newcombe's question was a test. He understood that Newcombe and Cam had the ability to get up and leave. "We were snowshoe camping," Ed said, gesturing back down into the west. "Me and the boys, my wife, and Samantha." He touched his shirt absently and the three square patches stitched onto his chest. 4. 1. 9. A troop number.

The girl was indeed sister and daughter to Brandon and Ed. Samantha and her mother had also been avid hikers and fishermen, and they'd tagged along for a week in the snow with the Scout troop. Ed was a roofer and usually worked straight through every summer, so the annual camping trip had doubled as a family vacation for years. His wife liked to say it beat the heck out of standing in two-hour lines at Disneyland. All of the kids were glad to skip school even if it meant extra homework afterward. Sam got to bring her iPod. Brandon had merit badges far ahead of his age. Both he and Alex had achieved the rank of Eagle Scout before the plague, and by Ed's estimation all of the boys—and Samantha—had long since qualified for Eagle Scout themselves.

They'd reached these low, tiny islands with three people they didn't know, Ed said honestly, when he could have lied. Cam didn't ask about the unlikely statistics. Why was it only the three strangers and Ed's wife who were dead? Either someone made a move for the girl or her mother, or someone started cheating with the food. Cam had committed murder himself for all the right reasons, and anyway the killing was long done.

The Scouts were perfect to help spread the vaccine, Cam thought, and it wasn't such a coincidence that he and Newcombe and Ruth had found this able group. No one else could have survived on these miniscule patches of ground.

"We need your help," Newcombe said, as he explained about the vaccine and the fight for control of it.

Ed and his wolf pack were aware of the sudden air war. At first, the surge of jets and helicopters had filled them with wild hope. They'd wanted to believe that a massive rescue effort was finally underway, but the batteries for their little radio had faded more than a year ago and they had only been able to guess who was fighting and why.

"You want us to go out there," Ed said uncertainly when Newcombe was done, but his son was more ready to get away.

"We know there are people over there," Brandon said, pointing across a narrow valley to the east. "We've seen smoke on two of those mountains."

At the same time, Samantha finally spoke up. "It doesn't look like your vaccine works very well," she said, gazing at Cam. "I'm sorry. I just have to say that."

"All of this happened before we got the nanotech," Cam explained, gesturing at his face, but it was no accident that he'd kept his gloves on, hiding his hands.

"The vaccine works," Newcombe said.

"This will be the most important thing you ever do," Cam said, meeting Brandon's eyes for an instant before turning to Alex and D Mac. They were the ones he really wanted, but D Mac was frowning and Alex seemed uncharacteristically quiet.

Alex was waiting for Samantha and her father, even as D Mac made his first small break from them.

"How do we get it?" D Mac said. "I mean, is it a needle?" he asked, and then Brandon and Mike filled the circle with words, leaning forward as they competed to be heard.

"So you're on the rebel side—"

"—but how do we know—"

"You have a duty," Newcombe told them.

"I'm not sure we want any part of this war," Ed said, and Cam understood. The man had seen these children through the entire plague year. His paternal instincts would be cut deep in him. He must have given up any hope of changing things and begun to plan through the grim, impossible chore of enduring in this place, breeding his daughter with each of the boys.

They'd surely talked about it—their limited genetics, the maximum population this string of islands could sustain. Cam couldn't see how else it would have played out. Ed must have used the promise of her to keep them patient until Samantha was old enough not to complicate her childbirth, and somehow their discipline had held. He'd done well, but now it was finished.

"You go or you don't get the vaccine," Newcombe said. "I'm sorry, but that's the way it has to be."

"We're not asking you to fight anyone," Cam said.

"You are," Ed said. "They're looking for you. They'll look for us, too."

"You're still Americans," Newcombe said. "You can be a part of that again. Just help us spread the nanotech. That's all we want. Just help a few people like we helped you."

"That sounds pretty good, Dad," Brandon said.

"But the planes," Ed said.

"You're still Americans," Newcombe repeated, looking around at their frayed uniforms and B.S.A. caps. He was obviously ready to draw on their past and their patriotism.

Cam could see it would be much easier than that. Alex might stick with Samantha. He was the tightest with her, but the other teenagers were restless and girl-hungry and excited. "Listen," he said. "Those other mountains over there are just the beginning. There'll be people everywhere who will be very, very happy to see you."

Samantha shook her head. "It's so dangerous."

Yes, Cam thought, looking at the boys instead of Ed and his daughter. "You'll be kings," he said.

It was early evening before Cam and Newcombe returned for Ruth, allowing D Mac, Mike, Hiroki, and Brandon to come along. The boys had looked like they were ready to fight to keep them from walking away. No promise to return would have been enough.

"We might drop below the barrier for an hour or more," Cam warned them, but D Mac shrugged and said, "We've done it before."

Even without Alex, the teenagers were extra noisy as they descended, questioning Cam and Newcombe about the war and the plague. They knew so little. They were still in shock. They were good kids, mostly, but it made Cam uneasy that Alex had stayed behind with Ed and Samantha and Kevin, the sixth boy. Kevin had big eyes and a small mouth. He was the bottom dog as far as Cam could tell, and he would probably do whatever Ed and Alex told him.

What if they decided to stay? They could be forced off of their mountain at gunpoint, he supposed. Either way, it would be better to give them the vaccine. Cam wouldn't abandon them here without it, but if Ed or the girl saw that, they would never leave. Not at first.

They won't stay here forever, he thought. Even if a few of them delayed for months, even if it took them the entire summer to become comfortable with the idea, ranging ever-farther below the barrier for food and wood, they would see the truth. Winter would drive them lower. And if Samantha did become pregnant, especially if most of the Scouts had left, wouldn't Ed want to find other people to help him raise his grandchild?

Cam smiled faintly as he led the boys across a field of rock and wild grass, listening to Newcombe fend off Mike.

"But if the president's in Colorado," the boy asked.

"There are at least two presidents now," Newcombe said.

"But if the real one is in Colorado—"

"President Kail died in the first month of the plague and the VP stepped up, but the Speaker of the House was in Montana, which went over to the breakaways."

"So the vice president is the real president."

"Look, kid, it's all fucked up, okay?"

He just needs to know he's on the right side, Cam thought, but they were within a quarter-mile of the camp spot and he wanted to be sure Ruth didn't run away. He cupped his mouth with his gloves and shouted, "Ruth! Ruth, we're okay!"

No answer. He felt a thread of nervous fear, but the whitebark forest was murmuring in the breeze, a sound like distant ocean surf, and they were still pretty far away. She might not have recognized his voice.

"Ruth! Hey!"

"There," Brandon said.

She'd gone to high ground, running to the splintered mess of a deadfall on the slope above them. She stood among the tangle of branches with a fresh red scratch across her cheek, her chest heaving for air. In her good hand was her pistol and Cam smiled again, glad for her. "It's okay!" he said.

"Are you all right?" she called.

The waiting had been hard on her. He realized that, but his heart changed as he closed the sixty feet between them. Ruth pushed off her goggles and he saw more than relief in her expression. Last night she had managed to hide it in the dark. Now he saw genuine affection, even attachment, which made him sick because he didn't know how to accept it. He knew that his bent, ragged hands on her would be repulsive.

Her eyes swept over the boys and also went to Newcombe, yet her smile and her tears were for Cam. "I was scared," Ruth said without shame. Her boots crunched in the twigs and pine needles. "You were gone so long, it was *hours*—"

Cam stepped back from her embrace. Her fingertips touched the back of his neck and then slid to his shoulder as he turned. His own arm came up briefly to her waist. That was all. Then he tipped his head at the boys and said, "We got lucky. These guys are great."

Ruth's face was torn with surprise and her lower lip hung open in a dull way that looked very much unlike her.

"Cam," she said, reaching for him again. She'd clearly made her decision. She was opening herself to him, and yet he had to say no.

"Let's get our packs. Come on."

"Cam, wait."

"It'll take us a while to hike back up again and we can have dinner there," he said as he moved away.

The four boys had shifted back from them, glancing at each other, but D Mac stepped forward as Cam went past, allowing Cam plenty of room. "Miss," D Mac said, ignoring the fact that Ruth was nearly twenty years older. "I'm D Mac. I mean Darren." He blushed and tried to cover it with a grin. "Thank you," he said. "Thank you so much."

"Yes." Ruth took the boy's hand, but Cam was aware of her gaze following after him.

They said nothing about who she was or the data index. They'd already risked enough, and they had to keep in mind that rumors would spread with the vaccine. They didn't want anyone else to come hunting them for any reason.

The wind continued to pick up as the sun fell. It scraped over the mountain, howling and cold. The wolf pack did not complain. They put on all of their extra clothes. Samantha kept herself very noticeable in a yellow jacket. Then they hunkered down behind their rock berms in twos and threes, using each other for shelter and heat. Cam found space for himself beside Brandon and Mike, leaving Ruth with Ed, D Mac, Hiroki, and Newcombe. The distance between the tiny groups wasn't much. Their camp barely covered thirty square feet inside the piles of rock, but he saw Ruth glancing at him again and again.

They threw a small party—a large fire and exotic food from

Cam and Newcombe's packs. Deviled ham. Canned pears. The fire snapped in the wind, throwing sparks and ashes, but Ed allowed the boys to use as much wood as they liked to keep the flames high. "There won't be much left for breakfast," Alex told him, and Ed said, "What the hell. We'll get more."

The boys hollered at the first can of food as if they'd never seen anything like it, but every one of them was careful not to dig out too much of the ham with their fingers. They passed the tin around so that everyone got some, even if Mike and Kevin had to lick the insides. It was the same with the pears, the crackers, the chocolate. Even faced with sudden wealth, they were careful. They were a team. Despite his raw mood, Cam was glad for their joy. He felt jealousy and pride.

The sky turned dark but held its blue half-light for more than an hour. Shadows grew in pockets across the land below, filling the leeside of every hill and low place like black lakes and seas, but there was nothing to shield this peak from the sun except the edge of the world itself. A few distant clouds glowed on the horizon.

"I say we take off tomorrow!" Mike still held one cracker in the frayed wool glove of his left hand, treasuring it. "That was the best food I've had in a year," he said. "We might as well hike on it."

"Yep."

"Makes sense to me."

That was Brandon and Hiroki, and Cam glanced up to find D Mac. He'd expected the boy to add his voice to theirs, but D Mac was quiet. A minute ago, Samantha had risen from her spot with Alex and Kevin to join her father, asking if she could brew some bark tea, but her real goal had been D Mac. She'd pulled him aside and Cam saw them whispering together. That must be how she operated. Just a private moment with her was an enticement and she had already drawn D Mac back to her side.

"We can carry as little as possible," Mike said. "Bedrolls, canteens, just one cook set. We can make it there in two days, don't you think?"

"Maybe you want to carry more," Ed said in his tentative way of moving around a problem. Cam had noticed that the man did not give absolute commands. He tried to nudge the boys with half-formed concepts instead, letting them come to him to complete his ideas.

"You mean in case there's a problem," Hiroki said.

"We don't know what's down there."

"Yeah. Fine." Mike nodded impatiently. "So we also take a tent. Extra food. We should still be able to get over there in two days. Maybe less."

"I just want you to be prepared," Ed said.

He's bending instead of breaking, Cam thought. The man had realized he'd never hold on to them, but he still hoped to rein them in a bit.

"It's been a long time," Ed said. "If it takes another week, what difference does it make?"

"Maybe just a couple of us could go first," D Mac said. "Someone should look around, you know. Look for food. There must be all kinds of good stuff down there."

Cam glanced past D Mac at the girl. It was her fear that D Mac was expressing.

"No," Cam said, pushing himself up. The wind was like freezing water in his hair and just the change from sitting to standing made a vast difference in the light. The orange heat of the bonfire only rose to his waist. Above it, the sky went forever, empty and cold. "You go or you don't get the vaccine," Cam said. "It's that simple, and every day matters. We told you. We're at war. Leadville could fly over this mountain tomorrow. And why the hell would you want to stay on this fucking rock anyway, when the whole world is down there?"

"That's right," Mike said, muttering.

"You go or you stay." Cam stared across the leaping fire at Ed and D Mac. "But you don't get the vaccine unless you go."

"You were careful with us," Ed said evenly.

"Yes." This wasn't a conversation that Cam wanted to have—the monsters they might find. "You can be careful, too," he said. "But you have to go. You have to try."

Cam noticed Ruth and Newcombe with their heads together and was immediately reminded of Samantha and D Mac, full of anger and suspicion. It was a weakness. He recognized that, but the destruction of his body had also destroyed something in his mind. He couldn't see how he would ever have a woman again and it colored everything about them both, the girl and Ruth.

The camp was settling down for the night. The fire had burned down to coals and only Mike and Brandon remained at the red glow of the pit, murmuring together. Ed, Alex, and D Mac moved in the darkness, carrying blankets from one tent to two others to make room for their guests. Ed's voice carried from the second tent as he argued with Samantha.

Cam knelt with his two friends. "What's up?"

"We've been talking," Ruth said. She seemed apologetic, even wary.

"You know we have to push these guys," Cam said.

"That's not it," Newcombe said.

"I think we'd better try for our rendezvous," Ruth said quickly. "The plane. I'm sorry, Cam. I'm sorry. My feet . . . I don't think I can hike any more. And these guys can spread the vaccine for us now."

I could, too, Cam thought, an instant before he understood that her worried frown held the same idea.

She didn't want him to stay behind, but he didn't want to keep going with her. She was his only hope of becoming whole again, developing powerful new nanotech to rebuild the damage to his skin and his insides, but how realistic was that? It was a dream. That was all. It would be years before scientists like her had any time or energy to spare, and even then what they knew best were weapons—simple, attacking technology like the plague and the vaccine. Sawyer had talked of immortality, but in the same breath he'd admitted he spent years just building the prototype that became the plague.

Cam didn't want to be her dog, and Newcombe could protect her, and these boys needed help. They needed someone to lead them. He could begin to reorganize the survivors here and take the first small, difficult steps to try to rebuild.

Even if the vaccine wasn't 100 percent effective, it was enough, and what if her plane was shot down? What if she never reached safety? It was crucial to save as many people as possible before next winter. Someone, somewhere, had to have a chance to reclaim the lowlands, and there might never be a better start than the opportunity presented by the Scouts.

"Newcombe still has his radio codes," Ruth said. "The Canadians can send a plane that can touch down on a road or a meadow. Somewhere close."

"As close as they can," Newcombe said.

Cam only nodded. *I should stay here,* he thought.

12

In the high mountains south of Leadville, the night was calm but vicious. Clouds blocked out most of the sky, heavy and still, but the temperature had plummeted, an invisible sort of motion as if the ground itself was lifting away. Major Hernandez clapped his gloves together and flexed his shoulders, not liking the impression of nervousness but too cold to help himself. "Better make this quick," he said.

"Hell yes, sir," Gilbride answered.

It was better in the bunkers. The holes acted like buckets, retaining the thin heat of the day, but they couldn't risk whispering through their plans with four or five other Marines packed in around them. The wrong word might ruin everything.

Two hours ago Sergeant Gilbride had barely made it back to camp before full dark, sweating hard, which could be dangerous in this environment. The moisture would freeze inside his clothes. Hernandez had ordered him to dig out a clean uniform and to get a little food and finally he'd gestured for Gilbride to step outside, nominally to help double-check the night watch.

"You're okay?" Hernandez asked.

"Yes, sir," Gilbride said, but his voice was a rasp and he'd been coughing when he returned to their peak. Gilbride couldn't stop scratching at his neck or the underside of his left arm, either, where his skin was dry and red. Their medic had smeared these irritated patches with gun oil, but Hernandez couldn't spare enough to constantly medicate his friend's rashes.

Gilbride was allergic to this elevation. That was the short truth of it, and yet Hernandez continued to make demands on his endurance.

"I don't know about Ward," Gilbride said, "but Densen is scared. I'm sure he'll want to talk more."

"They'll both send runners in a couple days?"

"Yes, sir."

"Then we'll just keep feeling them out," Hernandez said, watching the dark sea above him. The thick, unmoving clouds didn't smell like snow, but that could change and it would be a problem. It would keep them in their trenches and he couldn't afford the delay. "I've met Ward," he said. "He's tough."

"Yes."

Hernandez nodded unhappily. "And it's going to be as much like summer as it gets up here for the next few months. He might not come around. Not in time."

U.S. Army Lieutenant Ward occupied a ridge two miles to their east with thirty men. Marine Colonel Densen was positioned another four miles beyond Ward with a group of a hundred and fifty. All were artillery-and-infantry units—they were meant to harass an air invasion just like Hernandez—but the rebel assault out of New Mexico had yet to come and they didn't know why. Leadville had only told them to stay ready in the last radio alert.

"Walk with me," Hernandez said. He had to maintain the fiction that he'd gone outside to check on the other shelters, so they'd make an appearance at Bunker 4.

There was very little starlight, but the moon was rising in the east and had yet to disappear into the clouds. For another twenty minutes, the bone-white arc of the moon would remain visible between the jagged black earth and the smooth line of the clouds overhead.

Hernandez didn't look directly at the gleaming light because it would blind him. His eyes felt huge and sensitive. Instead he followed the muted thud of his own boots against the pale rock, moving slowly but with confidence. It was a world of silence and shapes. Gilbride stumbled and Hernandez turned and caught his arm. "Easy, Nate," he said.

He thought the attacks out of New Mexico might not come. It looked like something big was developing. The rebels must be aware of it, too. In fact, the rebels probably knew more than Hernandez, because they had satellite coverage, whereas he was still radio silent.

Three days ago, a huge flight of C-17 and C-130J cargo transports had lifted out of Leadville—forty-five planes by his count. The fleet went southeast in two groups, the C-17s outpacing the older, prop-driven C-130Js. Where were they going? Each group had also been accompanied by a fighter escort of six F-22 Raptors, but Hernandez didn't figure it was an offensive against New Mexico or Arizona. For one thing, an assault would have come back within hours.

Hernandez believed the Russian evacuation was finally in play. The transports must have gone around the world, but first they'd taken an angle to elude the rebels and the Canadians. So why didn't New Mexico attack? Leadville was short on air power and he wasn't sure the rebel leaders would hold back to avoid upsetting the diplomacy between Leadville, India, and the Russians. Or maybe they would. The rebels might hope to ally themselves with the new Indo-Russian state after defeating Leadville. They could be delaying to keep from threatening the Russian evacuation in any way. Far stranger deals had happened in other wars.

Hernandez was deep into a smaller conspiracy himself. For eight days now he had been using his sergeants to make contact with other nearby units. Delicate work. The first overture was simply that Gilbride and Lowrey went in person, off the radio. Then it was discussing each other's vulnerabilities and how to cover each other, what supplies do you need, I can spare some blankets if you'll give me aspirin.

The decision to send Gilbride and Lowrey as runners was also a cautious signal to his own troops. There was no way to conceal his sergeants' absence for two or three days at a time. More than that, simply by exploring around him, Hernandez had acknowledged the anger and the desperation of his Marines.

He'd also made twice as many field promotions as he'd intended, giving stripes to eleven troopers. Most of the new ranks were deserved. One was awarded in the hope of pacifying a troublemaker. It couldn't last. Very soon Hernandez would have to deliver something substantial, and he was reluctant to cross that line, because it would be a commitment. It would be treason. And yet the calendar was speeding by. June 2nd seemed like a long way from winter, but the seasons changed early at this elevation. Hernandez only had another ten or twelve weeks to figure out what the hell he was doing before snow was a certainty.

Stay loyal? Break away? He had no way to move south without being airlifted, and he couldn't see the rebel forces in New Mexico gambling even one plane to bring his Marines to their side. The best he might be able to do would be to move his troops out on their own, away from the war, but then what? How would they survive? At least here they had a steady supply of food, small but steady. Yesterday Leadville had even driven out two wooden crates containing stale coffee, fresh green onions, and a few bags of cow meat.

Leadville must realize how easily they could be bought, and Hernandez looked at Gilbride again as the two of them picked their way through the endless rock. *Thank you,* he thought. He knew his sergeants were working even harder than he was, not just the physical effort to scale across to the other mountains and back, but enduring the tension within their own squads. A war of nerves. There was no easy way out.

In fact, Hernandez had decided not to get out. The basic facts of the situation remained. Leadville was better prepared than anyone else to develop the nanotech, so he would stay and defend the city. The problem was in the leadership's decision to horde the vaccine for themselves. The only path to peace would be to share it, not only on this continent but overseas.

Hernandez was very late in coming to this realization. He wasn't proud of himself. It had been too easy to go along with them when he was on the inside. He had been a part of the problem. That was the truth . . . So he would stay, but in his mind he had already rebelled.

Given enough time, enough work, Hernandez was sure he could convince most of the other field commanders to join him. Eventually the chance would come; the chance to make an excuse to report in person, bringing Gilbride and a handpicked squad alongside him; the chance to imprison or kill most of the top leadership and then cement his takeover with the very same troops they'd positioned all around Leadville.

But he was out of time. Hernandez woke from a light, un-comfortable doze into frigid green daylight, the morning sun filtering through the command tent.

"Sir!" Lucy McKay shook his arm.

"Where is—" He heard fighters. "I want missiles right into them, do it now before—"

The scream of the jets was away from his mountain, receding quickly. Hernandez staggered up and grabbed his jacket and boots in a confusion of people as Anderson and Wang rolled out of their sleeping bags.

McKay looked wild with her hood down and her color high in her cheeks. "It's four F-35s, sir," she said. "They're ours. Looks like they're going east."

"Are there choppers out of New Mexico?"

"Command hasn't said anything on the radio."

He got outside with McKay still crowding his side. She was holding binoculars for him, their best, a pair of 18×50 image-stabilized Canons. Hernandez nodded thanks, although there was nothing to see. The jets were on the north side of the mountain. At a glance, the sky to the south was empty, too. There were less clouds than during the night. He studied the long slants of yellow sunlight.

McKay continued to fidget and Hernandez said, "Stay on the radio. Don't call. Just stay on it and shout as soon as you know something."

"Yes, sir."

He stepped past Wang at the .50-caliber gun, past Bleeker and Anderson with a missile launcher. Bleeker looked steady but Anderson's sun-scorched face was tight and Hernandez said, "You're doing fine, Marine."

Every alert wore them down a little more. When the fighters scrambled at night, there was the panic between getting outside and putting on enough clothes first. Four troopers had lost skin on their fingers when they ran to their weapons bare-handed. Another badly bruised her knee when she fell in the dark. But they had to respond. There was no way to know if Leadville was launching an attack or defending against one, and their own lives were on the line.

Hernandez moved completely out of the trench, stepping up above the rock wall. There was shouting across the hill and he used his binoculars to sweep Bunkers 5, 4, and 2.

Lowrey stood at the edge of 2, yelling at someone inside. Then he glanced up with his own binoculars. Hernandez raised one fist, then showed an open hand like a traffic cop. *Hold tight.* Lowrey repeated the gesture before he turned and relayed the command to Bunkers 3 and 6, which were beyond Hernandez's sight. It was ridiculous, but they only had one set of civilian walkie-talkies and just eight spare batteries. They needed to use hand signals or runners as much as possible.

Hernandez was pleased to see that his people continued to look ready, jumpy but ready, and he caught a few words of the hollering over in 2 now. "Up! Shut up so I can!"

They were shouting at each other to be quiet so they could listen for helicopters. Absolutely ridiculous. They needed radar, but all they had were two more binoculars, their naked eyes, and the broken land itself. The mountains channeled sound but also confused it, continuing to echo with the dull hammer of the jets. Hernandez scanned out across the upheaval of black spaces and snow and earth. The hazy sky. Nothing.

Forty minutes later he'd given the order to stand down as well as calling in his two lookouts. He was out of position himself. He could have kept his scouts in place but it was shit work, missing hot coffee and food. That was a leader's prerogative.

Hernandez had climbed up to the saddle of rock at the top of the mountain with his binoculars and a walkie-talkie, hoping for some clue down in the valleys around Leadville. Instead, there was movement far out to the east, a single cargo plane accompanied by a single jet.

At this distance, even the larger C-17 was little more than a dot, but Hernandez recognized the speed and shape of it. *That must be one of ours,* he thought, because no more fighters had scrambled to meet them. Still, the appearance of the transport was unusual. Nothing ever flew in from over the plains of the Midwest because there was nothing out there.

He thumbed his SEND button and said, "McKay, call in for orders. I have a C-17 and an F-35 coming out of the east. Tell them we're weapons tight. Permission to fire?"

The 'talkie crackled. "Aye, sir."

Hernandez didn't really have any chance at the planes. He estimated their range at twenty-five miles, although that might shrink to twenty if they continued in toward Leadville. Even if he'd brought a missile launcher, the surface-to-air Stingers had a max range of three miles. Still, he knew that a request to go weapons free would get a response.

It came in less than a minute. The 'talkie hissed again and McKay said, "Hold fire. Hold fire. They say it's a Russian envoy, sir. He's on our side. It sounds like there was some harassment from the breakaways out over the Midwest, that's why our jets went to meet him."

"All right. Thank you."

So the other fighters were providing a protective curtain far to the north. Hernandez felt a moment of empathy for the pilots. There was nowhere to eject if they were hit. Even when they were okay, they rode a tightrope above a world of ruins and death. For once he was glad to be on this mountain.

The two planes passed over the Continental Divide. The C-17 began to descend as its fighter escort pulled ahead. Hernandez couldn't see the marsh flats north of Leadville, but he'd watched enough to learn that the long highway had become one of the main runways for local forces. Leadville command seemed to be bringing the C-17 there, rather than using the short strip at the county airport south of town.

Suddenly the cargo plane dipped hard and Hernandez tensed against the frozen ground. Then the plane leveled out again, as if someone grabbed the controls. It circled uncertainly, casting left and right like a bird that had just opened its eyes. It flew like a different plane altogether. After the violence of its nosedive and the new way the aircraft handled, Hernandez did not doubt that a different pilot sat in the cockpit—and the real proof was in the change of flight path. The C-17 was already drifting toward the city.

The fighter was more than a mile in front but accelerated into a long, high loop, trying to swing back and catch the larger, slower plane. Too late.

Hernandez stared for one instant, his fingers clenched on his binoculars. Was it a September 11th–style attack? A heavy transport might destroy several blocks in the downtown area, but how could the Russians be sure that it mattered? Unless they got the leadership, it would a critical strike but not a death-blow. Unless the plane was loaded with explosives or worse. Some sort of nanotech?

A cold sheet of horror propelled him up from the ground and he turned to run, glancing back despite himself. His gaze fell briefly to the miles of up-and-down terrain between himself and Leadville and then Frank Hernandez sprinted away, screaming into his walkie-talkie.

"Cover! *Take cover!* Everybody down right now!"

13

In downtown Leadville, Nikola Ulinov emerged from a Chevy Suburban into the sound of aircraft. He carefully ignored it. His head wanted to turn up toward the distant thrum of jet turbines, but he kept his gaze on the sidewalk as he followed Senator Kendricks and General Schraeder from the car. It wasn't so difficult. The sound was everywhere, rolling from the mountains, and he didn't need to look. He knew what was coming.

"This way, Ambassador," said a young man in a trim blue suit. Pale and clean-shaven, the senator's aide had obviously never spent much time outside in this high place, and the lack of a beard was its own signal.

The men surrounding Ulinov all shared this luxury, like a uniform. It was the one thing in common between the security units that had accompanied Kendricks and Schraeder to the small plaza in front of city hall. The four civilian agents wore dark suits and carried only sidearms, whereas the two Army Rangers were in camouflage and boots and carried rifles, but they were all smooth-faced and none of them had that painful thinness he'd seen in so many other survivors.

"Well, it looks pretty good," Kendricks announced, surveying the bright ribbons and flags that decorated the plaza.

The lead agent said, "Yes, sir." But he was glancing over the rooftops, where soldiers stood in pairs in clear view. There would be snipers tucked into key spots as well.

So far as Ulinov knew, today was only the second time since the plague year that the top levels of the U.S. government would appear in public together. The layers of protection around this spot were intense. There hadn't been any need to come in two Suburbans. They could have walked. The city had been shut down and the streets were empty, except for the armor and machine guns at key intersections.

"Nice day for it, too," Kendricks said, directing a grim smile at Ulinov.

Ulinov only nodded. Kendricks seemed exceptionally pleased and was early for his little ceremony. He wanted to make this place his own before the Russian envoys were driven in from the airfield. The scene was well-crafted. Kendricks had transformed himself to match. He'd put away his cowboy outfit and donned a business suit instead, keeping his string tie but giving up his white hat, exposing his rich brown hair to the sun and the cool hint of a breeze.

The squat face of the city building had been lined with red, white, and blue bunting. In the open square in front stood a podium, four cameras, two clumps of folding chairs, and the beginnings of a crowd. There were the film crews and select media. Ulinov also saw a small pack of children with three teachers who'd wisely decided to keep the kids busy by talking to an Air Force general in dress blues.

Kendricks moved away from his Suburban in a phalanx of men. Ulinov limped after the group. Kendricks didn't look back, but Schraeder extended his hand to Ulinov's elbow.

"We're all the way in front," Schraeder said gently.

Ulinov nodded again, lost in his thoughts. As if it was possible to hide from the drone of the plane.

He looked exactly like these privileged men, he knew, sharp and tidy. That made him surprisingly uncomfortable. Yesterday, Schraeder had sent over two men with scissors, soap, a razor, and new clothes, and little by little it had felt like giving himself up. He didn't know why. He'd spent a lifetime keeping everything in its place. For a cosmonaut, neatness and details were critical, and yet Ulinov would have preferred to wear his nation's uniform. There had been more than one in his duffel bag in the *Endeavour*, but it was better for the Americans to feel that they controlled him down to the smallest details.

The only thing of lasting importance was his conduct. His heart. His memory. He knew he'd done well, and that helped him control his fear. More and more, he'd taken refuge in his past, recounting the people and places of his life, his father and sister and the simple comfort of home, his girlfriends, the magnificent killing beauty of space. He was glad Ruth wasn't here. He would have liked to listen to her tease him about his haircut and his suit, but the two of them had always been separated by duty and now he realized that it for the best. If she was still alive, he wished her nothing but success.

He thought of the other astronauts and the friendships they had shared in the ISS despite their differences. American. Russian. Italian. None of that had been a problem up there and it made him feel both wistful and glad.

At last, Ulinov looked up.

The noise was unending. Louder now. As the C-17 passed over the nearest peaks, the basins around Leadville had caught and echoed the sound. A moment ago there had been another subtle change as the hum of the engines deepened.

Kendricks missed it, making eye contact with a Special Forces colonel who stood near the last row of folding chairs. "Hello, Damon," Kendricks said easily, offering his small hand. "Early bird gets the worm, eh?"

"You and me both, Senator," the colonel said.

But at Ulinov's side, the lead agent put his fingers to his ear-mike and muttered, "Ah shit." Ulinov also saw several of the children lift their heads, restless in their perfect clothes. An eight-year-old boy poked an elbow into his friend's side and was reprimanded. "Stop it," their teacher said.

At the same time, the silhouettes of the men on the rooftops shifted and turned.

"Sir. Excuse me." The lead agent stopped Kendricks just as he began to stride through the corridor between the folding chairs. "Senator? We're on alert."

Schraeder reacted first. "Where?"

"The airfield. Their plane. It's not landing." The agent kept his left hand cupped over the side of his head, listening simultaneously as he talked.

The schoolboys traded jabs again. But their teacher was staring in the other direction.

"It's coming toward us," the agent said.

Kendricks's face shrunk into something made of stone. He shot a long, searching glance at Ulinov and said, "Are you trying to strong-arm us? Change the deal?"

Ulinov didn't answer.

Schraeder clutched his sleeve and yelled, "Damn it! Tell us what's going on!"

Kendricks seemed not to see any threat or triumph in Ulinov, however. Kendricks took aside the agent with radio connection and Schraeder ducked his head into the conversation, too, pausing only to stab his finger at Ulinov. "Search him," Schraeder said.

One of the Army Rangers touched his pistol against Ulinov's forehead. "Don't even breathe," the Ranger said as his partner shuffled his hands through Ulinov's clothes, looking for weapons or electronics. All gone. He'd destroyed his PDA and cell phone two nights ago and ditched the stolen 9mm Glock through a toilet seat into the septic tank beneath.

"Back in the car," Kendricks snapped.

The bass grumble of the plane rippled over the city, vibrating ahead of the slow-moving aircraft itself. Everyone looked up. Mixed with the sound was the higher, lifting whine of a jet fighter, but neither plane was yet in sight from where Ulinov stood inside the plaza. The row of flags undulated once in the breeze. Then a woman shrieked and Ulinov staggered as the Army Rangers hustled him after Kendricks and Schraeder, running back to the street. "Move! Move!"

The civilian agents also had their guns drawn, as if this could make any difference. It did. One of them reached the cars first and waded into the tightly packed vehicles, brandishing his pistol at a GMC Yukon that had just arrived.

"Move over!" the agent shouted.

"I'm with Congressman O'Neil," the driver said, but the agent yelled, "We're taking the car!"

Beside them, other units of men slammed into the parked vehicles, pushing and hollering. Within this small chaos, Ulinov's calm finally broke. *Please,* he thought. *Oh please*.

But it wouldn't stop. Their panic increased his own adrenaline. He saw two soldiers hauling a shoulder-mounted missile launcher out into the open. Some of the children screamed, their voices lost in the noise. Then the human sounds were punctuated by the explosive bark of recoilless rifles opening fire from the rooftops all around the plaza. Hidden weapons teams were trying to take down the plane—and for one instant, Ulinov hoped they would succeed.

Kendricks had been rough with Ulinov, outraged at his spying and deceit. Through him, Kendricks had pushed the Russian leadership hard, threatening to abandon them altogether. First he let them beg. Then he relented and agreed to honor their arrangement for U.S. planes to airlift the Russians into the Indian Himalayas. Anything beyond that must bear a steep cost. Limited munitions. Limited food. Leadville would not include any livestock and there would never be any weaponized nanotech.

That's it, Kendricks said, and the Russians had played into his power game. The Russians admitted they were desperate. They clung only to one additional point. Along with providing aircraft and pilots to help ferry their populace to India, the Russians also wanted the U.S. to accept fifteen hundred women and children as well as a few top diplomats directly inside Leadville, both to establish a small secondary colony and to assure the relationship between the U.S. and Russia.

Too many, Kendricks said. *We'll take a hundred.*

A thousand, the Russians bartered back. Then they sweetened the deal. Leadville would also be entrusted with the treasury and museum pieces of the motherland, and Ulinov wasn't surprised that this meant a lot to the Americans, capitalists to the end, no matter that the crowns and paintings of pre-plague history could feed and protect no one. To some minds, those artifacts would now be even more priceless.

The haggling went down to fifty people to make room for the money—fifty lives and tons of cold metal and jewels. They were more hostages than rescuees, of course. It went unspoken, but Leadville would have total control of their fates, and these fifty people were the wives and children of the premier, the prime minister, the generals, a famous composer. The exchange was supposed to be a new beginning, a mutual gesture of trust. The

Russians surrendered their families and their wealth, and in turn the Americans promised to allow five hundred more refugees to find safety in Leadville when the American planes finally returned from completing the Russian evacuation to India.

That's a generous offer, Kendricks said, but one plane cleared in through Leadville's defenses was all the Russians wanted. Just one.

It rumbled over the city, a snub black shape glinting in the sun. Ulinov closed his eyes against the noise and jerking of the security men, trying to quiet himself. This wasn't how he wanted to die, in a hubbub of rifle fire with Kendricks shouting at him.

"We'll leave every last one of your people to die, Ulinov!" Kendricks screamed as his men tore open the doors of the GMC. "Don't you get it!? You screwed your only chance!"

"Sir!" the lead agent interrupted, pulling Kendricks around the tall silver hood of the truck.

The bitter irony was that Ulinov thought perhaps he'd brought this on himself by relaying such huge numbers through his radio link, counting jets, reporting the buildup of armored reserves. His people must have decided there was only one way they could ever stand up to Leadville's strength.

The Americans would have scanned the treasure and reported it clean before loading it on the other side of the world. Somehow that hadn't been enough. Either one crate or more had been substituted before the plane took off, or one crate or more had been lined with dense, cheap silver that merely looked like Czarist-era relics in X-ray and infrared. The U.S. forces hadn't wanted to stay on the ground any longer than necessary, within reach of Muslim rockets and infantry charges, and of course they had the money on the plane. They also had the families, with every identity confirmed by state records and fingerprinting.

Ulinov did not doubt that these promising young sons and daughters were exactly who they were purported to be. It was only fifty lives—grandmothers, cousins, and wives. And yet he'd noticed one mistake among the dozens of the files sent back and forth. There had been one name that was never mentioned again after appearing on a single manifest, no doubt entered by a clerk who didn't realize what was being confirmed.

Kuzka's mother.

The name itself was not uncommon, and the early manifests were full of such listings, stressing the family ties of the proposed rescuees instead of their actual names. *Minister Starkova's aunt and son. Director Molchaoff's brother.* And yet put together, the words *Kuzka's mother* were also part of a Russian idiom that meant "to punish." More importantly, during the height of the Cold War, in a speech to the United Nations General Assembly, Soviet Premier Khrushchev had used the phrase as he warned the planet of an unprecedented, massive nuclear test to demonstrate the might of the USSR.

The bomb had been more of a stunt than a viable weapon, so grossly oversized that it could only be carried by a specially retrofitted tactical bomber. October 30, 1961. They'd detonated a fifty-megaton hydrogen bomb on an ice-capped strip of land above the Arctic Circle. By comparison, modern warheads ranged in yield from one megaton submarine-launched first strike missiles to ten megaton ICBMs.

Ulinov was both a patriot and a student of his country's rise to prominence. He'd caught the entry on the manifest that American analysts apparently had not, because he was certain of a double cross. Perhaps the Americans were too focused on their own rebels. Besides, the generations-old test was mostly remembered by its code name, "Ivan," or the nickname "Tsara Bomba," the Emperor's Bomb.

He could not gloat. Instead, he felt pity. Leadville had transformed some of the nearby old mines into command bunkers, and Ulinov believed there was also new digging and underground construction here in town . . . but it would make no difference.

The 1961 fireball had been seen farther than six hundred miles away, lifting nearly thirty-three thousand feet from sea level. The seismic shock was measurable even on its third passage around the Earth. To limit fallout, because most of the drift was across Russian Siberia, the bomb had used lead tampers instead of the more typical uranium-238. Ulinov assumed this device would be similarly modified. Land had become far too precious to contaminate hundreds of surrounding miles.

This was the final gambit. The Russians had been bled down to cold, savage veterans poised too long on the brink of annihilation, a stateless population of warriors with one chance at eradicating the only superpower left in the world. The plane must be carrying the largest warhead they'd been able to pry out of their abandoned stockpiles—or more likely several warheads—because a missile launch would have been detected and answered in kind. Now it was too late.

Ulinov fought them when the security unit tried to jam him into the truck after Kendricks. He wanted to feel the sky and the white mountains around him, no matter how foreign this place might be. He looked for the sun again—not the plane, but the warm, pleasant sun—as engines and shouts rose all around him. Radio static. The guns. It was the death-cry of a city.

For days, Ulinov had wrestled with his certainty and his fear, but he never tried to run. If he had, he would've alerted the Americans. But he hoped his people would understand. He knew what was coming.

He knew, and he stayed.

14

In California, Ruth flinched from the light in the east, an incandescent ripple like small suns popping suddenly in the morning haze. Three? Four?

At least four, she thought, trying to blink the hot white pinpoints from her eyes, but the light had been searing and unnatural. The fine hair on the back of her neck stood up like rigid metal pins. For several seconds, she didn't move. Didn't breathe. It was as if her body was a tuning fork, quivering and hyperalert. The rocky slope under her feet was still and cold, but the breeze out of the west made a tangle of currents as it swept through the tiny crowd surrounding her. Then the warm people reacted. The eleven of them clotted together, protecting each other, grabbing at backpacks and jacket sleeves to increase every connection.

"What the fuck was that!?" Alex screamed, and Samantha said, "Mike—"

"Aah!" Mike had twisted down onto one knee, clutching his face. By chance, he must have been gazing directly at the target when those man-made stars flared upon the earth.

Lord God, Ruth thought. How many more had exploded in other places? There could be strikes all across the planet, obliterating the last scattered fragments of humankind. What if India or the Chinese had finally convinced themselves to take that step before anyone else did?

The enormity of it walked through her like a ghost and Ruth staggered, numb and senseless, and then Cam was there like always, shouldering through the group to catch her arm.

Hiroki moaned as Cam jostled by, a low noise like a dog. The others were also beginning to wake from their shock. Alex and Sam knelt to help Mike, but Newcombe was checking his watch and Ruth didn't understand that at all.

"Mike! Oh my God, Mike!" Samantha cried.

Cam's expression was fierce. "Are you okay?"

"What?"

"Look at me. Are you okay?" His brown eyes were intent and unguarded, and Ruth stared at him. The wind felt clean in her hair. She smelled pine trees and damp earth.

They had hiked down the eastern slope beneath the Scouts' islands to give a send-off to Brandon and Mike, who planned to explore the nearest peaks across the thin valley, then return before showing themselves to anyone. D Mac was still undecided. The method for sharing the nanotech hadn't helped. Mike thought it was cool, but even Brandon had hesitated at drinking from the splash of blood that Cam drew from his left hand.

Ruth had considered less gruesome ways. The nanotech was smaller than a virus and could be absorbed through the slightest imperfections in the skin. They should be able to pass the vaccine merely by rubbing their spit against the boys' arms or with something as easy as a kiss, but they had to be certain. Smeared upon the boys' skin, the vaccine might drift away or remain inert, and a kiss might only leave the thinnest trace to be exhaled and lost. Ingesting the blood was foolproof. The nanotech was also much hardier than a virus, so it was sure to survive their stomach acids and move into the bloodstream.

Still, drinking it was ugly. The boys were scared despite Cam's encouragement, and Ruth had been bracing herself for his good-bye. He'd kept away from her all morning. He'd also brought his backpack. Cam and Newcombe agreed it was best to keep their weapons and gear with them at all times, no matter how much they liked the Scouts. Ruth had worn her own pack because of the data index, yet she could easily see how much Cam wanted to go east with Mike and Brandon. It would be very like him to attach himself to their task, offering his experience and his strength. He'd already given Mike his binoculars, two cigarette lighters, and a small amount of sterile gauze and disinfectant, equipping the boys as best he could.

But what if there are more bombs?

Ruth's terror was a huge weight and she reflexively pushed against Cam, trying to get past. He stiffened at her hands on his chest, misunderstanding. Then she felt the same bright fear transfer to him. There was a slanting pile of granite behind Cam and he pulled her toward it, using the rock as a blast shield.

"Here!" he shouted.

The others came after them, slow and dazed. "That was a nuke!" Alex yelled. "That had to be a nuke, right? They're nuking each other!" The boy set Mike against a boulder and tugged Mike's hands away from his wet face, trying to examine the damage. Brandon joined them and then Newcombe and D Mac. Ed directed Kevin and Hiroki into the safe space and everyone knelt down.

Even packed tightly together, they were a miniscule knot of lives and Ruth looked at the sky again with that quiet reaching feeling. Nothing had changed up there. A wisp of clouds ran on the breeze, impossibly calm.

Newcombe squeezed in beside Alex in front of Mike. "Open your eyes," he said. "You have to open your eyes so we can see, kid."

"I can't," Mike groaned.

Ruth laid her fingers over the etched stone in her pocket. "Was that Utah?" she asked. "Where was that!?" The need in her voice made her ashamed, because that scorching light was a horrible thing to wish on anyone . . . but if the flash had been in Colorado . . . if the holocaust was that far away . . .

"We should try the radio," Newcombe said. "Get the radio."

"Yeah." Cam shrugged off his pack and set it in Kevin's lap. They were clumped too close together for anything else. He pulled out a canteen and a bundle of cloth, then removed the thin control box and its aluminum headset.

"There aren't any burns," Newcombe said to Mike. "Can you see anything?"

"A little. I see shapes."

"Good, that's good." Newcombe bent around and extended one hand for the radio.

"No," Cam said slowly.

Ruth glanced back and forth between them, surprised that Cam would distrust him now, until she realized at the same time as Newcombe that Cam was no longer interested in them. She turned. They all did.

"Oh, fuck," Alex said.

Peering beyond the line of rocks, Ruth saw an immense arc of distortion in the atmosphere, a convulsing, tangled shock wave of force and heat. It spread like a circle on the surface of a pond, although it was so big that they could only see one part of the swelling hole in the sky.

Dully, she realized it must be hundreds of miles away—and hundreds of miles across. It was growing swiftly, rolling west against the normal flow of weather. It churned the air apart, wiping away the spotty clouds.

"Where was that!?" Ruth asked again, and her voice was high and sharp like a boy's.

"Oh my God, oh my God," Samantha said.

"What do we do?" Cam said, even as he looked down at the radio in his hand. He offered it to Newcombe, but the soldier was staring at the sky like all of them. He didn't answer until Cam pressed the gear against his shoulder.

"Yeah. Uh." Newcombe groped for the headset.

"The radiation," Cam said.

Then the side of the mountain across the valley from them seemed to jump. Dirt rippled up from the slope in patches and streaks. There were sharp cracks from the rock like gunfire. In the lower areas, trees swayed. Some toppled. To the southeast, a red cloud of bugs swirled out of the forest in confusion.

The quake shuddered down through fifteen miles of mountainside and valley in the blink of an eye. Then it raced over their peak. The ground lurched. One of the boulders above them scraped free and dropped—no more than inches, but it clapped against another granite slab with a bone-grating sound. Chips of rock pelted the group and opened two cuts on Brandon's cheek. Most of them screamed. Cam dragged Ruth away, stepping on Samantha, falling onto Ed and Hiroki.

The earth was already stable again. It was only their own crowded scrambling that extended the chaos and D Mac and Newcombe shouted at everyone else. "Stop! Stop!"

"We're okay, it's done!"

Then the ground shook again. Ruth gasped and stayed down, although this movement was very different. It was lighter, an aftershock.

"It's okay!" Newcombe shouted, but Hiroki had begun to moan again and Alex yelled and yelled without words.

"Yaaa! Yaaaa!"

Threads of dust and pollen came over the west side of the mountain behind them, lifted into the wind by the quake. It formed banners of brown and yellow, rushing east.

Ruth lay on her side in the open just beyond the pile of granite, watching the unimaginable dent in the sky. Cam moved to help her again. As his hands closed on her waist, she felt a glimmer of something other than mute animal fear. Gratitude. His attempt at escaping the rock hadn't amounted to much, but it had shown his priorities. He'd left everyone behind for her.

Samantha was weeping now and Alex paced in short vicious steps between the other boys, pressing his fists tight against his head. "Those bastards!" he said. "Those bastards!"

Everyone else was hushed. The instinct to hide was overpowering, and Brandon made little noise as his father dabbed at his cuts with a dirty shirt sleeve, trying to stop the bleeding.

"Nine and a half minutes," Newcombe remarked, studying his watch again.

His self-control was incredible and Ruth attacked it without thinking, full of envy and disbelief. "What are you doing!" she shouted.

"Approximately nine and a half minutes from detonation until the first quake," Newcombe said. He almost seemed to be talking to himself, as if memorizing the information, and Ruth knew he'd write it in his notebook as soon as he got the chance.

"What does that mean?" she asked. "It must have been close—"

"I don't know," Newcombe said.

"It must have been Utah or even someplace in Nevada!"

"I don't know."

Samantha tucked herself against D Mac, weeping. Hiroki and Kevin quickly scrunched in on either side and kept their heads down. Ruth discovered she was also crying. When had that started? She rubbed her hand against the wetness on her face and looked away from the children. She wanted so badly to lean into

Cam and close her eyes, but she hadn't earned the right. She could only cross her good arm over her cast and hug herself.

He was preoccupied with Newcombe and Alex anyway. The boy had crouched with the two men, forming a tense wall around the radio. They found nothing except crackling white noise, channel after channel. "David Six, this is George," Newcombe said. "David Six, do you copy?"

Static.

"Does anyone copy my signal? Come back. Anyone. Do you read me? This is California."

Static.

"I know it works," Newcombe said. "See? The batteries are good and we must've been far enough away that the circuitry wasn't shorted out by the electromagnetic pulse."

Alex said, "So what's wrong?"

"The sky. Look at it. Too much disturbance." Newcombe pulled his binoculars and dared a few glances to the east, then north and south. "That was very big," he said softly. "As far as I can tell, it was way out over the horizon, right?"

Ruth pleaded with him. "We couldn't even see it if it was in Colorado, could we? It's too far."

"I don't know." Newcombe unfolded their map of North America and set his notebook beside it, scribbling down 9.5. "Leadville is what, seven hundred miles from here? Call it seven hundred and twenty. But who else would be a target? White River?"

"Wait, I know this," Mike said with his palms still over his eyes. "With the curvature of the planet . . . Seven hundred miles, we could only see it if it was, uh . . ."

"White River already got their asses handed to them," Newcombe said. "Why hit 'em again? Especially with a nuke. Even a neutron bomb. The land's too precious."

"We could only see it if it was sixty miles high," Mike told them. "No way."

"It must have been in the mountains, though," Newcombe said. "There's nobody to bother with underneath the barrier, right? So the strike had to be at elevation."

"Leadville's only two miles up."

"But it looked like a flashlight, right? Shit, look at it now," Newcombe said, forgetting that Mike was half-blind. "It went straight through the sky."

"The atmosphere's just not sixty miles tall," Mike insisted, but he was wrong. Life-sustaining amounts of oxygen could not be found even as low as the tip of Mount Everest, at twenty-nine thousand feet, and yet Ruth knew that the gaseous layers enshrouding the planet actually rose beyond the orbit of the space station, more than two hundred miles above sea level, although the farthest reaches of the exosphere were thin indeed.

Ruth had to believe her own eyes. She couldn't ignore Newcombe's training. Leadville was the most powerful city on the continent—the most high-value target—and a doomsday bomb at that altitude might easily have sent its light all the way through the sky. Maybe the flash had bounced. There was no question that the column of heat behind the light had bubbled up far above the cloud layer, the force of it reverberating back and forth for hundreds of miles.

Would it reach them? *The radiation,* Cam had said, and Ruth felt the wild seesaw of emotions in her change again. She began to mourn. She hadn't made many friends during her short time in Leadville, but the ISS crew was there along with nearly everyone else she knew in the world, James Hollister, her fellow researchers, and other people who had done their best to help. Four hundred thousand men and women. In all likelihood they had just been vaporized—and yet she felt ambivalent about Gary LaSalle and the weapons tech he'd developed in support of the insane, brutal schemes of Kendricks and the president's council.

Was that what this was about? Who had launched the missile, the rebels? A foreign enemy?

Ruth laid her good hand on the dirt and traced her fingers through one boot print, as if the broken tread marks were some sort of Braille. As if there were answers.

"It couldn't be Colorado," Mike said.

"Look, kid, somebody just shot off a few warheads!" Newcombe yelled. "You—"

Cam stopped them. "Easy," he said. He had been quiet for several minutes and Ruth realized this wasn't the first time she'd seen him step aside to gauge everyone's state of mind before neatly solving a problem. "It doesn't matter," he said.

"It doesn't matter!?" Alex shouted.

"Whatever happened, we have to decide what to do. I say we all get moving. Today. Now." Cam gestured east into the valley below them. "We need to try to reach as many other people as possible and get off the mountains."

For an instant, there was only the wind.

"Before there are more bombs," Cam said.

"Yeah. Yeah, all right." Newcombe glanced at the Scouts and their stunned faces, Mike with his hands still on his eyes, Brandon squeezing his palm against his bloody cheek.

"We split up," Cam said. His voice was aggressive now, and he pointed at Ed and Alex. "Three groups. You, you, and us. That just makes the most sense." He kept his back to the hole in the sky, staring at them instead. "We have to do this," he said. "Get up. We're going."

D Mac and Hiroki chased Ed back up to their camp to grab the rest of their packs and sleeping bags as Cam unwrapped his left hand again. He reopened the knife wound he'd made earlier, bleeding too much into a tin cup.

"No," Samantha said to her brother. "Please, no."

Brandon shook his head. "We can't stay here, Sam. You know we can't."

Alex drank from the cup quickly and Kevin did the same, but Alex took it back from him when Samantha refused. "He's right," Alex said. "Come on. He's right."

"Stay with me," she said.

The ground trembled lightly again and they heard one of boys shout on top of the mountain. Then the earth heaved. Ruth was still sitting down but immediately lost her balance. She thought she bounced. Cam and Newcombe slammed down on either side of her and someone kicked her arm, a bolt of pain. Her mind went white. Somewhere there was screaming, Samantha and Brandon and herself.

Gradually she realized it was over. She looked for Cam and saw his face bent with his own agony. He lay on his side, picking dirt out of the cut on his bad hand. Kevin groaned, testing his ankle. Ruth heard more yelling from above and Mike said, "What's happening?"

"Every fault line on the continent might be letting go," Newcombe said. "That's my guess. Anyone see another flash?"

They shook their heads.

"You guys all lived here," Newcombe said. "Are we near any faults?"

"It's California," Mike said. "Yes."

"The first quake was the bomb. Maybe the second one, too. I don't know. Christ. Let's hope it's done."

"Behind you," Cam said.

In the east, morning had become night again. Ruth believed the vast distortion in the atmosphere was slowing down, but now a poisonous black stain crawled up from the farthest edge of the horizon, undulating after the shock wave. It rippled and popped, a thin, growing band of darkness.

It was fallout—pulverized debris that had briefly turned hotter than the sun.

Everyone drank, even Samantha, as they shouldered their packs and tucked away their knives and a few precious keepsakes. Hiroki had a shiny old quarter that he showed to Mike, then pressed into his hand as a gift. Brandon repeated the sudden gesture with his Giants hat, offering it to Alex.

Before they divided, the Scouts clutched at each other and shouted and cried. D Mac spontaneously turned to Cam and hugged him, too, and suddenly the children enveloped Ruth as well. Mike hurt her arm. Alex kissed her cheek.

It was the perfect farewell against the roiling sky. Ruth would not forget them or their courage, and she hoped that she would see them again. But as she started downhill after Cam, running east, Ruth clenched her fists and wondered how far west the fallout might come toward them against the wind.

15

"Wait." **Cam moved quickly** to his right, leading Ruth sideways over a log. The ropy brown snakes he'd seen probably weren't rattlers. Gopher snakes looked very similar and had been more common before the plague, but he couldn't chance it. Even nonvenomous bites would inject them with the plague and leave wounds that were vulnerable to more—and fresh blood might excite the bugs.

He helped her get her boots down. Then he kept his glove on her hip, looking for her eyes. Ruth was breathing hard inside her mask, but she kept her face down and all he saw was goggles and hood. His own gear seemed especially filthy after the night on the mountain, feeling the cold on his naked skin.

Newcombe climbed over the log behind them. Cam turned away and hurried in front again, moving east, always east, using himself to sound their trail through the forest. He was totally recommitted to her now. Any thoughts of sending Ruth away on a plane had been a fantasy. The idea that he could stay here with the Scouts, slowly beginning to rebuild, ignored the need and desperation of the rest of the world. He should have known better. Of course Leadville's enemies would attack. They'd only waited for the opportunity.

His guess was that it was the rebels. They'd taken out

Leadville to end the competition to get Ruth. That was a good thing if they'd succeeded. He had to act as if they hadn't. If help came, great. If not, leading her safely through this valley to the next mountaintop was all that was important. In twenty minutes they'd avoided a cloud of grasshoppers, more snakes, and two furious sprouts of ants bearing white eggs out of the ground. Black flies continued to lose and find them among the pine trees. Cam hoped the Scouts hadn't turned back. The quakes alone were bad enough and had yet to quit shuddering through the valley, agitating the reptiles and insects everywhere.

Newcombe was right. The bomb had acted like a hammer, triggering the worst fault lines. As those landmasses fell and clashed, they must have shoved against other regions and set off any weaknesses there. Once the chain reaction was done, California might be unusually stable for years, but for now the mountains rumbled and twitched. Cam was glad they'd escaped the lowlands. More of the failing dams and levees would collapse, adding to the destruction, and there must have been tidal waves along the coast and inside the Bay.

"Stay with me," he said.

Ahead, another huge tree had fallen. Cam angled laterally across the slope instead of risking a way through. There were snake holes in the earth and that made him nervous. He kicked his boot into the pine needles and dirt, showering the fallen branches with debris to scare anything curled up out of sight.

But the movement he expected was overhead. The trees stiffened. Daylight winked.

It was as if God had touched the sky. A new current shushed through the forest from the east, countering the breeze, and in that moment Cam felt himself lose hope. Everything he'd accomplished before today had been set against the vast, lethal reaches of the plague, a few small men and women surrounded by empty miles or dead cities, but he had always had a chance to influence his fate.

I think I just saw another bomb, he tried to say, before Newcombe grabbed at them both and dragged Ruth to the ground. "Down!" Newcombe yelled.

Then another invisible front shoved through the trees, far more violent than the first warm puff of air. The forest moaned, lashed with dust and bugs and flecks of wood and leaves. Cam rolled down and covered his face with his arms, choking despite his mask.

Just as swiftly the wind was gone. He stayed on the ground until his own paralysis scared him. He'd seen too many people give up, and that wasn't how he wanted to die. He moved. He moved even though there didn't seem to be much point, wincing at the abrasive grit in his eyes. He was caked in grime that he assumed was radioactive. The sun itself had dimmed, obscured by the sandstorm. Ruth and Newcombe hadn't fared any better, although there were clean patches on her side where Newcombe had covered her body with his own. Otherwise they were brown like Cam with filth in every crease in their jackets and hoods. It also stuck to the trees, discoloring the bark.

How long did they have left? Cam supposed it depended on how near the bomb had been. It might be days before the poison reduced them to bleeding invalids, but his next thought was the radio. He wondered if they could wire the extra batteries and rig it to broadcast for hours and hours after they were dead. Maybe there would be a survey plane. Maybe an evacuation out of Leadville's forward base would fly close enough to hear. Somebody might find them, bad guys or good, and he'd rather have anyone secure the vaccine than let it be lost forever in this narrow mountain valley.

Cam took off his goggles and clapped them against his leg, straining through the dust. "You okay?" he croaked, kneeling at Ruth's side. She nodded distantly.

Her goggles had failed, too, and were coated with grit on the inside. Cam eased the strap off the back of her hood. Then he pulled off his gloves and used his ugly, clean hands to brush at her cheek. He savored the small intimacy. Ruth was obviously stunned, but he could see that his attention helped her focus again. Her brown eyes went to his face. She might have tried to smile.

She glanced at Newcombe. "What happened?"

"Blast wave," Newcombe said, wheezing. He slapped at his hood. "Christ. I didn't think it would come this far."

"You mean from the bomb in Colorado? I—"

"What kind of radiation did we just get?" Cam asked with sudden urgency. Newcombe was too calm. The soldier didn't think they'd been hit again, and his demeanor set off the torrent of emotion that Cam had suppressed. He brought his hands back against his own body to hide his shaking. He was only beginning to dare to think he wouldn't have to shoot her and then himself before the vomiting and pain got too bad.

There wasn't a second bomb, he thought. *There wasn't.*

"This isn't fallout from another strike," Newcombe said, showing them one brown glove. "It was just hot air, mostly. From the first bomb. It took this long to get here. The radiation might be about the same dose we've been getting in ultraviolet every day. Not enough to kill us, if that's what you mean. Not at this distance." He looked at his watch. "Fifty-eight minutes. Christ. That nuke must have been gigantic."

"You're still sure it went off in Leadville?" Ruth asked. She'd finally started to pat at her own clothing and Cam used the excuse to lean away from her. He was trembling badly now and he didn't want her to see what must be in his eyes.

We're going to live, he thought. He almost wept. He was that deeply affected. He'd thought he had so little left to lose, but he was still a long way from being used up.

They stayed put for thirty minutes. Cam moved them a few yards from the snake holes onto a slab of rock, where they settled down to clean themselves, drink, and wash their goggles. Newcombe tried the radio again. He scrawled in his journal. Except for another passing quake, the forest was silent. The bugs seemed to have gone to ground after the blast wave and that at least was a mercy.

"You saw what happened to the sky," Newcombe said.

Ruth nodded but Cam's mind was still elsewhere. He looked up through the trees as they talked, absorbing the strange beauty of the dust. A brown fog continued to unfurl on the wind, affecting the sunlight, but they were three miles down into the valley. They'd lost their vantage point and could no longer see the torn horizon in the east.

"The quake hit first because vibrations go through solid things pretty fast," Newcombe said. "Air is different."

"The wind," Ruth said.

"That wouldn't make any difference up close."

"No. But the fallout," she said.

"I don't know."

"The wind will push the fallout away from us, especially the stuff way up in the atmosphere," she said.

They needed it to be true, but Cam kept his mouth shut. He was also worried about the plague. If the blast wave had truly swept across seven hundred miles, it would have also brought a massive storm of nanotech. A lot of the subatomic machines might have billowed up above ten thousand feet and self-destructed. Cam supposed the blast could have cleaned away as many as it deposited, but the Sierras rose up like a wall after the great basins of Utah and Nevada. The blast wave might have spent the last of its strength here even as these mountains acted like a comb, collecting thick films of nanotech out of the air.

He was in no hurry to start hiking again. If they'd ingested too much of the plague along with the dust, in another hour or two they'd be screaming with it. They could run back west up to the barrier.

It didn't happen. For once they had some luck. Cam supposed they were still close enough to elevation. Almost certainly there had been wild fluctuations of pressure inside the blast. Maybe the bomb had even sterilized a wide swath of the plague as a side effect.

They got up and hiked. They hiked, and after another mile Ruth began to limp, favoring her right foot. Gradually there were signs that the blast wave hadn't been so powerful down in the valley. The mountains across from them seemed to have deflected the wind, protecting this low area. There was less dust slammed into the sides of the trees. The normal litter on the forest floor had only been swept into curling fingers and dunes rather than completely lifted away.

In a stand of mountain hemlock, ants dropped out of the pine needles overhead like cinders, still alive. In another place Cam saw a yellow page from a phone book, just a single page, carried up from God knew where. Then they walked into a hundred yards of garbage strewn through the trees, mostly plastic bags and cellophane. It was new. The breeze was already pushing a lot of it free and one bag floated down alongside him as they walked.

The blast must have dispersed weird pockets of debris across North America. Cam wondered fleetingly about the ants in the trees. He'd figured it was a local colony that got swept up but maybe they were something else, like a desert species. The fragmented niche ecologies he'd seen everywhere might be facing yet another upheaval as new insects were dropped into the mix over hundreds of miles.

It would be worse on the other side of the bomb. The eastward flow of the weather would bend most of the dust, garbage, and bugs back over and around the explosion. Where the fallout didn't kill everything, the insects would begin a new and evermore savage fight for dominance.

There was no reason to care in the short run. Cam had learned very well to distract himself, but he couldn't escape the aching in his feet, knee, hip, hand, or neck for more than a few minutes at a time—or his concern for Ruth. They hiked. They hiked and found a sunlit meadow where the taller weed grass had been flattened in arcs like crop circles. Cam panicked again when his left hand began to throb suddenly, but after a few minutes the vaccine seemed to beat down the plague, and Ruth and Newcombe seemed unaffected. It was just a fluke infection.

They slept like the dead a good mile up the rising slope of the next mountain. They were all so tired that Newcombe nodded off on guard duty, something that had never happened so far as Cam knew. He opened his eyes to a black sky shot full of stars. The aspirin had worn off and he was dehydrated and cold, and possibly his subconscious had rebelled at the sound of two people breathing deeply when there should have been only one.

They were tucked into a crevice in a hill of granite, afraid of more nuclear strikes. Cam knocked over an empty food can and a full canteen when he sat up. *Damn it,* he thought.

They were dangerously low on water. They'd seen one pond but it had been hazy with bugs—and they were running out of food, too. Those basic needs wouldn't go away and Cam frowned to himself in the dark, counting through the miles left to return to the barrier. At daybreak he'd look for a creek while Ruth and Newcombe ate and packed and took care of her feet, changing her socks and applying the last of the ointment if she'd blistered again. He figured that even with a short nap at lunch, they should be able to reach the mountaintop before the sun went down again.

But there were planes at twilight. Drowsing in his sleeping

bag, Cam mistook the sound for a memory. So much of what he recalled and expected were nightmares.

The menacing drone grew louder.

"Wake up," he said to himself. Then he shifted his sore body away from the rock and spoke again, setting his glove on the other man's legs. "Newcombe. Wake up."

Both of his companions moved. Ruth sighed, a soft, melancholy sound. Newcombe rolled over and touched his hand to his mask and coughed. Then the soldier jerked and turned his face toward the gray sky. The valley was still dark, the dawn hidden behind the mountain above them. Cam noticed that Newcombe's gaze also went to the western horizon. He'd thought it must be a trick of the mountain peaks, reflecting the noise somehow, but the aircraft were definitely coming out of the west.

"What do we do?"

"Stay put," Newcombe said.

Their hole in the rock wasn't perfect but it would have to be enough. The planes were just seconds away. Newcombe found the radio and turned it on, then dug out his binoculars. Cam regretted giving his own to Mike. They watched the rim of the horizon as Ruth struggled into a sitting position between them, her naked cheek imprinted with red lines where she'd lain unconscious against her pack.

"You okay?" Cam asked quietly. She nodded and leaned against him. Her warmth was sisterly and good and for once he was able to let it be just that.

The engine noise spilled into the valley, a deep monotone thrumming. An instant later, brilliant new stars appeared over the peaks to the southwest. Metal stars. The planes lit up like fire as they flew eastward into the sunrise, gliding smoothly out of the night. Cam counted five before another batch came into view. Then the night sparkled with a third group much farther south, all of them coming out of the dark western sky.

This has nothing to do with us, he realized with a dull sense of shock. For so long, everything they'd seen in the sky had been hunting them. This was something else. He didn't know what, but it was an event like the quakes and the blast wave, too large to easily understand.

Newcombe also scanned up north, then turned back the other way. "Write for me, will you?" He didn't lower his binoculars as he fumbled at his chest pocket with one hand.

"Yeah." Cam took the notepad and pen.

"They have American markings," Newcombe said. "C-17 transports. Eight, nine, ten. They have an AC-130 gunship with them. Repairs on the fuselage. I also see a commercial 737. United Airlines. But there are six MiGs, too."

He said it as one word, *migs*, and Cam said, "What's that?"

"Fighters. Russian fighters. Christ. It looks like American planes with Russian escorts, but there's also a DC-10 that has Arabic writing on it, I think."

"Let me see," Ruth said.

"No." Newcombe turned north again and continued to gaze up the valley as he fiddled with the radio. There was just static. Cam didn't know if that was still because of atmospheric disturbance or because their transceiver only worked on Army bands that the planes wouldn't use—or because the planes were running silent.

"I know a little Arabic," Ruth said. She reached for Newcombe's shoulder but he shrugged her off. Cam was the only one to see two of the three groups change direction, the sun winking on their undersides as they banked away to the south.

"Now there are some north of us, too," Newcombe reported. "An old Soviet tanker. Three transports. Two fighters I don't recognize."

"A refugee fleet," Ruth said. "They took whatever they could find. But what's on the other side of the Pacific? Japan? Korea, too. There were U.S. military bases there. That could be where our planes came from."

"I think they're landing," Cam said. He pointed south, where the two farthest groups had already dwindled to pinpoints. Some of the glinting dots circled up into a holding pattern as others disappeared, merging with the ground. How? There were hardly any roads above ten thousand feet. Days ago, Newcombe had explained that C-17s were designed to land in very short spaces if necessary, but the 737 and the fighters would need runways of some kind.

Much closer, the third group had also leaned into a long easy curve, sweeping northward up through the valley. They would soon pass overhead and the vibrations of the engines ran ahead of the planes like another quake, trembling through rock and forest. Cam stared up at the machines. Then he had another thought. Maybe they were landing below the barrier wherever there were roads, as close to safety as possible. If they touched down with their cabins held at low pressure, the crews and passengers could line up at the doors, then crack the seals and run for elevation.

"I don't like this at all," Newcombe said. He gave Ruth the binoculars and immediately began to worm out of his sleeping bag. He grabbed the top and rolled it up, getting ready to go.

"They could be American," Ruth said. "Overseas military."

"No. We pulled everybody back. No way." Newcombe cinched his sleeping bag into a tight bundle and laid it next to his pack, strapping the two together. "This was choreographed with the bomb. Don't you get it? The electromagnetic pulse must have blinded our radar and communications across the entire hemisphere, which gave them a big fat chance to sneak in without anyone seeing them. First they stayed back far enough to make sure the EMP didn't hurt them. Now they're here. Shit."

"Aren't the Japanese on our side?" Cam asked. He didn't think Japan had nuclear weapons, or the Koreans, but China did and there was no way to know who had stolen what.

Newcombe grunted, *huh*. "Maybe it's somebody all the way out of Europe. We had a lot of bases there, too, and I know the plague hit before we cleaned everything out." He began to load Ruth's pack for her, picking up a can opener, a dirty fork, and a half-empty canteen.

A miniscule orange blossom licked up from a peak in the south. "They crashed," Ruth said.

Then there was another puff of fire and a third. To Cam's eyes, it appeared that the second explosion was in the sky. A missile? Someone was shooting at the new enemy.

"Leadville's forward base," he said.

"Yeah." Newcombe quickly returned to packing but Cam stared at the distant battle, wondering if there was any reason to cheer. An odd feeling. They'd been trying to avoid the jets and choppers out of Leadville's forward base for weeks, but now he was glad there was an American power in the Sierras.

The gunfire that hammered them was from behind. Cam whirled to see one of the new fighters strafing a mountaintop about four miles to the north. One of the larger planes also made a leisurely pass, its right side erupting with incredible force. Smoke and light burst from its guns. Each hail of bullets was as large and straight-edged as a city block, two huge rectangular patches.

The wind took the shredded brown earth away in sheets and Cam felt that paralyzing fear again. The new enemy was decimating any survivors who might resist after they landed, and there was nothing he could do against such strength.

He tried to shake his numbness. "We'll be okay," he said as much to himself as to Ruth. "They don't care about us. This mountain's too small."

"Okay," she said.

Someone was invading California.

16

The three of them strode onto the mountaintop with their
guns drawn. They made a triangle with Newcombe's assault rifle
in front and Ruth and Cam on either side. She knew they must
have looked faceless and alien in their masks and tattered gear as
they staggered into sight. Ruth felt her pulse slamming through
her limbs, but her good arm was anchored by the weight of her
pistol.

"Stop!" a man shouted. Thin, black, he had blots of pink rash
on his nose and chin. He'd turned his shoulder as if to hide the
stub of a knife in his hand—or to put his full weight into swinging it.

Behind him, a white girl crouched and grabbed up a rock, and
the rest of the loose crowd seemed to duck at the same time. The
sound was very human. Voices. Boots. They created a small rustle of bodies against the endless drone of the planes and suddenly Ruth was aware again of how exposed they must be on this
light-washed peak. The day was coming to an end. They stood
far above the sunset. Ruth's shadow stretched away in front of
her, joined with the outlines of Newcombe and Cam, whereas
the others' eyes and teeth glinted in the orange dusk.

Some of the strangers hid in their low stone-and-earth bur-
rows. Most of them spread out. Ruth focused on a limping man

who quickly reappeared from behind the nearest shelter. He paced sideways to flank her, holding a shovel like a spear. His face was lopsided by old blister rash and a badly cauterized wound. He had only one eye.

"Gun," Cam breathed. Ruth's gaze flickered left to his side of the rock field. There was a shaggy-haired man with a hunting rifle and her heart beat so hard that it felt like it had stopped, one painful throb and then nothing else.

"What do you want!" the first man shouted.

"We're American," Newcombe said, but the words came out like a bark. He was panting. Ruth and Cam, too. The rush up through the final hundred yards onto this island had taken everything from her. It was an effort just to stay on her feet. Each of them stood bent by their individual pains. Ruth hunched over her bad arm and Newcombe had set his rifle against his hip like a crutch. "American," he said.

The other man kept circling closer. Fifteen feet away. The round blade of his shovel was blunted but shiny, worn bright by the hard ground. Ruth twitched violently and straightened up through the pain in her side. She made sure he could see her pistol, but there was no change in his dead face.

"There might be more of them," the girl said, and the black man shouted, "Just get out of here!"

Cam found his breath first. "U.S. Army Special Forces," he said, tipping his head down at Newcombe's shoulder patch. His pistol never wavered. "We're here to help, so tell him to back off!"

"U.S. Army," the black man repeated.

"We can stop the plague." Newcombe took one hand from his rifle to push his goggles up, showing his face. "Look at us. How do you think we got here?"

"They're dropping people all over the place," the girl said to the black man. "They could be anybody."

The evening sky hummed with far-off jets. There had been a second wave of transports three hours after the lead groups, and then a few stragglers, and the invaders had kept a good number of fighters in the air. Mostly the noise was a distant soaring whisper. The jets stayed high, but if the wind faltered or if a jet crossed nearby, the sound could be intense. Twice more they'd seen mountains torn clear by gunfire. Just standing here was like stepping in front of a train, waiting to get hit. Ruth understood their paranoia, but looking at the one-eyed man's cold poise, she also had no doubt that the plague year had long ago turned some of these people into animals.

"We can protect you from the plague," Cam said. "There's a new kind of nanotech."

"We came to help," Newcombe said.

The black man shook his head slowly as if rejecting them. It was a signal. The girl lowered the fist she'd made around her rock and the one-eyed man paused in his closing arc toward Ruth. Nearby, another man and two women also relaxed, although they didn't drop their knives or clubs. One was hugely pregnant. The other had a fair complexion that had burned and peeled and burned again.

There were about twenty survivors here, Ruth guessed. Cam and Newcombe had made only a brief effort to survey this island before all three of them lurched into camp, still afraid that there could be Leadville troops lying in wait. Despite everything else, that threat was still very real.

Newcombe tipped his rifle down. Ruth let her pistol fall to her side, but Cam kept his weapon up. "We need to see everybody out in the open," Cam said. "Is it just you guys here?"

"What?" The man frowned, then glanced out into the great open space of the valley. "Nobody's landed, if that's what you mean. Not yet." He was delaying, Ruth thought, reluctant to put his tribe in a line in front of their guns. He gestured at the roaring sky and said, "What the fuck is going on?"

Cam refused to spend the night on the mountain. "We're leaving in five minutes," he said, kneeling as he unwrapped the dirty, stained gauze from his hand. One of the men had fetched a plastic bowl that Cam set on the ground beside his knife.

Eighteen survivors gathered before him in a half-circle. Ruth saw uncertainty and distrust in their eyes—and the first incredulous glimmers of hope.

"I know it's getting dark, but grab your stuff and get below the barrier," Cam said. "The vaccine works in a few minutes. Faster than the plague. The longer you stay, the better the odds that a plane's gonna come overhead and kill everybody. You've seen what's happening." He tipped his head north toward the blasted mountaintops, but only a few people glanced away.

He was trying to distract himself as much as convince them, Ruth thought. The cut hadn't had any chance to heal and the skin was angry and red, well on its way to infection. Cam sunk the tip of his knife directly into it. Ruth caught her breath and heard several of them react as blood ran down Cam's gnarled fingers into the bowl.

"We sure could use some help first," said the scrawny black man, Steve Gaskell.

Ruth looked up, furious that he was so indifferent to Cam's effort, but Gaskell's expression was wide-eyed and yearning. He stared at the neat, clear vinyl components of Newcombe's med kit, which she'd unfolded on the ground. Tape and gauze. Antibiotics. Salve. Ruth flushed with new stress. She was intensely aware of the bulk of strangers above her. Even with their packs nearly empty, the three of them must seem unbelievably wealthy—and Cam wouldn't stop pushing.

"There's no time," he said.

"We've got two pregnant women and three people sick," Gaskell said.

"We'll give you what we can spare, but get off the mountain if you want to live," Cam said. "Tonight."

Ruth wondered at Cam's disgust. Dealing with these people must be like staring into a mirror for him and he'd shown the same impatience toward the Boy Scouts for clinging to their islands. It was profoundly self-destructive. His behavior put them all at risk and she felt her own hot anger and fear.

The crowd shifted restlessly in the dusk.

Ruth looked for the rifleman.

"They can't leave," the girl said to Gaskell, and another man grimaced at Cam and said, "Wait. You can wait."

"We can't stay," Newcombe said.

"You don't have to, either," Cam said. "You can leave. You should."

"We'll come with you," Gaskell said.

"It's better if we split up."

"Just let us pack. Ten minutes."

"Try to reach as many other survivors as you can," Cam said. "Pay us back."

"Tony, Joe, Andrea, start getting our food together," Gaskell said, not looking away from Cam. Three of his people left the group and hurried to their shelters.

"There are others like us," Newcombe said. "We're all spreading out."

A woman said, "But who's in the planes?"

"We don't know."

"Tomorrow, send out a couple of your strongest guys," Cam said. "That's the best thing you can do. Find another group. Pay us back."

"We're coming with you," Gaskell said.

"That's okay tonight," Ruth told him quickly, before Cam could answer, and Newcombe said, "Yeah, fine, but then we spread out."

"We have to make sure somebody gets out," Cam said. "Drink." He'd squeezed his hand into a fist to stop the bleeding but kept his dripping knuckles over the bowl as he stood up, holding the scuffed green plastic picnicware with his good hand. He held the dark soup out to Gaskell.

"It's fine, you won't feel anything," Ruth said, trying to soften the moment, but these people weren't as healthy as the Scouts, and she thought again of the first mountaintop they'd found, wiped out by disease. As the vaccine spread, so might bacteria and viral infections. Anyone with a seriously compromised immune system was likely to have died long ago, but there were any number of slow-acting pathogens. Hepatitis. HIV. Too many survivors would be weak and susceptible. Some islands would carry their own kinds of death, but it couldn't be helped, not until they reached a place with a minimum of technology.

Gaskell drank first, then the girl and another man and another. Ruth saw no hint of horror in their faces. They'd seen and done worse to survive, and she turned away to stare into the last fading red coals of the sun.

Newcombe had offered to bleed himself, too. He'd taken Cam aside and said, *Fair is fair.* The two men had come a very long way, from allies to enemies to real brotherhood, and Cam just shook his head. *You still have two good hands,* he'd said. *It would be stupid to change that.* There was so much good in him. Ruth had to forgive his rage and his self-hate.

The woman with the belly hesitated when the bowl came to her. "What will it do to my baby?" she asked, looking at her husband and Gaskell and Cam.

"We don't know," Ruth said. "It will protect you both, I think. There shouldn't be a problem."

She was doubly glad she hadn't slept with Cam or anyone else. How much harder would their struggle have been if she was pregnant? Her first two periods back on Earth had been bad enough. After twelve months in zero gravity, both times she'd bled and bled through cramps and nausea—but each time it had only been four or five really bad days. What if she'd had morning sickness for weeks instead or developed complications like gestational diabetes or high blood pressure?

This late in her term, the pregnant woman would be having back problems and sore feet. A mother's bones began to soften noticeably in the third trimester to help the baby's passage through the pelvic bone. Trudging down the mountainside would be brutal for her, and yet a new generation was beyond price. This woman was exactly who they were fighting for, so Ruth forced a smile and said the words again like a promise.

"It will protect the baby, too," she said.

She lied again that night, huddled together with the others near eighty-five hundred feet in a clump of backpacks, tools, and weapons. Fighter jets crisscrossed the night, mumbling and echoing. The grasshoppers sang and sang. She told Gaskell they'd been given the vaccine by a squad of paratroopers, which was close enough to what had really happened to confuse things if the rumor ever caught up to the wrong people. She told him they'd survived the plague year on a mountaintop above one of Lake Tahoe's ski resorts, south of here, and Cam was more than convincing in discussing a few local landmarks.

The worst deceit was how Ruth explained their goggles. Gaskell's group had jackets and hoods and they'd torn up a few rags for face masks, mimicking their rescuers, and Ruth told Gaskell that her goggles and other gear were because of the bugs. There was nothing more these people could do to minimize their absorption of the plague. She didn't want to give up her own equipment and she didn't want to fight.

In the morning they left each other. Gaskell promised to send a few guys to another peak to the southeast. Ruth wasn't sure he'd do it but she was glad just to get away from them, not only because they scared her but because a crowd would be more easily noticed. A pilot might spot them or a satellite. It was good to hurry into the woods again with Cam and Newcombe. Still, in the first few hundred yards she glanced back a dozen times, a little afraid of herself. Maybe it would have been better if they'd all stuck together, but Gaskell's people seemed equally relieved to split up now that they had some answers.

We're all so much smaller than we used to be, she thought.

They worked their way north even though it brought them closer to the nearest launch-point for the fighter patrols. The jets seemed especially close on landing, groaning overhead, but the aircraft were thousands of feet up and miles away. That distance increased with every step down the mountain. Their plan was to curve eastward tomorrow. Ahead, the map showed a pair of valleys that fell all the way down into Nevada.

Ruth went into herself. In fact, her concentration wasn't wholly unlike sleeping. She moved in a trance, keeping just enough of her mind on the surface to be aware of Cam's jacket and the rough ground between them. Everything outside this tunnel she tried to ignore. Her thirst. Her feet. The sun was high in the forest and flies buzzed all around.

"Sst!" Cam turned and hooked his arm, catching her. Ruth immediately knelt with him beneath the scraping branches of a juniper, trusting his decision to hide.

Newcombe had ducked down across from them and continued to inch away on his knees and one hand, but he'd kept his rifle over his shoulder. He was still holding his binoculars, so Ruth nudged Cam, a silent question. Cam pointed out through the trees. There was smoke on another slope not far away to the north, nearly level with them. A fire? Ruth was too tired for fear. She only waited. Finally, Newcombe stood up and walked back to them, and she felt Cam relax when the other man rose from his position.

"It's a plane," Newcombe said. "A fighter. It's messed up pretty good, but from what I can see it's an old Soviet MiG. I mean really old, twenty, thirty years, like something they would have mothballed back in the eighties. My guess is it shorted out when he prepped to land or ran out of fuel before he got to a tanker. I don't know. We haven't seen any fighting, right?"

"Not close by," Cam said.

"He could have limped away from the Leadville base," Newcombe agreed. "But why come this far when they're on mountaintops all over the place? I think he just went down."

Ruth managed to talk. "Is he dead?"

"He probably chuted out. Hiked up hours ago." Newcombe knelt with them and shrugged out his pack. He found water and gave it to her. "You sound awful."

"I'm okay," she rasped.

"You didn't see me waving right in your face," Cam said. "Let's stop and eat. Thirty minutes."

"Make it an hour," Newcombe said. "I want to run over there and see if I can pull the radio. There might even be a survival kit if the pilot didn't get out."

First he stayed with them to eat. He shared the last dry fragments of beef jerky in his pack, spreading his map to show Cam and Ruth where he wanted to rejoin them. Chewing on the leathery meat made her jaws ache even as it softened and burst with flavor. Cam opened one can of soup. They also pulled several handfuls of grass and ate the sweet roots.

The radio spluttered beside Newcombe, catching erratic bursts of voices. American voices. All of it was thick with static, but they caught the phrase *saying Colorado* and then *to this channel* and Newcombe forgot about the wrecked fighter.

They needed to reestablish contact with either the rebel U.S. forces or the Canadians. A rendezvous seemed like their only option now. For twenty minutes Newcombe tried again and again to raise someone even though he didn't have the transmitting power, captivated by the possibility of real information.

All forces stand. Repeating this. Of civil.

Waiting was a mistake. They weren't the only ones who'd seen the smoke across the valley. "Turn it off," Cam said, shoving his bandaged left hand against Newcombe like a club.

Ruth jumped. There were other human sounds in the forest now. The voices called to each other, coming fast. She'd regained some energy with the food and water, and with it her senses had expanded again. The group was above them, angling across the slope. Was it Gaskell?

The three of them pressed in tight beneath the junipers. Newcombe's rifle clacked once as he braced it against his pack, but the group passed without noticing them. Ruth had a clear look at one man and glimpses of others, a white man in a filthy blue jacket with a rag over his mouth. No glasses or goggles. He did not appear to be armed and Ruth thought they were probably natives, not invaders. They spoke English.

"I said just stop for a minute—"

"—from the flies!"

They were loud to keep themselves brave, exactly like the Scouts had done. They probably couldn't believe anyone else was down here. They were still in shock at this change in their lives, and Ruth surprised herself. She smiled. She knew that if she popped up and yelled like a jack-in-the-box, they would absolutely shit themselves. That was kind of funny.

Newcombe stirred from under the tree and stood listening. Then he knelt and spread his map. "The Scouts must have reached this island here," he said. "We don't know those people."

"Do we talk to them?" Ruth asked.

"I say no. We don't want to get tied up with anybody."

Cam shook his head, too. "They already have the vaccine."

But the other group was obviously in fair shape. Ruth was sure that Gaskell's tribe couldn't hike at that pace. The lesson learned was that anyone who was weak, hungry, and hurt was fundamentally less trustworthy—including themselves.

She wished their little trio could have kept some of the Scouts with them. She needed help. The boys could have carried her gear and supported her.

"What about the plane?" she said.

"They're headed right for it and we can't wait," Newcombe said. "They might be there all day. It might attract others, too. This was a bad place to rest."

They slipped off carefully, keeping to the trees rather than moving into any open space. Ruth glanced back with the same regret she'd felt when they split from Gaskell's people, until she pulled together a more important idea despite her exhaustion. It was the real reason for her doubt.

If the vaccine's already spread to that many islands, the invaders might have it, too, she realized.

Gunshots rattled through the valley, two or three hunting rifles and then the heavier stutter of machine guns. Cam and Ruth immediately went to ground again and Newcombe joined them against a thatch of brush. They'd gone less than a mile since encountering the other group.

"Those are AK-47s," Newcombe said. "Russian or Chinese. Arab. That fits with the MiGs. I think it's one of them."

Meanwhile the echoes came and went, *pop, pop,* the lighter rifles mixed with the deeper *kng kng kng kng* of the other guns, a small, personal battle for territory inside the larger war. Ruth thought it was happening on a peak to the north behind them, but she wasn't certain that the fighting was above the barrier. They'd changed the world again. The plague zones were reawakening. For the first time in sixteen months, men and women filled the silence—murdering each other. The truth made Ruth sick in her heart.

"You said a lot of the planes are Russian, too," Cam said.

"Yeah, but they've been selling weapons tech in Asia and the Middle East for sixty years. Could be China."

They knew, Ruth thought, but she didn't want to believe it, so she spoke the words as a question. "What if they knew?"

"What?" Cam looked up from his boot, where he was tightening down his laces again.

"Why come to California if they didn't know about the vaccine?" It made too much sense. "Why not fly someplace where they wouldn't have to fight so hard?"

"Actually, this might be pretty easy," Newcombe said with a strange gleam in his eye. Pride. "Who's in their way here?" he asked. "A few red-blooded guys with deer rifles? Every other place above the barrier is covered with armies."

"But they're right up against the American military," Ruth said. "We're just a couple hours away for planes, right?"

"You mean from Leadville? They're gone. And don't expect much out of the rebels or the Canadians. The whole continent is still blind after the EMP and might be for days. It's perfect. They hit us hard, came in fast, and now they're digging in."

Ruth shook her head. "There was so much radio traffic before we went into Sacramento and probably ten times as much after we disappeared. They could have intercepted something or heard about it from sympathizers or spies. Maybe they even saw what happened with their own satellites."

They want me, too, she realized. *They're looking for me.*

That was why they'd preemptively killed everyone on so many mountaintops, not only to spare themselves a few casualties as they charged the barrier but also to keep the nanotech from getting away. They didn't know exactly where she was or how far the vaccine might have spread, and sorting through dozens of bodies would be far easier than chasing every American survivor into the valleys and forests.

The vaccine could be extracted easily from a corpse. In fact, with a little luck, the new enemy almost certainly hoped to find Ruth and her data index lying among the people they'd gunned down.

"She's right," Cam said. "You know she's right. We gotta figure they'll be under the barrier any time now if they're not already. They only need to find one person with it in his blood."

The emotions in Ruth were ugly and thick. She saw the same contempt in their eyes, too. All of their choices up until this point, all of their suffering—it was wasted. They had just given the West to the new enemy, not only the scattered high points along the coast but everything from California across to the Rockies. More. They'd given up the world.

Whoever the invaders were, they were about to become the first well-equipped population to own the vaccine. They could keep it for themselves, inoculating their pilots and soldiers. They could simply retreat to their homeland, taking the vaccine with them even as they pressed their war here.

It was an incomparable advantage. They would be able to land anywhere, scavenge fuel and weapons anywhere, move troops and build defenses anywhere, whereas the U.S. and Canadian forces were still limited by the plague.

My God, she thought, dizzy with understanding.

The invasion would already be a success if the enemy thought the vaccine alone was enough. If the enemy gave up on recovering her data index, the decision had probably already been made. They could nuke everything above ten thousand feet and scrape the planet clean of anyone else. They could do it now.

Ruth pushed herself up, staggering. "We need to get out of here," she said.

17

They should have stopped long before sunset, but Cam shared her urgency and they were so goddamned slow on foot. Every step counted. He wanted to get out in front again, ahead of everyone else. They had to assume that most people were also heading east, not just other Californians but the invaders, too.

They still didn't know who it was. Life wasn't like the movies, where heroes and villains came with stupid dialogue to make sure everyone understood what was happening. Maybe it didn't matter, but he couldn't shake the feeling that if they knew what they were up against it might improve their chances.

Behind them, the small arms fire had continued for nearly an hour, popping and cracking. More than once they'd stopped to look back, trying to place the fight. Cam also wondered how many other eyes were watching. Two groups besides Gaskell's? Could the Scouts have been that successful? He wasn't sure what he wanted the answer to be. The planes would drive any survivors into the same plummeting maze of ridgelines and gullies, and everyone was a threat of one kind or another. But they all deserved to live. Cam had been angry with Gaskell, and yet now that those people were behind him, he was glad.

He'd come full circle. Saving them was a way to save himself. Ruth would always come first, but the two goals were difficult to separate.

It was criminal to abandon anyone above the barrier. What could that possibly feel like, watching the invasion and then the activity in the valleys below with no way to move or save yourself? The idea left Cam shaking. They'd been so close. Another week, another month, and the vaccine could have reached survivors over an area of a hundred miles and thousands of lives. The invasion had stunted everything. Ultimately it might kill more Americans than had died in Leadville. Ruth was right. As soon as the new enemy immunized enough of their own men, they could put them on planes back to China or Russia to reactivate their missile bases.

How long would it be? Hours to cross the oceans, hours to power up their silos and retarget their ICBMs. The planes might have left California yesterday—but it wasn't impossible that the rebel forces in the U.S. controlled their own missiles, some fraction of the American arsenal. Maybe there had been nuclear strikes across Asia or Europe, destroying the enemy's capacity to hit North America again. Maybe the U.S. had already blasted the Himalayas or the mountains in Afghanistan. The invasion fleet might be the last remnant of the enemy, only powerful for the moment.

It was a cold thought, and it comforted him, because Cam was in agony. His ear smoldered with nanotech and a second infection had begun to spread through his fingers. They'd walked into a hot spot.

Ruth had it, too. She lurched like a crab, trying to stay off her left foot even as she bent to that side and thumped her cast against her ribs, beating at her own pain. Cam was to blame. He'd wanted to protect her. He'd stayed in a flatter area of the valley because the going was easy, ignoring the confetti of sunbleached plastic garbage in the trees. The blast wave must have eddied here, depositing trash and a higher concentration of the plague, and at sixty-five hundred feet they were far below the barrier. The trees had become ponderosa and sugar pine. The underbrush was often snarled and thick.

"'M sorry," Cam said, glancing through the long shadows. He was looking for garbage in the branches as an indicator, but his mask was damp and smothering and his goggles fogged as he tried to maintain a quicker pace, stupid with exhaustion.

He led them straight into an ant colony.

There were dozens of powdery brown cones on the ground, low circles of clean dirt as large as bread plates. Red mound ants. They had denuded the area of most of its brush and attacked many of the pines, too. Cam instinctively jogged into the clear space as he ran with his eyes up.

The colony boiled over their feet and shins before any of them noticed. Then Newcombe yelled as the ants rushed inside his pantleg, biting and stinging. "Yaaaa!"

Newcombe turned to swat his leg. Ruth fell. Cam clawed at her jacket but couldn't keep her off of the spastic earth. The bugs were a living carpet, shiny, red, wriggling. They surged over her on every side.

"God oh God oh—" she screamed.

They were in Cam's sleeves, too, in his collar and in his waist. He dragged Ruth up from the seething ants and flailed at her clothes with one hand. No good. They were both crawling with tiny bodies and the twitching mass surrounded them in every direction—the ground, the trees.

Newcombe seized Ruth from behind and Cam shoved the two of them away. "Move!" he shouted. He used his pack like a club, banging it against Ruth to clear as many ants as possible.

It was the gasoline in the outer pocket that he wanted. He splashed the fluid ahead of them, very close. He was clumsy with the pack hanging on one arm and the bites like nails in his cheeks, neck, and wrists. They were near the edge of the colony. Cam saw open ground, and yet there were still five yards of writhing bugs between them and safety.

He fired his pistol against the mouth of the empty canteen. The fire seared his cheek and hair as the fumes ignited. The small explosion kicked his hands apart and he spun over backward, knocking all three of them down into the spotty blaze.

"Up!" Newcombe yelled, but Cam chopped his arm at Ruth's legs when she staggered away. She was on fire—and the heat and the concussion had accomplished exactly what he'd hoped, shriveling the mass of ants beneath them. So he tripped her. He pushed her up and shoved her down again. They thrashed across the ground together, banging elbows and knees, both to put out the burning spots on their clothes and to crush the ants inside.

The colony wasn't done. Another red mass skittered toward them from the left and Ruth wailed, bashing her forearm against Cam's ear as she scrambled to her feet.

Newcombe leaned over them and shot into the dirt with his assault rifle. The weapon was deafening. He squeezed off a full magazine in seconds, using the bullets like a shovel to rip up the wave of ants. It only bought them an instant. The ants swarmed right through the broken earth, but it was enough. They ran. They were alive. And yet above them, the smoke was like a rising flag.

"We can't stop," Newcombe said, gasping. He tugged at Ruth and Cam, leading them downhill, and then Cam grabbed him, too, when he put his shoulder into a flexing pine branch and rocked sideways. "The smoke cloud," Newcombe said.

And our guns, Cam thought, but his head was a blur and he didn't even try to speak. The nano infections in him had quickly spiked. The ant bites had filled his skin with flecks like scalding water. It was gone now, after a short eternity, but the pain had cost each of them badly. They moved like drunks. Their feet dragged on the earth and Ruth bumped against Cam and then Newcombe, swooning. Her jacket had charred open on her upper left sleeve. Dirt and fire-black clung to them all.

Then she collapsed.

The valley filled with shadows as the sun went below the close horizon of mountain peaks—and a sheet of grasshoppers lifted up into the last rays of daylight, swirling out from a gray, ravaged stretch of forest a few miles across from them. There were enemy troops passing through the area, or maybe only more refugees.

"Go as far as you can," Newcombe said. "I'll find you."

Cam's attention was elsewhere. Ruth was conscious but still dazed. When he pulled back her hood and jacket to drop her body temperature, she moaned and said, "The senator. Two o'clock."

He could only hope they were out of the concentrated drift of the plague. Hyperthermia and dehydration would kill her just as well, and her delirium frightened him. He didn't think she was capable of more than a few hundred yards. He knew he couldn't carry her.

Newcombe planned to buy Cam and Ruth as much time as possible. They knew it was possible to use the bugs in their favor, so Newcombe would set out the last of their lard and sugar across the mountainside. A new frenzy of ants and other insects might divert whoever was coming. If not, he would try to lead them away, sniping at them with his rifle. Both men had one of their little radio headsets, and they'd divided the spare equipment and batteries evenly.

"Here." Newcombe weighed the two thin packets of Kool-Aid mix in his palm before passing one to Cam. "Eat this. Give most of it to her, but you eat some, too. It'll help." Then he stood and slung his rifle. "I'll catch up tonight," he said.

Cam roused himself in time to stop the Special Forces sergeant before he'd gone too far. "Hey," he called, thinking of all the things that should have been clear between them—the things he'd seen and meant but hadn't spoken of. "Be careful," Cam said.

Newcombe nodded. "Just keep going."

The two of them came to a road suddenly and Cam hesitated, looking up and down the smooth blacktop. The road made a small two-lane corridor through the forest and the temptation drew him sideways despite Ruth's weight. She nearly fell, sagging against him. Cam looked at the road again. They could walk far more easily on the flat, open surface, but it was also a good place to be seen. They had to stay in the brush and the trees.

"Fast as you can," Cam said, dragging her forward. Their boots clocked on the asphalt. They were across in seconds and then he glanced back at the sky. Twilight was giving way to full night. His guess was they'd gone no more than half a mile, which was more than he'd expected. The slope helped. Ruth moved like a broken doll. He didn't even think she could see where they were going. She just leaned against him and wheeled her legs as best she could, kicking at him.

They blundered on until Cam smashed them into a tree. It was like waking up. *Enough,* he thought. *That has to be enough.*

He angled uphill again into a clump of saplings that might hide them from anyone else heading down the mountain. Maybe he would hear them on the road, too.

Ruth fell onto her back, heaving for air. Cam dropped his pack and tried to find water. There was none. He still had one can of soup left, though, and found the can opener. Some of the precious juice slopped out when he wrenched off the lid.

"Ruth?" he said. "Ruth." He took off his own goggles first. The cold night felt amazing and strange and he breathed it in to be sure he'd feel a nano infection before her. Then he stripped her goggles and jacket. Body heat leapt from her like a phantom.

He helped her drink, cradling her cheek against his shoulder. Maybe ten minutes passed that way. A small peace. He ruined it himself. He thought to kiss her. It was a simple thing. She was the only softness in his world and he'd finally worn through his own defenses.

He studied her lips, still smooth and perfect despite the sweat, dirt, and creases left by her armor. She reacted. Her eyes shifted to his and he saw her recognize the intent in his face, the one spark of desire inside all his exhaustion and hurt. He turned away.

"Cam." Her voice was a murmur and she put her good hand on his leg. "Cam, look at me."

"I'm sorry."

"No." Ruth moved her glove to his rough, bearded cheek. "Please, no. I owe you everything."

I don't want it to be like this, he thought.

"Just once," she said. "Please. For luck."

Then she did exactly the wrong—or right—thing. She lifted her face and gently leaned her nose against his cheekbone, showing him what her skin would feel like.

Cam pressed his mouth to hers and it gave him new energy. It changed the long tension between them. All around them, things were worse than ever, but this one small act was sweet and right.

He arranged her pack for her like a pillow and set their guns on the ground beside them. Ruth was quickly unconscious. Cam briefly watched the stars through the trees overhead. Once

he brought his bandaged left hand to his ruined lips and the con-
cave on one side where his missing teeth had been.

She kissed him again in the morning without saying anything first, tugging her mask down and then reaching for his, a
quick kiss with her mouth shut. Maybe it was fortunate that
they had so many more pressing needs.

"We have to find water," he said.

"Yes."

Ruth kept close as he dug the radio out of his pack and he
looked sideways at her, distracted. They were both faceless again
in their goggles and hoods, but Ruth touched his shoulder and
nodded. Sunlight played on their filthy jackets, rocking down
through the trees. They needed to get moving, but he dreaded it.
His knee had stiffened, his back, his neck, and his feet were battered and raw.

The radio was full of voices on seven channels. Maybe it
had always been that way, but they'd been blocked from the
noise by the mountains and the jamming of Leadville's forward
base. Neither of those obstacles existed anymore.

All of the broadcasts were military. All of them sounded
American, too, except for one woman with an accent. "Condor,
Condor, this is Snow Owl Five, we can affirm One One Four.
Repeat, we can affirm One One Four."

"She sounds French," Ruth said.

Most of it was in similar code, numbers and bird names. It
should have been reassuring to hear so much commotion. America was still on its feet, even now.

Cam didn't trust them. He understood that if Newcombe
was gone, it was up to him to get Ruth to safety. He needed to
make contact with the rebel forces, but it would be very, very
difficult to take that gamble and reach out into the airwaves.
Worse, all of the frequencies Newcombe had said to use were
occupied. Cam's instinct was to stay quiet.

They shared three sports bars for breakfast and choked down
a handful of pills, too, four aspirin apiece and two antihistamine
tablets. The drug would increase their grogginess but the ant
bites felt awful and they were both scratching.

At last, Cam broadcast right on top of the other noise. "Newcombe," he said. "Newcombe, you there?" The voices didn't no-

tice. He lacked the transmitting power to reach Utah or Idaho and apparently there wasn't anyone listening nearby, either.

They were alone.

They hiked.

They hiked and Cam made sure not to rush her. The slower pace also allowed him to watch the terrain more carefully. They walked into a termite swarm and quickly backed off, not wanting to disturb the bugs. The front edge of the swarm rolled into the sky but Cam hoped the movement wasn't unusual enough to attract the interest of anyone watching the valley. That was important. He couldn't see much through the trees, but there were still planes overhead and the enemy must have observers on the mountaintops. Once a jet whipped past low enough to shake the forest. Had it been hunting them with infrared?

Cam led her to a creek an hour later and they both fell onto the crumbling bank. He leaned his mouth straight into the water. Ruth had a harder time with only one arm. She scooped her glove up to her lips again and again until Cam gained control of himself and filled her canteen.

"Not too much," he said. "It'll make you sick."

Ruth only nodded and laughed, splashing water on her face and scalp. The sound was a tired coughing but she laughed, and Cam was transfixed by it.

In some ways their wounds and exhaustion had left them childlike. Their vision was becoming more and more immediate, limited to the moment. Maybe that was good. No one's sanity could endure pain without end. It was a survival mechanism. But it was also dangerous.

Cam forced himself to get up and walk away from her to find a better vantage point.

"Wait." Ruth scrambled to her feet.

"I'm just looking—"

"Wait!"

He let her catch up. He found an opening in the trees where they could gaze back over the long rising shapes of the mountains both west and south. There was smoke in both directions, towering up from the forest.

"Let's sleep," he said. "Okay?"

Ruth nodded, but she waited to make sure he sat down before she did, too, leaning her shoulder against his. It was an odd kind of love. Sisterly, yes. They were both unreachable in their filthy armor, but that would be different at safe elevation and the thought of her was strong and good. It was a new reason to live.

Cam monitored Newcombe's channels again. Ruth napped. A cloud of black flies found them and buzzed and crawled but didn't wake her. Neither did the whispering radio. The sun hung at noon for what seemed like a very long time and Cam silently held her.

He woke himself when Newcombe said, "David Six, this is George. Do you copy? David Six."

The transition from sleep to consciousness eluded him for too long. Cam fumbled the headset over his hood and upped the volume, thumbing his SEND button. "This is Cam. Are you there? Hey, it's Cam."

David Six was their call sign for the rebels, but Newcombe was gone. The light had changed. The sun was near the high line of the mountains in the west. Dusk stretched over the long slopes and pooled in the valleys, revealing the far-off glow of wildfires.

Cam stared at the thin control box. Should he switch frequencies? "Newcombe!" he said on 6, then changed to 8. "Newcombe, this is Cam."

Ruth said, "Are you sure it was him?"

There was a man on 8 reciting coordinates, but a different voice broke over him. "Cam," the radio said. "I hear you, buddy. Are you guys all right?"

"Oh, thank God." Ruth squeezed Cam's arm in celebration.

But he'd gone cold. "Shh," he said, turning to look into the woods with a flicker of panic. *Buddy*. Newcombe had never said anything like that before and Cam shifted with restless fear. What if Newcombe had been captured?

"I'm pretty sure I picked up your trail," the radio said. "Why don't you stop. I'll catch up."

The two of them had probably kicked over every pinecone,

rock, and fallen branch between here and the road. Jesus. And he'd *slept*. He'd sat here and slept for hours.

"Cam, can you hear me?" the radio said.

"You need to answer him." Ruth was quiet and tense. She had also turned to gaze into the shadows behind them and Cam reluctantly nodded.

He spoke to his headset. "Do you remember the name of the man who got us off the street in Sacramento?"

"Olsen," the radio said. One of Newcombe's squadmates had given his life to delay the paratroopers who cornered them in the city, and Cam did not believe that Newcombe would disgrace his friend's bravery. Not immediately. It was the best test that he could manage, providing Newcombe a chance to get it wrong if the enemy had a knife to his throat.

"Okay," Cam said. "We'll wait."

They tried to set up an ambush just the same, hooking back above the trail they'd left. They waited in a jag of earth with their pistols, but only one man came out of the night.

"Newcombe," Cam said softly. The soldier ran to them and gripped Cam's hand in both of his own, eager for contact. With Ruth, he was more careful, touching his glove to her good arm.

He was different. He was chatty. Cam thought Newcombe had been more scared than he would ever admit. He seemed to notice the change in them, too. As they ate the last of the packaged food, Newcombe looked up from his dinner repeatedly to peer at Cam or Ruth in the darkness—mostly Ruth. Cam smiled faintly. He was glad to have anything to smile about and he saw a tired, answering slant on Ruth's mouth as they shared two cans of chicken stew from Newcombe's pack.

"The bug traps worked," Newcombe said. "Worked like crazy. There were ants coming out of the ground over a mile away. I had to circle north, that's why I got so far behind you."

"Did you ever see who was coming down the mountain?"

"No. But the radio says it's the Russians."

"The Russians," Ruth said.

"Yeah." Newcombe had left his set on, squawking beside him. Cam thought he'd probably been making calls the entire time just to hold on to the illusion of another human presence.

Only bad luck had kept them from hearing each other. Newcombe said, "It sounds like they fucked us in some land deal and brought the nuke into Leadville with their top diplomats and a bunch of kids. Their own kids. I—"

The dim murmur of voices was overcome by a louder broadcast, a woman speaking low and fast. "George, this is Sparrowhawk. George, come back. This is Sparrowhawk."

Newcombe dropped his stew and grabbed the headset, talking before he'd even brought the microphone to his face. "George, George, George, this is George, George, George."

The three of them were so intent on the radio that at first Cam didn't realize there was another sound rising over the forest. A distant, familiar roar. He looked up through the dark trees.

"I need confirmation, Sparrowhawk," Newcombe said, before he turned and muttered, "It's our guys. It has to be our guys."

The world exploded around them. A jet ripped overhead, dragging a wall of noise behind it. The rush of turbulence crashed into the mountains and echoed back. Dry pine needles and twigs showered onto Cam's hood and shoulders.

"Hotel Bravo, Bravo November," the woman said, "Hotel Bravo, Bravo November."

"There are runners at third and first," Newcombe said urgently. "The batter is Najarro. The pitcher is a Yankee. The ball goes to third."

Her engines were red-white fire in the night, curving upward suddenly in a hard leftward arc. Was she coming back again? Newcombe's broadcast couldn't reach more than a few miles, but if she circled she'd give away their location—She was performing evasive manuevers. There were more fires in the sky. A peak to the south had lit up with searing yellow trails and the jet's engines flared as the pilot boosted away.

"Missiles," Cam said, because Newcombe's head was down, concentrating on his message.

"The ball goes to third," Newcombe repeated.

Static. Her engines whipped down against the black earth and vanished behind a hill. Then an explosion skipped up from the terrain. Cam and Ruth reached for each other. "No," Ruth said, but the engines rose into sight again, swiftly dwindling into the east. It was a missile that had struck the ground.

Cam decided this couldn't have been the first scout that U.S. forces had sent blitzing into California, its cameras snapping like guns. "Baseball," he said to Newcombe. "You think the Russians are listening, too."

"Maybe not."

"You used my name." Cam had never been on the radio, and wouldn't have been a part of any manifest before the expedition into Sacramento. "The pitcher is a Yankee. New York."

"You want to go north again," Ruth said. "Where third base would be from here."

"Northeast. Exactly. There's a county airfield near Doyle, not far inside the California-Nevada border. It's right in line with the grid I just laid out."

"What if the pilot doesn't remember?" Cam said. "Or if she didn't even hear you?"

"She'll have it on tape. They'll figure it out."

"Unless she was out of range."

Newcombe shrugged confidently in the dark. "It doesn't matter," he said. "They'll be back."

18

Six days later they were within two miles of the airfield and Ruth split away from Cam as he went to ground in a cluster of red desert rocks. Neither of them spoke. They simply acted. He picked his way into the small maze of boulders and Ruth hunkered down a few yards to his flank, watching their back-trail as Newcombe trudged past and then took his own position on Cam's other side.

The triangle was their default and their strength. It was as close to a circle as the three of them could manage, turning eyes in every direction.

The path behind them was hazy with orange dust and the breeze had been erratic today, calming early in the morning. It might be hours before the fine, dry grit settled down again, but they couldn't afford to wait for the weather to change. Instead, they watched for other dust trails.

No one, Ruth thought. *There may never be anyone out here again.*

To the west, the Sierras were a staggered wall of blue shadows and dusky forest. That color lightened and broke apart as it spilled down into the arid foothills. Their guess was that most survivors would move north or south along the edges of that uneven line, and if Russian troops had come in pursuit, they'd obeyed the same border.

Ruth, Cam, and Newcombe were miles beyond any hint of green. The plague had been catastrophic in this place. Even the weeds and hardy sagebrush were dead. All that stood were a few dry stubs of windswept roots. Several times they'd seen the desiccated remains of grass and wildflowers laid on the ground like stains, brittle and black. In the heat, the insects had been destroyed, which in turn condemned the reptiles and the vegetation. Lacking any balance whatsoever, the biosphere tipped. The earth baked into powder and superheated the air.

It drew moisture from every seam in their armor. Ruth was stripped down to T-shirt and undies inside the grimy shell of her jacket and pants, and still she broiled.

Drinking water had become life-and-death. Every day they needed more than they could carry. Fortunately they'd also returned to civilization, passing through the outskirts of little towns with names like Chilcoot and Hallelujah Junction. Highway 395 paralleled their hike north and was spotted with cars and Army trucks. They scavenged new clothing and boots. They also found bottles and cans easily enough, although many had swelled or burst in the sun.

The highway was no protection from the dust. Red dirt and sand licked across the asphalt. It piled against cars and guardrails, forming dunes and bars. There were soft pits where culverts had been and other hazards like fences and downed wires. Once she'd cut her ankle on a fire hydrant concealed in the sand, so they usually went cross-country.

They had yet to see another dust cloud. Most days had been windy, which erased their trail but would also confuse the dust kicked up by anyone else. They worried constantly about planes and satellite coverage. Were the flags of dust running up from their feet noticeable from above? There was always movement around them. Huge whirlwinds walked in the desert and vanished and then leapt up again, especially to the east. Their hope was that they only looked like another dust devil.

"Sst," Cam whispered. Newcombe repeated the all clear and then Ruth, too. They drew together in a band of shade and Ruth blessed the wind-blasted rock for its size, glancing up along its pitted surface as she set her good hand against her pants pocket and the hard, round shape inside it. She still had the etched stone she'd taken from the first mountaintop. More and more she was treating inanimate objects with respect, making friends or enemies of everything that touched her.

Part of her knew it was stupid. But she'd grown superstitious. There was no question that some things liked to bite. She would be a long time forgetting the rigid edges of the fire hydrant against her pantleg, so didn't it make sense to feel obliged to benign objects like her little stone and the much larger shape of the desert rock? The idea was as close to faith as she'd ever been, a heightened sense of connection with everything around her.

Maybe there really was a God within the earth and the sky. He would exist immaterial of whether religions were right or wrong. People tended to believe in what they wanted the world to be instead of looking to see what it was, inventing tribal power structures, skewing observable facts to make themselves important. Before the plague, in fact, the most successful religions had existed as shadow governments, transcending nations and continents. What fathers believed, they taught their sons, and they were encouraged to have as many sons as possible. Who honestly thought that the Catholic edict against birth control was based on the lessons of Christ? Or that the enforced ignorance of women in the Muslim world was holy in any way? Large families were the quickest way to expand the faithful— and yet none of these human blunders meant there wasn't some kernel of truth to the idea of a greater being.

Hundreds of forms of worship had been born throughout history, and new religions had surely begun since the plague. Why? Despite the suspicion and greed of the monkey still inside them, people could be smart and honest and brave. Had the best of them truly perceived some link to the divine? Ruth was beginning to think *yes*, although her sense of it was doubtful and faint.

Earth was a very late planet in the life span of this galaxy, flung deep into its spiral arms. If there was a God, maybe he'd used the farthest, most forgotten worlds of his creation for experiments, knowing that most of them would be half-perfect mistakes. What could He hope to learn? The limits of their imagination and strength?

Her little stone, etched with crosses, had become more than

a reminder. It was a talisman. It had power. She could sense it. The stone protected her.

"What do you think?" Cam asked.

Newcombe was peering north through his binoculars. Ruth turned and squinted into the desert herself. The town of Doyle was a squat collection of buildings like boxes and square signs elevated on long metal poles. Mobil. Carl's Jr. Beyond it, brown hills and ridges rolled upward into the dazzling light.

Newcombe shrugged and traded Ruth the binoculars for a plastic bottle of mineral water. She swung her gaze away from town to the few structures of the airfield, feeling both wary and hopeful. She couldn't deny that she was also pleased. The men were beginning to trust her as much as they relied on each other, and she'd earned it.

Her transformation was complete. Ruth had always been tough but now she was a warrior in every aspect, lean and hard and too sensitive all at the same time. To say that she was twitchy would not be incorrect. And yet the twitch was a cool, distant feeling, insulated by experience.

She let her eyes drift over the airfield's fences and high buildings. "Looks good," she said.

Still they waited, drinking more. Newcombe passed around some candy for quick energy and dug out the radio, too. He didn't speak. He only clicked at his SEND button a few times, transmitting three short ticks of squelch. It meant *I'm here* but there was no reply, only empty white noise.

They'd established direct contact with the rebel forces twice more, once for nearly a full minute with a fighter that jettisoned an automated relay. Both times Newcombe had talked nonstop, accepting the chance of being triangulated or overheard, using as much slang as possible in case the enemy was recording him. He had never been explicit, though, and the pilots had also hedged their language. No one ever came right out and said *the Doyle airfield* or *June 11th, before noon.*

"Okay," Newcombe said. "You know your marks."

Cam nodded. "Ten minutes."

"Thirty," Ruth said.

Newcombe touched her shoulder and then Cam's before he moved out, intending to reconnoiter wide around the airfield. They were badly hamstrung by the short range of their equipment, and the relay had vanished in the dust. They just didn't know what to expect. U.S. soldiers couldn't wait below the barrier, unless a pilot had landed in a containment suit with a stack of air tanks. That seemed unlikely. They'd had the airfield in sight for a day and a half now with no sign of activity, but there were any number of ways the Russians could stop them.

Because they had the vaccine, the enemy might have left men at every airport within a hundred miles. Or they could have simply dropped motion detectors or antipersonnel mines. An effort that widespread would have used a lot of fuel and gear, of course. It was a good bet that the invaders hadn't done it. The stakes weren't quite so high for them.

The same couldn't be said for the United States, because the U.S. had yet to gain possession of the vaccine. The two fighters they'd spoken with weren't the only ones Newcombe identified as their own. Four days ago, a trio of F/A-18 Super Hornets had slashed into the mountains. Yesterday, a lone bomber came limping out of the southwest before two MiGs overtook the wounded aircraft and gunned it down.

Their side was trying to cover them and misdirect the enemy. They'd been surprised to find an ongoing exchange between a weak transmission from a man who said he was Newcombe and a stronger signal urging him toward a pickup in Carson City. The weaker transmissions were still more powerful than their own, and so more easily overheard, and Carson City lay sixty miles away from Doyle in the direction they would have gone if they'd chosen to head south instead of north. It was a neat trick, and Ruth appreciated the help—but meanwhile other people were sacrificing their lives.

Larger conflicts were taking place in Yosemite and farther south. The Russians had been airlifting the rest of their people into California, which was good and bad. It meant the enemy was preoccupied with shielding their planes from American and Canadian interceptors, but they were also growing stronger and better established.

The U.S. was crippled in meeting the enemy. A large part of the nation's air force had disappeared with Leadville—and for hundreds of miles, the surviving planes were only so much aluminum, plastic, and rubber. The EMP had burned out electronics even below the barrier, where U.S. forces might have scavenged new parts and computers.

Estimates on the radio said the Russians had already landed

tens of thousands of troops and civilians. More were on the way. In fact, their numbers were surging. There were more and more planes every day, because the Russians had carried the vaccine overseas. The Russians had freed every available pilot and engineer to scavenge below the barrier, lifting aircraft out of the Middle East and their homeland.

Ruth was certain her tiny group couldn't stay ahead of the invaders much longer. The Russians would spread out if only to improve their defenses and food stocks. They would find her.

She still kept her grenade with the data index and slept with both under her head.

She also worried about her arm and whether it was healing correctly. How would they know when to cut off the worn, stinking cast? The men could fashion a splint easily enough, but their opinions differed on when she would be ready to lose the fiberglass sheath. She was honest. She explained that the doctors in Leadville had been concerned about her bone density and said the break might be a long time knitting together. It still hurt, which couldn't be a good sign.

"How's he doing?" Ruth whispered. Cam didn't answer. Her job was to continue to guard behind them, but it took all of her self-discipline not to turn and watch Newcombe. That was Cam's responsibility, studying the area between them and the airfield in case Newcombe flushed any threat. The ground was deceptive. The desert blended into a single red expanse, but the flats weren't flat, as they'd learned too well. The land rolled with hidden pockets and gullies and rock.

Ruth said, "Hey, are you listening?"

"He's fine."

The sun flashed across her goggles as she leaned too far from the boulder, glancing sideways, but Cam didn't look at her. Empty static on the radio. Warm sweat down her ribs.

You're angry with me, she thought.

Sleeping side by side now carried an electric charge, and more than once she'd been restless despite her exhaustion. Their situation was still the all-time worst for romance, caked in dirt, strung out on adrenaline, in danger of bugs and enemy troops. The friction between the two of them was maddening.

They both found excuses to get away from Newcombe. Scavenging for food was a good one, or calling a short rest as Newcombe scouted ahead. There had been more kissing and careful hands. Ruth enjoyed pressing her body against Cam's despite all their bulky gear. At night she'd considered more. They could touch each other, at least. Was it worth risking the machine plague? No. But she knew their clothes only gave them the slightest protection. She thought about it incessantly. *If I push down my pants and he takes off his glove . . .* Two nights ago, when Cam was asleep, she'd rubbed her fingers in her crotch to no satisfaction, her blunt glove against her jeans.

"Remember our signal," Cam said, handing her the binoculars.

"Be safe," she answered.

He didn't seem to want more. He dropped his pack beside Newcombe's and quickly loped away, circling out to the left to form a pincher with the other man.

Ruth trapped her peppermint against the back of her teeth and set her good hand against the inside of her hip, centering herself, touching her frayed pants and the round stone in her pocket. She should have jumped him. That was what she would have done in her old life, take the opportunity, have some fun. They could both be dead in minutes.

Cam faded into the terrain, leaving only dust. The horizon shimmered in the heat. Ruth kept her head on a swivel, trying to cover a full three hundred and sixty degrees now that she was the last one in hiding, and yet she caught herself looking after Cam more often than not. She smiled grimly.

You're not in love with him, she thought.

The sky shook before her thirty minutes were up. Jet fighters lanced out of the northeast in three arrowheads, barely off the ground. One group was different than the other two. She'd come to recognize the twin vertical tails of F-35s, but the third group consisted of a sharp-nosed model she'd never seen before, with lean, swept wings. It didn't matter. Ruth felt her heart leap with elation—and a new concern.

The planes weren't slowing. They ripped past and cut into the Sierras, transmitting in bursts: "Hotel Yankee, Bravo Quebec. Hotel Yankee, Bravo Quebec. George, respond. This is Flicker Six."

Ruth gawked at the thundering sky. She thought wildly of leaping onto a rock and screaming for Cam and Newcombe, maybe firing her pistol, but there was still no guarantee that the three of them were alone out here. She couldn't chance giving them away. The decision was hers, and the simple code matched what Newcombe had told her.

"This is Goldman, confirm, confirm," Ruth told the radio. She bent to take the men's packs with her own. Then the desert shook again. The mountains behind her rattled with sound and motion, enveloped in torn cyclones of dark lines and fire—jets and missiles.

Somehow the same voice acknowledged her, even though the fighters were engaged. "Roger, George, your retrieval is in fifteen. Repeat, your retrieval is in fifteen." The rebels had come in force. There was no way to hide a plane over the basins of Nevada, so they were using themselves as a battering ram, clearing space between the enemy and the Doyle runways.

Ruth hiked with her pistol out and the radio hissing softly beneath the roar of the jets and a distant explosion—a smoke trail down into the mountainside. Somehow she turned her back on the spectacle and kept moving.

There was a rifleman in the desert. *Oh please, no,* she prayed even as she freed her gun hand.

It was Newcombe. "What are you doing!" he shouted, glancing away from her to the mountains. Ruth did the same. The air war was fast and terrifying and had visibly separated into two conflicts now, bright specks and smoke.

"Where is Cam?" she asked, panting. "Plane for us. Twelve minutes. We need to get to the airfield."

Newcombe took the radio from her but simply walked away from his pack and Cam's. "We can't mess with this stuff. You have the nanotech, right?"

"I'm not leaving him!"

"Do you have the nanotech?" Newcombe said. "He'll see us down there. Come on. Goddammit, come on. There's no point running around looking for him. We could miss each other and miss the plane!"

Ruth nodded, but the irrational feeling stayed with her as they ran. She hadn't understood how deeply she was attached. She had been fooling herself pretending that her relationship with Cam was just physical, just circumstance, just anything. She would have paired herself with Newcombe if it was really only about a warm body.

Too soon another plane darted out of the heat, smaller,

slower. The fighters had come in very low, but this one kept within a few feet of the terrain, swerving and diving like an old barnstormer. The buzz of its engine was very different than the high scream of the jets. It was a stubby little Cessna.

Newcombe banged against a chain-link fence and cursed, rocking the wire violently. "Damn it!" They were a hundred yards from the airfield with no way through. He could have climbed it with no problem, but she had her arm.

Ruth glanced out into the rocks and bare earth again. *What if Cam ran all the way back to our hiding place for me?* she worried. She wanted to shout. *Where are you?*

Newcombe led her forty yards to a gate. He put his rifle barrel against the lock and fired. They hustled between two long aluminum hangars as the Cessna droned into the open space ahead, but suddenly the plane lifted away.

"Wait, wait, we're here!" Newcombe yelled into the radio. Then they got past the hangars and saw the runways were drifted over with sand. The desert had long since reclaimed this field exactly as it had buried the highways. The plane swung back again in a loop and Ruth glimpsed black skids against its belly. Of course. They knew what to expect from satellite photos. Their first pass had only been to get a closer look.

"Stay back," Newcombe told her, maybe thinking of fire and shrapnel if it crashed.

The white Cessna kicked up sand as it touched down, bouncing. Newcombe waved and yelled as the plane trundled back around for takeoff, but he was looking past her shoulder. Ruth turned to see Cam behind them. She touched her hand to her chest as if to hold the warm feeling there.

"I told you," Newcombe said. "Move!"

She resisted. She wanted to help Cam, but he waved her away so she turned and ran. The door of the plane was open. Ruth tried to climb aboard with Newcombe's help. A man leaned out and grabbed her jacket.

Ruth looked up. "Thanks—"

There was something wrong with his face. A bandage. He was not wearing a containment suit or even a gas mask. She glanced at the cockpit. In the pilot's seat was another man with the same perfect wound. No. The first man wore a square of white gauze over his right eye, while the second had a square taped over his left. Otherwise they seemed unhurt and even clean. New uniforms. Both of them held submachine guns.

Ruth began to push back against Newcombe, but he was stronger and the other man yelled, "Let's go, let's go!"

"Come on, Ruth!" Newcombe shouted.

She leaned inside despite her instincts. Maybe it was okay. The man in the cockpit had lowered his gun, and the first guy reached down to help Newcombe and Cam, too. No one else was aboard. The less weight, the longer their range. In fact, the thin carpet was spotted with holes where rows of seats had been torn out.

Ruth took one of the few that remained, and Cam fell heavily beside her. Newcombe dropped into a seat behind them. Then the other man bolted the door. "Strap in," he said as he ducked into the cockpit.

The pilot was already accelerating. The plane slammed against the dunes and a familiar cold weight filled Ruth's chest like a ball of snakes, choking her. She'd forgotten. Her long months in the space station had left her uneasy with tight places. The rattling cabin felt like a deathtrap. Then they heaved into the air.

"What happened to their eyes?" she asked Cam, mostly to be close to him. The pilots' wounds were too symmetrical, which made her wonder if they were self-inflicted. Why?

Cam only shook his head, still gathering himself. Then he turned to Newcombe and indicated his face.

"Nukes," the soldier said quietly. "They're afraid of more nukes. The flash. If they only lose one eye, they can still land the plane."

Lord God, Ruth thought, fighting her claustrophobia. She leaned her goggles against the window as if to escape, but the air beyond the scratched Plexiglas was a tangle of far-off jets and burning mountain peaks.

19

Cam's seat belt cut into his hips as the plane jerked and bumped. The pilots had shoulder restraints. The rest of them did not and the flight was like a roller coaster, tipping and diving. Again and again his seat snapped away from him, even with the belt cinched down.

Hills and rock whipped past the windows. A city. Once they paralleled a line of utility wires for a few seconds, dozens of poles stuttering by. It was a disappointment. They'd suffered so badly to get here and they still weren't safe, although they were free of the plague. The Cessna 172 was not a pressurized aircraft, but the cabin windows and the cockpit glass had been sealed with silicon caulk, as had the instrument and control pass-throughs, the hatches, and one of the two doors. There was a vacuum pump bolted to the floor, exhausting to the outside. It was a crude fix, but it worked. The pilot had leveled out for two minutes while the copilot applied a fast-setting caulk to the inside of the remaining door. Then they'd lowered the air density within the plane to the equivalent of eleven thousand feet.

"We're okay!" the copilot called back, reading from a gauge strapped to his wrist.

Cam tore off his goggles and mask, scrubbing his bare hands against his beard, nose, and ears in a frenzy of relief. Ruth removed her gear more woodenly and he saw that her face was drained white.

"Look at me," Cam said, leaning close to be heard over the engine noise. Then they tumbled left and banged their heads together. "Don't look at the windows, look at me."

She nodded but didn't comply. Beneath her matted brown curls, her eyes were wide and dull, as if she was seeing something else. Cam knew the feeling. They were incredibly low. One mistake could fly them into a building or a hillside, and the back of his neck crawled with nervous strain. Would they know if missiles were closing in?

"We'll be fine," he said.

"Yes." Her voice was shaky and she clenched his hand in her own, bare skin on skin.

"Where are we headed?" Newcombe yelled toward the front. Cam felt a pang of worry for his friend. Newcombe didn't have anyone to comfort, and Cam would have grabbed his arm or his shoulder if Newcombe were in the same row.

"Colorado," the pilot shouted.

"What? Isn't that where the nuke hit?"

"Leadville, yeah." The plane veered left again and then jackhammered up and to the right. "We're out of Grand Lake, about a hundred miles north of there," the pilot shouted. "The fallout didn't reach us."

He answered their questions as best he could during the two-and-a-half-hour flight. The plane settled down once they were out of the desert, but he obviously shared their tension and welcomed the distraction. He knew who they were. He was proud to serve. "You guys look like shit," he said like a compliment.

Grand Lake was among the largest of the U.S. rebel bases. They landed on a thin road and Cam saw a scattering of jets and choppers on either side, many of them draped in camouflage netting. Nearby stood four long barracks of wood and canvas. There were no trees. The land was trampled brown mud. There were people everywhere. These peaks were inhabited over an area of several square miles in a shape like a horseshoe. From the plane, Cam had seen tents, huts, trucks, and trailers spread across the rough terrain along with hundreds of ditches and rock berms. Latrines? Windbreaks? Or did those holes and simple walls serve as homes for people with nothing better?

Grand Lake had been a small town set on the banks of its namesake, a fold of blue water caught in a spectacular box canyon just nine miles west of the Continental Divide. It sat at eighty-four hundred feet elevation and couldn't have supported many more than its original population of three thousand in any case, but during the first weeks of the plague, its streets had served as a staging ground for convoys and aircraft. The roads and trails that rose into the surrounding land became lifelines to safe altitude. Soon afterward the town itself was demolished for building material and other supplies.

From above, the movements of the first evacuation efforts were still visible, like tidemarks in the sand. Many of the vehicles didn't look as if they'd moved since then, packed in among the refugee camps. In places the trucks and tanks also functioned as barriers, squeezing the population in some directions while protecting the people on the other side. There were also open areas where they seemed to be farming or preparing to farm, digging at the mountainsides to create level patches. Some looked better planned than others.

Cam's impression was one of entrenched chaos, but he felt admiration that they were here at all. They'd done so much better than anything he'd known in California. They had more room and more resources, but more survivors, too. They could have lost control. They could have been overwhelmed. Instead, they'd kept tens of thousands of people alive even as they maintained a significant military strength.

The chaos had increased nine days ago. Cam saw that, too. Grand Lake was only ninety-six miles from Leadville. They had yet to recover from the damage. Many of the shelters were still being rebuilt and there was litter everywhere, often in long patches and streamers that ran northward in the direction of the pulse. The blast wave had swept through this area like a giant comb, tearing away fences, walls, and tents—and aircraft.

As they taxied and braked, Cam noticed a jet fighter up the slope that had overturned and caught fire. Nearby, another F-22 still hung in a cradle of chains attached to a bulldozer as a team of engineers struggled to excavate beneath the plane, trying to right it again without damaging its wings.

"I'll run interference for you if I can," their pilot said, gesturing to the other side of the Cessna.

"Thank you, sir." Newcombe spoke for them all.

At least a hundred men and women stood beside the road, grouped among the trucks and raised netting. Cam was on edge. The crowd was five times as many people as he'd seen in one place since the plague. In fact, a hundred people were nearly more than he'd seen alive at all, not counting helicopters and planes. He touched his face. He turned to Ruth. She was what mattered, and he saw a different strain in her eyes as she clutched her backpack and the data index.

She was breathing too fast. Her chest rose and fell against her T-shirt. Her arms were scored with red marks where she'd been scratching. They'd taken off their encrusted jackets and Ruth was slim and firm but absolutely filthy, speckled with old bites and sores and a few spots of blister rash.

"The man in the dark suit is Governor Shaug," the pilot said. "Small guy. Not much hair."

"I see him," Newcombe said.

"Let's head straight for him, okay?" The pilot had removed his eye patch and pocketed it as he walked to the door of the plane. Newcombe and Cam stood up. The copilot joined them.

Outside the round windows, Cam saw a team of Army medics and a gurney off to one side. That was good. They'd anticipated the most obvious need, but he resented the mob. He wanted food and sleep. But they wanted the vaccine. He had no right to blame them. The circus seemed like a bad idea, though, despite the netting that concealed most of them from satellite coverage. The Russians might be looking and listening. The best thing would be for Ruth to disappear.

Their pilot opened the door. The air felt wonderful on Cam's skin, but the crowd stopped them close enough to the plane to feel the hot stink of the engines. Most of the people were in uniform, yet it was a civilian who took charge, a clean-shaven man in a smudged white dress shirt. Many of the others were bearded and sunburnt. This man was pale.

"Missus Goldman?" he said.

"We have wounded," the pilot said. "Let us through."

"Missus Goldman, I'm Jason Luce with the U.S. Secret Service. Are you okay?"

"She's hurt. Let us through."

"Of course," Luce said. His men slipped in between Ruth and the copilot as they walked and then a man in Army green drew Newcombe away from her, too.

"Staff Sergeant?" the man said.

"Sir." Newcombe saluted, but visibly hesitated as the space between himself and Ruth filled with people.

It was hard to let go. They had been bound together through eight weeks of desolation and misery and yet this was exactly what they'd fought for, the chance to pass the vaccine to someone else. Cam told himself to be glad. It was over. They'd won. Grand Lake had the men and the aircraft to spread the nanotech—and to protect Ruth.

"Wait." She pulled back from Luce. She'd regained some of her color, but her expression was afraid.

"She needs medical attention," Newcombe called.

The pilot said, "They all do. Give 'em some room."

"We have doctors and food and you can rest," Luce said, "but you have to come with me."

Cam didn't argue. His role had changed as soon as they boarded the Cessna. The power he'd wielded for so long was meaningless here, and he didn't know enough about this place to decide if he still belonged in her life. But she wanted him. That was enough. He held on to Ruth's narrow waist and supported her as they moved into the shade beneath the netting, where Governor Shaug advanced with both hands out.

The governor was in his sixties, short and balding. He was also the oldest person Cam had seen in sixteen months. In California, unending stress had swiftly killed off the children and the middle-aged. Shaug was one more indicator of how different things had been here.

There was real strength in his smile. "Thank God for everything you've done," Shaug said. "Please. Sit down." He gestured to where steel benches and tables lined one corner of the shaded area. The nearest had bottled water, Cokes, and four cans of sliced peaches. A small feast.

Cam nodded. "Thanks."

"We'd like blood samples immediately," Luce said, waving for the Army medics. "Please."

Please. From him, the word was loaded with tension. Cam tightened his arm on Ruth and her dirty backpack, glancing at

Shaug to see if the governor would intervene. He'd thought the medics were assembled to care for Ruth. It felt like a lie. But Ruth only nodded and said, "Yes."

Richard Shaug had been the governor of Wisconsin, displaced like so many survivors. He was nominally the top man in Grand Lake, and yet Cam wondered if Shaug and Luce were working against each other. There would be factions among the leadership. That went without saying. Every day was a test, and they would have different goals. Was it something he could exploit? Which man had the real power? Cam imagined that it lay with the Secret Service agent. He thought Luce was more likely to have allied with the military, and he'd seen how the armored vehicles and barricades divided this makeshift city.

He was wrong. The medics drew four slim vials of blood each from Ruth, Newcombe, and himself. The twelve plastic tubes were set in four racks and Luce said, "Take three of those to the planes."

Shaug held up his hand. "No."

"Governor," Luce said.

"No. No yet."

"We have to get it to as many people as possible. We could fly it to Salmon River, at least," Luce said.

"What's going on?" Ruth asked. Her face was paler than ever. She hadn't been able to afford even 30 ccs of blood and looked nauseous, although her eyes were angry and alert.

Two of the medics hustled off with the blood samples, leaving their cart and equipment behind. A full squad of troops moved with them through the crowd. They were headed for the labyrinth of shelters, not the runway. Cam's gaze shifted to the needles and tubing, and then to Luce. Did the man realize how little blood was necessary?

"Let's get you inside," Shaug said, offering Ruth one of the cans of peaches. "Do you want to eat a little first? Please. I can see you're very tired."

"I don't understand," she protested, but she was hardly a fool or a helpless girl. She was trying to draw him out.

Shaug didn't bother to answer. "Clean that up," he said to the remaining medics, pointing at their trays and equipment. Then he looked back at Ruth like an afterthought. "Let's get you inside," he repeated, glancing at another man.

It was the officer who'd stopped Newcombe by the plane. A colonel. "Let's go," the colonel said, and Cam watched the crowd separate as men and women in uniform stepped forward and Luce's civilian agents held back. Had Luce really expected to outmaneuver the governor?

Ruth was being used for barter or political gain, he thought. Shaug wanted to hold on to her and the vaccine in exchange for guarantees from the other Americans and the Canadians, and it was true that Grand Lake had rescued her when no one else could. But it was divisive. That was why Luce had rushed their plane. Luce hoped to spread the vaccine before some catastrophe destroyed it altogether, another bomb, or a Russian assault.

Cam wanted him to succeed, and maybe that was all Luce had intended to accomplish—to make a friend. Shaug probably couldn't control the vaccine no matter what he did. The three of them were exhaling traces of it just sitting here. As soon as they showered or went to the bathroom, the vaccine would be in the water and in the latrines. In fact, their jackets must be crawling with it, rubbed inside and out with blood, skin, and sweat. If they only knew, Luce and his people could slice the jackets into pieces and package the material aboard any number of jets. They could even ingest a pinch of the dirty fabric themselves and then set out below the barrier on foot.

Cam didn't say it out loud. There was another way. He coughed and brought his hand to his mouth, spitting lightly into his palm.

"Have you heard from Captain Young, sir?" Newcombe asked. The colonel only frowned. "My squad leader in Sacramento," Newcombe explained. "He and another man went south."

"I don't know, son."

"We saw fighting on May twenty-third, west of the Sierras. We thought it was them."

Cam paced through the soldiers and made eye contact with Luce, extending his hand. "Thank you," he said.

"Sure," Luce said doubtfully, yet he reached out and Cam completed the gesture, pressing his wet palm against the other man's dry skin. The uncertainty in Luce's expression deepened, but then he nodded. It was done. The vaccine was loose in Grand Lake.

A blue-eyed soldier with sunburn on his ears and cheeks took Ruth's pack. Cam would always remember his face.

"We have a small lab," Shaug said. "There are some people who'll start looking things over tonight. Tomorrow you can help them."

"Yes." Ruth nodded, but her mouth was set in a grimace and Cam felt no better, watching the soldier turn and go. They'd carried that battered green pack for hundreds of miles and now it wasn't theirs anymore.

Newcombe disappeared with the colonel. A persistent nurse also tried to separate Cam and Ruth in the small, overcrowded medical tent, where row after row of people lay groaning on blankets and cots and the bare earth, mostly soldiers. Even with the tent sides rolled up, the air was putrid. Stomach flu. But this was where Grand Lake had an X-ray machine.

The nurse said, "We really don't want anyone in here who doesn't need to be here."

"No. I'm staying with him," Ruth said.

"We just want to take a quick look at—"

"I'm staying with him."

The nurse checked with three doctors before turning on the X-ray, which was isolated in its own tiny space by hanging blankets. This tent was hooked into Grand Lake's power grid, fed by turbines far below in the river, but the amperage on their line was weak and couldn't support more than a few pieces of equipment at once.

While the film was developed, Cam and Ruth were led to a second tent where they were given antibiotics. Ruth grabbed something from her pants before a man took their filthy clothes away. A rock. She tried to hide it, but Cam recognized the lines scored into the granite.

"Jesus, Ruth, how long have you been . . ."

"Please. Please, Cam." She wouldn't look at him. "Please don't be mean about it."

He nodded slowly. The rock was obviously safe. Otherwise

they would have gotten sick weeks ago. *But why would you want to take anything from that place with you?* he wondered. Maybe she wasn't sure, either. "It's okay," he said.

They were given stinging sponge baths with soap and water and rubbing alcohol. Then their multitude of wounds were treated, stitched, and bandaged. Ruth wasn't shy about her body, although there were half a dozen people in between them and Cam turned his back, trying not to stare.

The medical staff wore cloth masks and a hodgepodge of gloves, some latex, some rubber. They were almost certainly exposed to the nanotech. Cam coughed and coughed to purposely infect them. The vaccine wouldn't replicate inside them because there was no plague here for it attack, but he wanted to spread the technology to as many people as possible.

A man with glasses came in and said, "Goldman? Your arm's healed fairly well, but I'm going to recommend a brace for at least three weeks. Don't overuse it."

They cut off her battered fiberglass cast and Ruth gasped at the sight of her arm. The skin was wrinkled and albino pale, the muscles wasted. Trapped sweat had puckered her skin and in places the doughy tissue was infected. She wept. She wept and Cam knew her tears weren't for her arm, not entirely. She was finally able to let go of all the horror she'd repressed.

Cam hurried through the strangers and held her. Neither of them wore anything except a flimsy hospital smock. Ruth's clean-smelling hair had fluffed up in waves and curls and Cam kept his nose against the top of her head, marveling in the small pleasure of it.

Things got worse. The two of them had already received a fortune in pharmaceuticals and the medical staff refused to give her painkillers before they cleaned her arm. "It's superficial," the surgeon said. He scraped at her mushy skin and swabbed the wounds with iodine as Ruth screamed and screamed, clinging to her little rock.

"We need to rest," Cam said. "Food and rest. Please."

"Of course. We can follow up tomorrow." The surgeon was testing Cam's left hand now, pricking the scar tissue, but he turned and gestured at a nurse, who left the narrow room.

Ruth had lain down, shaking. Her forearm was wrapped in a

black fabric sleeve reinforced with metal struts, although the surgeon had said to take it off as much as possible to let her wounds breathe.

The nurse returned with four soldiers. Cam recognized one of them from the landing strip and fought to hide his reaction, bristling with distrust and aggression. It was misplaced. It came too easily. "Can you help her?" he asked.

"Yes, sir," the squad leader said. "Ma'am? Ma'am, we're going to carry you, okay?"

Cam and Ruth were dressed in Army green themselves, old shirts and pants—old but clean. The nurse hadn't been long finding things in their exact sizes. Cam tried not to dwell on the fact that the spare clothes must have come from dead men. It wouldn't have bothered him except that he didn't want to offend the soldiers for any reason.

Cam leaned on one of the young men as they left the tent. Ruth was half-conscious in their arms. Outside, a blond woman stood waiting in the last light of the sun, her chin tipped up almost combatively. From her rich hair and complexion, Cam thought she was in the prime of her early thirties, a lot like Ruth. She was beautiful, but she wore the same Army green as all of them beneath a white lab coat and it was the coat that unsettled Cam. Was she from Shaug's nanotech team?

Just go away, he thought.

The woman's legs scissored as she moved into their path. There were nonreflective black bars on her shirt collar and the squad leader said, "Excuse me, Captain."

She didn't even look at him. "Ruth?" she asked. "Ruth, my God." Her smooth hand went to Ruth's shoulder, as deft as a bird.

Cam said, "Leave us alone."

"I know her," the woman insisted.

He would have shoved past, but Ruth wriggled free of the soldiers and took one step, unsteady, smiling, before she buried her face in the woman's long hair and embraced her. "Deborah," she said.

The wind picked up as the light changed, fading to orange, but Ruth clung stubbornly to her friend in the same way she'd refused to lose sight of Cam.

"Please, ma'am," the squad leader said.

"Can't you just bring our dinner here?" Ruth asked. She sat between Cam and Deborah on the tracked bare earth near the corner of the surgical tent, where they were mostly out of the breeze but could still look across the mountains in the west.

"Ma'am," the man repeated, but Deborah said, "Just do it, Sergeant. Send one of your guys. The rest of you can keep her plenty safe for a few minutes."

"My orders are to get her inside, Captain."

"I like the air," Ruth said distantly.

Cam worried that she might be confused, but Deborah only repeated herself in that haughty way. "A few minutes," Deborah said. "Go on."

The squad leader jerked his thumb at one of his men, who moved off. There were other people passing by, two doctors, two mechanics, a teenager in civilian clothes.

"What can I do?" Deborah asked softly. "Are you okay?"

"I'm cold," Ruth said, still gazing at the horizon.

Deborah glanced past her at Cam with a worried look and he felt for the first time that they might be friends, too, although it was strange. If he remembered right, the two women had been adversaries before today.

Deborah Reece, M.D., Ph.D., had been the physician and a support systems specialist aboard the International Space Station. All of the astronauts had worked two or more jobs to maintain the station, and she was a formidable woman. Most impressive of all was that Ruth had last seen her in Leadville. Somehow Deborah had walked away from the nuclear strike, and yet Cam held his tongue, watching the people come and go until Ruth shook herself, coming into focus at last.

"Deb, what are you doing here?" she asked. "I thought Grand Lake was a rebel base."

"It's not important. Did you get what you went for?"

"Yes. Yes, we did." Ruth set her good hand on Cam's knee and squeezed, although she didn't look at him.

Deborah noticed the contact. She glanced past Ruth again, and Cam tried to smile. "We need to know everything about this place," he said.

"I'll tell you what I can." But mostly Deborah talked about Leadville. She had yet to make peace with it, Cam realized, and that was no surprise.

"Bill Wallace is dead," she told Ruth, counting friends. "Gustavo. Ulinov. Everyone in the labs."

Nikola Ulinov had sacrificed four hundred thousand people for the Russians, saving only one. Playing on the authority he'd once had aboard the ISS, Ulinov quietly suggested that Deborah volunteer for a combat unit. Her medical training could be of real use, he said, helping the men and women on Leadville's front lines rather than babying the politicians in town.

"It was a warning," Deborah said. "It was the best he could do. If he ran . . . If our entire crew disappeared, Leadville would've known. They would have shot down the plane that brought in the warhead."

Cam let her talk, watching the fine wrinkles that appeared at the corners of her eyes and mouth as she struggled with herself.

"When I think of him waiting," Deborah said. "When I think of him being sure, but still waiting . . ." She leaned against Ruth and sighed, blinking back tears even as her eyes sparked with rage.

"It's okay," Ruth said. "Shh, it's okay."

Cam frowned and turned to gaze out across the mountains again, wondering at the man's determination in bringing such force down on himself. He had seen all kinds of bravery and evil. Sometimes they were one and same. The only difference was in where you stood, and that made Cam uneasy. He believed in what he was doing, but maybe it was a mistake.

He coughed hard into his palm. Then he touched the back of Deborah's hand as if to comfort her, infecting her with the vaccine. "I'm sorry," he said.

Grand Lake had gone underground. Many of the trailers and huts concealed tunnel entrances. On their way from the medical tent, Cam saw a wide shape of camouflage netting that covered new excavations. Work had stopped for the day, but it looked as if they'd dug a fifty-foot pit by hand and were still hacking at one edge while other teams built wooden frameworks into which they'd pour concrete. He supposed that after the boxy shapes of the walls had set, they'd add ceilings, then pile the dirt back in to hide and insulate the bunker. A wasted effort.

You can all go back down again, he thought. *You should all be able to walk off this mountain.*

That was probably why Shaug sought to control it. If too many people ran, he'd lose his fighting force. A mass exodus down from the Continental Divide could be its own disaster, because without an organized military, they would be helpless against the Russians.

Maybe the governor was right.

Cam felt new adrenaline as the squad leader led them to a sun-faded mobile home with a tarp for an awning, hiding its door. Deborah had already left, promising to visit Ruth again before breakfast, and Cam was glad that someone else knew where to find them. What if Shaug meant to lock them in?

He was unarmed and outnumbered. He went through the door when the squad leader gestured. Inside, the prefab home was little more than a shell, no furniture, no carpet. Most of the wall panels had been torn apart for firewood and to get at the wiring and plumbing. Only two light fixtures remained. The kitchen was gutted of its cabinets, sink, and counters, and in this bizarre scene stood a short-haired Asian woman with a cigarette. The home was only here to cover the stairwell and the ventilation holes in the floor.

Cam hesitated at the top of the dark stairs. "I need to talk to Shaug," he said. It was all he could think of.

"We'll walk you over in the morning, sir," the squad leader said.

Ruth glanced into Cam's eyes, ready to play along, but the noise from below did not sound like a prison and the woman with the cigarette was disinterested and relaxed. Cam heard laughter as a man shouted, "Five bucks! That's five bucks!"

They went down nearly twenty feet. The walls were unfinished concrete lined with a single black wire. Two lamps had been bolted to the ceiling. Eight doorways filled a short hall, hung with blankets, and Cam worried at the damp cold.

"This is you, sir," the squad leader said, pointing at the first door. "We'll be right across, okay?"

"Yeah. Okay." Cam led Ruth into their room. It was cramped but private, and equipped with an electric coil space heater. He turned it on. There was also one narrow Army cot and four blankets, although he was too keyed up to sleep.

Ruth gently touched her fingers against his chest and kissed him. "Thank you," she said. "Thank you, Cam."

He only nodded. There was no anxiety in the moment. That made him feel pleased. She trusted him and he was very glad for his sense of kinship and safety.

Ruth lay down on the cot and Cam sat awake on the floor, his mind churning. Deborah had vouched for Shaug. *I think he's a good man who's done his best with very little,* she said, and she knew more than he did. She had been here for two days before they arrived, and her medical training had been a ticket straight into the middle echelons of the leadership.

After the bombing, Deborah's unit had surrendered to the large contingent of rebels aligned under Grand Lake, the nearest surviving American stronghold. Loveland Pass had burned, too close to ground zero, and White River might as well have been on the moon because of the huge plague zones in between—but Deborah said there had been similar movements up and down the Continental Divide as the American forces rejoined. Grand Lake's fighting strength was actually larger than it had been before the bombing, although most of the new troops were infantry or light armored units. The surprise attack had done that much good, at least, pushing most of the shattered United States back together once more.

Now the vaccine would turn everything upside down again, as would the data index. Ruth believed that researchers everywhere must be on the verge of weaponized nanotech like the snowflake. Could her presence here become the boost that Grand Lake's small lab needed?

When she kissed him, Cam had seen the haunted, rising dread in her eyes. He finally recognized the distance he'd heard in her voice outside the medical tent. It was the fear of so much responsibility. Given a moment to reassess, given a full lab and equipment, he wondered how Ruth would change the war.

20

There was a second nano in Cam's blood sample, a new machine shaped like a twisted X. Ruth had never seen it before, although she immediately thought of the dead mountaintop etched with thousands of crosses. The emotions in her now were the same—lonely confusion and despair. She leaned back from her tunneling scope and clenched her left fist in her brace, unable to get past the truth. It should be impossible, and yet the strange nanotech existed in his blood alongside the vaccine. His, but not hers. The nanotech was benign for the moment. Ruth expected it was waiting for some trigger.

Where had it come from?

"Let me out," she said suddenly, turning to the microphone on her left. The clean booth was equipped with two open mikes, one to record her observations, the other to keep in contact with the outside because this booth was too small to enter or exit without help. For a laboratory, Grand Lake had built a reinforced steel box too small to hold all the equipment they'd gathered. A rack of electronics partially blocked the door and the bulk of an electron microscope crowded Ruth on her right, but the lab was sterile and well-lit and could draw more power than she needed, even to purge the box.

They knew the danger in some of what she was doing. The workbench was rigged with X-ray and ultraviolet projectors, which should at least slow an uncontrolled nanobot if not destroy it outright, and the air-conditioning could briefly jump to eighty-mile-per-hour winds if necessary, vacuuming up any stray particles. It didn't bear thinking about. The radiation would be bad enough for anyone inside the lab. Ruth expected the vacuum would also lift the scopes and machining tools in an upside down rain of metal, hard plastic, and lashing power cords—and of course if that didn't eradicate any threat, they could just weld the box shut forever. It was like working inside a coffin.

"Let me out," she said.

"What's up?" McCown asked.

Ruth touched her white gloves to her mask. "I forgot my notes, I'm an idiot," she said, fighting to hold down the cold, bright edge of her claustrophobia.

Most days, that particular fear was only a scratching at the back of her mind. She had been enthralled to return to her work. It was unspeakably good to be in control again and Ruth had always excelled at ignoring everything beyond her microscopes, at least while she was making progress. Sometimes she lacked momentum. More than once her nerves leapt with a memory of planes or gunfire. Another time, she saw ants that didn't exist from the corner of her eye.

Ruth thought she had been very brave to step into this cramped box day after day, but now it was all that she could do to keep her heartbeat from affecting her voice.

"Please," she said. "I know it's a hassle."

"Why don't we have somebody get your notes for you," McCown said. "We can read anything you want."

"No." The word came out too fast. "No," she said carefully. "I should have worked through a couple ideas before I even bothered today. I was too tired after dinner."

"Um. All right." McCown sounded like he was frowning. "Give us a second."

Ruth sagged against the workbench but caught an atmosphere hood with her elbow, a small glass sheath meant to snap onto the tunneling scope. The hood clanged and Ruth jerked and hit her head on a shelf. "Oh!"

McCown came back on the intercom. "Ruth?"

"Oh, shit," she said, with just the right tone of casual disgust. "This place is like a shoebox." *Get me out,* she thought. *Get me out. Get me out.*

"Five minutes, okay?" McCown said.

"Yes." Ruth looked up at the harsh lights in the ceiling and then back and forth at the cluttered walls. Trapped. Then she leaned over the slim, elegant shape of the microscope again. It was her only escape.

McCown would probably be ten minutes, in fact. First he had to call for power to ramp up the air filters in the prep room outside the lab. Then he'd run his clothes and especially his hair and hands against a vacuum hose before he stepped inside, locked the door, and repeated the process with another vacuum. Next he'd take his clothes bag down from the hooks on the wall and don his hairnet, mask, gloves, and baggy clean suit. It was only after this meticulous checklist that he would unlock Ruth's door and help her stow her own suit.

She didn't want him to see her panic. She needed to bury the feeling deep, but her best-learned coping mechanism left her in direct confrontation with the source of her fear.

Who made you? Ruth wondered, peering into the scope. The new nanotech was a ghost. It shouldn't exist at all. *Who could have made you, and where was Cam exposed?* His blood sample contained only two of the new machines that Ruth had isolated so far, among thousands of the vaccine nano, but the ghost was very distinct. The ghost resembled a bent snippet of a helix, whereas the vaccine was a roughly stem-shaped lattice.

The ghost was beautiful in its way and Ruth briefly forgot herself, caught in the mystery. She couldn't help but admire the work it represented. Her quick estimate was that the ghost was built of less than one billion atomic mass units, which was damned small. The vaccine was barely under one billion AMU itself and as uncomplicated as they'd been able to make it. Could the ghost be a failed effort? Maybe the pair she'd found were only fragments of something larger . . . No. The two samples were identical. Even more interesting, the ghost had the same heat engine as the vaccine and the plague, which meant it had been built after the plague year by someone who was both capable of identifying the design work and reproducing it. The heat engine was a top-notch piece of engineering. Like Ruth and her colleagues, the ghost's creator had seen no reason to reinvent the wheel. He'd put his energy elsewhere. This was obviously a functioning nano and it was biotech just like the vaccine, designed to operate inside warm-blooded creatures.

But what does it do? Ruth worried. The fear in her head felt like clots and lumps now, straining her ability to think.

What if the individual ghosts were meant to combine into a larger construct? Its helix shape could lend itself to a process like that. The trigger might be nothing more complicated than a heavy dose. Saturation. Cam appeared to have a low and ineffectual amount in his blood, but what if he absorbed more? Would it activate?

Whatever the ghost is for, it's able to function above the barrier, she thought. *So there's no way to stop it.* Then the latch in the door rattled and Ruth jumped and turned to shove herself against the heavy steel panel, nearly slamming it into McCown's surprised face.

"Don't touch a fucking thing," she said.

Ruth walked through the cold white sun in her Army jacket and thin pants, needing air, needing him. For the past three days she'd imprisoned herself for hours at a time. She'd barely seen Cam at all, which she regretted. They'd been so close to a relationship, but her schedule was practically nonstop—work, work, collapse, more work. Cam had moved out after the second morning, joining an effort to trap and inoculate rodents and birds in an attempt to reestablish some kind of ecology below the barrier.

The vaccine was widespread in Grand Lake. Cam had won that battle quickly, even though he'd appeared to be nothing except helpful and obedient. All of his coughing in the med tent. He'd outsmarted Shaug as easily as that, which was sort of funny. He always found a way, and she missed him now that their paths had separated.

Other people were moving apart, too. The exodus had been limited so far, but McCown said there were deserters in the military and Ruth could see for herself that the refugee camps were quieter than usual. Normally the two peaks across from her were busy with farming efforts. Today one of the terraced gardens was empty, and the work crews on another were definitely understrength. Ruth understood. The temptation was too great. She was surprised that so many stayed. The new supplies were a help. Scavenging efforts had increased beneath the barrier, from organized convoys and helicopter runs to small handfuls of people who carried up as much as possible. Grand Lake had retained most of its population, at least for the short term. The habit was long ingrained. No one who'd survived would ever trust the world below ten thousand feet again, and the vaccine did not offer complete immunity.

At meals, she heard talk of relocating everyone to Boulder. Denver was much bigger, but it had taken fallout. There were also rumors that the Air Force would take a more aggressive stance and move a number of their people down into Grand Junction, a hundred and fifty miles to the west. Maybe it was even happening. Fighters and larger planes constantly roared away from the mountain and came back and left again and she couldn't say if the amounts were the same. Some of them never returned because they were shot down, but maybe others were finding new stations.

Snap decisions were a way of life up here and Ruth supposed she shouldn't have been surprised to find herself propositioned by one of McCown's assistants and then by the man who had the room next to hers in her shelter. They all felt like they had nothing to lose, and she was new and seemed unattached.

She stopped at the nearest mess hall. Snares and wire cages had been laid along the base of the long tent. A rat thrashed at the end of one line and Ruth stared at it with a weird mix of disgust and something else—her loneliness.

You got one, Cam, she thought.

There had never been much living up here, chipmunks, marmots, elk, and grouse and several other species of birds. Nearly all were extinct. The human population had tracked and killed every species beyond the point of sustainability. There might be a few grouse and chipmunks left in the region, but nobody had seen one for months. Occasionally birds still flitted overhead. And there were vermin. Rats were not indigenous to this elevation, but there must have been a few among the endless crates of FEMA and military supplies that were airlifted into the area during the first days of the plague.

The rats had flourished in the crowded conditions and in the grime. Ruth supposed they should be glad. Had anyone, anywhere, managed to save other kinds of mammals? She wondered again at the bizarre world the next generation would inherit, assuming they didn't finish what the plague had started with a new contagion. Rats, birds, bugs, and reptiles made for a bleak and virulent environment, and yet it would be more stable than one without any warm-blooded creatures at all. Conservation efforts would become a way of life for centuries. Any dogs or horses or sheep that had survived would be priceless beyond measure. They must be out there in small numbers, hidden or lost on mountaintops around the world, which made it all the more important to preserve every single one.

The rat squirmed and clawed at the wire, snapping at its own leg. Ruth looked away from the ugly thing and saw two soldiers approaching. The man in front had unslung his rifle, although he held the barrel toward the ground.

"This is a restricted area, Private," he said. "You know that. Lunch isn't for two hours."

"Yes." Ruth wore no insignia, so they thought she was a recruit looking for a way to steal or barter for extra food. She was probably lucky she was a woman, or they might have been rougher. McCown had given her a badge that showed her actual status, but Ruth saw no reason to take it from her pocket, which would create a record of where she'd gone.

She tried to smile and turned to leave. Then the soldier noticed the rat and glanced after her, his eyes hardening. *He thinks I was planning to take it!* she realized. That had been another benefit of the vermin. The rats had damaged crops and food stocks, but the rats had become food, too.

"I'm looking for Barrett's group," she said quickly. "Do you know if they've been through here today?"

The soldier relaxed slightly. Barrett was one of the leaders of the repopulation project, a civilian leader, although there were also troops assigned to the effort. "You're late," the soldier said, gesturing downhill to the west. "I saw some guys with cages at least an hour ago."

"Thank you." Ruth walked away. They were releasing the first rats into the old township in the hope that the little monsters would breed and continue down the face of the Continental Divide, clearing the area of insect swarms. It was a crazy idea. It was necessary. Rats were adaptable and cunning, which made them perfect to go up against the insects. Birds would be great, too, if Cam and his friends could ever catch and infect enough mating pairs.

Ruth already knew she could make some improvements to the vaccine. She'd begun to work through new sensor models that would bump up its target-to-kill rate, but at Shaug's insistence she'd set aside her theories to build and culture the snowflake instead. There was no room for moral qualms. The world wouldn't wait. The United States needed new weapons, because spy planes and satellites showed that the Russians already had close to fifty thousand troops on the ground, along with nearly half that many support personnel and refugees. The distinction was tough to make. During their endless struggle in the Middle East, the Russian population became a war machine, with everyone in combat or preparing for it.

U.S. and Canadian interceptors had begun to have more luck with hitting Russian transports before they reached the coast, but the invaders were flying in from all directions now, down from the Arctic and the Bering Sea, up from the South Pacific— and they could land anywhere, not just in the mountains. Their planes hid and rose and hid again, deceiving North American radar and pursuit.

Two spearheads of Russian infantry had spread into Nevada while California burned. Uncontrolled blazes exploded through the diseased forests, both hindering the invasion and providing them with some cover. Ruth had seen the photos herself. Twice she'd sat down with generals and civilian agents to discuss the vaccine's parameters and what kind of casualties the enemy could expect.

Ruth estimated the Russians' short-term losses at 5 percent. Over a period of years, if the technology didn't improve, there was no question that the internal war between the vaccine and the plague would lead to significant traumas and deaths, but in the meantime the invaders would merely be uncomfortable. Except for anyone who stayed in a hot spot, mostly they'd suffer only minor hemorrhaging and blister rash. Sometimes an unlucky individual might experience a bleeding eye or a stroke, perhaps a cardiac arrest, which could be costly if it was a pilot or a driver who was suddenly incapacitated.

The Russians were willing to pay that price. Their advance

was staggered at times, but they'd claimed hundreds of miles, absorbing dead cities and airports, quickly motorizing their troops with abandoned vehicles and American armor—and they must have used the promise of the nanotech to win reinforcements.

The U.S.-Canadian net had detected huge flights of Chinese aircraft rushing across the Pacific to strengthen the Russian foothold. Large naval fleets came behind. The enemy already held Hawaii. They'd attacked the tiny American outpost on Mt. Mauna Loa during the blackout after the electromagnetic pulse, risking an alert to the mainland. The islands were an ideal stepping-stone. The Chinese probably hadn't thought twice about it. With the vaccine, they could win their fight in the Himalayas even as they helped the Russians take control of industry-rich North America, its superior croplands, its military bases. The new allies could divide everything however they liked, unless Ruth stopped them. The snowflake might be the only way for the U.S.-Canadian forces to regain the West, short of poisoning it with their own nuclear strikes.

She'd done it. She knew exactly how the snowflake killed, but she'd rebuilt it with the same blind will of the rat in the snare. It hadn't even felt like her decision. Millions of people needed the weapon's power to survive. Millions more would die. The holocaust would always be her responsibility, but so were the lives she'd save. Her guilt colored everything she did. It affected her sleep. It kept her from approaching Cam even when she needed him more than ever.

The snowflake was more of a chemical reaction than a true machine. It was originally one of several ANN developed by the scientists in Leadville, an anti-nano nano meant to destroy the plague. Composed of oxygen-heavy carbon molecules, the snowflake was intended to disable its rival nanotech by drawing the plague into nonfunctional clusters. Each bunch would recombine around the original seed and shed more artificially weighted grains, which would attract more plague, and so on. The process was termed "snowflaking" by its creator, LaSalle, but he had never been able to limit or regulate the effect.

The snowflake tore apart all organic structures. A single wisp of it would liquefy all living things within hundreds of yards, people, insects, plants, even microbes and bacteria. Fortunately the chain reaction broke down in an instant. The snowflakes tended to glom onto each other as well as foreign mass and became encased in free carbon of their own making.

Cultivating it was extremely delicate work, for which Ruth donned one of Grand Lake's few containment suits. One mistake could kill her. But the snowflake did not attack rubber or glass.

She was forced to start from scratch. The data index included notes and information stolen from Leadville, but LaSalle's files had been unavailable. It didn't matter. Her memory was nearly photographic and she'd helped LaSalle with early models of his baby. In fact, after the president's council realized the true might of the snowflake, Senator Kendricks had tried to recruit Ruth into LaSalle's weapons group with the threat of losing a new arms race to the Chinese. At the same time, James Hollister had insisted that the Asians were years behind U.S. research.

Ruth didn't know who to believe anymore. By itself, the new technology she'd called the ghost was proof enough that other scientists were still at work. The nanotech war had begun, almost unnoticed within the larger conflict. She was afraid they'd already lost. The hundreds of sick people in the medical tents . . . The thousands of others who'd died undiagnosed in the long winter . . . How many of those casualties could be attributed to some as-yet-unknown effects of the ghost?

In three days she'd spent less than three hours trying to improve the vaccine. The rest had gone into preparing a genocide. It was a real chore to assemble the snowflake by hand with inadequate gear and her first four efforts failed, too imbalanced to retain their purpose. Finally she had a single working snowflake and locked it in a glass cap, carefully exposing it to a handful of weeds inside a larger glass. Breeding more was that easy. The weeds disintegrated and suddenly Ruth had trillions of the killing machines, although many of these new snowflakes were dead or half-strength. Ruth had to discard two hundred before she quit trying to sort through the mess, but during that time she found seven more snowflakes that were whole. Each of them went into a cap. Then she exposed those seven, too, after which she divided each of her eight teeming glasses into hundreds of smaller vials. Cluster bombs. Fifty vials to a case.

The snowflake would also be effective in stopping the massive fires across the West, she'd realized. If they dispersed the nanotech along the front lines of a blaze, it would smother the inferno by reducing its fuel to dust. Maybe there were other peaceful uses.

If nothing else, she needed the snowflake for testing. Eventually she hoped to design some way to protect people against it, like a weapon-specific ANN, but the damned thing was just too basic. There was no proof that Ruth could imagine. Not yet. In time she might design a supernano that was capable of holding a person together against anything, even a bullet. It would be a form of immortality, an augmented immune system capable of sustaining good health.

Most important to Ruth, it would be the incredible technology to save Cam, using the blueprint of his DNA to restore his body and completely heal his wounds.

She found him where the soldier had said, hiking up from the broad valley where the town once stood. Footpaths and crude jeep trails lined the slopes by the hundreds. Mud slides slumped across the barren earth. Here and there, stripped vehicles marred the land, cars and trucks that had bogged down or run out of gas during the first sprint for elevation. They were empty shells. Everything had been ripped away from them, seats, tires, hoods, doors, bumpers. The need for building material had been that severe. Far away, all that remained of the town were the right corners and straight lines of its foundations and streets, a small maze of squares set against the uneven shore of the lake. Several concrete structures remained, as did the fenced-off tarmacs of its three gas stations, but anything that was wood or brick or metal was gone.

Ruth felt nearly as forlorn. She worried at the choices she'd made. She could have had Cam, even for a moment, but she'd run to her work instead. It was the same choice she'd always made, even when one sweet hour together would have left her rested and better focused.

She didn't want to die alone.

The sun had fallen away from noon in a hazy sky laced with contrails. Helicopters chattered somewhere in the north and Ruth wondered what they would do if the war suddenly fell on top of them. *Run down,* she thought. *Run to him and keep running.*

There were more than a dozen people with Cam, but Ruth recognized the way he carried himself even though his body was top-heavy with equipment. He'd slung a rack of wire cages over his shoulder. He wore a pack, too, and there were thick leather gloves tucked into his belt. Her chest lightened at the sight of him so clearly in his element . . .

Cam was laughing with a young woman. Ruth frowned. She had waited nearly an hour, holding her stone in her left hand, pressing its gritty surface into the soft, tender skin of her palm. She could have trudged down after him instead of staying with her thoughts, but she was sure he would have made the same decision. Be patient. Don't risk infection.

Ruth tucked her rock into her pants pocket and walked to meet him, ruffling her fingers through her bangs when the breeze tugged at her jacket and her curly hair. She needed a barber. When her hair got too long, it fluffed and made her look like Jimi Hendrix, which wasn't particularly flattering. Still, the primping was unlike her and she knew it.

"Cam," she called. He didn't react. The wind was against her and he walked in the middle of the ragged group—ragged but in good health. Their voices were loud with the satisfaction of a job well-done, and yet Cam only directed his words at one of them. Allison Barrett.

"Next time just drop the cage," he told her.

"That little fucker wouldn't have made it anywhere near me and you know it," Allison said, and Cam laughed again.

The girl was in her early twenties, Ruth thought, with a wide mouth and great teeth that she liked to show in a confident animal smile. Bad skin. Most of it was sunburn but there were threads of plague scarring, too, especially on her left cheek. Her blond hair had been bleached almost white by the sun.

Ruth only knew her because Allison was one of the mayors elected in the refugee camps. After Ruth's second meeting with Governor Shaug, Allison and three others had waylaid her escort in strident voices, demanding information. Shaug hadn't dismissed them either, taking the time to introduce Ruth and to settle their questions. The refugees had clout if only because there were so many of them, and yet Ruth suspected the "mayors" had been a large part of Grand Lake's ability to endure. For example, the trap-and-release project was absolutely genius. It showed the capacity to look ahead instead of allowing their many immediate problems to blind them to everything else.

Allison was clever and tough, exactly like Cam. *Like the*

rats, Ruth thought, but that was uncharitable. She made herself smile as the work crew approached, carrying Allison and Cam along in the middle. Their heads were still turned toward each other. Allison noticed her first.

"Hi," Ruth said.

Cam hesitated. His body language toward Allison was calm and open, but his eyes grew troubled. It was a complex exchange and Ruth missed none of it.

He said, "Ruth, what are you doing here?"

"I need a minute."

"Okay." He set down his cages and his gloves. That he didn't question her at all made Ruth feel good. They could still rely on each other, no matter what else.

Ruth caught his arm and drew him aside, glancing at Allison to make certain the girl didn't follow. Stupid. If she and Cam had touched each other—if they were having sex—Ruth would need to test Allison for the ghost, too, but her instinct was to protect Cam and that meant keeping the contagion a secret as long as possible.

She let go of his sleeve. Being close to him evoked more feelings than she was ready for and she was glad to move into the wind.

I'm jealous, she realized, too late.

Ruth had been using samples of his blood and her own because they were the original carriers of the vaccine. It was widespread now, but that was just good science, and a good excuse to see him.

"There's a problem with your work," Cam said, watching her. His intuition was straight on the mark and Ruth was suddenly afraid of what else he might see in her.

"Where have you been?" she asked, harried and intense.

"We took some rats into town," he said. "There's still a chance—"

"Where have you *been*, Cam?" Ruth clutched his wrist to make sure she had his attention, searching his brown eyes. He stared back at her, a little frightened now. Ruth said, "In the lab in Sacramento, did you go anywhere? Did you open anything?"

"What are you talking about?"

"There's something else inside you, a new kind of nanotech. Maybe a weapon. There's something else besides the vaccine and I don't know what it is."

"I—Oh my God." Cam stepped back from her, staggering. Ruth quickly moved after him, but he brought his forearms up between them, looking at his hands as if he thought he could possibly see the subatomic machines.

"You know I'll do everything I can," Ruth said, sharing his fear. It was strange. She felt a very welcome intimacy in the moment. On some basic level, she had learned to associate Cam with tension and pain, and now they were bound together by those feelings again.

Hurting for him, she watched his face. She also was aware of his friends shifting behind her, and she was glad for their voices and the rustle of their boots. Standing apart from them only heightened her sense of rejoining Cam.

"What do you remember about Sacramento?" she asked.

"I don't think I went anyplace that the rest of us didn't go, too," he said. Then, more fiercely, "I didn't. I swear."

Ruth matched his quiet tone. "We'll figure it out," she said.

Allison intruded. Allison edged past Ruth, walking like a cat. The girl held her body low but kept her shoulders up, her hands ready to grab or punch. It was a posture that she must have learned in the camps, Ruth thought, light-footed and able.

"What's going on?" Allison said. Her voice was as full of challenge as the way she held herself and Ruth met it without thinking.

"I'll need blood samples from you, too," Ruth said, trying to scare the girl.

Allison only grinned at her. "Is that why you're here?" Allison asked. Then she took Cam's hand in her own and stood with the shoulder of her tattered blue sweater against his Army jacket.

"There's a new kind of nanotech," Cam said, explaining to Allison.

The two women never looked away from each other. Ruth tried not to let her defeat show in her face—or her respect. Allison was plucky and bold. In fact, the girl reminded Ruth of herself at her best, but she just wasn't that confident anymore. Allison was willing to rush an opportunity. Ruth was not. Otherwise she wouldn't have missed her chance before Cam and Allison met.

Watching him with the girl made it clear. Even with his rugged looks, there had been no shortage of attention for who he was and what he'd accomplished, and their acceptance of him was exactly what he'd missed.

And you deserve it, Ruth thought.

Still, she was crushed. Cam must have exhausted his patience with her during their long run, and yet this was the only time she'd known him to veer away from what he really wanted. In some way, Ruth supposed he was trying to punish her. She saw that now. His decision to pair up with Allison was self-destructive, complicating his relationship with the woman he really wanted. Ruth knew that he loved her. Finding someone else, simply taking the opportunity, was an attempt to reject Ruth before she had the chance to say no. But she loved him, too. Couldn't he see that?

She didn't doubt that Allison's attraction to him was genuine, but she was suspicious of the girl's reasons. Allison would always be looking to strengthen her faction here in Grand Lake, and Cam was both a celebrity and a veteran survivor. So the girl had tied herself to him.

"You better come with me," Ruth said, looking away from Allison to include the others in the group. "All of you. I need blood samples before you go anywhere else."

She turned her back on Cam in a daze. She knew what she had to do. A discovery as criticial as the ghost could not be left for later, so Ruth went forty-eight hours with only a few catnaps and two big meals, hiding herself in the lab.

Was the ghost a Chinese construct? She knew that in Leadville, intelligence reports had put China's research program at the top of the list after Leadville itself. The plague year had badly confused things, of course, and a nanotech lab could be small and easily hidden, but at the same time, the world had shrunk to a handful of island ranges. There were fewer places to watch. Their list of competitors was very short. China. Brazil. India. Canada. There was a displaced Japanese team on Mt. McKinley, Alaska, and a British group in the Alps. All except the Chinese had been considered friendly. Regardless, Ruth didn't think any of them except the Chinese were capable of building the ghost, so it must be a threat.

She had been wrong in her initial assessment. The ghost was 15 percent smaller than the vaccine, but more advanced. It was a high-level construct and in its complexity Ruth was able to discern the tiniest changes. Generations. A few blood samples from McCown and his assistants seemed to indicate that it had spread through the local population in waves. An early model was followed by another. Possibly more. Cam had probably gotten it from Allison, and Ruth continued to fear that the ghost was only waiting to reach some critical mass before decimating Grand Lake.

Was it everywhere across the Continental Divide? Shaug allowed her to send radio queries to the labs in Canada, and the answer was no. So where had the technology come from?

The ghost was in Ruth, too. It appeared in her blood on their fourth day, just a half step behind Cam's infection, which fit with her hypothesis. The count in Newcombe's sample was also low. They hadn't brought it to Grand Lake. Grand Lake had infected them.

After that, her tactics changed. Ruth insisted on blood samples and basic information from a thousand soldiers and refugees, beginning a crash program to backtrack the ghost's origins. For two more days she dedicated computer time to the task along with most of McCown's group and dozens of overworked medical staff. She was fighting her own people. Shaug and the military leaders pressed her for new and better weapons. Ruth refused. It was the wrong priority.

Deborah Reece became a crucial ally and volunteered to oversee the blood work. Ruth let herself be interrupted to monitor the snowflake production, but mostly she'd handed that effort off to McCown.

The land war was rapidly escalating to the brink. The Chinese naval fleet swarmed into San Diego and Los Angeles and dispersed tens of thousands of infantrymen, armored units, and aircraft, opening a new front against the United States. Meanwhile the Russians continued to push through Nevada—and the invaders were winning the battle for air supremacy. The Russian air force was full of relics and mismatched planes, and the Chinese had similar problems, but even at half strength they dominated the United States, especially as America continued to shuffle working aircraft into key positions.

Each side tried to protect their planes and fuel supplies even as they sent fighters slashing into each other's territory. Each side rushed to claim airports and old U.S. bases, destroying some, protecting others, a game of chess with negotiations flaring and failing. The U.S.-Canadian forces threatened full-scale nuclear strikes on mainland China and the Russian motherland if the invaders did not immediately pull back to the coast, while the Chinese swore they'd respond in kind, plastering the Continental Divide at the first sign of an American missile launch.

It should have been insignificant, but Ruth also had to confront Allison every morning as Cam and Allison helped to deliver the samples and geographical data from hundreds of refugees. Ruth couldn't help believing that Allison and Cam were a good match, both of them scarred but still young and strong, savvy and dedicated.

In fact, Ruth went to Allison first after she'd made her decision.

She caught her just after sunrise. Cam and Allison were inside a broad tent where they'd set up a dozen benches, a dry-erase board, and four desks to process the refugees who came in exchange for a granola bar or an extra piece of clothing. There was already a crowd forming outside.

Cam had his head together with an Army medic over a clipboard. Ruth walked past them. She felt ill with tension and lack of sleep and Allison grinned at her. It wasn't a mean gesture. The girl knew she'd won, and Ruth thought she was only trying to be friendly. Possibly there was just the smallest hint of amusement or pity in the way she treated Ruth for being older, too old for Cam.

"Hello," Allison said.

"We need to get out of here," Ruth said bluntly. She was angry that anyone could seem so content, and took satisfaction in wiping away Allison's big smile.

"Oh shit," the girl said. "Cam told us it was probably a weapon—"

"No. No, I still don't know." Ruth shook her head at herself. She had no right to blame Allison. But she had her suspicions about who had designed the ghost. She recognized the work. Every machinist had his or her own style, exactly like painters, writers, and musicians. The ghost wasn't Chinese. It was American. The new technology belonged to Gary LaSalle, and Ruth said, "I think it came from Leadville. I think Leadville cornered our friends before they made it into the Sierras and then they had the vaccine, too, which means they could have run spin-offs for at least a week and a half before the bombing."

"I'm sorry," Allison said. "Who had the vaccine?"

Ruth realized she wasn't making sense. Cam would have understood, but Allison hadn't been there. "I need your help," she said.

"You bet." Allison nodded, watching her face closely. The girl had finally noticed Ruth's exhaustion.

"There were two more people with us who made it out of Sacramento," Ruth said. "A soldier and another scientist like me. They had the vaccine. Leadville caught them. That was about two weeks ago, and Leadville must have started running trials and new versions based on that technology."

There were four different strains of the ghost. Ruth had solved that much of the riddle without coming any closer to knowing what the ghost was supposed to do. At the same time she'd also identified, very roughly, four infection points that had since blended as the remnants of Leadville's armies split and surrendered and migrated away from ground zero. The leadership there had been secretly testing new models of the ghost on their own people. They'd dosed forward units to see what would happen—and yet the ghost was not a perfect vaccine, even though it should have been easy for them to improve the crude, hurried work that Ruth had done in Sacramento.

The teams in Leadville never would have left the vaccine exactly as it was, not bothering to improve it. Ruth knew that much. A better vaccine must exist. Leadville's machining gear far exceeded anything that Grand Lake had been able to steal or buy. Leadville also had the expertise of fifty of the best minds in nanotech. A vaccine that offered full immunity against the plague would have been their first priority, but they must have kept it for themselves exactly as she'd feared. Then they'd begun to experiment with other nanotech.

What did the ghost do? Could she recover the improved vaccine somewhere? Ruth would never be able to match their work or recreate it on her own, not for years or decades, but there might be survivors from their inner circle or molecular debris that had been thrown clear of the blast and absorbed by the nearest refugees. She was certain she could find other traces of their handiwork, if only she looked.

"We have to get out of here," Ruth said, "and I need you to

help me convince Shaug to let me go. I need an escort. Cars. My equipment."

"That won't be easy. I can talk to the other mayors."

"Thank you."

Ruth needed to follow the muddled, invisible trail back into the south to see if she could recover LaSalle's best work before it was lost forever. There wasn't anyone else who could sort through and identify the nanotech.

"Do you think Cam . . . Will he come?" Ruth ducked her head from Allison's gaze and spoke to the floor. "He's finally safe here. And he has you and his other friends."

Allison waited until Ruth looked up again, then shook her head and smiled once more. This time the smile was sad, and Ruth understood that Allison carried her own resentment. In fact, Allison would have been glad to see her go.

"Try to stop him," Allison said.

21

"**Move away from the** jeep," Cam said, holding his carbine on the burned man. Beside him, Corporal Foshtomi aimed her submachine gun at the man's teenage sons. They stood in the middle of a small crowd. Cam and Foshtomi had their backs against their jeep, with Sergeant Wesner perched above them—but when Cam risked one glance, he saw that Wesner had turned away to cover the other side.

There were at least seventy refugees on the hill. Most of them gathered in a clump at the first of the three vehicles, where Ruth, Deborah, and Captain Park were drawing blood. Some people had already hurried away with a can of food or a clean sweater, their reward for cooperating. But there were others who'd drifted out of line. The burned man and his sons had reached into the back of the second jeep to grab whatever wasn't tied down until Wesner shouted at them.

"We need it more than you," the burned man said.

"Move." Cam pulled the charging bolt of his M4, a harsh metallic *clack*, but the burned man only stared at the supply cases as if convincing himself. "Move!" Cam yelled.

"Get back! Get back!" Wesner shouted, supporting him, and at the head of the column, six more Army Rangers took up the warning, suddenly pushing into the crowd.

The noise from the refugees was less powerful, although the Rangers were badly outnumbered. Cam saw Deborah grasp at a starving woman to keep her in their canvas folding chair. Captain Park was inoculating everyone with the vaccine after Deborah drew a blood sample, but the stick-figured woman thrashed away from Deborah, screaming. At the same time, Ruth lurched back from the crowd and drew her pistol.

Good girl, he thought. His divided attention nearly killed him. The burned man stepped in with a knife and Foshtomi shifted her weapon.

"No!" Cam said, jostling Foshtomi's arm. Foshtomi was small and tightly built. She probably weighed a hundred and five in her boots, but she was quick as hell. She bent away from Cam and swung her gun up again, jamming its snub nose into the man's ribs.

"Don't fuckin' move," she said.

Cam covered the two boys with his carbine. There was more shouting at the head of the column, but he kept his eyes locked on their faces. The burns were radiation. They'd been close enough to the flash that their skin had seared. Now they wore permanent shadows like cracked brown paint. Where was the boys' mother? Dead? Only hiding? This family had seen the world end twice but still had the determination to fight their way north, and Cam did not want to hurt them. He'd felt it before—this sensation of staring into a mirror. It was only a wild chain of luck and circumstance that had put him on the other side of the glass, well-fed, in uniform, and armed.

"Just go. Please." Cam almost reached into the jeep for a few cans of food, until Foshtomi added, "You're lucky I didn't blow your guts out through your spine."

Foshtomi continued to glare after they'd left. She was trembling, though, and Cam smiled to himself. Of all the good men and women who'd volunteered to leave Grand Lake, this brash little Ranger was his favorite. Like so many of the best survivors, Foshtomi possessed certain traits. As the only woman in her squad, she could be crude at times, even heartless, as if compensating for her small size, but Foshtomi was also smart, active, and tough. In fact, she often reminded Cam of Ruth, in the same ways Allison did, except that the only history he shared with Sarah Foshtomi was uncomplicated and new.

*   *   *

Being with Allison had changed him. His self-image was still shaky, but his confidence was growing again. He wasn't so bitter or afraid. Maybe he should have been. He'd taken the first hesitant steps toward building a normal life in Grand Lake, only to leave her. Allison had stayed behind and he didn't blame her. She had other responsibilities. He'd realized his place was here.

He made a point of finding Ruth that evening in camp. She looked up from her maps and Cam glanced left and right, feeling like he was on stage. The three jeeps sat in an open triangle with firing positions at each corner, in the middle of a long, slanting area of low brush and rock. The space inside was no more than ten yards across at its widest point. Twelve people made for a good crowd, even though most of them were either sitting at the guns or sacked out in their bedrolls. Cam saw Captain Park and another man watching him.

The Rangers were curious. They'd gambled their lives for Ruth and they weren't quite sure how Cam was attached to her— and he was obviously with her, no matter that he'd given his oath and wore their uniform. Cam was a Ranger in name only. He was still learning to disassemble and clean his weapon, the 5.56mm M4 carbine. He was slightly more familiar with the older M16, which had been carried by the troops out of Leadville, like Newcombe, but although the two models were very similar, Cam had never trained with one. The difference was unexpected. He knew the plague year had forced the military to draw on old stockpiles and equipment, yet it surprised Cam to learn that rebel soldiers were better armed than the troops had been in the capital, at least in this instance.

Most of the Rangers were friendly, like Foshtomi. They were willing to teach him, but they wanted to know how he fit into the puzzle. So did he.

The look in Ruth's eyes was wary, though she tried to hide it with a smile. "Hi," she said.

"How are you doing?" Cam paused at the edge of her notes. Then he crouched on the far side of the battered sheaf of paper.

Ruth began to tidy up and seemed glad for an excuse to avoid his gaze. She pointed at the map. "We haven't found anything new yet," she said.

That wasn't what he'd asked, but he nodded.

Ruth shook her head. "I didn't really expect to. We haven't covered enough ground."

"We will," Cam said.

The sunset had that lasting quality he'd only found at elevation. Her hair shone in the twilight, and when she looked up, her brown eyes were dark and beautiful and so very serious.

She deserved better. She should have been able to remain in Grand Lake, and Cam wondered at her insistence that no one else could screen the blood samples for nanotech. Ruth was still punishing herself. Why?

The drive had been tough-going. They had the ability to drop below the barrier but they wanted to meet people, and the vaccine had yet to spread south of Grand Lake except where they'd distributed it themselves. There were no refugees below ten thousand feet. Regardless, the roads were jammed with stalled traffic. Mostly they went cross-country. In three days they'd gone just twenty-four miles, most of that weaving like a snake. Once they'd had to winch the jeeps down a broken mountainside. Several times they had to reverse direction and find another way. They didn't have enough people to send anyone ahead as a scout, and even the best maps had become unreliable as mud slides or refugee encampments blocked the way.

They avoided the largest groups. Twice they'd fled below the barrier after being surprised by shantytowns. Ruth wanted as many blood samples as possible, but they were afraid they'd be overrun. The squad carried four M60 machine guns in addition to their carbines and two snub Mac-10s that Foshtomi called "meat grinders," but twelve people could never be a match against a thousand. Their supplies made them a target. Fortunately they'd kept ahead of word of mouth. Their vehicles were a huge advantage, and almost everyone they met was learning about them for the first time.

Their group was small for several reasons. They needed to be able to scavenge enough food and fuel to keep going. It was also important to avoid the attention of Russian-Chinese planes and satellites. A large convoy would have been more visible, and the sky was a greater threat than any starving survivors.

Much like the expedition into Sacramento, this squad was all chiefs and no Indians. Foshtomi and Ballard were the only corporals. The others were sergeants of various sub-ranks, and John Park and Deborah were both captains, although it had been made clear that Park was in command.

Deborah was an outsider like Ruth and Cam. She was never far from her friend. The tall blond had been charting her own notes, but now she got up and walked four paces and sat down again, joining Ruth. "Can I talk to you about the second group today?" she asked, interrupting whatever else Cam might have said.

On purpose, he thought. Deborah had been quietly writing by herself for twenty minutes. She'd only stepped in after he came over. Had he missed a signal? Ruth might have looked past his shoulder and caught Deborah's eyes . . . No. Ruth answered Deborah with a nod, but she turned to Cam and gave him an apologetic look. She wanted the chance to talk, even if he made her nervous, and Cam frowned to himself as he watched the two women. His rivalry with Deborah was just getting worse.

"Four of those refugees also said they'd come from the east," Deborah said, touching her notepad. "Do you want me to put their samples with the first group?"

"Absolutely not," Ruth said. "Let's make a subset, though. Cross-reference them."

"Okay. And everyone out of the south has priority."

"Yes."

Deborah's job had become more difficult when they packed up and ran this afternoon. Keeping the samples organized was vital to their mission, but that wasn't why she'd intervened.

The two of them were like moths competing for a light. Cam had seen the same polarizing effect between himself and Mark Newcombe. Deborah was here to protect Ruth. Her motivation was much like his own. Being with Ruth was a chance to share her incredible sense of purpose.

"I should get ready for my shift," he said. It was partly true. He stood up and Ruth rose with him.

"Are you—" she began, but Cam stopped her.

"It's okay. You have a lot of work to do."

Her face was uncertain, but she nodded. She hadn't even unpacked her microscope yet. The night before she'd taken hours to screen less than twenty samples, huddled beneath a silver foil survival blanket to hide her flashlight, and today they'd accumulated thirty-one vacuum caps of blood. Tomorrow there

would be more. The job was already too big for her, even with
Deborah and Captain Park as assistants. Ruth was too thorough.
Cam would have taken half as many samples and doubled their
travel time, but she was terrified of missing any clue.

It would be perverse, but Cam also wondered if she was upset because she wasn't responsible for the advances that had
brought the nanotech this far. Life wasn't like TV, where every
success belonged only to the hero. Sometimes you could only
react to other people's accomplishments. They'd seen enough
twists and surprises to know that was true. Cam thought Ruth
had learned not to let her own ego work against her, and yet the
fact remained that she was playing catch-up to other people's
work, when for most of her career she had been the hotshot.
That must be tough, so he only smiled at her.

"Sit with me for breakfast," she said.

"If I can." Cam was important to the job, too, standing guard
in three-hour watches just like the other Rangers, supporting
the team and contributing to their ever-changing plans. Given a
moment of privacy, Cam would have said more. *You know why
I'm here,* he thought, but Deborah stirred beside Ruth with her
chin tilted up in that aggressive way, so Cam only smiled again
and turned to go.

Deborah disapproved of him. Their backgrounds could not
have been more different. The basic EMT classes he'd taken before the plague were a joke compared to her years of education,
and he was definitely not a book that was judged well by its cover.
A haircut and a clean uniform had only made his scarring more
prominent, whereas Deborah's skin was clear and unblemished—
and Ruth's temples and left cheek remained lightly marked from
their long run in goggles and masks.

Whether she realized it not, Cam thought that on some level
Deborah was pulling at Ruth to keep her from becoming any
more like him. Deborah was a good friend to Ruth. Cam liked
her for it even if they didn't get along. The bottom line was that
Deborah Reece could be arrogant, even rude, but she had been
safe in Grand Lake and she'd walked away from it for the
greater good.

Cam still wondered how close Ruth had come to being told
she couldn't leave. Governor Shaug hadn't wanted to see Debo-

rah go, either, or the elite troops or the atomic force microscope that Ruth demanded.

In the end, Ruth convinced him there was far more worth to be had if she succeeded. She had also lost her value as a bargaining chip. Shaug could no longer fly her to the labs in Canada in exchange for food or weaponry, because Grand Lake's allies had issued a quarantine. The ghost nanotech seemed limited to Colorado. They didn't want to be infected themselves. They continued to coordinate their militaries with Grand Lake, but planes out of Colorado were no longer permitted to divert anywhere else even if they were hit or low on fuel. Colorado ground troops in need of help would not see reinforcements except from other Colorado units.

Governor Shaug must have been desperate to change that edict, and Ruth could be forceful when the mood struck her. In Sacramento, Cam had seen her yell at seven armed men when she disagreed with them, so it intrigued him that she was tentative with him.

There was no reason to ask him to join her except that she trusted him. Loved him. The Rangers were a top-notch escort, whereas he was a complication.

Newcombe had opted out. Cam was disappointed, but he couldn't resent the soldier for his choice. Newcombe had fit himself back into the larger whole of Grand Lake exactly as he'd always intended. Newcombe just didn't have the same ties to Ruth. During all their time together, she'd chosen Cam instead, and he hoped she would do it again if Deborah continued to force the issue.

She did. The next morning she brought Cam tea and oatmeal as he helped Wesner and Foshtomi load their gear into the jeeps. Later that day she even used Allison as an excuse to talk to him about their days in Grand Lake. She took another blood sample herself. She said she had to monitor how they were being exposed themselves, dealing with the refugees, but Foshtomi noticed that she let Deborah draw blood from the rest of the group.

Foshtomi was delighted by their slow-motion romance because she was just one of the guys in her squad, Cam thought. She kept tabs on Ruth because it allowed her to be a woman.

That Ruth was watching you again last night, Foshtomi would say, or, *Did you see how that Ruth waited to eat until you were done helping Mitchell with the fuel cans?*

It was true. "That Ruth" found time to be with him despite everything else, even if it was just for a few minutes—and she had to be the one who approached him, because Captain Park gave her all the latitude she wanted, whereas Cam was always busy as a member of the squad.

In many ways he enjoyed that pressure. The Rangers were a well-oiled machine. Their power appealed to Cam. They imposed order and direction on their world, which was a remarkable feat.

By their fifth day, the land above the barrier pinched into a thin neck of ground along the Continental Divide, forcing them to turn west below ten thousand feet. Highway 40 ran eastward through the sheer peaks, zigzagging up through to the other side of the Divide and the refugee populations that had formed above the small cities of Empire, Lawson, and Georgetown, but the highway was thick with old traffic and new rockslides. Fires had blackened the mountainsides even where there was nothing to burn except damp moss and weeds. Ash and dust lay across the earth in vast streamers. It whispered up beneath their tires and boots. Three of the Rangers now wore radiation badges clipped to their jackets and Captain Park also had a Geiger counter that chittered and clacked at times. They seemed to be edging through an area where the fallout had settled after the explosion. They were lucky the prevailing weather was out of the northwest, behind them. It had carried most of the poison east, but the radiation was another reason to go west from the Divide.

They spent two days in a long, green valley cut into the mountains by a good-sized creek that had briefly become a colossal flood. Nearer to ground zero, most of the snowpack had been vaporized, but at this distance the snow immediately slumped away as water and slush, increasing the landslides caused by the quake. Their jeeps rocked and crashed through banks of gravel, muck, and driftwood. They broke one of their four shovels digging a way through. They also encountered three groups of survivors. This valley faced north and had escaped the worst of the damage. Many of the aspen and spruce were still standing and the water ran clear—and there was nothing in this place to attract the air war, only wilderness.

Finally they made it up through the Ute Pass, where Highway 9 arrowed south toward Interstate 70. On this high point, the blast wave had lifted cars by the thousands, overturning the old metal shapes. The road was a mess of broken glass and odd drifts of rust and paint flakes, and Captain Park took them back north instead of following the highway toward Leadville. He refused to move deeper into the blast zone. Ruth's few protests were soft-spoken and confused.

Ruth was haggard beneath her sunburn. She worked nights with her AFM and tried to nap in the day when they were on the move, but it must have been like sleeping on the back of an elephant. The jeeps bumped and seesawed on the rocky earth, stopping and starting as the Rangers jumped down to push wrecks or boulders out of the way. She was exhausted. She carried that goddamn stone everywhere.

She thought she'd failed. Two of the refugee groups they'd met in the valley had been clean. They'd infected those people themselves. Yes, she'd given them the vaccine, but at the cost of tainting them with the ghost, too. *We couldn't have known,* Cam told her. Ruth only grimaced and shook her head. They seemed to have lost the trail.

They were running out of time. Open broadcasts out of Grand Lake constantly advised American forces of enemy action, and Chinese armored units had pushed into Colorado.

The Chinese had taken southern California and most of Arizona with relative ease. There was no one to oppose them except the tiny populations on the few peaks east of Los Angeles, who were quickly burned away. The Chinese armies numbered at least a hundred and fifty thousand soldiers, pilots, mechanics, and artillery men—and their naval fleets were rushing away for more.

Interstates 40 and 70 became the lifelines of the invasion. At low elevations, the freeways were mostly clear, except where American fighters had destroyed bridges and causeways. Planes from both sides clashed above the desert while, far below, Chinese combat engineers struggled to move their trucks and APCs across every break in the road.

The Chinese armies were also disrupted by hot spots. There had been huge drifts of the plague out of the L.A. basin and it scattered the Chinese reserves, overwhelming the vaccine. At the Arizona border, the Colorado River was also seething with nanotech. U.S. surveillance put the enemy's casualties in the thousands, and North American Command did their best to channel the invader into these death zones.

The Chinese couldn't slow down. They also had the bugs and the desert heat to contend with. Their best strategy was that of momentum and speed. They plundered every city and military base within reach and they were briefly rich for it, squandering fuel and ammunition.

Flagstaff only lasted five days. While Cam and Ruth were in their quiet valley just west of the Continental Divide, the Chinese effectively claimed Arizona and turned toward the Rockies in full strength.

The Grand Canyon served as a critical defensive line. This deep, ancient gash in the Earth stretched for hundreds of miles through Nevada, Arizona, and Utah, and not a single bridge or dam survived the American strikes. It split the Chinese in two. The enemy could provide air support for themselves across the entire Southwest, but their generals were faced with a decision as far back as Las Vegas, at the mouth of the Canyon, beyond which their armies were no longer able to reach each other.

The Russians helped them in Utah, pounding at the largest American outposts in the mountains east of Salt Lake, but the enemy bogged down there. Interstate 70 ran north from Vegas and stayed tight along another high range for nearly a hundred miles before it squeezed into a series of passes and bent east toward Colorado. The Chinese advance was hit every step of the way.

If they'd tried to charge through, they probably would have succeeded, with heavy losses, but the northern Chinese group didn't want Utah at their backs as they assaulted Colorado. They appeared to settle in for a long fight.

Their southern force had always been the larger one, however. It was also where they directed all reinforcements. The thrust by their northern army was only to hold Utah in check. Meanwhile, their southern force angled up into Colorado on as many smaller highways as they could access, swarming north and east as the roads curled away from the vast, sprawling bulk of the front side of the Rockies.

Bombers out of Canada, Montana, and Wyoming struck the Russians and the Chinese from behind. Attack choppers out of New Mexico harassed the Chinese in Arizona, but New Mexico was preoccupied as smaller Chinese landings on the coasts of Florida and Texas began to launch their own assaults, picking at the U.S. forces from behind.

Colorado armies still held Grand Junction, which straddled I-70 near the Utah border. The all-important airfields in Durango, Telluride, and Montrose had fallen. The Chinese were rapidly securing their grasp on the southern part of the state, and Cam was glad again for the insignificant size of his squad. Every day there were jets close overhead. More frequently, they heard distant planes or saw contrails or bright metal dots.

If they were noticed by an enemy fighter, they would be dead in seconds. There had been reports of the Chinese strafing refugee camps simply to create more chaos, expending ammunition on nonmilitary targets because the survivors fled for the protection of Army bases, where they made trouble for the soldiers and pilots. Unfortunately, most of the people in this part of Colorado still did not have the vaccine. Grand Lake had flown it to military personnel across the United States and Canada, thoroughly screening those vials of blood plasma for the ghost nanotech. Soldiers everywhere had spread the vaccine to nearby refugees if they could, but Cam's squad saw no one whatsoever for the next day and a half as they circled west and then south again below the barrier.

Interstate 70 rolled nearly dead-center across the middle of the state. Reaching it was their first goal. Captain Park planned to join the freeway in the town of Wolcott, jog west, then continue south again on dirt roads and trails as they worked their way back toward elevation. They knew there was a large conglomeration of American infantry and armored units in the area, coordinating with Grand Lake command. West of Leadville, the mountains surrounding the once-famous ski town of Aspen were poised to become a stronghold against the Chinese.

Ruth hoped to find her answers there. If not, the expedition was wasted. Everything boiled down to whether or not she'd guessed right—but if, for example, Leadville had only tested its nanotech on its troops along its northern border, they'd come all this way for nothing. There would be no perfect vaccine. They would have no explanation for the ghost nanotech and Ruth would be more alone than ever, as the last top scientist in the United States.

She snapped at them and then apologized. She obsessed with

her maps even when they hadn't taken any new samples since the Ute Pass. Cam tried to kiss her that night and Ruth grabbed a handful of his jacket and used her arm like a piston, shoving him back. But first she pulled him closer and opened her mouth. He was sure of that.

Ruth was a mess, strung out and unsure even of herself. Cam had never felt so clear. He knew he'd been right to come. The Rangers were committed but Ruth needed friends, not only protectors. He regretted adding to the demands on her. There was no time or privacy for them to pursue whatever was happening between them, and she wouldn't relax until they'd found the remnants of Leadville's military.

Unfortunately, Wolcott was a swamp. The town sat in a steep channel along the Eagle River. The quakes and floods had turned this gorge into a muddy lake. It was June 27th. Their only choice was to turn back and fight around the water to the east, where they stumbled into a hot spot as they winched their jeeps up an embankment. Ballard was distracted, infected in his ear and hands. He caught his sleeve in the winding cable and the winch snapped his elbow before Park shut it down.

Escaping the machine plague had to be their first priority. Ballard toughed it out, cursing himself, and eventually Deborah and Sergeant Estey reset his joint on a lush mountainside spotted with white and yellow flowers. Cam stared at the little blossoms. This place seemed completely untouched by the vast conflict of men and machines, and he imagined there were other safe pockets everywhere, even beyond enemy lines.

The thought shouldn't have made him sad. Angry and sad. *If we'd just shared the vaccine,* he thought. Had the entire war really hinged on that one decision? Where would the fighting stop? Even if Ruth was successful, even if she developed a perfect vaccine, that didn't seem like enough of an advantage to push back the Chinese. Cam saw no end to it.

They stayed in the meadow for lunch, bolting down a meal of tinned ham and fresh, bitter roots as distant percussions echoed from the mountains. Artillery fire. Cam looked out into the pale blue sky but saw nothing, no smoke, no movement. The war was still hidden down in the west, but it was hurrying closer even as they drove toward the U.S. lines.

Park expected it would be at least another day before they reached the northern edge of the Aspen group. They were only six miles from the nearest secured area, a base on Sylvan Mountain, but they weren't moving much faster than a person could walk. The terrain was too rough. Park stayed on the radio constantly, trading coordinates with flank units and requesting information on the Chinese. He could call in air support if needed, if there was time, but until they reached Aspen Valley, ultimately they had no one to rely on except themselves.

On the morning of the 28th that wasn't enough.

The hillside erupted in geysers of fire and dirt. Four or five towering blasts appeared out of nowhere, bracketing the jeeps, hot and bright. Then the explosions seemed to walk together like two drunken giants, stomping through the vehicles and then back again.

One of the jeeps flipped. Captain Park's? Ruth's? In the third jeep, separated from the others by curtains of debris, Cam lost track of the two vehicles ahead of him. He'd gone deaf in the ringing impacts, yet he was aware of rocks and earth clattering against the jeep. The hood twisted up and stopped again, a jagged metal sheet. In the driver's seat, Wesner twisted sideways as something whipped into his head. Cam was struck in the arm and chest, but the other man shielded him from the worst of it, even when the windshield cracked and imploded. Bits of fender and other shrapnel had rattled through the torn shape of the hood. Wesner took most of that, too.

He was still alive. He pawed feebly at the steering wheel as Cam grabbed the biggest wound on Wesner's neck, trying to stop the bleeding.

"Get out!" Foshtomi yelled, directly behind Cam in the backseat. She sounded like she was at the bottom of a well and it wasn't until she bumped past that Cam realized they'd quit moving. His inner ears were in shock. His balance was gone and he swayed as if the ground was an ocean wave when he left the jeep, dragging Wesner behind him.

Foshtomi helped as best she could for fifteen staggering yards, screaming with effort. Her cheek was cut and there was blood in her hair, too, but she kept her arm around Wesner's back.

Cam glimpsed other people to his left, partially eclipsed between smoke and daylight. Friends? Enemy troops? *Ruth,* he thought. Her name was like a small cool space inside his panic. He slowed down, intending to run in that direction.

Foshtomi tripped him. Foshtomi stamped her boot down on his ankle and the three of them fell behind a bump of granite as the giants pounded the vehicles again. The sound was enormous. Cam jammed his hands over his ears without thinking, uselessly trying to block the hypersonic blows.

The wetness on his palm reminded him of Wesner. He turned to apply pressure to the man's wounds again, but Craig Wesner was dead, slack-faced with dirt in his eyes.

Foshtomi shouted distantly. "Break!" she cried. "Okay?" She leaned close and Cam watched her mouth as she repeated it. "We run again in the next break!"

"No!" Even his own voice had the faraway quality, and Cam gasped at a stabbing pain in his left side. A broken rib, maybe. "We need to find Ruth!"

"We can't help her!"

Cam shook his head and twisted awkwardly to look up, keeping his body flat. He hadn't seen or heard any planes, but the sky was dark with windswept banners of pulverized dirt and smoke.

"The jeeps!" Foshtomi yelled. "They're shelling the jeeps, not us! We have to—"

But the giants danced away suddenly, spreading across the hillside. Half a dozen fireballs punched into the green earth in what appeared to be random lines, moving southward and down the mountain. Chasing someone? Cam knew from talking with the Rangers that modern warfare could take place over a range of tens of miles. Tanks and cannon were capable of remarkable precision at that distance. Their jeeps had been spotted by a forward observer or a plane or a satellite. Somewhere, Chinese artillerymen were lobbing shells at a target they couldn't even see, simply obeying a series of coordinates.

There was no way to fight back, other than to radio for help. Foshtomi was right that they needed to get out of the grid, but the Chinese seemed to be hitting the entire mountainside now, mopping up. If they ran, they could just as easily move into the next salvo as move to safety.

Cam wasn't leaving without Ruth. The thought steadied him and he risked another glance up the hill.

It was the lead jeep that had overturned. One wheel had

blown off and the axle was ripped away. There was only one body in the open, a man lying in a dark blotch of fluid. The second jeep, Ruth's jeep, had crashed into the destroyed vehicle but looked abandoned. She'd gotten clear.

She must have gotten clear, Cam thought. But the giants were coming back again, slower this time. The explosions picked their way along the slope, lifting brush and rock in powerful, bone-shuddering detonations. Cam pressed himself into the earth. Each breath was laced with smoke. Then the impacts were past and he was up and running.

He fell. His balance was still off and he discovered that he needed to stay bent over his left side. The ground was littered with dirt clods and rock, sometimes in large hunks. Then the ground itself jumped. Cam was barely halfway on his feet again. He managed not to collapse onto his bad side. He rolled into a crater and found Estey and Goodrich hunched against the fresh, crumbling earth.

Estey was trying to staunch a wound on Goodrich's forearm and didn't see him. Goodrich shouted but Cam only heard his warning tone, not the words. He'd gone less than thirty feet. It felt like another world, especially in the buzzing silence. The artillery had briefly concentrated here and the hill was a moon-scape.

Ruth should have been with them. She rode with Estey, Ballard, Mitchell, and Deborah in the second jeep, but they'd obviously scattered in all directions. Cam wondered what he was going to do if she was uphill of the vehicles.

He kept looking for her across the wasted ground. He fought off Estey's hand when Estey tried to drag him down. He'd spotted another human shape in the dark, drifting clouds, one running man followed by another. The giants were gone. The sun split through the dust and Cam scrambled out of the crater, only to throw himself down again and claw for his pistol. He'd lost his carbine with the jeep, but Estey still had his weapon and Cam glanced back and screamed, "Look out! Estey!"

There were at least ten human shapes dodging through the haze, far more than the missing part of his group. Their yelling was muffled and strange. They were also the wrong color. Cam's squad wore olive drab, whereas these people dressed in tan camouflage and seemed to be misshapen. Uneven brown rags hung from their heads and arms, and Cam did not recognize their long rifles or submachine guns.

He took aim but didn't fire as someone else stood up in another crater in front of him. Deborah. Her blond mane was filthy, but still unique. Cam lifted himself to run to her, sick with fear. He was certain that he would see her gunned down. Then she waved to the approaching troops, and Cam struggled to discern the men's voices.

"U.S. Marines! U.S. Marines!"

He lowered his pistol and ran to the crater.

Ruth embraced him and hurt his ribs and he laughed, breathing in the good, complex smell of unwashed girl. She was alive. She'd escaped with scrapes and bruises and one peppered rash of shrapnel on her hip, where she would need surgery not just to remove the flecks of metal but also the fabric from her shredded uniform, which had been imbedded into her wounds.

Others hadn't been so lucky. Park and Wesner were dead and Somerset was critically wounded in the belly and face. Hale, also from the lead jeep, had broken his collarbone and both legs when the vehicle went over. It was only a bizarre miracle that Goodrich was only cut on his arm.

Cam absorbed most of this information through the aching cotton that blocked his ears, but they were all yelling. Most of them had difficulty hearing and everyone was wild with adrenaline. They knew the artillery could start again any time.

"My rock," Ruth said. "I lost my rock!"

She must have known it was irrational—even crazy—but she pawed at her clothes anyway, staring helplessly across the torn hillside.

"Shh," Cam said. "Shh, Ruth."

Their first decision was to move everyone who could move except Mitchell and Foshtomi, who volunteered to stay with Somerset. "We're not leaving him," Foshtomi said, and the Marine captain nodded and gave them his radio.

The scout/snipers belonged to a long-range SR patrol sent to look for defensible ground above Interstate 70, although their mission changed when Park's squad drove into their sector. They'd moved to cover the Rangers if possible. Two of their

men had been hurt in the shelling, too, because they'd run into
the killing field instead of turning away. Cam marveled at their
courage and discipline.

Their strength was crucial to evacuating Ruth, her gear, and
the battered Rangers. Estey was nominally in command of the
squad now, despite Deborah's rank, yet it was Deborah who
walked back to the second jeep with Goodrich and Cam to be
sure the Marines recovered everything Ruth needed.

They might have driven away—they might have used the
jeep to carry Somerset—except the front axle was broken and
the radiator was torn. Some of the paperwork was confetti and
the sample case had four ragged holes blown through it that
were leaking blood, but Deborah insisted on wrapping everything up just the same. Then she sagged and let a Marine get his
arm around her. She was bleeding herself from a nasty lacera-
tion up her back.

Ruth wept openly. Before they walked away, Cam squeezed
Foshtomi's hand and the young woman nodded tersely. She had
already taken Park and Wesner's tags. She planned to bury her
friends in one of the craters, and Cam suspected that within a
day at most she would bury Somerset as well.

Three men carried Hale on a short, broad stretcher they'd
fashioned from a blanket and two rifles. Cam and Goodrich
lugged the AFM. Other men had dumped precious rations and
clothing from their packs to make room for the blood samples
and paperwork. Ruth limped by herself, her teeth gritting in her
pale face. They'd covered less than a quarter-mile when a pair
of F-22 Raptors soared out of the northeast, ripping down into
the valleys far below to hit the Chinese artillery.

His right ear improved. His left did not, and the uneven
sound of the people around him continued to affect his balance.
Another fighter rushed overhead and Cam was unable to place
it until he saw the others looking east. It scared him.

They managed to keep going for thirty minutes before Ruth
and one of the Marines needed to rest. Cam didn't think they'd
reach the secured area before dark, no matter that it was still mid-
morning. Too many of them were hurt. They were carrying too
much. But within a few hours, they were met by a pair of trucks.

Late that afternoon they rode in past line after line of earthworks and razor wire.

These mountainsides faced west and hadn't burned in the nuclear strike. In the following weeks, however, the land had been reduced to sterile mud slopes. Defensive barriers ringed the mountains as far as Cam could see, many of them studded with gun emplacements and vehicles and wreckage. Enemy planes and artillery had pounded the hill repeatedly. Nearly as much damage had been done by thousands of American feet and the weight of their trucks, tanks, and bulldozers.

The rutted earth stank of fire and rot, and the smell thickened as they drove into the series of berms. There were dirty people everywhere, some of them eating, some of them digging. They might have been living in any preindustrial age. It was the radar dishes and tanks that looked out of place.

At last the trucks drove into a prefab warehouse, hiding from the sky. Somehow Ruth had fallen asleep. Cam tried to protect her from the jostle of Rangers and Marines as everyone stood up. No good. Her eyes widened with fear. Then she saw him and smiled wanly. Cam set his hand on her knee. Meanwhile, a medical team quickly unloaded Kevin Hale, who was feverish with trauma.

"Clear a hole, clear a hole," a man said, pushing through the other medics and officers. Something in the man's lean build was familiar and Cam tipped his head to stare through the many soldiers, dazed with exhaustion.

It was Major Hernandez.

22

Ruth struggled up from the slat bench in back of the truck and forced herself to walk on her stiff, throbbing hip. "Watch out," she said. "Please."

Sergeant Estey had moved to the rear of the vehicle with the scout/sniper captain, speaking urgently to the uniforms gathered below. "I left three men in the field, sir," Estey said, repeating the most important part of his report, which he'd called in hours ago.

"We're still trying to get a chopper," one of the officers replied, extending his hand to help Estey down.

"Please!" Ruth craned her neck to see.

Then the scout/sniper captain stepped off the back of the truck. Estey and Goodrich followed. The warehouse echoed with voices and movement. Somewhere a door banged and a distant set of artillery fired several rounds, and Ruth heard none of it.

She knelt clumsily in the truck to bring herself level with Frank Hernandez. A spasm went through the gashed muscles in her hip, but it was the surge of emotions that nearly made her fall, remorse and joy and a powerful sense of déjà vu. She stammered, "Huh, how did you—"

"Hello, Doctor Goldman," he said in his smooth way.

Ruth had first met Hernandez from the back of an ambulance

in Leadville, faint from the pain of a newly broken arm and the body-wide shock of returning to Earth's gravity. For a brief time they had been allies. She respected him more than he might have believed, even after she betrayed him. He was a good man, but too loyal, supporting the Leadville government without question. They'd last seen each other in the lab in Sacramento, at gunpoint. Newcombe's squad had killed one of Hernandez's Marines before leaving him and three others immobilized deep within the invisible sea of nanotech, tied with duct tape, their radio cords severed, with less than two hours of air inside their containment suits.

Ruth and the other traitors had not intended for him to smother, and the death of his Marine was a mistake. They told Leadville forces where to find Hernandez, using him as a decoy as the fight began for possession of the vaccine . . . and Ruth had always hoped that he made it out, although later she assumed that if he was rescued, he must have perished in the U.S. capital when the bomb went off.

It was like finding Deborah. It was like finding family. This was the second time she'd rediscovered someone she thought was dead—until she realized that to some extent she'd been right. His appearance was very different. The man she'd known had been as neat as the U.S. Military Code, healthy and trim. He was skinny now, and the brown hue of his skin was tinged by an ugly gray pallor. The mustache he'd worn was a full beard and it concealed burns that reached up his left cheek like dribbles of pink wax, though he wore his field cap low as if to hide his scars.

Blinding tears filled Ruth's eyes and she didn't even try to hold her feelings back, allowing the droplets to fall into the narrow space between herself and Hernandez. "You." She hesitated, then lightly set her fingertips on his uniform. "I never thought I'd see you again."

He smiled. He could have responded in so many other ways, but perhaps he felt the same welcome sense of familiarity. He could have blamed her for everything and Ruth would not have disagreed. What if he'd taken the vaccine back to Leadville? What if the president's council had been able to deal with the Russians from a position of absolute strength, rather than scrambling to put down the rebellion in the United States at the same time they were negotiating overseas? And yet his smile was genuine. It touched his dark eyes and softened his posture, too.

It felt like forgiveness, so Ruth was surprised when Hernandez stepped back and let another soldier lift her down from the truck. Was she wrong? No. His gaze flicked away from her with something like embarrassment.

Hernandez wasn't strong enough to hold her weight. The burns. His bad color. He had radiation poisoning, but he swiftly covered the moment by looking past her at Cam and Deborah.

He didn't seem to recognize Deborah—they'd barely known each other—but Deborah moved protectively to Ruth's side while Cam crouched at the back of the truck with his left arm tucked against his ribs. One of the Marines helped Cam down and Hernandez said, "Hey, *hermano.*"

Brother. The two men had their Latino heritage in common, when so many of the other survivors were white, which had formed an additional bond between them.

"Mucho gusto en verte," Cam said.

Ruth didn't know what that meant. She was hardly listening anyway. She had touched Hernandez with such care, thinking her own tentativeness was for other reasons, although it was obvious once she realized how his clothes hung on him.

"I'm glad you're okay," she said.

He was dying.

"Yes. You, too." Hernandez surveyed her tears before he smiled again. "Let's get you patched up. You can rest. Then we need to talk."

"I want blood samples from everyone here," Ruth said.

"You can start that later, okay?"

"You do it," Deborah told him. "Sir. You do it while we're with the doctors. Otherwise there might not be time."

Hernandez said, "You're the astronaut. Reece."

"Yes, sir."

He rubbed at the gray hollows under his eyes and shook his head. "Grand Lake didn't say who was coming. A tech with an escort. If I'd known, I would have moved more people to try to run off the Chinese, but they've got us outnumbered almost everywhere." He said, "I'm sorry about your friends."

Ruth nodded. While they were safe, Somerset lay bleeding out on the mountainside, but Grand Lake had kept quiet about their mission because there was such a concentration of electronic surveillance focused on the Rockies. It would have taken just one slip. One clue. If the Russians or the Chinese learned she was on the move, the enemy might have redirected their entire force to kill or capture her.

"The people we left behind," she said. "Can you get them?"

"I sent another truck hours ago. We don't know if they'll be able to drive through a few places, but if the terrain's too hard they'll hike the rest of the way to your guys."

"Thank you."

"I'll get some teams on the blood samples. Can you tell me what we're looking for?"

"Nanotech. I—"

"I know that. Otherwise you wouldn't be here." Hernandez let them see some of the warrior inside the gentleman, challenging her with a stare. "But we already have the vaccine, and you weren't driving around out there because you didn't rate a helicopter—"

Ruth interrupted, too. "I don't need more than a drop from each man. Needle pricks are fine. Just make sure you isolate each one and make sure you tag them with the man's unit, where he is now, and where he was before the bombing."

"Before the bombing," Hernandez said.

"Yes." Ruth cleared her throat. She didn't want to hurt him any more, but he deserved the truth. "Leadville was testing new technology on its own people," she said.

They were led to a crowded tent and her sense of déjà vu continued. She almost laughed, but that would have been crazy. Too many times she'd found herself surrounded by medical staff, like a damaged race car that had to return to the track. She hoped she'd never need this sort of attention again, and yet more blood was all she saw in her future. Kill or be killed. What else would end the fighting? Surrender? She didn't know if the enemy would even allow that.

A man helped her undress and then gingerly scrubbed at the smoke-blackened earth and blood on her hip. Ruth wore only her T-shirt and socks and wasn't embarrassed except for the xylophone of ribs that showed when she lay down on her good side and her shirt rode up. Nearby, Deborah was topless, stripped to her undies as they assessed the wounds on her back—and even after so long on minimum rations, Deborah looked good. Really good. She was long and smooth-skinned with small, perfect breasts.

Ruth saw Cam glancing at Deborah's figure and suddenly he caught her looking, too. Ruth blushed. The medical staff didn't notice the exchange. They must have seen thousands of patients come and go. As a doctor herself, Deborah also seemed aloof. Ruth thought that was a shame, the human body reduced to a vehicle or a tool. She was glad to be a woman stealing glances with a man. She worried for him. Cam rubbed his left ear again and again, reaching across his scarred chest with his right hand. Estey had said he thought Cam's ribs were only bruised, but it obviously hurt Cam too much to lift his other arm and he said he was still deaf on that side.

Her surgeon arrived, a sick man with a face like wet ash. The radiation. He coughed and coughed inside his mask, holding his breath to steady his hands for a few moments at a time. Ruth would have asked for someone else, except that a nurse leaned down and whispered, "Colonel Hanson is the best."

He was even worse off than Hernandez, and yet he'd stayed on duty. Ruth wondered how many others were already buried or on their deathbeds. She knew she could never stop going until she was killed herself.

He shot her hip full of novocaine, a dental anesthesia. Nothing more. They were down to the very last of their supplies and every day there were more wounded. Ruth shrieked at the grinding pressure against her pelvic bone as he dug out the shrapnel, but it was Cam's hand wrapped tightly in her own that she remembered later.

Hernandez sought them out again after dark. Ruth had forced herself to eat a cup of broth despite her nausea. She lay on a cot with her eyes half closed, hovering somewhere between her pain and the dim, ever-changing light.

They had been taken to a different tent, one that was longer, colder, and more crowded. The only illumination was a single lantern at the far end. Nurses periodically walked through the light, and dozens of patients shifted on the beds and on the floor, drawing long black shadows across the tent.

Cam and Deborah made bookends on either side of Ruth,

both of them stiff with their own wounds. The two women shared the bed, spooning for warmth. Deborah lay on the outside to protect the stitches in her back. Cam sat against the thin metal frame of the cot with his shoulders nearly touching Ruth's feet, asleep with his head on his knees. Ruth would have asked them to switch places if she weren't afraid of offending Deborah, but Deborah couldn't sit against the bed. Putting her on the floor would have been inexcusable and Ruth had already been cruel enough to Cam, pushing him away, drawing him in.

She'd never intended to be a tease. She wanted to cement their relationship even if it was nothing more than a quick fuck. When had there ever been time? She supposed the Rangers would have averted their eyes if she and Cam bundled together in a sleeping bag, but she would have felt so vulnerable. Worse, someone had stolen the box of condoms from her pack while she was in the medical tents in Grand Lake.

Ruth wondered what Cam and Allison had done together. Had they limited themselves to oral sex and hands or had they engaged in full intercourse? Ruth wanted to be better. She wanted him to want her more than the younger woman, and she thought of Ari and the fun little kinky things they'd played at, stroking each other, licking and kissing. The memories made her uncomfortably aware of Deborah sleeping against her back. She pressed her thighs together as snugly as the stitches in her hip would allow, trying to contain the warmth there.

She thought she'd been more hesitant with Cam than she might have been with anyone else because he'd seen her at her worst, but there was always something else holding her back. It would be frivolous. It would be wrong. She didn't feel like she deserved the relief, much less any pleasure, when it was her mistakes that had led to the war and killed a tremendous number of people across the planet.

Ruth bit her lip and watched the man in the next cot, an Army trooper with gashes on his chin and nose. She'd seen a nurse changing bandages along his collarbone, too, before replacing his blankets. His skin was yellow-gray in the dark, but his breathing was steady and Ruth tried to wish as much of her own strength into him as he needed.

Hernandez came slowly through the gloom, stopping to murmur with someone a few rows over from her. He stopped again before he reached her cot, peering down at the three of them.

"I'm awake," Ruth said.

Hernandez nodded. He had a plastic canteen with him and held it out. Ruth felt the bottle's heat even before she touched it. "Soup," he said.

"Thank you, General."

He didn't react to what she'd meant as a compliment. He glanced at Cam again, who was still sleeping, and then to the trooper on the next cot. He seemed as reverent as a man in church. He was definitely not impressed himself. More than anything, Hernandez was unwilling to disturb their rest, and Ruth knew very well the crushing sense of connection that she saw in everything he did.

Sergeant Estey had also checked in with her an hour ago. Ruth appreciated the update, even though Estey was all business. The two of them had never had any reason for small talk and Ruth knew that attitude to be an excellent coping mechanism. Still, she'd tried to soften him. She wanted to be more than a job to Estey. She'd asked him to give her best to Hale and Goodrich, but he only nodded and moved on to other useful data.

Frank Hernandez was now a one-star general. He had become third-in-command of the central Colorado army, in part because there was no one else left, but also because he'd succeeded when the situation demanded it. Hernandez had been instrumental in reorganizing the area's ground forces in time to meet the enemy. Many of the Guard and Reserve officers who technically outranked him had stepped aside.

It was his decisions that won or lost many of the battles along Highways 50 and 133. Whether an infantry company was in the right place or an artillery unit had the tools to maintain its guns, Hernandez was the key in every equation. His ability to anticipate the terrain and the capacities of his own people made every difference to hundreds of thousands of lives.

He was inextricably tied to them. Ruth thought it was this sense of obligation that had really brought him to the front line. Hernandez wasn't supposed to be here. Sylvan Mountain had experienced a huge increase in attacks as the Chinese pressed north, spearing toward I-70. Local U.S. command was hidden deep in the Aspen Valley in a larger, more secure base. Hernandez had risked his life to drive across. He'd insisted on meeting the survivors of the Ranger squad, but he couldn't have been sure that Ruth was among them. It was an excuse. He needed to see the troops he'd known only as numbers on his maps, and she respected him for it.

He spoke in a whisper. "We've started taking your blood samples right here in the tents."

Ruth nodded. Good. This is where the bulk of their medical staff could be found, along with the few rosters and charts they'd kept despite being overwhelmed.

"What else do you need?" he said. "We're refrigerating the needle pricks, but I don't know if we're capable of building a clean room for you."

"Don't waste the refrigerator space. Room temperature is fine, and any work space is great. It doesn't have to be much. I've been getting a lot of my work done from the back of a jeep."

"Then I'd like to move you tomorrow. Their planes are hitting us everywhere, but this base gets too much artillery. I'd rather have you somewhere farther back."

"Okay. Thank you." Ruth wasn't going to pretend to be so brave that she didn't want protection.

He looked for her eyes again in the shadows. Then he set his hand on the cot near her face. The gesture was almost aggressive, she realized, a display of his ability to corner and control her. "What am I up against?" he asked.

"General—"

"I need to know, Ruth."

She winced. Hernandez had never used her first name before and the informality was at odds with his little show of strength. He was trapped. He had to help her and yet he remained suspicious, either because of her treason in Sacramento or because of the staggering power of nanotech. Probably it was both. Ruth might as well have been a witch from the way that Hernandez treated her, with a mix of reverence and mistrust. He understood men and guns. She represented a different threat.

"I don't have an answer for you," Ruth said. "I swear. But I don't think the ghost is a weapon. I think Leadville was experimenting with new vaccine types."

"That's the only reason you're here?"

"Of course!" She forgot to keep her voice down and Deborah stirred against her, drowsy and soft. Cam was already awake. His eyes had turned to study Hernandez, and Ruth said, "What are you really trying to say?"

"We've been through your notebooks."

"A lot of that is speculative." She sounded defensive even to herself.

"I need to know about the saturation trigger."

Ruth stared at him, her mind racing. What guesses had his people made from her numbers and shorthand? It seemed unlikely that Hernandez had anyone trained in nanotechnology. Had he simply asked combat engineers or computer techs to figure out her notes as best they could? Based on its helix shape, Ruth had theorized that the ghost might be designed to coalesce into larger structures after crossing some threshold of density in a population . . . but that idea was still nothing more than an idea.

Firmly, she said, "If you read everything, you know I had serious questions about that line of thinking. And I gave it up days ago."

"That's not what my people tell me."

"Then they're wrong."

Cam said, "What is he talking about?"

"Doctor Goldman has considered a way of stopping the Chinese army that would also kill everyone in these mountains," Hernandez said. "Some kind of critical mass."

"You don't believe that," Cam said, taking the argument upon himself.

"I believe Grand Lake would do anything to win," Hernandez said, and Ruth finally grasped the sheer depth of the changes he'd been through. He was the one who'd lost in Sacramento. He was the one who'd watched Leadville vaporized. Hernandez was testing her. If she failed his questions, if he truly believed that Grand Lake intended to destroy him, the American civil war might erupt again when they could least afford it. Even joined together, the forces in Colorado were barely holding a line against the Chinese.

"You think we came all this way just to die?" Ruth asked with biting sarcasm. "Like we thought a suicide mission was our best choice?"

"I know you have a lot of guilt." He cut through her scorn as easily as that. "Your friends wouldn't have to know what you were doing," Hernandez said, and he was right.

He turned her contempt into self-doubt and she immediately reached for Cam. "It's not true," she said.

"I know." Cam covered her hand with his own.

Behind her, Deborah lifted herself on one elbow to gaze at Hernandez. She laid her other hand on Ruth's waist. It was an affectionate moment and Ruth would never forget their loyalty to her. She was grateful for it, because she still had one secret.

"I came to help you," she told Hernandez. Her voice was tight with tears. "I came to help everyone," she said, and slowly Hernandez began to nod in the darkness.

"I'm sorry," he said. "I had to be sure."

"You . . . But we didn't . . ."

"I'm sorry." His hand rose uncertainly, as if to find a place on her and join the small chain that connected her to Cam and Deborah. Ruth wished he would. Instead, Hernandez lowered his arm to his side. "My first responsibility is to the people here," he said. "And your notes are terrifying."

"Yes."

They were quiet for an instant, listening to the restless sounds in tent—the rustle of wounded soldiers who were alone and cold despite sharing this nightmare.

"You shouldn't get in her way," Deborah said. "Ruth is the best chance we've got."

"We'll see." Hernandez stood up.

Ruth reached after him. "Wait. Please."

"There's too much to do."

"I don't want you to leave like this," she said honestly. "Please. Just a few minutes."

"All right." Hernandez sat again.

Ruth struggled to find something pleasant to say. "Do you want some of the soup?" she asked.

"No. It's for you."

But there were too many important things to know and never enough time. "We thought you were in Leadville when the bomb went off," she said.

Hernandez nodded. "I was."

His company only survived because of the mountains surrounding the capital. The enemy plane must have been well below those fourteen-thousand-foot peaks when it detonated its cargo. The high ring of the Divide had acted like a bowl, reflecting the explosion up instead of outward. U.S. intelligence estimated the blast at sixty megatons. A doomsday device.

There was no reason to pile so many warheads into the plane except the Russians must have been concerned they would be turned back or shot down. With an airburst of that strength, they might have leveled the city from fifty miles away or damaged it at a hundred.

Hernandez was lucky they'd gotten so close. Aerial and satellite reconnaissance showed nothing but slag at ground zero. There was no longer the slightest trace of anything human in that valley. The land itself was unrecognizable. Untold amounts of earth and rock had been vaporized, and the remainder briefly turned liquid. The eerie new flat land was studded with lopsided hillocks and dunes. It almost looked as if someone had dumped an incredible flood of molten steel from the sky. The effect was uneven. The shock wave had roared through every low point and gap, washboarding against the terrain. It was what had saved Deborah. The blast leapt and splashed and bounced, devastating some valleys and sparing others.

Hernandez had been on a south-facing slope away from the flash. The long series of ranges between his position and Leadville redirected the worst of it. Even then his escape was a near thing. Impact jolted his mountainside sharply enough to close many of his fighting holes like hands snapping into fists. He had five dead and seventeen wounded in those first immeasurable seconds. Daylight turned to black. Then the windstorm hit with choking heat and dust.

They ran downhill, abandoning everything but their wounded. They were afraid of the machine plague, but they knew they would smother if they stayed. Later they realized the atmospheric pressure had plummeted over an area of tens of miles as the nuclear reaction sucked air into an immense, superheated column. It was the slightest bit of good fortune. The region was temporarily wiped clean of the plague. Once they reached the base of the mountain, they were able to stay on Highway 24, hurrying along the buckled asphalt. Then the mushroom cloud fell in on itself and collapsed, blanketing them in ash and unseen bands of heat.

Hernandez was sick like so many of his troops, which made it easier for the Chinese to surge northward against them. None of the surviving American forces had been any closer to the strike than his unit, but nearly a third of them had been exposed to the fallout. It ravaged their effectiveness. They were unable to mount the counteroffensives they needed simply to shore up their defensive positions, and the Chinese generals knew it. The Chinese continued to race past American emplacements, leaving their supply routes vulnerable but accepting that risk in exchange for the gains in territory.

The central Colorado army was being encircled. Soon the enemy would reinforce its advance units on I-70 and face Aspen Valley from three sides. There were other U.S. populations throughout the state, but other than Grand Lake, none of them had significant military strength.

The tipping point was here. That seemed to be why the Chinese gambled. Their need for fuel, food, and tools was part of it. Every small town they absorbed was a help, and they made it tougher on the American Air Force by sprawling out. Widespread targets were harder to hit and had more time to cover each other, but Ruth wondered if the Chinese were also pushing so hard in this area because, like her, they hoped to recover some trace of the nanotechnologies developed in Leadville.

They might have already found it in the American dead. Here and there, they would have taken prisoners, too. In fact, it wasn't impossible that the U.S. had transmitted the nanotech to the Chinese with their bullets and missiles. Every time a soldier loaded his weapon, each time a ground crew rearmed a jet, their skin, sweat, and breath were tainted with it.

Ruth had no way of guessing if Chinese researchers were outpacing her or if the enemy had already developed new weaponized nanotech themselves.

"You know about the snowflake," she said to Hernandez. She needed to warn him to be careful of his own planes if it looked like he was losing his fight to keep the enemy from I-70.

If the Chinese flanked the Aspen group, if Grand Lake thought this was the last place to catch the Chinese in a bottleneck before the enemy surged toward the new capital, there was no telling what they might do. The snowflake was the easy solution. There was no way to defend against it, and after its initial burst, the snowflake was clean.

"The weapons teams were trying—" Ruth said, but she stopped when she realized she was distancing herself from what she'd done by using the past tense.

"I've heard about it," Hernandez said. "I don't think Leadville ever let the nanotech out of their control."

He was trying to help. He thought the snowflake was gone forever. For a moment, Ruth couldn't even speak, overcome with self-loathing and embarrassment. His troops had saved her, and in return . . . "Grand Lake has it now," she said. "I built it for them."

His dark eyes stared at her in the gloom.

"I didn't know what else to do," Ruth said, and Cam murmured, "Jesus Christ."

She hadn't told him. What could he do? It had seemed like the right decision at the time. She'd thought she was providing her country with a powerful new deterrent, and that was still true, but now everyone in this place was in jeopardy.

Hernandez looked away from her even as his hand tightened on the edge of the cot. It was almost as if he swooned. He understood. Ruth saw it in his gray face. He was a tactician, and throughout the civil war he'd seen his people turn on each other again and again.

Grand Lake had always had the option of nuking the enemy. There were still USAF officers in the sealed missile bases in Wyoming and North Dakota, but the Rockies would be downwind of any target in the western United States. Worse, the enemy would almost certainly answer in kind.

The snowflake was different. A nano weapon would be an escalation. Using one would run the chance of a nuclear response, but desperate men might convince themselves that it would scare the enemy enough to stay their hands. Desperate men might believe that an unparalleled new weapon of mass destruction was exactly what could win the war.

It left Hernandez in a terrible dilemma. He needed to keep his guns and infantry in close to repel the Chinese, but at the same time, if he overcommitted, his troops would have no chance to pull back before Grand Lake dusted the area. And yet he needed to commit every last man. If he lost another battle, if Grand Lake panicked or simply lost patience with the limited strength of Aspen Valley, the jet fighters that had aided Hernandez might instead bring death to everyone beneath them.

The bombing would not be indiscriminate. Ruth hoped they'd have the brains to drop their capsules on the far side of the Chinese, but their pilots had no experience with the snowflake. Their pilots would be accustomed to hitting their targets straight on. Regardless, the chain reaction was inherent to the technology. It would reach American lines.

"The best thing we can do is tell Grand Lake I've found what I need," Ruth said.

"You haven't even started—" Hernandez shook his head at himself. He was clearly still stunned. "Of course. Okay."

Lying isn't easy for him even now, Ruth thought, *despite how many times people have failed him.*

He stood up. He seemed glad to move away from her. "What can I say on an open frequency?" he asked.

"Tell them I have what I was looking for. Just like that. It should buy us more time."

"I'll call them now."

"I'm so sorry," Ruth said. "I am." Words were inadequate. Once again she'd hurt the very people who were risking everything to help her.

23

Chinese artillery pounded the land in the distance, a staggered thumping that came and went. Three or four explosions hit together, followed by a pause, then ten or more impacts in a rush. In the brief quiet, Cam heard American guns returning fire. His left ear was still partly deaf but the outgoing shells made a distinct *crack. Crack crack.* Then the heavier explosions picked up again, battering the other side of the mountain a few miles to the west. Cam wished they'd driven farther from Sylvan Mountain. He constantly expected this narrow rock gorge to erupt with death. They were still so close, and the enemy had begun a new offensive with reinforcements out of Arizona.

The war was always there. Smoke and dust poisoned the evening sky, drifting toward them on the wind. Cam stared at the sunset, a sooty orange glow beyond the dark peaks that formed the horizon—but people were dying in that spectacular light, he knew, and the beauty of it upset him.

He turned the other way, looking for Ruth in the gorge. He was huddled with Foshtomi and Goodrich along a split face of granite, cleaning half a dozen carbines. Busywork. Otherwise the waiting was impossible. Hernandez had ordered them to sit tight. Estey wanted to run patrols through the area—he was as restless as any of them, Cam thought—but they were behind their own lines and Hernandez insisted on as little activity as possible to keep from drawing the enemy's attention. It was bad enough that they'd rolled away from Sylvan Mountain in two trucks and a jeep, with Ruth, Cam, Deborah, and the five Rangers supported by a Marine platoon and Hernandez himself.

Hernandez intended to take Ruth all the way to the command bunkers at Castle Peak, but they'd already lost too much time. If she could produce an answer, he needed it now. So they waited. They ate. They tended each other's wounds and tried to catch up on their sleep.

It had been nearly thirty-six hours since they'd hidden in this jagged gully. Cam ached with tension. More than anything else, the plague year had taught him to act. The urge to stay ahead of every threat, whether real or imagined, was exactly why he'd left Allison. He still wondered at himself. He'd given up her smile and her warmth in exchange for nothing except more hardship, blood, and glory. That was not the decision of a well-grounded individual. At the same time, he wasn't sure what kind of man would have let Ruth go alone.

"Hey, take it easy," Foshtomi said, pressing her knee against his.

The slight movement made Cam realize he was as rigid as the rock itself, his body hunched as if to jump up. His jaw hurt from grinding his teeth. *She's right,* he thought. *You're actually damaging yourself.*

"Sometimes the only thing you can do is wait it out," Foshtomi said, returning her work. She was inspecting an M4's bolt carrier group, yet Cam saw her hazel eyes lift to his face once more as if to catch him disobeying her. Sarah Foshtomi was a good squadmate. Cam almost smiled. There were worse things than sitting here with this resilient young woman. That much was true. But he didn't have the benefit of Foshtomi's years in the military. She knew how to do her job and only her job, accepting her place in the larger whole, whereas Cam had learned nothing except the self-reliance of a loner.

He had never felt more apart. Two of Hernandez's Marines remembered him as an enemy. Nathan Gilbride was among those Cam had betrayed in Sacramento, and neither Gilbride nor Sergeant Watts seemed as ready to forgive him as their

commanding officer had been. Worse, they'd told their fellow
Marines. It was an unexpected strain. Cam had never imagined
he would see any of those men alive again. He kept his mouth
shut and his eyes down. Even Ruth had been taken from him.
Ruth had the only tent in camp, a lean-to they'd erected against
one of the trucks and disguised with netting and dirt, blending
the long shape of the vehicle into the rock. In a day and a half
Cam had seen her just twice, both times in conference with Deborah, Hernandez, and Gilbride—and yet as much as he wanted
to touch her, he'd stayed back. Her work came first. Cam was
jealous of Deborah for being so necessary. Deborah served as
Ruth's assistant, organizing the blood samples from Sylvan
Mountain. Deborah wasn't above fetching Ruth's meals, either,
or emptying the bucket that served as her latrine.

Cam had to be careful. He'd made a mistake the last time
they were in this situation. When Ruth disappeared into her lab
in Grand Lake, he'd found Allison.

"Okay, let's pack up," Goodrich said. He slung two of the
M4s over his shoulder and Cam and Foshtomi stood with him,
gathering their own carbines. Sunset was giving way to night. In
thirty minutes they were on watch.

As he walked with Foshtomi to the second truck, Cam could
not stop himself from gazing at Ruth's tent. It was a flimsy structure in which to house their best hope. They could never protect
Ruth from artillery or planes, whether there were twenty soldiers
here or five hundred, and he knew that he was the least useful of
all, with minimal training, one good ear, and the quiet animosity
between himself and the Marines.

He might have left on his own if he had anywhere to go, if
only to get moving again. The urge ran that deep. He recognized
the feeling for what it was, nerves and doubt and old trauma, but
he wondered if he would ever be able to settle down. Even if
Ruth gave him the opportunity, or Allison or anyone, Cam wondered if he would always be trying to get away from himself.

"There she is," Foshtomi said as lantern light spilled through
the gorge. Two silhouettes held open the side of the tent, Deborah and Ruth.

Directly in front of the two women, a Marine ducked his

head, pinned in the yellow light. Hernandez had ordered a total blackout. "Hey!" someone shouted. Ruth's shape hesitated, but Deborah's taller figure let go of the tent flap.

Cam set down his canteen and started toward them, blinking to regain his night vision. "Cam, wait," Goodrich said. He didn't stop. If the sergeant pressed the matter, he would say he hadn't understood because of his ear.

"Where is General Hernandez?" Deborah asked the soldiers in front of the tent. She was supporting Ruth as well as speaking for her. Ruth stood awkwardly, protecting her hip, and Deborah kept one arm around her waist. Cam edged through the few Marines to reach her side. One of them said something that Cam only caught part of, "—ight now," but the man pointed as he spoke and that was enough. Cam was more interested in trying to assess Ruth's health in the dark.

She noticed him and smiled.

"How are you?" she asked. Then they were separated again as Deborah guided Ruth forward, walking through the Marines. Ruth looked back once, her curly hair like a soft tangle in the moonlight.

What did you find? Cam thought. He knew her moods well enough to recognize this exhausted pleasure. Good news. It was good news, and that meant none of their losses had been in vain. The thrill of it made him grin as he strode after the group. The wind sifted through the gorge, cold and alive. Cam was aware of another kind of motion around them as other soldiers got up and paced alongside them. Most of the twenty-six Rangers and Marines were in foxholes outside the gully, but Ruth drew the remainder to her in twos and threes.

Like the trucks, the jeep was also draped in netting. Hernandez slept beside the vehicle and its radio. A Marine corporal sat nearby, leaning against a tire with his submachine gun in his lap. He woke Hernandez, who coughed and pushed himself up. Then he coughed again, uncontrollably.

Deborah let go of Ruth and knelt close to him, laying her hand on his back as he rasped for air. "General," she said.

"I'm fine." He choked the words out.

Deborah stayed with him. She was obviously trying to gauge the strength of his breathing and Cam didn't like the obvious tension in her shoulders. Shit. Hernandez had hidden his respiratory

problems from them, but even if it was just a cold, not radiation
sickness, the man was in dangerously bad shape to be fighting off
a virus.

Hernandez was gaunt and pale. "Doctor Goldman," he said,
quickly locating the most important face in the crowd.

"They trusted you," Ruth said. "They trusted you more than
you think."

"I don't understand."

"Leadville," she said. "The labs."

To the west, a clump of explosions flared up from the black
mountains. The booming reached them an instant later as Ruth
knelt, too, twisting to protect the wounds in her left hip. Some of
the Marines also crouched down and Cam was not surprised by
this sudden intimacy. Everyone wanted to hear.

"They were testing nanotech on forward units," Ruth said,
"but they must have been almost certain how well the new vaccine would work. They trusted you."

"A new vaccine," Hernandez said.

"Yes." Her eyes were large and childlike. "There are two
nanos in you right now, and they're both different from anything else I've seen."

Hernandez coughed again, wincing. Beside Cam, one of the
Marines touched his own chest and several others glanced down
at themselves or fidgeted with their hands, afraid of the machin-
ery that they could not see.

"They targeted you deliberately, General," Ruth said. "They
trusted you. We've taken hundreds of blood samples and no one
else had the vaccine or a working ghost."

"What does that mean?" a woman asked behind Cam. It was
Foshtomi, and he turned to see that she stood away from the
group, as if that could possibly save her. But she was loyal and
brave. The wind blew Foshtomi's dark hair across her face and
she strode forward with the rush of the breeze, joining them despite her nervousness.

Ruth glanced at the younger woman, then turned back to Hernandez. It might have been Cam's imagination but he thought
Ruth looked at him, too, after dismissing Foshtomi. Why? Because she didn't like it that he and Sarah were friends?

"How long were you stationed outside Leadville before the
bombing?" Ruth asked Hernandez. "Were you above the barrier
that whole time?"

"What are you saying—we were immune to the plague?"

"At some point. Absolutely. The atmospheric effects of the bomb had nothing to do with the fact that your troops were able to run below ten thousand feet and survive."

Hernandez shook his head. "We would have noticed."

"No. Not if you never tried it. You wouldn't have launched any attacks below the barrier until after Grand Lake brought you the vaccine that Cam and I carried out of Sacramento, right?"

"We mounted a few strikes. We thought there were still areas where the bombing had wiped out the plague."

"You were immune. The vaccine out of Grand Lake wasn't half as good as what you already had." Ruth laughed, but it was a melancholy sound. "You must have gotten it some time during the two weeks before the bomb. Leadville caught our friends in the Sierras, which is where they got the early model of the vaccine. Then they infected you with an improved version and a spin-off technology to see how the two would interact."

The soldiers moved uneasily again. "Jesus," Watts said with his hand at his mouth. It was another protective gesture, no different than the way Foshtomi had hung back from the group. These men and women still thought of the nanotech as a disease.

Ruth said, "Did they give any kind of inoculations or pills? Something they said was a vitamin?"

"No."

"It could have been in your water or your food. As far as I can tell, the improved model has the same weakness as the first generation. It only replicates when it's exposed to the plague, which means the infection would have been sporadic unless you all ate or drank the same thing." Ruth paused, embarrassed. "After the bomb, when you left your mountain, did you lose anyone?"

"It was chaotic," Hernandez said. "And dark and very hot."

Ruth reached for his arm, making contact. "Is there any way to know if some of them died because of the machine plague?"

He looked down at her hand. He shook his head.

"Please," Ruth said. "This is important."

"It was chaotic," he repeated, and Cam marveled at the understatement.

"We have to assume it's a possibility," Ruth said. She glanced at Deborah, as if resuming a different conversation. Or maybe she couldn't bear to face Hernandez anymore.

The general still had his head down, either wrestling with his illness or his grief. He appeared uncharacteristically weak and Cam also turned away. The soldiers had done the same. Their respect for Hernandez demanded it, and Cam wondered what they would do when he was gone.

"I'll need blood again," Ruth said slowly. "We need to make sure we get the new vaccine to as many people as possible, and I think . . . I'm sure the second nano is the only reason you're alive."

"They brought us steak a few days before the bombing," Hernandez said. "Fresh steak. Not a lot. But we were surprised."

"That was probably it," Ruth said.

"We'd already started communicating with other units up and down the line. I . . . We were talking about leaving our posts."

The emotion in his eyes was both haunted and amazed. Hernandez was glad to be wrong, Cam realized. Despite everything else that had happened, he took comfort in discovering that Leadville continued to rely on him.

"We thought they were punishing us," Hernandez said. "We thought the meat was only a way to keep us on a short leash."

"They trusted you."

"I was already committing treason," he said, looking left and right at his Marines. He was using his confession to bring them closer to him. He had recovered from his shock, and again Cam was stunned by the man's abilities. Everything was a lesson to him. His entire focus was on his troops and the never-ending process of improving them—and he was stronger for it. Not for the first time, Cam envied Hernandez.

"Sir, a lot of us were looking to the rebels," Watts said, and Deborah added, "It wouldn't have mattered. You had nothing to do with the bombing."

"It does matter," Hernandez said. "I should have stuck it out. What if the president's council heard some rumor of what I was doing? What if that's why they didn't tell me about the vaccine? Think what we could have done with it if we'd known. We could have moved down onto the highways. We could have dug in and stopped the Chinese cold."

Cam frowned to himself. It was true that a lot of good opportunities had been missed, but it troubled him that Hernandez could ignore the way he'd been used as a test subject. It was a blind spot. His fealty was the real difference between them, and Cam was angry for him. Cam was angry *at* him.

"You said they gave us two kinds of nanotech," Hernandez said, coughing again as he turned to Ruth.

She nodded. "We called it the ghost when we found it in Grand Lake. Nobody could tell what it did, and Leadville must have put it through several generations in a hurry. We isolated at least four strains before we got here."

"But it's not a vaccine."

"No. Yes. In a way, yes. I kept thinking that most of the radiation victims we met weren't as bad off as they should have been, but no one had a real idea how close they were to the blast. No one except you."

Above them, the night rippled with birds, an unexpected, darting swarm that lifted a shout of warning from one of the Marines. Cam flinched.

Ruth barely reacted to the interruption, her voice hushed and intense. "Sir, you should be dead. The rads you took are off the scale, but you also have the most advanced version of the ghost I've seen. It's some kind of overall booster. I think it's a prototype that was intended to protect against the snowflake. Soldiers carrying a perfect version of it could probably hit the enemy with the snowflake and not see any effects themselves . . . and I think it's helping your tissues stay intact despite the radiation damage. It's gradually cleaning your cells." She tipped her face up toward Cam, then looked back at Hernandez and said, "It's rebuilding you."

"But I'm sicker than ever."

"I don't think it can keep up. It's an early model."

Hernandez didn't say anything else, although his mind must have been racing. Cam was still trying to make sense of everything they'd heard and he hadn't just learned that he belonged in his grave.

"I'm sorry." Ruth reached for Hernandez again, and the general took her hand.

She could fix us, Cam thought.

"I'm so sorry," Ruth said, but Hernandez pressed his lips into a thin smile and said, "They kept us alive longer than we had any right to expect." He meant himself and the survivors from his company. He was still drawing connections between himself and Leadville, taking comfort in the past.

"Can you save him?" Cam asked, because it would have been awful to say what he really wanted to know. *Can you fix me?* He was ashamed to be so selfish, because Hernandez continued to put everyone else first. Hernandez wouldn't plead with her, not for himself—but his troops spoke on his behalf.

"Make the nanotech better," Watts said. "Please," Foshtomi added, as another man said, "The thing already works pretty good, right?"

Ruth ducked her head. Every day she seemed more humble, which was strange in someone so masterful. Her little habit of turning away came frequently now and Cam remembered the gesture especially from the day she'd first met Allison, avoiding the younger woman. Ruth was learning to evade challenges, which was dangerous for all of them, and Cam shared some of the blame for her indecisiveness.

"Maybe," she said at last. "Yes. The potential here is incredible. The model you have inside you represents the best work of the top people in nanotech, fifty researchers with full machining gear and computers."

She meant that she was alone. She was still hedging her words, as if there were any possibility they wouldn't back her into this corner. Their lives depended on it. More importantly, her work would shape the outcome of the war. Mankind would rebuild on North America. There was no question of that, but the color of the natives' skin and the languages they spoke would depend on Ruth's success or failure.

The ability to move freely in the plague zones was only the beginning. A nanotech capable of healing even serious wounds would make them unstoppable.

Cam flexed his ruined hands and glanced at Deborah, Ruth, and Hernandez, all of them hurt in different ways. What if they were able to stand up again after being shot or burned? They would be superhuman, and Cam tried to form a prayer to all of the scientists who had been killed in Leadville.

Help her, he thought. *You can help her somehow.* Shouldn't they be able to talk to Ruth through their work? There would be clues and other evidence in the nanotech, obvious problems to fix and improvements to be made.

"You've done it before," Cam said.

"I've seen it," Watts agreed.

In the lab in Sacramento, Ruth had quickly drawn together

and improved the work of four science teams, building upon the original *archos* tech to create the first working vaccine. Of course, she had also had the help of two specialists, D.J. and Todd, both of whom were either dead or hopelessly lost.

"A lot of people are depending on you," Hernandez said.

Ruth wouldn't look at them. "I need time," she said. "Maybe too much time. And I don't have any equipment here."

"You do in Grand Lake," Hernandez said.

"Yes. Some."

"We can get you there."

They ran northeast on the morning of July 1st, moving downhill before the dawn lifted over the horizon. The mountains in the east topped out at fourteen thousand feet, hiding the sun. Cam felt his gaze drawn again and again to those peaks. It was difficult to tell in the brilliant new light, but those mountains looked unusually smooth along their southern edges. They were *melted*. Their bulk was all that had spared Aspen Valley from the bombing, channeling the worst of the blast away. Even so, Ruth's escort had quickly hiked into an area where the ground was a marsh, still waterlogged from the floods of snowmelt, and yet the fallen trees were brittle and dry.

"Watch out." Foshtomi stopped Cam from following Mitchell. Mitchell had stepped over a dead gray stump into an ordinary-looking puddle, but the surface was deceptive. Mitchell sunk to his hip. He twisted to grab the stump and Foshtomi splashed forward to help, both of them coated with the spotty black muck of eroding bark. "Hang on," Foshtomi called.

Cam looked back. They were in the middle of the group to assist Ruth while most of the squad ranged ahead, but Ruth was already looking for another way through, talking with Deborah. She pointed and moved left.

"Wait!" Cam said, hustling to join her.

A few trees still jutted into the sky, leafless and broken. This long mountainside was covered with blowdowns. Fortunately the spruce and aspen forest had been thin at ninety-five hundred feet, because moments after the blast wave knocked them over, the floods had locked the shattered trunks and branches together in a treacherous puzzle like pick-up sticks.

The undergrowth was a different matter. Most of the brush

and grass had survived the heat and the windstorms. In many places, they weren't drowning either. The trees and rocks formed thousands of small dams, directing the water into rivulets and swamps—but even where the ground bumped up, the brush was sickly. When he touched one, the leaves crumbled away like confetti. Every minute on this ruined slope, Cam was sure they were absorbing radiation.

He reached for Ruth's arm as she began to crab her way over a pair of logs after Deborah. "You have to wait," he said.

Her dark eyes flashed at him. They no longer wore their goggles and masks. There was no need, so he got the full brunt of Ruth's expression. *"Let go,"* she said. "Let go of me!" She climbed across, peeling bark away in clumps beneath her damp gloves and boots.

Cam followed her. "Goddammit, wait," he said, looking for Deborah's eyes instead of Ruth's. He was slowed by his ribs and Ruth had already limped to the next blowdown, grabbing for handholds among its jagged branches.

She'd been like this ever since Hernandez left them.

"You have to talk to her," Cam said, striding alongside Deborah, but the tall blond only shrugged, almost indifferent.

"I think she's right. We need to keep moving."

"If she breaks her leg," Cam said, raising his voice.

Suddenly Ruth stopped in front of them. Cam looked out across the hillside. Forty yards ahead, Estey had raised his hand, signaling for them across the snarled trees, mud, and water. In the space between, Goodrich and Ballard also stood waiting. The soldiers made three strong human shapes among the debris.

Cam waved back at Estey and said, to Ruth, "It's stupid for you to walk in front. We have to get back to the others."

But that wasn't what had stopped her. She'd found a bird. "Oh," Deborah said softly as Ruth knelt and reached for the pathetic creature.

The finch couldn't have been in the plague zone very long because it was still alive, although its feathers were molting from its belly and neck. It flopped weakly in the muck, trying to escape. It had no strength in its wings and it might have been blind, too. The bird's eyes were a cloudy blue-white that Cam had never seen before.

"This way!" Estey yelled, and Cam waved again, although

he wasn't sure if Ruth would obey. She hesitated with her gloves on either side of the bird. He thought she must not have seen the bloated chipmunks they'd passed fifteen minutes ago, two little bodies that had washed down the mountainside together. The chipmunks would have stopped her, too, and he preferred her wild impatience.

Ruth could be careless of her own safety when she was manic, but it also made her dangerous to anything in her way. They couldn't afford for her to fall apart. They needed to harness her expertise one more time—and they were still an hour from their rendezvous. Cam hoped to God she'd make it.

"Look at him," she said. She meant the bird.

"We need to go," Cam said, and Deborah added, "Ruth, the sun's coming up."

"Right." She didn't move at first. "You're right. It's just a fucking bird." Ruth stood up and pushed past them with her trembling, filthy gloves.

They were on foot because Hernandez had driven back to Sylvan Mountain, both to rejoin the base and as a decoy for enemy satellites. His trucks were far more likely to attract attention than a handful of people, especially since his vehicles were moving toward the front. If there was an attack, Hernandez wanted to draw the fire to himself. He was buying time. He'd organized a flight of helicopters to take Ruth north again, but he didn't want to risk a pickup too close to Sylvan Mountain. The Chinese had too many guns focused on the area. The invaders had also continued to push their advantage in the air war. Helicopters would be vulnerable no matter what he did, but Hernandez intended to lead a massive counteroffensive to push the Chinese back. A diversion.

You just make sure you do your best, Hernandez had said as Ruth leaned over his forearm, jabbing the inside of his arm with a needle that she immediately sank into her own wrist. That was why she was so upset. It was clear that Hernandez didn't expect to see the outcome of her work, and Cam thought he would probably ask all of his sickest men and women to follow him in the front waves of the assault. Cam thought they would say yes.

The worst that Ruth faced were scratches or a turned ankle, and she seemed eager to hurt herself, shoving through the branches and mud. They were incubating. They'd dropped below the barrier forty minutes ago and the perfected vaccine would beat out the earlier model, swiftly multiplying as it was first to disassemble the plague. At the same time, the booster nano should help protect them against the radiation.

Hernandez would give his life for hers. With more time in the labs in Grand Lake, Ruth had the ability to turn the war in their favor by improving the booster nano. There seemed to be no limit to what it could do. Accelerating a man's capacity to heal was only the beginning. She might be able to double their strength, their reflexes, their sight. But as always the problem was contamination. If they could pass an improved booster among themselves, they would inevitably spread it to the enemy. Supersoldiers would have the advantage only for a short period before the enemy rose up with the same new traits. The United States would need to launch their new attacks in a single coordinated thrust, if there was time—if there were still enough Americans left.

The swamp turned black as Estey led them into an area where the collapsing forest had ignited and burned before the floods extinguished the fire. Cam saw another dying bird. Then he spotted a blue Pepsi can and wondered how it had gotten there.

From somewhere north came the long, shuddering wake of jet fighters. "Down!" Estey screamed. Most of them splashed into the charcoal-encrusted grime. Ruth stood looking up. Foshtomi grabbed the back of her jacket. "Get down, you idiot," Foshtomi said, but the thundering sound was far away and getting farther, fading into the night sky behind them.

Cam turned to see the dark west horizon stutter with orange bursts of light as gigantic explosions filled the valleys beyond Sylvan Mountain. U.S. fighters were slamming the Chinese again, preparing the way for the ground assault.

Hernandez had some advantages. He had elevation. It was ironic. The Colorado armies had stayed above ten thousand feet because they were afraid of the plague, ceding most of the lowlands and highways to the Chinese, but now they would crash into the enemy with all the momentum of superior positions. *Not for her,* Cam thought. They weren't only doing it for her, although Hernandez might have tried more conservative tactics if he hadn't wanted to protect Ruth above everything else. That was why she was so unsettled. Thousands more would die to serve her, no matter if it was her decision or not.

The sun touched them at last as they hiked out of the swamp onto a ridgeline. The light felt warm and clean—and the wind began to carry the sounds of artillery. Then there were more planes. The clamor of war followed them for miles and Ruth kept her head down, limping through the rock and scorched grass as fast as she was able.

The thrum of helicopters echoed from the shallow mountain pass in front of them. It became a roar as three snub-nosed Black Hawks surged out of the landscape ahead. Estey knelt with his radio as Goodrich waved both arms over his head, so Cam was surprised when two of the attack choppers banked away and kept going. More decoys. The third helicopter came straight for them and flared hard, lowering its skids to the earth as the crew chief banged open the door.

"Do you trust me?" Ruth asked, leaning close enough that her hair whipped at Cam's face. He barely heard her. On the flight deck, the sound of the rotors was bone-jarring. The turbines screamed each time the chopper lifted and swung through the terrain. Cam looked out from the noise at the quiet world flitting by. The shapes of mountains heaved up and down, but the desolation was constant. Endless miles were burned or flooded or brown with dead trees.

Ruth leaned away to see his face. There was something new in her eyes, excitement and fear, an idea, and Cam nodded. He let her brush her lips against his good ear again.

"I need you to trust me one more time," she said.

Estey's Rangers were separated from each other as soon as the chopper landed in Grand Lake. Cam and Deborah were pulled into the effort as well. Special Forces medics drew several hypodermics of blood from each of them. Other soldiers led them to command shelters and barracks, rapidly pricking the insides of their arms with needles, then stabbing those bloody slivers into other men and women. It was almost funny. Cam was badly worn and the process had a madcap feel that reminded him of the bumbling clown shows he'd seen at various fairs and amusement parks when he was a kid.

Where did that memory come from? he wondered, pressing a

gauze pad to his bleeding arm as three soldiers rushed him toward another bunker. They shouted once at a civilian. The man tried to grab Cam but the soldiers punched him in the face.

Grand Lake was in turmoil. Most of the area was evacuating. Cam found himself in a tent crowded with pilots in full flight gear, all of whom ran from the barracks as soon as they were inoculated. Cam also passed through two shelters full of officers where he learned as much as he needed, listening to them confirm signals and rendezvous dates. A full platoon had taken Ruth to her lab. Some of the top commanders were also staying, at least until alternate bases were established below the barrier. They were trying their damnedest to get out of here without crippling their defenses. That was impossible. The transition would be a staggering amount of work exactly when they needed most to focus on the enemy, but they were too vulnerable on these peaks. Chinese fighters had broken through to Grand Lake eight times in the past two days, strafing its makeshift air bases and ground crews. Enemy planes could come again any minute.

Cam knew something they didn't. Neither sides' efforts would matter if Ruth was successful. She no longer planned to improve the booster. She imagined a way to remove the enemy completely, and yet there was no guarantee that her scheme would work. Until then, Cam could only do his part.

He spotted Foshtomi once in between the tents, running with her own bodyguards. Another time he saw a mob on the hillside across from him, a near-riot in the refugee camps that must have gathered around another of his squadmates. A lot of the refugees were already gone, taking their chances with the early model of the vaccine. Some had stayed, however, either from inertia or to help organize the rest.

Allison Barrett was one of those who'd remained. She found Cam that evening as he ate with Ballard and Goodrich. The rest of their squad had yet to reappear, and his heart leapt at the sight of a familiar face. Cam stood up from the table and walked past his guards, embracing her.

"Come with me," Allison whispered. Her blue eyes were bright and urgent.

He shook his head. "I can't." He thought she meant outside the tent, but Allison had larger plans.

Allison bared her teeth in her fierce, beautiful grin and said, "You can help us. Please. Regular people are important, too. We need more leaders and you've been under the barrier so many times. You know what to expect."

"I'm sorry."

"Please. We're going east." She kept her arm cinched around his waist. "This place will get hit again. You know it will."

"Yes."

Ballard said they'd used the snowflake. The ground assaults out of Sylvan Mountain had failed almost immediately, beaten back by Chinese air superiority as Hernandez must have expected. Hours ago, Grand Lake had dusted the Chinese as they pursued Hernandez back into the mountains, decimating many of the U.S. forces as well. It was a desperate show of strength. Both sides were frantic and outraged. The rumor was that the launch codes were locked. There could be a nuclear exchange, and Grand Lake was surely a prime target.

"You should go," Cam said.

"You can't help her any more. You've done enough." Allison bared her teeth again in her aggressive way. "She's not in love with you."

"What?"

"She doesn't love you. Not like that."

"That's not what this is about," Cam said honestly. The connection he felt with Ruth was much more than as a lover. It was layered and powerful. Yes, they had been physically intimate, touching and kissing. Maybe there would be more. But his feelings for her went beyond that. He had to see this through.

"You can change your mind," Allison said. "You can come with us anytime."

Then she walked away. Cam went after her, although he stopped at the wide door of the tent. Two of his guards had followed him and he glanced out at the hazy night, searching among the busy lights of American planes. Would there be any warning?

Maybe it would be better just to vanish in a single white instant of nuclear fire. They wouldn't suffer. They could stop running at last.

Cam thought of Nikola Ulinov, whom he could never meet. He thought of Ruth, furiously trying to outrace the tide of war. Despite everything, he felt still and quiet. He'd done what he could. Now it was out of his hands again. One way or the other he'd do everything he could to help Ruth. He continued to wait and watch as Allison joined the bustle of soldiers rushing to get out of this marked place.

24

The command bunker was hidden beneath an ordinary-looking Winnebago camper, like so many of the shelters in Grand Lake. Ruth almost didn't get inside. The four soldiers stationed at the camper door were USAF air commandos and they'd unsafed their weapons as Ruth approached, which made her nervous and angry.

"I'm under orders, ma'am," their captain said.

"Goddammit, so am I."

"This is Dr. Goldman," Estey said beside her, but Ruth thought her escort was part of the problem. Cam had asked Estey, Goodrich, and Foshtomi to stick with her. By now, the Rangers were accustomed to protecting her. Unfortunately, the USAF captain's first responsibility was to consider everyone a threat.

"She's the nanotech lady," Estey said.

"I need to see Governor Shaug." Ruth had new identification and showed it to them.

The captain didn't move to take it, although one of his men turned his submachine gun aside and reached for the paperwork. "Call it in," the captain told him. "The rest of you, back off a little, okay?"

"Okay," Ruth said. They were all tense. They all expected to die and maybe it was worst for the USAF squad, standing with their backs against a safe hole—if the hole was safe. Ruth did not doubt that the bunkers could withstand conventional bombs or artillery, but Grand Lake's engineers had almost certainly lacked the resources to build deep enough to survive a nuclear strike.

She glanced at the sky again and Foshtomi unconsciously mimicked the gesture beside her. The impulse was too powerful. Camouflage netting stretched from the camper to a nearby trailer, however, forming a roof over its door and the space in between. Ruth felt blind. It was silly, but it calmed her when she could see empty sky and she looked up again even though she knew the netting was there. *Stop it,* she thought. She turned to watch the USAF troops instead. The man with her paperwork had gone to a phone mounted on the camper wall, and Ruth tried to figure out how the command shelter maintained links with its radio, radar, cell, and satellite arrays without creating a hub of electronic noise for the enemy to pinpoint. Maybe they'd run lines all over the mountain to disperse their signals, hiding their dishes and transceivers in other campers and tents. Did it matter?

She missed Cam. They should have been together at the end, but he'd quietly listened to her and he'd nodded and then he was gone. Deborah hadn't been so easy to convince, but she'd left, too, and now Ruth was alone. The Rangers weren't friends. They had never warmed to her, despite her respect for them and the blood loss they'd shared.

"Foshtomi," Ruth said. The young woman turned, and Ruth tried to smile. "Thank you," she said.

"Sure."

No, I mean it, Ruth thought, but the USAF trooper hung up his telephone and said, "Goldman, you're clear."

"I need these three," Ruth said.

"No, ma'am," the captain said. He waved for her to walk forward from the others. "We going to pat you down. Take off your jacket, please."

"I need them," Ruth said tightly, hoping not to let her adrenaline show in her voice. "Tell Shaug."

"We're locked down, ma'am."

"Tell Shaug I need them or I can't guarantee the next step of the booster will work. They're some of the original carriers." The last part was almost true. Another scientist might have questioned her, but she didn't think Governor Shaug or the military command would argue. They were too desperate for any advances in the nanotech.

"All right." The captain pointed for his man to return to the phone. Meanwhile, he slung his weapon and ran his hands closely over Ruth's body, not shy at all about her crotch, waist, or armpits. He noticed her cell phone, of course, and pulled it from her front pocket.

"I need that to call the lab," she said.

He did not find the tiny glass welds she'd made on the back sides of two of her shirt buttons.

The stairwell went down farther than Ruth had anticipated. Her phone almost certainly wouldn't work. That was a serious problem. Ruth looked back once before the door scaled, rubbing her thumb inside her palm as if she still had her etched stone. Then the cold in the tunnel raised goose bumps along her arms and neck and she stumbled on the concrete steps.

Estey caught her. "Careful," he said.

The stairs were very steep. Ruth quickly passed through four giant steel doors, each one about a full story below the next. They made a series of buffers meant to absorb and deflect a blast. Maybe the bunker would survive. Each of the barricades had to be opened and then dogged shut again by the USAF colonel who'd come to lead them inside.

A fifth door led to a room about the size of a small house. It was crowded with computers, display screens, and people. The uproar of voices was amplified by the bare concrete walls and ceiling. This place was a box, and Ruth guessed that it held more than a hundred soldiers. Most were seated along the banks of equipment. Others stood or walked in the paths in between. The vast majority of the uniforms were Air Force blue, but there were also people in tan or olive drab and Ruth saw more than one knot of civilians.

"This way," the colonel said.

Ruth went left when he moved right. He seemed to be heading to a door across from them, but Ruth had seen Governor Shaug inside a glass-walled office. She walked straight at him.

"Dr. Goldman?" Estey said, and the USAF colonel hollered, "Stop that woman!" The busy people clotted around her. Two men and a woman caught her arms, one of them dropping a handful of printouts on the floor. A fourth soldier rose from his seat with his headset cockeyed around his neck.

"Let go of me!"

"Sergeant? What's going on?" The colonel directed his words at Estey instead of Ruth. It was another way of containing her, she realized.

"Sir, I'm not sure," Estey said, but he gestured at the glass office. None of the people inside had noticed them yet. "I think she was just trying to talk to the governor," Estey said.

"That's right," Ruth said.

The colonel stared at her. "You don't go anywhere I don't tell you. Understand?"

"Yes. I'm sorry."

"They'll join us in a minute," the colonel said. "I'm taking you to a spare office."

"Okay. Yes." *No,* she thought. Ruth wanted to be in the heart of their operations when she spoke with Shaug and his generals. If there was any hope of silencing her, they would take it. She couldn't afford to be isolated.

She got lucky. The governor finally noticed the disruption out in the main room. He strode to the glass door of the office. Perfect. As he pushed through he lifted his hand, *hello*, not understanding the situation. A man in a blue uniform walked after him and then a woman in Army green.

The soldiers released her. For a moment, Ruth was free. One of them bent to gather his printouts from the floor, and the data tech returned to his seat. Ruth yanked her cell phone from her pocket. "Stop right there," she said. She pointed the small black plastic casing at Shaug like a gun, yelling now as the soldiers converged on her again. "Stop!"

They came very close to taking her down. The data tech froze with his hand on her sleeve. Another man stood at her shoulder, and the colonel had drawn his pistol. They couldn't know what she intended, but in the twenty-first century, a phone could be a weapon. A phone could trigger explosives or signal troops.

"Everyone get back," Ruth said. She turned slightly to aim her fist at the data tech, stepping away from him and the other man, creating a thin space for herself in the crowd. "Listen to me. The war is over."

They didn't hear her. "Put it down," the colonel said, and Shaug called, "What are you doing?"

Other conversations continued in the room. Except for a few men and women immediately beside her, the soldiers were absorbed with their work, and Ruth wondered how many lives she'd already jeopardized across the U.S. by interrupting radio calls. One girl remained at her console, talking into her headset even as she watched Ruth's face. "That's a roger, Jay Three. Expect them on your north side," the girl said.

Ruth winced and clenched her fist again on her cell phone. She needed to steady herself. "The war is over," she said. "I'm forcing a truce."

"You can't," Shaug began.

"Put it down." The colonel aimed his gun in her face. Three other soldiers had pulled their sidearms, but Ruth continued to hold up her phone.

"It's the only way," she said.

The colonel racked the slide of his 9mm Beretta without pointing it away from her first, chambering a shell. Ruth felt herself go white as something in her chest lurched—heart, lungs. "I'm not warning you again," the colonel said.

Estey stepped in front of her. "Wait." He'd lifted his arms from his sides, making himself bigger as he walked into the muzzle of the colonel's gun.

Goodrich did the same on her other side. "Everyone just wait," he said, increasing the safe zone around her.

Ruth was astonished. She had wondered long and hard why Cam asked these three to escort her and only these three, excluding Ballard and Mitchell. She wouldn't have thought that Estey could let go of his authority, and yet Cam had been very right about him, his exhaustion and his grief. Estey wanted to believe that she knew some way out.

Foshtomi acted alone. Foshtomi grabbed Ruth's hair and spun her sideways, chopping her arm down on Ruth's hand. She knocked Ruth's phone into the row of computer consoles. Then she slammed Ruth's hip and shoulder blades down onto the hard shapes of the desk, a keyboard, two card cases, and a PDA.

"No," Foshtomi said. Her lovely face was twisted with fury as she cocked one fist high behind her own ear. Ruth tried to block it and missed. Foshtomi's knuckles glanced off her teeth, cracking her skull back against the messy surface of the console.

Goodrich clawed at Foshtomi, but he was dragged back by another man. Estey didn't even get that close. One of the other soldiers clubbed Estey with his pistol and Estey banged into an overturned chair.

"Wait—" Ruth coughed, spitting blood.

"You crazy bitch. We _died_ for you," Foshtomi shouted, and it was true. Wesner. Park. Somerset. Ruth didn't know how many more had been hurt or killed with Hernandez in the ground assaults out of Sylvan Mountain, but that number must be in the thousands. They were exactly why she was here.

"Nanotech," Ruth said.

Foshtomi only struggled to hit her again, wrestling with the men who'd surrounded them. "No!" Foshtomi yelled, not at the soldiers but still trying to deny Ruth. Cam had misjudged her— maybe because she was cute. Maybe she'd never invested as much hope in Ruth as the rest of them. It didn't matter. Foshtomi's left hand was snarled in the front of Ruth's shirt, bumping and pulling at the buttons Ruth had altered with liquid glass, creating miniscule air bubbles against the plastic.

"I'm wearing nanotech!" Ruth screamed. "Get her off! Get her off me _now_!"

The USAF colonel threw Foshtomi aside but leaned into her place himself. He pressed his weapon against the underside of Ruth's jaw, forcing her head back. She was too scared to hold still. She tried to pat at her shirt to see if the buttons were there and the colonel immobilized her wrist with his other hand, bent over her body and the computer console. He twisted her arm—her bad arm—and Ruth cried out. Then someone else caught her other hand. She saw Estey pinned to the computers beside her, a submachine gun at the back of his head. No less than a dozen USAF commandos stood behind the colonel, and yet Ruth grinned at them over the smooth-edged bulk of his pistol.

"Let me up," she said.

"Where is Cam!?" Foshtomi yelled, imprisoned herself by three soldiers. "Where's her friend?"

"The war is over," Ruth told them, bleeding and desperate. She licked at the coppery warm gore on her lips as if the wounds belonged to someone else. She was even glad for the pain, because it hurt less than the ice in her heart. "Listen to me," she said. "There's no other way. I have nanotech that will push the Chinese all the way back to California, but unless you do exactly what I say it'll kill our side, too."

The colonel did not release her, although he glanced down at her shirt. "Oh, shit," he said.

Ruth Goldman had turned traitor again.

"Why are you doing this?" Shaug asked, and General Caruso said, "Think what you're doing. It's not too late. We could use this to surprise them."

"No." Ruth tried to hold still in her chair. She wanted to project only strength, but she couldn't get comfortable. Her back was covered with bruises. Her lips were torn and swollen. A medic had treated her quickly, putting one stitch in her upper lip and then covering it with gauze and tape. The bandage felt awkward against her nose. She kept lifting her good hand to fidget with it.

"If we had time to coordinate," Caruso said. "If you just gave us a few days."

"No." Ruth was anxious, but that worked in her favor. They were jumpy, too, because she held one of the buttons between her finger and thumb. With every gesture, they flinched.

Shaug had been the first to recover after the colonel let her up. *We can get someone to take care of you,* he'd suggested. He wanted to move her into the glass-walled office, but Ruth declined. She needed witnesses. She needed the leadership to have as little control over this information as possible.

The data tech who'd joined the struggle was back at his console, and the girl beside him never stopped talking into her headset, coordinating with fighter teams out over Nevada. Everywhere in the large room, people had returned to their tasks—but they were aware of Ruth. The din of voices continued to lull. They were talking about her. Some of them had heard what she'd said. They told the rest, and from here the truth would eventually reach U.S. and Canadian populations up and down the Continental Divide. From here, she could reach the enemy.

"This is treason," Caruso said.

This is the real start of it, Ruth thought. *Not the bombing. Not the invasion. Today. This is peace.*

The pride she felt was inescapable. It burned brightly inside her, competing with her fear and her shame, because more people would die because she hadn't been able to do this sooner. Her anguish reminded her of her time in Nevada, thirsty and hyper-aware of her connection with everything around her.

Everything she'd done in thirty-six years had led her to this point. All of the false turns and mistakes seemed not to be mistakes in the end. Each discovery had added to her skill set, no matter how small. This was the reason for her life.

She badly wanted to convince these men of it, but if necessary she would force them instead.

"I want that cell line open," she said.

"You haven't thought this all the way through," Shaug said, trying again to distract her.

"Open that cell line now. Are you listening to me? If I don't talk to my friends in the next twenty minutes, the nanotech will hit us first. It'll work in the enemy's favor. Please. Put me on the phone."

The command bunker was too far down. Her phone was useless, but she knew they could connect her to the cell towers outside through any of a hundred comm lines. They were dragging their feet. They'd run her request over to a man in the next row of equipment, distancing it from her. Then another soldier came back to say the towers were overloaded and they'd patch her in as soon as they could interrupt the call traffic up top.

They were probably searching for the physical location of the two cell numbers she'd given them. Was that even possible? She had to assume yes. If they couldn't trace those phones electronically, they would be organizing troops and helicopters. It was a mistake to let them have any more time.

Ruth got to her feet. "Don't push me," she said, looking for Estey and Goodrich. She'd demanded their release and the two Rangers stood nearby.

Foshtomi was gone. Foshtomi had cursed all three of them until Shaug cut his hand through the air and the USAF commandos led her away, wild with scorn. *Why are you helping her?* Foshtomi shouted. Goodrich especially seemed to be uncertain. Estey looked straight ahead, nearly holding himself at attention, whereas Goodrich watched the floor, unable to meet the eyes of the other soldiers gathered in front of them.

Ruth didn't doubt that both men regretted what they'd done, but she was hopeful. History was behind them. Today was July 2nd, close enough to the Fourth, the birthday of their nation, and in a very real sense their actions were a revolution. If they could end the war, it meant freedom, not only from the Chinese but from their own leadership.

"I'm making my calls," she said.

Caruso stood up as if to block her way. "We just don't use the cell network down here," he said. "We need a few minutes."

"No." Ruth held up her button. Caruso backed off. Then she walked through the dense rows of men and women, doing her best to ignore their faces. Estey had the right idea. These people were hostile and confused, and she couldn't let any of it affect her. She stopped beside the comm specialist who had been given her numbers. Caruso and Shaug were right behind her, along with Estey and most of the USAF commandos.

"Goldman!" Shaug said.

She raised her voice to match. "If I crack this seal, everyone in this room will be breathing nanotech in seconds. Put me on the phone. Now."

"It will get you, too," Shaug said.

"I knew that when I walked in here." Ruth blinked suddenly, not wanting him to see her tears—but her honesty rattled them more than any threat.

"Okay," Caruso said. "Okay. Just wait."

Ruth held two swords at their throats. The tiny glass packets she'd worn into the bunker were only the first of her weapons, because given the choice, she'd realized there was no choice. She needed to honor the effort and sacrifice of people like Hernandez and the Boy Scouts and every nameless soldier who'd died in the attempts to rescue her, even the invaders—even Nikola Ulinov. She wanted to save all of the survivors of the machine plague and the war.

Ruth had used the great leaps forward she'd found in the new vaccine and the booster, but instead of improving the booster she'd created a very dangerous new ANN, a parasite capable of interfering with and shutting off both versions of the vaccine. Permanently. The parasite had no other effects or functions, but that was enough, forever denying the world below ten thousand feet to anybody it touched. Someone with the parasite inside them would never be able to host the vaccine again. It would ruin the armies spread across the western United States, robbing them of artillery and armor and far too many more lives as they scrambled back to the barrier.

It would briefly cause the fighting to intensify. In Utah, the Russians' only choice would be to charge into the guns of the American positions east of Salt Lake City. In Colorado, the

Chinese would face the same problem. Their reserves and supply chains throughout the Southwest would be devastated. The advantage would swing to the United States, and yet that first day would be horrific. The losses on all sides would be crippling.

Ruth had sworn to do this unless there was a cease-fire and unconditional withdrawal. Unfortunately, she needed some cooperation. The enemy would take any threat of nanotech seriously, but words alone wouldn't stop them. There had to be proof, so she'd also designed a second model of the parasite. This one had a strict governor. It would only affect an area the size of a few city blocks, instead of replicating without end.

It was this second ANN that she'd worn into the bunker. She had also left four capsules of it for them to find in her lab. They would need jets equipped with missiles that had been stripped of explosives, carrying only the nanotech—and even as America announced its ultimatum, they could hit four places deep inside enemy lines, delivering incontrovertible evidence of the parasite's strength.

There were too many details for it to be done instantly. Ruth expected to have to push them every step of the way, holding Grand Lake hostage for hours or days. That was the real reason for the first, ungoverned version of the parasite. This morning Cam and Deborah had both left the mountaintop with capsules full of billions of the parasite, running in opposite directions. They would disperse it on Ruth's command or if anyone found and cornered them, or if she failed to make contact at all.

"Call the eight four six number first," she said, studying the complicated radio console. "Give me your headset." If they had someone tap the line, she wouldn't know, but she didn't want to be on an open microphone.

The comm specialist obeyed. He punched in the number and Ruth heard a normal telephone ring tone, once, twice. It was a stranger who answered. "Burridge," a man said, and Ruth went cold.

She yanked the headset away with her bad hand. "This is the wrong number," she said, whirling on the specialist.

"No, ma'am. It's correct."

"Burridge," the man repeated as Ruth pressed the earpiece back against the side of her head, breathing deep in an attempt to control her panic. *My God,* she thought. *Lord God.* He was a

soldier or an intelligence agent. Ruth knew they answered calls
with their last name, so she responded the same way.

"This is Goldman," she said, testing him.

"We have your friend in custody, Dr. Goldman. And the nanotech. We—"

"Let me talk to her."

"We know where the other man went—"

"Let me talk to her!" Ruth shouted. The triumph on Shaug's
face made her flush with rage. She nearly snapped the glass
pack in her fingers. Instead, she looked away and inadvertently
found Estey. His mouth was open with fear. He understood.

Without the outside threat, Ruth would not be able to control
them. Even if she infected the people inside this bunker, they were
already trapped by their duties here. They could quarantine themselves. It had always been a weak threat to tell them they'd have to
stay, and Ruth sagged as Estey rushed to hold her arm. *My God.*

Finally, Deborah Reece came on the line with none of her
usual arrogance. "Ruth, I," she said. "Ruth, I'm sorry. You can't
do this."

Deborah had been uncertain. That was why Ruth called her
first. She didn't worry about Cam, but the look in Deborah's
eyes still lingered in her mind. When she passed over the vials
she'd smuggled out of the lab, Deborah had closed her fingers
on the small plastic capsules as if to hide them. *This doesn't
seem right,* Deborah said, and Ruth covered her friend's hand
with own. *We can stop the war,* Ruth said, but she hadn't been
able to say enough.

Deborah had turned herself in.

"It's over," Shaug said, gesturing for the headset.

Ruth stepped back from him. "You don't have my other guy,"
she said. She'd almost used his name. Maybe she still should.
Foshtomi had immediately guessed who was helping her and it
might improve her stance if they knew who held the parasite—
one of the few men who'd walked out of Sacramento. "Make the
call," she said. "You're short on time."

"We'll find him," Shaug said.

"I don't care. If he pops the capsule, that's it. The nanotech

hits us first. You lose everyone who's evacuated and every forward unit across the Rockies."

Caruso grimaced. "This is insane."

"Make the call," Ruth said to the comm specialist before she
turned to Shaug and Caruso again. "Don't you get it? If you do
it my way, the Chinese retreat. We win. Please." She stared into
their faces. "Please."

The headset only rang once.

"Yeah," Cam said, as steady as always. His voice set her
heart thumping again.

"Are you okay?" she asked, too loud.

"Yeah. What's going on?"

Ruth found it very easy to picture him alone with nothing
except his rifle and his pack, hurrying across the mountainside.
After all this time, he belonged out there, whether he wanted it
or not. He would have crossed below the barrier hours ago, losing himself in the trees and rock, but he was no longer wearing
goggles or mask, his face exposed to the wind . . . and in
Ruth's imagination, his dark eyes lifted at the drumbeat of helicopters . . .

"I need you to go through with it," Ruth said gently. Then
she realized how that might have sounded. "No, I mean, just
keep moving, but I need you to stay ready."

"If you—" Cam said.

Another voice broke in. Grand Lake's people had been listening all along and Ruth felt a sickening bolt of panic as a new
man on her headset said, "Najarro, this is Major Kaswell. Stand
down, soldier. Do you understand? Stand down. If you let her
use that nanotech, you'll kill thousands of your own people."

Cam didn't even respond to the other man. "If you think it's
best," he said.

"I do," Ruth answered like a promise.

He was the perfect one to shoulder the responsibility. He
was accustomed to relying only on himself and to being apart.
Maybe he even resented them because he wanted so much to
belong but always felt on the outside.

"Cam," she said, without thinking. Then she repeated it.
"Cam, thank you." She knew they had to keep their conversation short to prevent Grand Lake from triangulating him, and
she wanted to make their connection as real as possible. "Don't
worry about me," she said.

"You'll be fine." Then his tone changed. "You let her go or I'll release the nanotech anyway," he said to everyone else on the line. Then he hung up. There was so much more to say and they'd never had the chance.

Ruth was shaking. She nearly dropped the button. But she had learned to channel the force of her emotions and she turned it on Shaug and Caruso. She let the tremor show in her voice. "I'll give you one hour," she said. "Get your planes ready. We'd better have them in the air before we warn the Chinese, or they might just sterilize this place with another nuke."

Caruso said, "We need longer than that!"

"One hour. I'm through arguing."

"Goddamn it, this is insane."

"We win," Ruth said. "Do this and we win."

The parasite had it all, the advanced targeting of the new vaccine and the unparalleled replication speed of the machine plague. Because it lacked the hypobaric fuse, it would spread worldwide in far less time than it had originally taken the plague, filling the atmosphere, riding the jet stream. The nanotech would hit Europe and Africa in days instead of weeks, dooming everyone to the tiny fragments of land above ten thousand feet. With their other war in the Himalayas, the Chinese couldn't risk it even if the Russians might—and without their allies, the Russians would also fold.

"Think what those bastards did to us," Shaug said. "You're going to let them keep California?"

"Some of it. For now. What does it matter?"

"It's our home! It's ours."

"They'll go back to their homes if we let them. If we give them a little time. They'll go back or I'll wipe them out. Just them, don't you get it?" Ruth knew she could design a new plague to eradicate the enemy—only them, all of them—a smart bug that understood geographical limits. The parasite was merely the first step in a stunning new level of nanotech.

"Then do it now," Caruso said. "Kill them now."

"No."

He was as exhausted as all of them, she realized at last, and since the invasion he'd seen little except defeat. He would grasp at any straw, but she would never start a genocide if there was any other option. Even a new plague would not be instantaneous. The Chinese would have time to launch their missiles.

The desperate nations around the world simply could not continue fighting. The cost was too steep and there was no end in sight except total collapse.

"It has to stop somewhere," Ruth said, blazing with sorrow and faith. "It stops today."

25

The mountainside was busy with people, a confusion of dark shapes against the lighter earth. Hundreds of them formed two slow-moving chains, following the long *V* of the two gullies cut into the slope. Dozens more picked their way down through the hills outside of the ravines. Daylight flashed on weapons and equipment. The late afternoon sun was nearly gone from the eastern face of the Rockies, and its low rays turned everything to shadows or sparks.

Cam stood motionless above a short cliff, squinting into the light. "So many soldiers," he said.

Allison grinned. "That's good."

He shook his head. Grand Lake seemed to be losing a significant number of troops to desertion and their uniforms added to the disorder. Most of them had taken off their helmets and field caps. They'd donned civilian jackets or hats. And yet they stuck together for the most part, making concentrations of Marine or Army green despite their efforts to blend. The other refugees tried to avoid them, which was impossible, creating knots and jams within the migration.

There was no fighting that Cam had seen. Everyone was too busy, loaded with packs and slings, but he'd noticed more than one collision. The nearest ravine had a crooked drop in it. Again and again people tripped and fell there, jostling in the crowd. Cam supposed it was only a matter of time before someone's frustration led to blood. He worried that a lot of the troops were still organized squads. He was especially interested in the loners and small groups who chose to hike through the rougher terrain outside the ravines. Not all of them were heading down. Here and there, tiny figures trudged upward against the larger trend. Why? Allison thought they were giving up. Others were probably looking for places to camp out of the wind, but she agreed that some of them must be hunters sent by Grand Lake to get to Ruth first.

Cam tugged restlessly at his carbine's shoulder strap. Then he swung his binoculars to another man standing on a high point across the slope, one of Allison's people. Cam signaled with his arm straight out from his side, holding the pose until the man saw him and returned the gesture. It meant "I haven't seen anything."

Shit, he thought.

They should have planned to meet Ruth somewhere else. This pass was a madhouse, although Cam didn't know where the situation would be any better. Even the western faces of the Divide must be covered in people. Ruth could walk right past and they'd never see her, but Cam did not complain out loud. Allison and the other mayors had done more than he had any right to expect, mustering nearly forty armed men and women who were willing to stay and watch. They were still at least a day's hike from Deer Ridge, the nearest town where there would be shelter from the bitter nights, and meanwhile the refugees who'd gone ahead would claim all of the available food, clothing, and other gear.

"I should try to talk to them," Allison said. She meant the soldiers, he realized. She was staring into the gully below, where four men in coveralls and a USAF jacket moved among the other people. Allison's scarred cheeks had lifted in another confident grin and Cam smiled at her ambition.

If Ruth got free, it would be due in large part to the other woman's efforts. Cam was grateful. Allison could have walked away, but she was selfless enough to feel her own kind of gratitude. She was smart enough to see an opportunity.

It had been three days since Ruth walked into the command bunker and ended the war. Cam had shut off his cell phone to avoid being tracked, yet they knew from radio reports that the test strikes had been a success. One of the American planes was shot down before delivering the parasite, crashing in the wilderness, but in three spots the Chinese and the Russians suddenly found themselves overwhelmed by the machine plague. Some of them survived. That only helped Ruth's scheme. The invaders' aircraft were turned away by their own people in the mountains in Arizona and California, but they managed to find safe ground just the same, landing on isolated peaks—and they continued to report their survival.

The cease-fire was established hours later. The withdrawal began the next day. Ruth remained in the command bunker throughout their negotiations, staying the hands of the American officers who wanted to chase the enemy back into the desert. Cam had spoken with her twice more, turning on his phone again at midnight on the second day and at noon on the third. She was okay. And then she was outside.

"Come with me," Allison said, tugging intimately at Cam's gun belt. He was aware of her blue eyes, but he continued to sweep the mountainside with his binoculars.

"Let's give it another hour," he said.

"It'll be dark before then."

"You can talk to those guys after they've made camp. They wouldn't listen to you now anyway."

"Come with me," Allison said, drawing Cam near enough for him to notice her good, female scent despite the wind. She said, "It's not safe for us to be alone out here at night."

The pace of the crowd was increasingly anxious. Some groups were already staking claim to the flatter areas inside the ravines, blocking the flow of other refugees, erecting lean-tos and tents. There was no firewood. There was no food except whatever they carried and weeds and moss. Water seeped from the earth in a few muddy trickles but Cam saw a pack of men and women in Army uniforms settle down on top of one spring, denying it to anyone else.

Yesterday at dawn, the sun had found several cold bodies among the thousands of those still breathing. The war was over, but the dying went on. Not all of the sick or injured would survive the trek down from the mountains, and Allison's people had dug in against a low knoll away from the ravines, stacking rock to form windbreaks and filling every canteen, cup, pot, and plastic bag from their own spring, buying the goodwill of nearby refugees with water and advice.

Allison kept her hand around his waist. "I know what you're thinking," she said. "We're doing what we can. If she made it this far, we'll find her."

"Yeah."

There were so many things that could have gone wrong. Grand Lake might have captured Ruth as soon as she called to say she was clear, gambling that Cam would never release the parasite. They could have tracked her by satellite or plane despite his warnings to let her go. The refugees worked to conceal her, but at the same time, the crowds were another danger. A woman by herself would be a target.

We should have gone after her, Cam worried, but Allison had had her hands full organizing her camp and her sentries. Cam couldn't have hiked back into Grand Lake himself. He still carried the nanotech and he didn't trust it with anyone else. Allison's people were ready to embrace Ruth as a savior for forcing the peace, but they didn't know about his involvement. He'd told them Ruth did everything herself.

"We'll try again tomorrow," Allison said. She finally let go of him. She held both arms over her head, calling in the line of sentries. The nearest man didn't notice, his binoculars aimed up the mountainside, but on a hump of granite beyond him, the next woman saw Allison's signal and repeated it. Those two had even farther to walk to camp than Cam and Allison, and he was glad they'd stayed as long as they had.

"Thank you," he said, taking Allison's hand. He would repeat the words in camp, too, as he asked them for one more day. They were all discouraged—but the nearest man was waving off Allison's signal.

The man raised his left fist, then turned and pointed at the mountainside. Cam immediately twisted away from Allison, though not so fast that he didn't see the emotion in her face. She covered her hurt with her grin, but he knew he'd done a little more damage. For the moment, he didn't care. He brought his binoculars to his eyes and tried to find what the man was indicating.

About a mile up the hill, outside the ravines, a trio of uniformed figures had stopped to gaze back at Allison's sentries with their own binoculars. That was not unusual. Both the civilian refugees and the AWOL troops reacted uneasily to the lookouts. There was nothing distinct about this threesome, two men and a woman, filthy and tattered like everyone else, but they'd recognized Cam. They all had their hands up. It was Ruth and Estey and Goodrich.

"Ha!" Cam rolled his arm in a big *this way* gesture. Then he turned to go, wild with excitement.

Allison didn't follow, exchanging semaphore with her sentries on either side. Cam should have waited. Instead, he scrambled down a rocky bluff.

He had to cross the nearest gully, which was thick with refugees. He stalked into the crowd with his weapon up. No one moved to stop him. In fact, four women stumbled away from their blankets and packs to keep their distance. Cam thought to apologize, but it was better if these people were afraid. Allison and her sentries would cross behind him and they didn't need any trouble. It was a strange feeling. Everyone on this mountainside was alive and free because of one woman's strength. They should have been celebrating. *Ruth,* he thought, but he wouldn't yell her name. "Estey!" he shouted.

The three of them walked together in a way that reminded Cam of himself and Newcombe. He wondered briefly if Newcombe was alive and if he was still a friend or if he'd chosen another loyalty, like Deborah. Their days together seemed very distant, and Cam marveled at the unity he saw in Goodrich, Ruth, and Estey.

He hadn't been sure if any of his squadmates were helping Ruth. She'd kept her phone calls to a few seconds each. Where was Foshtomi? Dead? The other two Rangers appeared to have committed to Ruth entirely during their standoff inside the bunker, and they would be a welcome addition to Allison's group. They might help Allison reach out to other deserters, bolstering the future of the refugee crowds, but as Cam got closer, he forgot everything except Ruth.

She ran to him, laughing despite her obvious exhaustion. She was horribly pale, yet her brown eyes were alive with pleasure and hope. Cam didn't hesitate. He stepped right into her arms and they clung to each other, their chests pressing tighter each time they spoke and drew breath.

"You did it," he murmured into her curly hair. "You did it. You did it."

"Cam," she said. "Cam." But she let go of his waist.

Allison strode in behind him with six men and women, each of them brandishing a shotgun or a rifle. Several more spread out across the hill, forming a defensive line. "We're with him," Allison told Estey and Goodrich, and Cam nodded quickly and said, "It's okay, they're here to help."

"Great," Estey said. "Thanks."

The two women looked each other up and down as Cam kept his arm around Ruth's shoulders. Then he stepped away from her toward Allison. Ruth was worn and tense, but he saw the disappointment in her eyes before she concealed it exactly as Allison had done.

"Yes, thanks," Ruth said to the younger woman.

Cam had been sleeping with Allison again. For one thing, she was capable and smart and beautiful—and the fact of the matter was there hadn't been any guarantee that Grand Lake wouldn't go up in a nuclear fireball or that Ruth would escape even if she took control of the war. Regardless, Cam had decided he'd better do everything possible to entangle himself with Allison again. They needed her.

"There are some people watching us," one man said.

"Let's go," Allison said. "We have food and water and a few tents out of the wind."

They got moving. Cam and Allison walked together as the group hurried toward the ravine, but as they began to spread out he glanced sideways for Ruth. She met his gaze silently. Maybe she understood. He wished things were different.

"How are you?" he asked.

"We're okay. We're all tired." Ruth glanced at Estey and Goodrich, including the Rangers with herself. *We.*

Not long ago she'd spoken about him the same way, but he had to be careful. Allison and the other mayors would be a major force in establishing the townships they intended to build on the plains east of the Rockies, far away from the foothills, where the summers were probably too hot for the bugs.

Allison could be the key to keeping Cam and Ruth hidden. They knew they would always be regarded as criminals by some. They hoped to keep their heads down until the situation improved, and meanwhile there were hundreds of other problems. Except for a few wild crops, there was little to feed anyone beneath the barrier. Farming would be a long-term challenge given the insect swarms, widespread erosion, and the utter loss of some plant species. The nearest cities had already been heavily scavenged during the plague year. Entire neighborhoods had been destroyed by fire, floods, bugs, and fighting. They couldn't rely on the old world to sustain them for long.

Perhaps most importantly, there was also the next-generation nanotech that Ruth had said must be designed as fast as possible. The war was over, but there were still large Russian and Chinese populations throughout the West. They would play for every advantage as they gained and developed their own nanotech, dragging their feet to leave U.S. soil, haggling and bargaining, looting, even digging in for a new fight.

"Tomorrow we'll make it to Highway 34 and Deer Ridge," Cam said. "It'll get easier."

"Mm." Ruth was noncommittal.

She'd stopped looking at him, and Cam felt a deep pang of his own longing and disappointment. They'd won. They'd lost each other. He couldn't even make an effort to correct that loss. He knew her too well to believe that she would ever disappear into the ruins with him, just the two of them together. Ruth needed people because she needed electricity and food and protection. She needed equipment if they could find it, and Allison's network might prove more useful in acquiring the basics of a nanotech lab than any raids led by Estey and Goodrich.

The sun touched the ragged line of peaks above them, casting shadows across the slope like massive teeth. They were still in the light, but Cam could see the border approaching rapidly as the shadows grew. The wind tugged at his jacket. The cold increased.

"I'll see you in camp," Cam said, watching Ruth's face, and for an instant she smiled at him again. Then he turned and caught up with Allison.

They walked into the darkness to find their way safe.

Acknowledgments

More than anyone else, I want to thank my wife and sons for their remarkable patience and support.

Sweetheart, I really do love you more than my computer.

I'd also like to express my gratitude to the experts who shared their education with me. Any mistakes are mine. Fortunately, no one really knows what would happen to the environment or to the geopolitical world if you removed all warm-blooded life below ten thousand feet. My thanks go to Mike May, Professor of Entomology at Rutgers University; Harry Greene, Department of Ecology and Evolutionary Biology at Cornell University; Major Brian Woolworth, U.S. Army Special Forces; Lt. Colonel J. Brian "Bear" Lihani, USAF (ret.); and to my father, Gus Carlson, Ph.D., engineer, and former division head at Lawrence Livermore National Laboratory. All of these people were instrumental in shaping *Plague War*.

A huge thanks also to the Ultimate Grandparents Club: Patti, Ute, Char, Bill, Byron, and my father, Gus, again. The extra days and hours you provided, whether babysitting, grocery shopping, or taking us away for a weekend of fun and rest, were crucial to finishing this book on time.

There are other people deserving of mention—our friends Adad Warda and Charlie and Violeta Escobar, for their help and support; Judith Murello and Eric Williams, who have done a sensational job with the covers for the series so far; Meghan Mahler, for her maps; and John Robert Marlow and Janet Lewis, for maintaining my web site at www.jverse.com. Come see what they've done. The site offers free fiction, interviews, tour dates, and advance information on upcoming books.

As always, I want to acknowledge my agent, Donald Maass, and Cameron McClure and Stephen Barbara in the office.

Thank you to everyone at Penguin USA. My editor, Anne Sowards, went the extra mile, and my publicist, Valerie Cortes, has been outstanding. I also appreciate the help of Ginjer Buchanan, Cam "The Other Cam" Dufty, and the rest of the good people behind this novel. They say a writer works alone, but the truth is that a small army put their smarts and energy into producing *Plague War*. I hope you enjoyed it.